GIRL
UNSEEN

PRAISE FOR ATHENA DANIELS

The Seer's Daughter

"…the perfect culmination of paranormal mystery with steamy and sensual romance and just enough suspense and intrigue to guarantee a chilling, goose bump-invoking, story line… *The Seer's Daughter* would be a brilliant option for adaption to screen—there's a television series/movie in here for absolute certain."
—*AusRom Today*

"…as chilling as it is sexy… This is much more than a romance. The paranormal aspects along with the secondary characters really make the story. The descriptions, language, emotions, dialogue… are all cleverly written to keep you engaged and the pages turning, while the suspense will make sure you read this story with all the lights on."—5-star Top Pick, *The Romance Reviews*

"If you are looking for a book to give you goose bumps and keep you watching over your shoulder, then I can recommend this one! … I got dragged away from this book late in the evening by my husband, as I had an exceedingly early start the next day. This didn't stop me from thinking about the book and what I had read for well over an hour after the lights went out, as well as dreaming about it!"
—Archaeolibrarian, 5 stars, Amazon review

"I love paranormal books, especially when there's romance thrown in, and this… will send a chill up your spine, raise the hairs on your neck, and make you tremble with emotions. What a rush! One of my most favorite reads this year! … It's almost like Stephen King meets Christina Dodd… I loved it; can't wait for book two!"—5 stars, Amazon review

"…a perfect blend of paranormal fiction and romantic suspense that had me completely captivated to the very last page… flawlessly delivered."
—Faridah, 5 stars, *Readers Favorite*

"One of the best ghost/demon stories I have read in a while! It had romance, witches, demons, AND ghosts! Absolutely loved it!"—5 stars, Amazon review

The Alchemist's Son

"…go the hell out and buy both of these books now because they are freaking FANTASTIC. I am not exaggerating when I say this is some of the best romantic suspense I have ever read, paranormal or otherwise; I literally couldn't put down *The Alchemist's Son* until I got to the final, thrilling climax."—5 stars, Amazon review

"This book is as good as the first, with twists and turns! You get the good ol' creepy feels! You may be wanting to look behind you, or not go in your attic or basement anytime soon! I wish this author could write as fast as I can read; I would never put her books down!"—5 stars, Amazon review

"Kept me on the edge of my seat. Several scenes I was holding my breath reading what was happening next…."—5 stars, Amazon review

"This book had my hair standing on end and gave me chills from start to finish. Once again I could not put it down, and loved how, no matter how hard I tried, I just couldn't guess ahead what was going to happen next."—5 stars, Amazon review

Girl Unseen

"For paranormal fans, *Girl Unseen* can't be beat! The depth of emotion with which Athena Daniels fills her characters provides such intensity that you feel their pain and heartache… Just make sure to leave the lights on! Fabulous read! I couldn't put this down and can't wait for more!"—5 stars, *Readers Favorite*

"A wonderful, spooky story with lots of action. A murder mystery to solve and a scorching hot romance. It has everything and will keep you guessing all the way through. I loved it."—5 stars, Amazon review

"I loved it so much! For me, this book covers a lot of ground when it comes to romance + something else. You like a little bit of scary? You've got ghosts and spirits. You like a little bit of detective work? You've got a badass PI trying to solve the mystery… You want romance? Well, you have one amazing medium falling for the PI, while trying to help out a lost soul. Oh, and maybe, just maybe, you want all these with nice writing? You've got author Athena Daniels. Congratulations for your future book to read!"—5 stars, *Lilly's Book World*

Desperate

"What can I say other than I absolutely loved this book from the start, and the prologue really set the pace for a fast-paced plot with lots of suspense and the right touch of romance. The plot was strong and progressed well and I loved the flirty banter between Eric and Ivy, which added to the growing relationship between the pair and provided a few good sex scenes illustrating their intense chemistry… the author has done an amazing job of penning this novel and I can't wait to read more of their work in the future."
—*The Romance Studio* (TRS), 4 stars

"Suspense and steamy romance line the pages of this fast-paced thriller, with action and drama from start to finish…. If Athena Daniels keeps it up with writing like this, I have no doubts that she will establish her place amongst the most well-known authors of erotic literature…. If you're a fan of romantic thrillers, I would definitely recommend giving this one a read."
—Official Review, *Online Book Club*, 4 out of 4 stars

ALSO BY ATHENA DANIELS

Novels

The Scream Behind Her Smile

Desperate

Beyond the Grave Series

The Seer's Daughter (Book One)

The Alchemist's Son (Book Two)

Girl Unseen (Book Three)

When Darkness Follows (Book Four)

GIRL UNSEEN

BEYOND THE GRAVE
BOOK 3

ATHENA DANIELS

Sunset Coast Publishing

This book is dedicated to everyone who has read the series so far and has taken the time to tell me they loved it. A writer is nothing without readers, and you are the ones who make this journey possible. I appreciate each and every one of you.

ACKNOWLEDGMENTS

Thanks to the dynamic duo, Dana Delamar and Kristine Cayne, for their sharp eye for detail and for polishing my words and making them flow. A special mention must go to my phenomenal editor, Dana. Thanks for not letting me get away with *anything* and for teaching me so much along the way. Your unwavering belief in me gives me strength and courage in this journey. Thanks for always being available and for being as passionate about the series as I am.

My love and appreciation, as always, to Leah for making time to do a first pass read of the book and for your feedback and suggestions. It can't be easy being the sister of a writer in the process of releasing a book. Thank you for the daily dose of sanity!

Love and appreciation to my daughter Alicia for listening to my early plot ideas and for your ideas and suggestions. Thank you for your constant encouragement.

To my boys, Theo and Steven, who are too young to read my books, but cheer me on regardless. Your enthusiasm and support warms my heart and spurs me on.

To my husband, who understands how important this journey is to me, and for supporting this writing thing even when it's hard.

And to my Nanna, who I somehow know is still with me and cheering me on from beyond the grave.

Paranormal
adj. (*Oxford Dictionary*)
Denoting events or phenomena such as telekinesis or clairvoyance that are beyond the scope of normal scientific understanding.

Hidden in the shadows of our everyday lives, invisible forces travel amongst us. The paranormal is entwined within the fabric of our very existence. We share this earth with things most cannot see. Others choose not to see.

Some don't get that freedom.

CHAPTER ONE

TWO A.M.
LIGHTHOUSE KEEPER'S COTTAGE
LEEUWIN ROAD, LIMESTONE COAST
WESTERN AUSTRALIA

Soft footsteps crossed the timber floor overhead. Pia Williams, psychic medium for the paranormal-investigations TV show, *Debunking Reality*, looked up at the rough-hewn ceiling.

Are you the one trying to reach me?

There was no answer, just as there was no one in the attic. No one in the house, other than her and the team.

The footsteps were the first sign of paranormal activity. Well, the first sign the others would have picked up on. Ever since Pia had entered the house, something, *someone*, had been trying to reach her, snatching at her with wispy fingers, trying to pierce the veil that separated the living from the dead.

A gust of wind whipped against the weathered wooden exterior of the 1896 timber cottage before dropping off abruptly. *Like the slap of an angry hand.*

Across a small cove, a short distance away, Cape Leeuwin Lighthouse stood, proud and tall, glowing stark white against the stormy black of the unsettled sky.

Many memories were buried within the walls of this haunted old cottage. Few of them good.

Tonight, however, they were of little interest to Pia.

1

There was something else she was supposed to see… something that fluttered just out of reach.

Pia was sitting and staring out the window of the recently renovated lighthouse keeper's cottage when she and the entity finally connected.

Though Pia's physical body was in the room, her mind was elsewhere, listening to a tragic echo from long ago. Images, objects, places, were coming to her. She strained to listen, struggled to find coherence in the disjointed pictures pressing into her mind.

Reaching out through an otherworldly resonance, a hazy imprint of souls departed, Pia found a clarity. The spirit who sought her. As though it were her own, anguish tore through Pia's body. Such heartbreaking despair. A sense of hopelessness, bitter loneliness. Abject misery.

Who was calling out to her? A woman? No, younger… a girl.

The footsteps crossing the attic were hers.

There was something important, something urgent, the girl wanted Pia to know. The cause of her pain.

What is it? Tell me.

Concentrating harder, Pia pressed her fingertips over her eyes. Her chest squeezed, and she felt overwhelmed with suffering not her own. She had to push through the thick saturation of emotion, reach out through the anguish with her mind.

The girl was crying. Not a trickle of tears, but huge, gut-wrenching sobs, the kind that ripped your heart out.

What happened to you?

A door slammed, and Pia jumped, the sound coming from overhead momentarily confusing the past and present.

Lowering her head into her hands, Pia retrained her focus. Ignored the pain she felt as keenly as though it were her own.

Show me a little more. Just enough to see.

The blade of a knife, an ornate wooden handle carved into the shape of an eagle. A mouse. A filthy, soiled mattress. A doll with long blonde hair. Shackles and chains.

And blood, so much blood.

What are you showing me? Pia asked without words. *Who are you?*

"Pia?" Someone was shaking her. Shouting in her ear.

"Go away!" She threw out an arm. She wanted to see. To understand.

"Pia!" Someone slapped her face. Her eyes sprang open, the sting jarring her back into the present.

"Damn it, Pia. Look at me." Mark Collins, *Debunking Reality*'s lead investigator, was staring into her eyes, his hand warm and firm against her stinging cheek. "You're scaring me."

Pia brushed away a rush of annoyance. Mark had every right to be concerned. She took a series of deep breaths and got herself under control. The fragments of herself began to regather as she shrugged off the heavy sadness of the past.

"I'm good," she said.

Mark's brows drew together into a frown, his eyes scanning her face.

"I heard activity in the attic," Pia said. "Shouldn't you be checking out the slamming door and the footsteps?"

Debunking Reality had been hired by Chad and Monique Reynolds to investigate claims of possible poltergeist activity in the house. The Reynolds had two daughters, Cassandra, nine years old, and Rebecca, who was only seven. The activity had increased to such a degree that the parents were concerned about their girls' safety.

The team could now remove "possible" from that statement. Something was definitely sharing this house with the family. It was the team's job to investigate what. And, if possible, cleanse it from the Reynolds' home.

"I was on my way up when I saw you with your head in your hands," Mark said. "You almost fell off the chair."

"I did?" She must have been more out of it than she'd realized.

Overhead, the floor creaked, and a muffled cry seemed to reverberate out of the ceiling.

"Oh, for heaven's sake. Stop fretting about me and get up there."

"I'm still worried about you."

Pia stood, wiped her damp palms down the sides of her jeans, and gave him a brief smile. "I'm fine. Now go."

As a team of seasoned investigators, it was rare for one of them to be overcome or affected during an investigation. But it had happened on occasion. And Pia's abilities made her more susceptible to certain energies than the others were. Mark had mistaken her deep concentration for something more sinister, and after a particularly terrifying experience the team had had six months ago, he had good reason.

Something shattered and broke upstairs. Like glass being dropped on the floor. No, it was angrier. *Like glass being hurled against a wall.*

Mark briefly touched Pia's shoulder. "That's my cue. Shout if you need me." He rushed to the stairs, signaling for Ryan Donovan, the team's cameraman, to resume focusing the handheld night-vision video recorder on him.

"The time is two-thirty a.m.," Mark spoke to the camera, "and we're heading upstairs to investigate a series of unexplained crashes and doors slamming coming from the attic. The house has been in complete lockdown since eight p.m. and is still secure. As you can see, we are all present and accounted for, here on the first floor."

Ryan panned the camera, showing the positions of Mark, Pia, and Joe Clarke, their electronics whiz, monitoring the various static night-vision cameras positioned around the house. "Joe, grab that spare camera and join us," Mark said. "I want to maximize our chances to capture everything possible tonight."

"Coming, Tom?" Mark called from the stairs.

With a nod, Tom Kelly followed the team upstairs. Sixty-five years old, with leathery skin, a white beard, and hard eyes, Tom looked every inch the weathered rock lobster fisherman he'd once been. Tom had stayed in the cottage on occasion with the original owners, Simon and Meg Farrell, thirty-plus years ago. Rock lobster, or crayfish or crays, as the locals liked to call the tasty saltwater shellfish, was a profitable business, and Tom had been part of Simon Farrell's cray-fishing crew.

Mark had talked Tom into doing a set of pre-investigation interviews to add a little background to tonight's show. Pia wasn't sure why Tom was still here; it was rare for Mark to allow others to stay after the lockdown, not wanting to risk interference or contamination of evidence.

Something about Tom Kelly raised the hairs on the back of Pia's neck. Survival instinct. And Pia trusted hers implicitly. She just didn't know why Tom Kelly stirred hers. Yet.

The team's voices faded away as they moved upstairs with Tom. Pia stayed by herself on the ground floor, grateful for the moment alone. The truth was, she was still shaken from what she had seen in the vision.

What she had *felt*.

The girl had reached out to her, tried to give her a message.

The air in the room turned still.

Something was… *off*.

Muted sounds of talking and movement filtered down from the guys upstairs. Pia's stomach clenched. With every breath she took, her sense of unease increased.

A tingle slid across the skin of her cheek and over the back of her neck. Pia let out a breath. The connection she'd made with the girl had not been fully severed.

Not one to tolerate failure, Pia wouldn't leave tonight without understanding not only who was at unrest in the house, but why.

Breathing deeply, Pia once again reached out with her mind and opened herself up. She likened the process to becoming a receiver of a radio station, tuning herself in to a frequency slightly out of phase with normal reality.

Feeling herself being called toward something, she followed her intuition. She picked up a night-vision camcorder and used its greenish-hued viewer to navigate the dark room. She found herself standing in the doorway to Cassandra Reynolds' bedroom. The room was typical of your average nine-year-old girl—stuffed toys and dolls everywhere. Why was Pia being drawn here?

The team had been in the house for over six hours so far, video rolling continuously from seven separate units and eight audio recorders. Tomorrow, Joe and Mark would begin the arduous task of replaying the footage, editing it down, and overlaying the highlights with Mark's commentary to create a concise, forty-minute episode for the television network.

There had been lots of activity tonight, much of it captured on film. Mark would be pleased, but to Pia these investigations were more personal. It wasn't enough to simply capture evidence of the paranormal. Considering Pia's abilities, she didn't need proof of that.

There were reasons so-called "hauntings" occurred. Reasons a spirit remained trapped on earth. Sometimes it was due to a sudden violent death, like a car accident or a murder. And sometimes spirits didn't realize they were dead. Pia could often help those lost souls to find the light and the peace waiting for them on the other side. Some spirits knew they were dead but were unwilling to leave loved ones.

And some stayed because they had unfinished business.

Despite the danger of being a *sensitive* in this line of work, Pia had never considered doing anything else. The spirits she could help were what compelled her to keep investigating with Mark and the team.

So few true mediums existed in the world. Even fewer were willing to take the risks she did to reach the dead. Often, she was the only hope for many of these trapped and wandering spirits, and the only one who could—or would—give them peace. How could she possibly turn her back and walk away? For better or worse, she'd been given her abilities for a reason, and she put her heart and soul into helping the ones she could.

What am I dealing with tonight?

Pia pushed off from the doorframe, stepped into Cassandra's room, and instantly sensed she wasn't alone. The temperature in the room plunged, and Pia pulled the sides of her jacket closed. Ice trickled down her spine and spread through her body, a bone-aching chill seeping into her marrow. Her heart raced, and she was instantly alert and on edge.

The room smelled of strawberry lip gloss.

And death.

Something moved in the far corner of the room. Pia resisted the impulse to turn on the light and instead pressed Record on the camcorder and peered through the night-vision viewfinder.

On a wicker chair was a carelessly tossed cardigan.

And a doll in a long white dress.

Was that what she'd seen in her vision? She thought she'd seen a girl, not a doll. But the two looked identical. Pia moved deeper into the room, careful not to trip over the corner of the bed.

The strangely intelligent eyes of the doll tracked her every move.

Pia's heart pounded in her chest and sweat prickled across her forehead. Steeling herself to remain calm, she sat on the ruffled pink bedspread, lifted the doll off the chair, and held it out at arm's length. The doll was large, surprisingly heavy, and emitted the aroma of laundry detergent and disinfectant. But then that scent faded, and Pia psychically picked up something that turned her stomach. The sharp, ammonia-like smell indicative of mice. And beneath that, the hint of something putrid. Fresh blood and the pervasive odor of death.

What was this disturbing doll doing in Cassandra's room?

Pia placed the camera on the bed and used two hands to examine the strangely lifelike toy. Delicate features etched the face, the head fashioned out of porcelain, not the lightweight plastic used in factory-made dolls. The hair was blonde and so silky soft it had to have been real. The dress consisted of flowing layers of intricately delicate lace, in a style of years gone by. A machine had no part in the making of this doll. Every inch of it had been crafted by hand. Out of love. It also hadn't been made for the girl who slept in this room.

This doll was not Cassandra's.

Yet it belonged in this house, just the same.

A music box turned on in the corner, and Pia almost dropped the doll. Lights in the ornate wooden box flickered, and a ballerina began twirling to the melodic notes of a piano, the tune's tempo a fraction too fast.

The air vibrated, crackling with the tension that precedes a destructive storm. Mark's muffled voice through the overhead floorboards sounded even farther away.

Pia didn't yet know what type of entity she was dealing with. Or what it wanted. Setting down the doll, she curled her fingers around the black tourmaline crystal pendant she wore for protection and cautiously picked her way across the room. The music box was ice cold, and when she turned it over, she discovered the bottom panel was missing, revealing an empty battery compartment.

But the music continued to play, eerily out of tune. Pia wouldn't be shocked to learn that the song playing wasn't even the one that came with the jewelry box.

Her heart fluttering wildly, Pia shivered against an arctic chill. Tiny hairs on her arms stood on end, her chest tightened, and she sensed she wasn't alone.

Something was behind her, its eyes boring holes into the back of her head.

Show no fear.

Evil entities fed off fear and could attach themselves to the weak and vulnerable, leading to oppression, or worse, possession. Until Pia knew what this entity was, she could reveal nothing, not even a hint of her nerves.

"Who is here?" Thank God her voice came out loud and clear, projecting a confidence she didn't feel. To the untrained eye, Pia would appear visually alone in the room, but the space around her was anything but empty. The air was thick and heavy, depleted of oxygen, and seemed stale, as if she were trapped in a tiny closet.

Her knees turned to water, and she quickly sat down on the bed. The mattress next to her dipped. Pia's throat closed over, and her fingers gripped the quilt.

Something Pia couldn't see, and still couldn't get a read on, had sat down beside her. The doll rolled away from Pia, seemingly of its own accord.

Something didn't like her touching the doll.

The owner of the object?

"Who are you?" Pia asked, softer this time, her tone cajoling. "Don't be scared of me. You can talk to me. Tell me who you are."

Sarah. The name pressed into Pia's mind.

"Hello, Sarah." Pia sensed this was the same girl she'd seen in her visions. The girl who had reached out to her. "What are you doing here, Sarah?"

Can you see me? the entity asked.

"No." Pia concentrated. She could often see those who had died, but this time no images formed.

A rush of highly charged energy blasted her, and Pia instinctively gripped the bed to brace herself. Her head spinning from dizziness, she clutched the black tourmaline pendant and visualized surrounding herself in a protective white light.

What the hell is this entity? Pia's answer, that she couldn't see the entity, had triggered a flood of rage from her unseen companion. Why?

Show no fear.

Pia stood, her fingers tightening on the tourmaline. *Keep me safe. Keep me strong.* She chanted the words in her mind.

"Don't," Pia said firmly, addressing the entity. "Don't do that." The energy blast had hit like a physical blow. What was she actually communicating with? A young girl who'd died long ago?

Or is this entity demonic?

Demons were masters of manipulation and often disguised themselves as children. Such a ruse frequently allowed them to get close to humans, to infiltrate the lives of the living before they realized what had happened.

Pia tugged her jacket tightly closed and glanced around the room warily.

You can't see me, the entity claiming to be Sarah said. *It doesn't matter. No one ever did.*

Deep sadness had replaced the abrupt flood of anger, the complete swing unnaturally immediate, like shutting off one tap and turning on another.

"Who didn't see you?" Pia asked, striving for this to make sense. Hoping to keep this entity calm until she worked out who—or what—she was dealing with.

No one saw me.

"Who? Who didn't see you?"

And they must pay. He *will pay.*

"He? Who are you referring to?" As she spoke the words, she knew.

Tom Kelly, the cray fisherman Mark had invited to join them, was the current subject of the entity's anger.

The old man was in danger.

"Tom!" Pia shouted.

The air turned thick, so viscous, it became almost impossible to breathe. Pia tried to call out again to warn Tom, but the words stuck in her throat.

Terror's icy talons clawed at her skin and raked her spine. The situation was going from bad to worse. Pure unadulterated hatred speared the air with needles of menace.

Pia braced herself against the onslaught. Her head pounded, threatening to explode, while improbable gusts of wind whipped strands of hair against her face. A draft was impossible; the windows weren't open. The artificial wind was electrical energy generated by immeasurable, inhuman anger.

Despite the howling wind, Pia heard footsteps on the upper floor. She turned to look. Tom stood at the top of the stairs. He must have heard Pia call out his name and was coming to see what she wanted. When he took the first step down, he cried out. His head twisted one way, then the other, then he doubled over and clutched his stomach, as though he were in the ring with an invisible professional boxer. Losing his footing, he tumbled to the bottom of the stairs and landed in a heap of tangled limbs.

A visible manifestation, a young girl—Sarah?—appeared in the doorway and stared at Tom's motionless form.

The entity's hair was blonde, the same color as the doll's. The girl's smile was thin and tight. Chilling. She wasn't merely a spectator to the tragedy; she was the instigator. Harming Tom had been her intention all along.

Pia raced to help Tom, but was thrown backward against the wall outside the door to Cassandra's bedroom, able to see, but unable to help. Trapped and helpless, she saw Tom being picked up off the floor and thrown back against the wall, where he was held fast, his feet six inches off the ground. Tom fought his unseen attacker, crying out and coughing, blood trickling down his chin to splatter in gruesome patterns across the floor.

"Stop!" Pia demanded, struggling to overcome the invisible force keeping her in place. Turning her head, she focused on the entity of the young girl, who was most certainly at the center of this power.

"Stop!" Pia shouted. "You can talk to me. You said no one can see you. I do now. I see you."

You do? A dangerous glint flickered in the entity's black, soulless eyes when she turned them in Pia's direction.

"Yes!" Pia forced through a constricted throat. "Stop hurting Tom. You don't have to do this."

Yes. I. Do!

A series of loud crashes assaulted Pia's ears. Tables overturned, and cupboard doors flew open, their contents spewing forth to shatter on the floor. Chairs floated up into the air before hurtling at high speed to splinter into ragged pieces against the walls.

A victorious growl rose up through the floorboards, and a tornado raged through the air. Thunder boomed, echoing throughout the eaves of the house as the maelstrom reached its crescendo.

Tom's limp and battered body was lifted off the wall and sent hurtling forward. He was slammed against the opposite wall, his body falling to the floor, a twisted and lifeless heap of flesh and bones. A wicked-looking knife with a carved eagle head materialized on the hallway table, then flew like an arrow to land dead center in Tom's chest. He cried out once, thrashing briefly before going utterly limp. The entity's intentions were absolute.

"Why?" Pia cried.

It was a long time coming.

The pressure holding Pia against the wall released her. She bent forward, drawing in huge lungfuls of air.

The house stilled. Everything fell into absolute silence around her, the only sound her own ragged breathing.

Then the chilling, disembodied laugh of a young girl trickled through the air, before bleeding into the darkness.

Finally able to move, Pia stumbled across the room, desperate to help Tom. Though she reached him in seconds, there was no saving him. Mark, Ryan, and Joe came rushing down the stairs, arriving seconds after her.

For a long, terrible moment, no one spoke. No one moved. They simply stared at Tom's lifeless body. Too stunned to explain, Pia silently made her way to the front of the house, groped in her handbag for her phone, and with trembling fingers, placed the emergency call to triple zero.

She turned and met Mark's wide-eyed gaze.

"What the fuck just happened?" His voice shook as he spoke.

Pia couldn't answer. What could she say?

What the fuck did *just happen here?*

How could a standard paranormal investigation go so horribly wrong?

Who—or what—was the girl she'd seen standing in the doorway? The same entity who'd reached out to Pia for help. The entity Pia had felt sorry for.

Was the entity in the image of the doll in Cassandra's room truly the spirit of a lost girl?

Or was it something far more sinister?

The trapped, earthbound spirit of a young girl wouldn't kill someone on purpose. Would it?

Anger had poured off the spirit, a vortex of hatred that had seemed directed toward Tom Kelly.

But why? Who was Sarah?

And why was she on a quest for revenge?

CHAPTER TWO

Pia was not under arrest—yet.

The document she'd signed stated she was at the Margaret River Police Station voluntarily. Mark and the team had all signed similar documents before being separated. Pia's fingerprints had been taken, and she was now sitting in a small room with bare, cold walls and a two-way mirror. She'd been asked to stay, but she didn't believe for one moment she'd had a choice.

She might not yet have official charges laid against her, but if the demeanor of the cops she'd spoken to so far was anything to go by, that particular detail was only a matter of time.

Placing a hand on her churning stomach, she breathed deeply. She didn't want to be here. Couldn't be here. This was a waste of time. She needed to understand what had happened last night, and to do that, she needed time alone to think. To get back into the house and reconnect with the entity.

Nearly all the evidence pointed to it being demonic. Typically, entities didn't hurt people, much less kill them. In fact, such behavior was extremely rare.

But the emotions she'd felt from the entity had been so human. So real. Genuine sadness lay beneath all that hatred.

What were they dealing with?

Pia was tired, hungry, and frustrated. Vivid memories of last night replayed in her mind, mixing and mingling with the visions, the imprints of images the entity had shown her. Short stories, jumbled scenes without context. The soiled and tattered mattress, the shackles and the blood. The doll. The manifestation of the girl—Sarah—at the door. The subsequent chaos, the violence of the attack. Tom at the top of the stairs, his violent death. The eagle-handled knife that had materialized and had somehow flown off the hallway table to pierce his heart.

What does it all mean?

It didn't make sense, like a jigsaw puzzle before you put its pieces together.

If only she could get somewhere alone. Get some time and space to think. The detective she'd met when she was first brought in, Detective Chief Inspector Darren Johnson, entered the room, his expression grim and formal. He took a seat across the table from where she'd been sitting in a strategically uncomfortable, cold plastic chair. Johnson was followed by his partner, Detective Inspector Terry Mulgrave.

The Detective Chief Inspector did not like her. Pia didn't need to be psychic to know that. He looked at her with poorly concealed contempt. He'd met Pia's explanations during informal questioning with derision, repeating her answers slowly, in a way that said, *Do you really expect me to believe this crap?*

While Johnson took his time pulling out his notebook and pen, Pia focused, using the moment to get a "read" on him. A little over fifty, married with three kids, Johnson was good at his job, uniformly considered the best in the station. He had a full caseload and wanted this homicide wrapped up swiftly.

He'd already made his mind up that the ghost hunters were responsible for the death, the most obvious suspect being Pia. She'd admitted to calling Tom Kelly away from the others.

I don't believe in ghosts. The thought replayed over and over in Johnson's mind. *Only nutjobs believe in ghosts.* And it was his job to decide which nut on the ghost-hunting team had done the killing.

One of the ghost hunters had killed Tom Kelly, or at the very least had seen the perpetrator. Pia was of the most interest. There were holes in her statements given at the scene. He was going to pick at them until she broke. He'd done so many times. Johnson could have his grandmother confessing to murder if he put his mind to it. He'd have this nut cracked by the end of the day. He smirked at his own joke.

The cop sitting next to him was Detective Inspector Terry Mulgrave. About a decade younger than his superior, Mulgrave was seemingly content to take a step back and watch the interview unfold. He was bored, restless. He had much-needed annual-leave break coming up in two weeks, and the ghost-hunting aspect of this homicide was an amusing twist to the day-to-day repetition of crime he'd seen lately.

Mulgrave's phone flashed, signaling an incoming message. He swiped the phone off the table, glancing at the screen briefly, before sliding it into his top pocket. The message was from Danielle, and a thin layer of sweat broke out across his forehead.

Mulgrave was having an affair, and lately Danielle had been pressuring him to leave his wife, something he'd promised her many times in the heat of passion, but never intended to do. His stomach burned, and he popped an antacid. How the hell was he going to break it off with Danielle and not have this whole situation blow up in his face? Men had affairs all the time. Why had this turned to shit for him?

Pia forced her attention back onto Darren Johnson, who'd begun speaking into a small black recorder, stating the time he was resuming the interview and indicating who was present in the room.

Johnson was ready to wrap this case up. He had irrefutable facts and hard evidence. Details he would lay out on the table, truths she would be forced to agree with, then he would move in for the kill. The victory swing of the sword. He'd danced to this tune many times, and he had his moves down to a fine art. No matter how much trouble Pia Williams was, he'd have official charges laid by the end of the day.

Until this point, he'd been playing too nice. He needed to rile the suspect. Angry people were careless. All he needed were a few ill-chosen words, and it would be case closed.

Pia stopped probing and shut her abilities down. Knowing what was in the detectives' minds combined with her own anxiousness to leave were making her nervous. A reaction they'd interpret as guilt.

She was innocent, but being in this room, knowing how determined the detectives were to lay charges, made her *feel* guilty. Why was Johnson so determined to convict her of this crime? There was something else there, something she couldn't quite see. Something about this particular case that was… *personal?*

Johnson was talking. She cleared her mind of Johnson's thoughts and focused on her own.

Stay calm.

Johnson spent some time formally going over the facts of the case as he knew them to be, and then he asked her officially if she'd killed Tom Kelly.

She replied, for the umpteenth time since last night, that she had not.

Johnson then asked her directly if she knew or had seen who'd committed the murder.

Pia stated, again for the record, that she had not.

Johnson did not appear surprised at her continued denial, nor did he appear to believe it.

"Ms. Williams, can you explain, for the record this time, exactly what it was that you were doing at Chad and Monique Reynolds' house at two o'clock in the morning?"

"We were conducting a paranormal investigation." Pia answered the question in the same formal tone he'd used. She'd already answered these questions, and her patience was hanging on by a fraying thread.

"Hunting for ghosts, you mean?" Johnson asked, deliberately placing an inflection on the word "ghosts." Baiting her.

Mulgrave began singing the theme to *Ghostbusters* in his head, *Who you gonna call,* and Pia shut him out, erecting a psychic wall that stopped her hearing his thoughts.

"I don't *hunt ghosts,*" Pia replied, taking a breath. She reminded herself that Johnson's attitude was deliberate. He wanted her angry, reckless. And Mulgrave was enjoying the show.

She fought for patience. "Our team, *Debunking Reality,* the number one paranormal-investigations show to a *major network,*" she added with emphasis, "investigates unexplained events that could be attributed to the paranormal."

"*Riiiight…*" Johnson flicked an amused gaze at his partner. "So your clients believe their house is haunted?" he raised an eyebrow in question. Pia kept her gaze even. Johnson cleared his throat and continued. "They call you out to chase away the ghosts. Would that be correct?"

Pia folded her arms across her chest. "Phrase it however you need to make it easier for you to understand."

"Answer the question, Ms. Williams."

"I prefer my answer to your paraphrased one. It's more accurate. Feel free to rewind the tape if you need to hear it again."

A muscle in Johnson's jaw twitched, and his pen tapped the lined pad in front of him.

Mulgrave was still humming *Who you gonna call*, this time out loud, but when Johnson tossed him a pointed glare, then looked at the recorder, Mulgrave fell instantly silent.

"What exactly do you do in these ghost hunts?" Johnson asked.

"Paranormal investigations," Pia corrected him with emphasis. "Using state-of-the-art equipment, we record and capture EVPs, electronic voice phenomena, measure EMFs, electromagnetic frequencies, and capture unexplained noises, voices, and movements that otherwise can't be attributed to what most consider to be normal reality."

"I don't believe in ghosts," Johnson said. "I believe only in facts and hard evidence. I need to see something before I know it's real." He leaned back in his chair and crossed his arms over his chest.

"Congratulations," Pia said.

Johnson narrowed his eyes, leaned forward, and placed his elbows on the table. "What makes you think you can get irrefutable evidence of anything? Don't you think if ghosts existed, scientists would have proved it by now?"

Pia didn't need proof of anything. On a daily basis, she experienced what mainstream science couldn't explain. But there were new branches of science, new technologies being developed, that could potentially measure and prove the existence of life after death. Pia hoped to see more leaps of scientific advancement in her lifetime and hoped evidence from *Debunking Reality*'s paranormal investigations and her own abilities would provide valuable assistance in such research.

Pia eyed Johnson across the table. "Your scientists can't prove the existence of God," she said carefully, not intending to insult whatever belief system he might have.

Pia herself believed in a higher consciousness, a power greater than human life. Her point was merely about believing and knowing something to be true without requiring confirmation by modern science.

Still, her comment had offended him. His face reddened, and the look he gave her was one a headmaster would give a recalcitrant child before using the cane. *You have no one to blame but yourself for what I'm about to do.*

"So, you claim to be a… psychic medium?" Johnson asked.

"If you say so." *Stop trying to aggravate me and get to the questions about Tom Kelly's death.*

Johnson tapped his manila folder with his pen. "Says so in here."

"Well, then. If it says so in there, it must be true."

"What are Saturday night's winning lotto numbers?" Mulgrave asked with a smirk.

Pia closed her eyes, made a low humming noise, and held out her hands like a fortune teller in an incense-filled room behind a curtain. "Twenty… fifteen… thirty-eight… two stupid detectives in a room."

Pia opened her eyes, amused to see Mulgrave had actually been writing the numbers down. He ripped the page from his notebook, scrunched it up, and tossed it at the wastepaper basket in the corner. It missed.

Johnson slowly and deliberately placed his pen on the table and met her gaze head on. "This is a homicide investigation, Ms. Williams."

"Then I suggest you stick to questions that relate to that."

"I don't need you to tell me how to do my job, Ms. Williams."

"Clearly you do."

He tapped his pen on the table. *Tap. Tap. Tap.* Irritation rolled off him in waves, and Pia fought the impulse to back away. Not from his questions, but his energy. Johnson was a powerful man, his presence forceful to people in general, and Pia felt it even more keenly. She steeled herself the best she could.

"You lock all the doors and secure all windows, exits, and entryways during your ghost hunts," Johnson stated.

"Paranormal investigations," Pia corrected him. Again.

"Answer the question."

"Phrase the questions correctly and I will."

"What time did you lock yourselves in the house?"

"Eight p.m."

"And no one entered or left the building after that time."

"To the best of my knowledge. Until we let you in."

Johnson made a show of checking his notes, although he knew what time the police had arrived without having to look it up. "The call to police came through at 3:11 a.m. and the first unit arrived on scene at 3:17 a.m. Is it usual practice for you to ransack a house you're investigating?" Johnson whipped his gaze from the paper to hers, as though attempting to catch her off guard by the sudden change in direction.

Pia held his eyes without flinching. "No."

"Then why did you do so last night?"

"I didn't."

Johnson stared at her. "If no one else could enter or leave the building, one of you had to have torn the house up. Who was it?"

"None of us."

"Then how do you explain the contents of the house getting so damaged?" Johnson spoke slowly, as though addressing someone of compromised mental capacity.

"If you view the footage we took of the night, you'll see and hear the unexplained things that we captured. You'd see for yourself what was happening in that house. You've confiscated the tapes. Do yourself a favor and watch what's on them."

Johnson shifted in his seat. "You could have tampered with the footage. You were after all, making a TV show. Theater is make-believe."

"We didn't have time, not that we would have tampered with it anyway. The time and date of the recording is on all the footage. There were several cameras running, capturing events from different angles, from different parts of the house."

"You can rest assured the footage will be analyzed thoroughly by experts. At this stage, I can't rule out the likelihood of you staging it."

"Why would we do that?"

"To cover up a crime, Ms. Williams."

Pia narrowed her eyes. "I did not commit a crime."

"That is yet to be determined."

"Detective, I have not only answered your questions about what happened, I have also given you evidence in the form of digital recordings."

"Evidence?" Johnson coughed and took a sip of water.

"Yes, evidence. As good as surveillance cameras in any location. You use video evidence in a court of law all the time. We were investigating last night, just like you do."

"Investigating *just* like me?" His lips twisted.

"Have you taken a look at the footage?" Pia demanded. They hadn't had time to review what they'd caught in the final moments; she had to hope they had something substantial. Something that could clear them all of a possible murder charge.

"Yes."

"Well?"

"Well, what?" Johnson shrugged. "Looks like it would have been a spooky show. But I'm talking real life here, Ms. Williams. A man was murdered. I need facts. Evidence. I need you to start telling the truth."

"Did the camera in the hallway capture what happened to Tom?" Pia sat up straight in her chair. All they had to do was prove the footage hadn't been tampered with, and they'd be clear.

"At 3:01, the cameras went staticky, then died. What are the chances of all the cameras running out of batteries just moments before Mr. Kelly died? The house was in perfect order at that time, I might add. Someone really messed up the house between 3:01 and 3:17."

Pia rubbed at her temples. "All the cameras?" It was not uncommon for entities to use electrical equipment nearby to help get the energy required, particularly for a manifestation, as when "Sarah" appeared in the doorway next to Pia.

"All the cameras," Johnson said, as though that proved his point and not hers.

"How could we possibly turn off seven different cameras in various locations at precisely 3:01 a.m. when there were only four of us?"

"How did you?" he asked.

"It's not possible."

"Very little surprises me these days, Ms. Williams. If I were to take a guess, I'd say you turned them off remotely."

Pia clenched her jaw and remained silent. There was no argument she could make that he would believe. He'd already determined her guilt.

"I put it to you, Ms. Williams, that you or one of your team killed Tom Kelly, quite violently I might add, then ransacked the house in an attempt to cover up or destroy evidence."

"I did not."

"Then who did?" Johnson asked. "All of you? There was a lot of destruction for just one person. I fail to see how just one of you could have done it and the others not be aware of it." He paused. "I'm going to ask you one more time. What happened to Tom Kelly, and who caused the damage to the house?"

"I don't know."

"For a psychic, you really don't know much, do you?"

"For a detective, you are slow at connecting all the dots."

"What dots would those be?"

Pia averted her gaze. Six months ago, she'd gone through exactly the same thing with another set of detectives, Ethan Blade and Nate Ryder, on a different investigation back in Cryton, South Australia. It was almost impossible to convince skeptics of what they chose not to see.

"Precisely where were you when Tom Kelly was killed?"

The question was fired at her like a bullet from a gun, and Pia whipped her attention back to the room. "I told you, I was just outside the daughter's bedroom. Cassandra Reynold's room."

"From the doorway of that room, you have a straight line of sight to where Tom Kelly's body was found. Am I right?"

"Yes."

"And yet, you didn't see anything at all?"

"I saw lots of things," Pia said.

"Would one of those things be who murdered Tom Kelly?"

"No."

"Because it was you."

"It wasn't me."

"So Tom Kelly was killed in front of you, but you didn't see who did it. Supposing that's true, what I don't understand is why you didn't do anything to help him?"

I couldn't. I was pinned against the wall. "I guess I must have been in shock." *What else can I say that he'd believe?*

"What were you doing in Cassandra's room all alone?" Mulgrave asked. "When the rest of the team was upstairs?"

Pia stretched her neck. This situation was not looking good. What defense did she have if the detectives wouldn't believe there was something paranormal involved?

"Playing with her doll collection," Pia said, her flippant comment annoying both detectives to judge by their reddening faces. *Stay calm.*

"So if you didn't kill Tom Kelly, and you claim the rest of your team didn't, what do *you* believe happened to him?"

"An unfortunate accident as the result of violent poltergeist activity," Pia said, in echo of Mark's observation while they'd been waiting for the police to arrive. She had nothing to lose, so she'd put that theory out there. And stand by it.

"So you're suggesting that a… *ghost* did it?" Johnson sneered.

"Woo ooo ooo," Mulgrave said in an imitation of spooky music under his breath.

Pia rubbed her temples. She hadn't slept at all last night, and after what had happened during the investigation, she was emotionally exhausted. Impressions were starting to bombard her. She was tiring fast and could no longer maintain control of her filter. Images, phrases, voices were coming at her thick and fast. From this room and from the corridor behind her.

Calling it the "interview room" did little to change the fact she was as trapped here as she would have been in a locked cell. A cell like the one Detective Johnson believed he was taking her to after the interview. When he arrested her.

Mulgrave's phone vibrated in his top pocket. He pulled it out and looked at a text message. Danielle again. He needed a cigarette. He wanted to think. He had to work out a way to break off the affair without it blowing up in his face. He could lose everything.

"And you'd deserve it," Pia said.

"What?" Johnson asked, brow wrinkling.

Mulgrave's eyes widened, before narrowing suspiciously.

"Just to make sure I've got this right," Johnson said. "Mark Collins, Ryan Donovan, Joe Clarke, and Tom Kelly were all upstairs, and you were the only one downstairs. Is that correct?"

"Yes."

"Moments before the tapes went out, your voice is on the recording calling out to Tom Kelly. Why did you call him downstairs?"

Pia closed her eyes, but that wouldn't help her. When Sarah had been standing in the door, Pia had had an overwhelming sense that Sarah's anger was directed at Tom. Pia hadn't known why—she still didn't—but it had been only instinct that had made her call out to Tom. To warn him.

"So you called for him to come downstairs," Johnson pressed on, taking her silence as confirmation of her guilt. "And then you beat him up and killed him. Why?"

"I didn't beat him up or kill him."

"So you called him, but remained just outside the girl's bedroom where you somehow didn't see or hear who beat him up and then killed him?"

"It wasn't me."

"Wasn't it?" Johnson cleared his throat. "Then tell me who it was," he demanded, leaning forward with his elbows on the table. "You were meters away, and you didn't see anything? All that noise. All that chaos happening right in front of you, and you didn't see a damn thing?"

When she didn't reply, he continued. "The front door was locked, and you said you had to unlock it to let the police in."

Pia's stomach knotted.

"Why did you call Tom Kelly to come downstairs?"

Pia couldn't hold Johnson's gaze. What reason could she give that he would believe? His questions were getting louder, more demanding.

"What were you doing after you called out for Tom Kelly to come down?"

How could she explain that she'd been pressed against the wall, unable to move?

"You were the only one downstairs; everyone agrees that the rest of your team was upstairs at the time of the incident. You called for Tom Kelly, for a reason yet to be determined, then all of a sudden Kelly is dead. And you, Ms. Williams, by your own admission, were the only one downstairs."

Johnson looked down at his notes in faux confusion.

"But you claim you didn't kill him...."

"I told you what I believe happened," Pia said, struggling to talk past the constriction in her throat.

Johnson went back through his notes, pretending to concentrate as though he'd missed something. "Oh that's right," he said, tapping the note with his pen. "According to you, a *ghost* killed him."

Oh, she was so screwed.

She should have called a lawyer. Clearly, attorneys were not just for the guilty. But who could she call? Pia didn't know any lawyers. And this wasn't a standard crime.

Who would believe her?

She could just imagine the lawyer suggesting their strategy be an insanity plea.

Pia released a long, slow breath. *Stay calm.*

"I want a lawyer."

Johnson and Mulgrave exchanged satisfied looks.

"Look, Ms. Williams," Mulgrave said. "You are entitled to a lawyer. But we're only asking a few questions. Trying to clear things up. We can start again at the beginning. Perhaps there's something you've missed."

There was nothing Pia could say that would make things any clearer for the detectives. She opened her mouth and said the first thing that rose to mind.

"The feng shui in here is terrible."

Johnson blinked. "The what?"

"The feng shui," Pia said, waving her arms to encompass the room. "The steel gray walls are too harsh; they would benefit from being painted a more soothing color. A soft blue perhaps. Something that sets people at ease. If you create free-flowing positive energy, you might find interviewees more forthcoming with their answers."

Johnson gave her a hard look. "Would you be more forthcoming if the walls were a different color?"

"You should put a plant over there." Pia pointed to the corner adjacent to the door. "Soften those hard corners. The furniture should be rearranged. This desk needs to be shifted so that your back is not to the door. You should—"

"Ms. Williams!"

"See, you're frustrated," Pia said with faux sympathy. "A nice picture of a waterfall trickling into a calm pond would do wonders for your nerves."

She could almost hear his teeth grinding.

"You won't be such a smart-arse when I arrest you for murder."

Pia shrugged. "I didn't do it."

"You think you're the first person to protest their innocence?" Johnson smirked.

Pia held his gaze, refusing to be intimidated. The moment drew out. Much to her surprise, he was the first to look away.

"Tell you what," Johnson said. "You work out how to bring that ghost in here for questioning, and if he admits guilt, we'll lock him up. In the meantime,"—

Johnson leaned forward, elbows on the table, his eyes taking on a hard glint—"you can do us all a favor and confess. I'll take you to a different room. Never know; that one might have better foong shuwi."

"It's pronounced 'fung shway.' And spelt F.U.C.K.Y.O.U."

Johnson's face turned purple.

"I want to call my lawyer."

Johnson turned the tape off, then he stormed out, Mulgrave on his heels. Mulgrave slammed the door behind him.

Pia pulled her mobile out of her bag and stared at it.

She could call Sage Blade, the friend Pia had helped with the demonic entity in September last year. Sage's husband, Ethan, had been in Special Operations with the South Australian Police Force. He might be able to help.

But Sage was pregnant and had been in the hospital recently. Pia couldn't pull Ethan away from Sage's side.

Pia closed her eyes, concentrated, and a picture of a business card she'd received six months ago came to the forefront of her mind.

She shook her head, dispelling the image.

No. She couldn't call *him*.

There had to be someone else.

She leaned forward, face in her palms. What was she going to do? It didn't take a brain surgeon to realize she was in trouble.

Big trouble.

Mark and the team were in the same situation. Mark would be firm in his claim of poltergeist activity. And why not? He believed it to be the truth. But what did you do when you couldn't use the truth?

She couldn't bother Sage and Ethan. And that meant she knew only one other person who was in a position to help.

Him.

Her stomach twisted.

She dialed the number she'd remembered. When she heard the smooth, deep voice on the recording that answered her, she closed her eyes and gripped the phone tight in her hands, her heart pounding.

"Hi, it's me. Pia. I need you. Your *help*, I mean," she rushed to say. "I need your help."

CHAPTER THREE

Nate Ryder was working a private case when a call came through, and he let it transfer straight to voice mail. He couldn't be interrupted at the moment.

Former Detective Senior Constable of the South Australian Police Force, ex-Special Operations unit, Taipan, Nate and the team had formed their own company and worked independently of the government now. Since they no longer needed to keep the unit's identity secret, they'd kept the name Taipan as a tribute to fallen team member Jake Brown, who'd died in the line of duty last September.

"I have visual." Sam Wells whistled in appreciation through the headset in Nate's ear. "Nice birthday present. Thanks." Today Sam turned twenty-six.

Nate barked a short laugh. They'd just located—and were about to steal back—a rare, 1969 Ferrari convertible stolen from a very wealthy private client of Taipan Security and Investigations, TSI. The car's worth had been pegged at around three million dollars.

Straightforward case—for TSI anyway. To men as highly trained as Sam and Nate, a simple seize-and-recover operation should be a breeze.

The slight complication in the case, if you could call it that, was that the Ferrari had been stolen nine months ago by one of the biggest drug lords in Australia, Wild Wilson.

Nate had been handed the file less than twenty-four hours ago, and with the assistance of their technology wizard, Zach, and his less-than-legal methods of gaining access to information, they had located the rare gem secured in a large shed hidden in bushland on a secluded country property a hundred kilometers south of Perth.

Another minor hitch was that the shed was wired to blow. When Aussies referred to a shed, they typically meant an aluminum structure with a rusting tin roof. This "shed" was a fortress by comparison. A secure facility surrounded by industrial-strength razor-wire fencing.

The Ferrari was protected in the shed's center by bulletproof glass wired to explosives, ensuring that any intruders would die before getting close, while also ensuring that the Ferrari wouldn't suffer so much as a scratch.

Nate looked around. Secure structures off to the side of the shed no doubt contained ingredients for the drugs made in the adjacent building. Zach's intel had informed him the nearby residence was a suspected state-of-the-art drug lab, but Nate was no longer a cop. Drugs were no longer his concern.

Nate's only interest was the swift retrieval of the stolen Ferrari.

Wild Wilson was currently less than three hundred meters away in the main house. Nate had assisted Wilson's rather grumpy guard dogs to sleep temporarily, giving him and Sam just enough time to disable the security, disengage the explosive device, and remove the Ferrari before the dogs woke from their slumber.

That was the plan, anyway.

Nate moved silently and set to work. It took several seconds longer than anticipated to disable the intricate alarm system and deactivate the explosive device.

"One dog is waking up," Sam said via his earpiece. "Shall I put it back to sleep?"

Nate looked at his watch. "No." There was no time. They needed to be gone in less than five minutes. Wilson would have two armed guards patrolling past in exactly six. At any moment, Wilson could discover that his security monitor was down and come to investigate.

"Clear to enter," Nate said. Now that Sam was in sight, they would switch back to hand signals.

Tall, lean, and athletic, Sam had scaled the outside of the shed to enter through a roof-height window. There was a reason he'd earned the nickname Spiderman. Using his jacket to protect his hand, Sam broke out the glass.

Nate's pulse raced. Experience had taught him never to be overconfident or let his guard down. He remained predator-still, listening for the tell-tale click of a tripwire, or some other trap he hadn't seen on previous scans.

Sam slipped in through the window. Moments later, the lock on the shed door disengaged, and when the door opened, Nate stepped inside to see a grinning Sam, who remained by the open door to stand guard.

Two minutes.

Nate hot-wired the Ferrari; the low rumble of the engine, as beautiful as it was, was deadly at the same time.

A guard dog came rushing toward the shed, barking furiously. A door slammed open and someone shouted from the house.

"Get in!" Nate ordered Sam.

Nate revved the engine just as two armed guards reached the open shed door and aimed shotguns in their direction.

"Come on, baby. Show us what you're made of." Nate put the pedal to the metal, asking the question, and the Ferrari answered. Thrown back in their seats, Nate and Sam hurtled out of the shed, the guards jumping out of the way. Spewing rocks and dust behind it, the Ferrari ate up the driveway, Nate deftly navigating the deliberately unkempt dirt road.

In the rear-view mirror were several pissed-off bikies who sent bullets flying in their direction. Nate felt at least one hit the vehicle, possibly near the driver's side taillight.

Not bad collateral damage, considering. Without physically checking, Nate believed the car to be in an otherwise undamaged state.

Finally on the open road, Sam fist-pumped the air. "Yeah!"

Nate eyed him and grinned. There was nothing like the thrill of a successful mission. It didn't hurt that their reward was driving a rare Ferrari worth several million dollars back to South Australia. They could open it up on the flats of the Nullarbor Plain, see what it could do.

His phone vibrated in his pocket, and he fished it out and handed it to Sam. "It's Blade," Sam said. He answered and updated Blade on how the op went. When he finished, Sam turned to Nate. "You've missed a call. I don't know who it's from, but there's a message. Want to hear it?"

"What's the number?"

Sam recited the digits, and a tingle of awareness spread through Nate's body, his muscles tensing. He recognized that number. How could he ever forget?

His heart pounded in his chest. "Play it."

Sam hit speaker on the phone, and a soft, husky female voice filled the small space. He hadn't heard that voice since September last year. Except during quiet moments shrouded by the privacy of night. A voice, a face, a woman Nate would never forget.

But never thought he'd see again.

"Can you drive this baby back to SA on your own?" Nate asked Sam.

"You betcha!" Sam didn't appear at all displeased with the idea. "Sounds like you got somewhere else you need to be. Let me know if you need a hand."

"Thanks mate. Drop me off at my place. Tell Blade I might be out of action for a little while."

———◆———

It had taken some doing, but Nate managed to arrange Pia's release even though he was no longer officially on the force. You didn't become part of an elite special operations unit without making friends along the way. People in high places who owed you a favor or wanted one up their sleeve. Nate, in his current line of business, was a powerful friend to have.

Plus, a tip-off on the whereabouts of a certain crime lord's drug lab with a currently disabled security system was highly influential currency.

And of course, there was the fact the police had no solid evidence against Pia. Charges had not been laid, although that had certainly been Detective Chief Inspector Darren Johnson's intention. But with no eyewitnesses, no motive, no blood on her hands or clothing, and no fingerprints on the murder weapon, there was simply nothing concrete to pin her as the killer. Just a whole lot of circumstantial evidence that didn't look good.

Circumstantial evidence notwithstanding, Nate didn't believe for a second that Pia was capable of murder, or the cover-up of one. Nor the others members of the

Debunking Reality team for that matter. Nate and his business partner, Ethan Blade, had come to know Mark Collins and the rest of the Paranormal Research and Investigation (PRI) team extremely well during a case in Cryton six months ago, the same case Nate had been on when he'd met Pia. A unique situation dealing with a dark paranormal entity where they'd all been forced to depend on each other for their very lives.

Nate took a moment to observe Pia through the two-way glass of the investigation room. Crimson hair spilled in silken waves over her shoulders and down her back, and she was currently securing it into a ponytail. Her nails were still long and painted glossy black. Her face was strained, pale and so beautiful, it made something deep inside him physically ache.

When she finished with her hair, she sat rigid in the chair, her arms folded across her stomach, sharp green eyes narrowly focused on Johnson, who was avoiding eye contact with her. Nate suppressed a grin. He remembered all too clearly how it felt to be the recipient of that piercing emerald gaze.

"After you locked yourselves in, no one came in or out during your... investigation," the detective said. Nate had discovered Pia had held back on retaining a lawyer for now, freeing Johnson to ask her more questions. Or rather, the same questions over and over, looking for even the slightest variation in the story. It took a lot of energy to maintain a lie, especially when pressed constantly for tiny details.

"How many more times are you going to ask that same question?" Pia's soft voice was slightly husky, and a lot pissed off.

Outwardly she showed little sign that she'd been interrogated by Johnson for over six hours. After an all-night paranormal investigation she was holding up well, Nate thought with a surprising touch of pride. Johnson had a reputation for breaking suspects quickly.

"Then how do you explain the dead body?"

"No matter how many times you ask, I can't give you the answer you want."

"The problem is, your answer doesn't make sense to me, and I've been in this game a long time. No one came in, no one went out, the house ends up trashed, a man ends up dead. You were the only one on the same floor with the victim, yet you claim not to have seen what happened."

"I explained what happened. You just don't want to believe it."

"If not you, then which one of you killed the guy?"

"None of us."

"But there was no one else in the house," Johnson pressed, allowing his frustration to show. "All the evidence points to you. If you didn't do it, you'd better tell me who did, or you're going to go to jail for a long time for something you didn't do."

He doesn't believe she did it either. Nate listened for a while longer and knew by the way Johnson was questioning her that he thought she was covering for someone. Perhaps one of the team members.

He doesn't believe she did it, and yet he wants to pin her for it. He wants this case closed swiftly and neatly.

Nate's instincts prickled. *Something isn't right here.*

"I told you everything," Pia said. "I won't change my story. I can't. It's the truth."

"You're seriously not sticking by your ghost theory."

"You have a better one?" Pia spit the words at Johnson.

"Yes. You, Ms. Williams."

No, you don't believe it, Johnson. Scaring her won't work either. Pia's too strong. She won't break.

"I believe you did it," Johnson continued, leaning forward in an intimidating manner, "and it will be only a matter of time before the evidence will prove it."

"I believe you're an arsehole, and I already have the evidence to prove that."

Johnson's face reddened.

Nate needed to put a stop to this before she did something Johnson could actually charge her with.

"You have a smart mouth," Johnson said between clenched teeth. "You won't be so cocky when I throw you behind bars. I have a cozy little cell waiting with your name on it. You'll love your cellmate. Can't wait for you to meet her. One look at you, and she'll eat you for breakfast. Too bad I won't be able to respond to your cries for help until it's too late to be of any assistance."

Nate's fists clenched at his sides, and he forcibly restrained himself from going in there and tearing Johnson apart, limb from limb. If Johnson so much as laid a single finger on her…

Nate's sudden rush of possessiveness was powerful. And not altogether surprising.

It had been the same last September. That rush he got every time he saw Pia. The heated thrill that went through him, an electrical charge that caused his body to heat and his jeans to feel way too tight.

Nate thrust a hand through his hair, took a deep breath, and forced his feelings toward her aside.

For now.

Right now, his number-one priority was getting her out of the police station. Numbers two and three were ensuring her safety and proving her innocence.

And then?

Then he'd consider the best way to get her into his bed. And keep her there.

Nate pushed on the door and entered the room.

CHAPTER FOUR

Pia froze. A heartbeat… two….

Nate Ryder stood in the doorway, the brilliant glare of fluorescent light casting him in a silhouetted glow. She'd known he was outside an instant before she saw him, and still, the knowledge did nothing to lessen the impact of him actually standing there. Over six feet of powerful male entered the confined space. His presence washed over her, stole her breath.

"Are you all right?" His eyes immediately sought and connected with hers.

"Just peachy."

Her curt tone wasn't due to her situation, although he'd likely interpret it that way; it was because of the effect he had on *her*.

Pia tentatively reached out, tried to see what he was thinking. Nothing. She couldn't tell if he was pleased to see her or pissed off that she'd called him.

It had always been that way, ever since she'd first laid eyes on him last September, in Cryton, South Australia. There had always been something different about Nate; he affected her in a way no one else did. Pia could usually "read" people, picking up what they were currently thinking about, as that was what radiated off them most strongly.

But not Nate.

Nate Ryder had been a mystery to her then, and his presence here today confirmed he was just as much an enigma now. Nate was a closed man to her, a black box.

Having Nate simply standing there in such close proximity made it hard for her to breathe. That was what had driven her crazy six months ago, and it drove her crazy again now.

"Peachy is good," Nate replied, a nearly imperceptible twitch at the corner of his lips.

His voice was deep, slightly gravelly, and carried an easy-natured confidence that only truly powerful men had. Nate Ryder was a force of nature. He knew what he wanted and had the ability and authority to get it.

Her pulse ratcheted up a notch and her skin heated. His hair was longer than when she'd seen him last, less professional and more sexy… scruffy. She meant scruffy.

She shifted in her chair, her fingers twisting the ponytail lying on her shoulder, a nervous habit she'd switched to in an effort to replace nail biting. Taking a deep breath, Pia forced her hands flat on the table in front of her, every muscle in her body alive. Aware of *him*.

Nate and Johnson finished exchanging their brief greeting.

"A word in private?" Nate said to the detective.

Johnson clenched his jaw as he rose, his annoyance at the interruption evident to Pia but outwardly concealed by a cool professional mask.

Although Johnson knew Nate, clearly respected him and his status, he was also extremely irritated that he was here. Johnson regretted not charging her now. Even if he would've had to trump up the evidence. Let the lawyers fight it out in court. What the hell was Ryder doing here? Why was a man of his status interested in this case, murder or not?

Curious. Wouldn't Johnson consider the extra assistance helpful, especially from someone of Nate's caliber? Pia couldn't shake the feeling that Johnson was taking this case personally.

But why?

At times, Pia found Johnson almost as difficult to read as Nate. Perhaps that was a sign of an experienced cop, trained to school his thoughts and emotions. But her difficulty likely stemmed from her emotional investment in her predicament. To get a clear read on a situation, Pia needed to be detached, to let the impressions form without preconceived notions or desires. Strong emotional responses blurred her judgment. Were the impressions she got real, or were they generated by her fear?

Mulgrave hit the "off" button on the recording device after announcing the time and that the interview was being paused. Then he followed Johnson and Nate outside.

Alone in the cell disguised as an interview room, Pia slumped in her chair and took a few deep breaths. As crazy as Nate made her, she was grateful he'd come. He'd been in South Australia when she'd seen him last, and there'd been no guarantee when he'd receive her voice message, or if he'd even come when he did.

Actually, that was not entirely true. Pia felt sure he'd come. Something strong had sparked between them last September; she just didn't know exactly what it meant. Despite her inconvenient and intense physical attraction to him, she'd kept him at arm's length. They were not friends in the usual sense of the word. Definitely not "have a drink on Friday night" type friends. Their friendship had been forged out of crisis, the unique connection that surviving a life-threatening situation can create. People tended to instantly bond when thrown into life-and-death situations.

Or was it something else? After all, Pia hadn't had the same reaction to the other men involved…

Nate was back at the door, Johnson and Mulgrave nowhere to be seen.

"Let's go."

Pia stood, grabbing her handbag. "I can leave? Just like that? No more questions?"

Nate nodded, but there was something serious in his eyes. "Just mine." He held the door as she walked through it.

"What about Mark, Ryan, and Joe?" Pia asked, feeling a rush of anxiety. "Did they get out too?"

"I arranged their release when I first arrived. They left about half an hour ago. None of you have had formal charges laid. But that doesn't mean it won't happen."

"I haven't done anything. None of us has." She started to say more, but he held up a hand.

"I need to take you somewhere we can talk in private." Nate swiftly navigated the narrow corridors, Pia struggling to keep up with his long strides. After all those hours in interrogation, her release was happening fast.

Pia's head spun, and she focused on Nate again, but still couldn't tell what he was thinking. Was he angry with her? Annoyed she'd called and interrupted whatever he'd been doing? Or worse, did he have some misguided idea that he was obliged to help her?

As she hurried to keep up, she tried repeatedly to reach out. Nothing. Pia recognized the wall Nate slid behind well; she had one of her own.

This situation aside, Pia had no idea what Nate thought of her on a personal level. His words, his actions, made her feel he barely tolerated her. Yet sometimes, the looks he gave her, the heat in his eyes, scorched her skin.

A woman appeared in the doorway of a side office. She was tall, dressed in jeans, a fitted shirt and a suit jacket, her rich chocolate hair tied back into a stylish knot. She had the self-assurance of someone comfortable in her skin, in her authority. A woman with power. A detective. Nate had the same way about him.

Nate paused, leaning his shoulder against the opposite wall. "Hi, Tash."

Tash tilted her head toward Nate and smiled. "Didn't know you were back in town." She used a tone that suggested familiarity of an intimate kind, her eyes traveling down his body in a deliberate way, as though undressing him by memory, not imagination.

Something twisted in Pia's stomach, and she felt a rush of possessiveness at odds with any sense of logic or reason, considering most of the time she'd spent with Nate they had been arguing.

"Not by design," Nate replied easily. "I'd intended to be half way across the Nullarbor by now."

"I've sent you a few emails." Tash's voice was low, carefully neutral.

"I've been busy."

"Setting up your new company, I heard. Congratulations. How is it, going out on your own?"

"Pretty good, actually. You know how much I love my freedom." He put a slight emphasis on the last word.

"Heard you've picked up some impressive clients." Tash smiled knowingly.

"Can't discuss our clients." But he gave her a small smile.

"I miss you." Her voice dropped to a husky whisper.

Ah, geez. "I'm standing here too," Pia grumbled under her breath. She could have throttled the woman. And Nate hadn't bothered to introduce her. Was she not important enough to warrant a simple introduction?

"Can I see you later?" Tash asked.

"I'm busy."

Interesting. Was he brushing Miss Gorgeous Detective off?

Tash let her gaze wash over Pia for the briefest of moments before she focused on Nate again. "Later then, when you've finished with business?"

Pia shook off an unwanted vision of Tash and Nate together.

"Pia's not business," Nate said. "We go way back."

Pia's body warmed, ridiculously pleased by his not entirely accurate response. They went way back, if "way back" was six months. However, during that brief time in Cryton they'd been through more together than most people who'd spent an entire lifetime in each other's company.

Tash smiled and touched his arm. "I have to see you," she said softly. "Before you leave. Call me."

Tash tried to hold eye contact, but Nate looked away and didn't reply, shifting his body so that her hand fell from his arm.

Tash's gaze flicked back to Pia, lingering this time. The woman's thoughts bombarded her: *He couldn't possibly see anything in her. Look at how much eyeliner she wears! She's short, and that hair color isn't even real—*

Surprised at the sudden rush of nastiness, Pia quickly closed herself down. Intense emotions like anger and jealousy were difficult to keep out, especially when aimed directly at her. Gorgeous Tash had another side, and it wasn't pretty.

Had Nate seen it?

Nate grabbed Pia's hand firmly and pushed off the wall. She raced to keep up as he made a swift line for the door. A couple people called out to him, and Nate said a few words without missing a step, brushing them off in the most efficiently polite manner she'd ever seen.

Outside the station, Nate tugged her to a stop off to the side of the concrete steps, just out of sight of passersby in the street. His body briefly touched hers when he stopped, and her heart skipped a beat.

She took a step backward, bringing her flush against the concrete wall. The heat radiating from his body washed over her. Pia was more sensitive to energies than most, but there was something about Nate's presence that was always a little too much. The fresh air outside did little to cool her heated skin or calm her nerves.

He let go of her hand. She could still feel the warmth that had been transferred from his body to her skin.

"Where shall we go?" His steel-blue eyes searched her face.

Where shall we go? Pia tried to order her thoughts. *Of course, you idiot, he needs to talk to you about what's going on.* Damn it! Why couldn't she maintain her sense of equilibrium around him?

He knocked her for a loop, again and again.

This was why she'd kept him at a distance six months ago. His mere presence was a distraction; she couldn't afford that then, and she couldn't afford it now. She had to think clearly, and she had to get over whatever this was with Nate, and fast.

His phone buzzed, and he took it out of his front pocket. "Sorry, just need to give an update." A lock of hair fell across one eye as his fingers tapped the screen.

She took a moment to compose herself. She needed to put the situation in perspective. Nate was a handsome man; it was only natural her feminine interest would be piqued. What woman wouldn't be interested? Just because she'd sworn off men didn't mean she was made of stone.

Denim jeans hugged him in all the right places, and he wore his tight black T-shirt untucked to hide the concealed weapon she knew he carried on his hip.

He finished his message, and she took a deep breath.

"Thank you for coming," Pia said, keeping her voice even while he slid the phone back into his pocket. "I wasn't even sure you'd get the voice mail."

"I happened to be nearby."

"I didn't know who else to call," Pia said, shuffling her feet. "I thought about calling Ethan, but Sage's been in hospital recently. It just didn't feel right to divert his attention from where it should be. And I could have called Sean, Sam, or Daniel," Pia continued, referring to the other members of Nate's team, "but I didn't have their numbers, and that would have meant going through Ethan…" She was rambling. "You once gave me your card. I hope you don't mind that I remembered your number."

"I'm glad you called me." The intensity of his gaze blazed against her skin. "I'd have been pissed if you hadn't."

Pia's pulse fluttered. Deliberately, Pia thought of Tash. Even if things were different, Nate was way out of Pia's league. Six months ago was the past.

Focus! She was about to be accused of murder, and Nate was the only one who could help. She was not going to screw this up.

"I'm not going to ask you if you did it," he said. "I know you didn't."

"Thank you." Some of the tension coiled inside her eased. After being around so many people who were convinced of her guilt, it was nice to have someone who believed in her.

"But we do need to talk. Someplace private," he said, his expression grim.

Despite everything they'd gone through six months ago, Pia realized how little they knew about each other. He probably wanted to take her to her place, but he didn't even know where she lived. How much should she tell him?

Nate appeared to sense her hesitation. "You live in Adelaide. Where are you staying while you're here for the investigation?"

She suppressed a laugh. Of course Nate would know where she lived. He'd probably compiled a dossier on the entire PRI team as part of his investigation last September in Cryton. *She* was the one who didn't know much about him.

"Mark booked a holiday rental in Dunsborough for the team. Can you take me there? I really need to talk to them." She hoped the guys were faring okay after their time with the investigators.

"Not a problem. But let's go to my place now. I want to talk to you alone first." Nate slipped his dark sunglasses out of his top pocket and put them on.

He grabbed her hand and began walking briskly down the street.

Now just a bloody minute!

"Wait." Pia yanked his arm to stop him. Nate was a man used to being in control, used to giving orders with the expectation they'd be followed without question. That she was not the kind of girl who followed just added to their long list of incompatibilities.

"What?" Nate turned, his eyes narrowed.

"Have you just decided we are going to your house when I asked to be taken to Mark and the team?" She was leaving one situation she wasn't in control of, only to be put into another.

"Yes." Nate stated this like it was the most logical conclusion in the world.

Pia glared, and he had the audacity to appear surprised.

"I'm not sure I understand the problem," Nate said slowly. "It makes sense. I have all the resources I could possibly need at my fingertips. You'll be safe, and we can have privacy while I work out how we can untangle you from the mess you've got yourself into."

I hardly got myself into this! Pia's head spun again. His reasons were sound. Rational. But the thought of going to Nate's house? When she couldn't catch her breath being near him already? She needed space to think clearly. And she couldn't do that around Nate.

She broke his gaze and stepped back.

He took a step toward her, closing the distance she'd put between them. "I don't understand the problem," he repeated.

"Look, Nate." Pia began. Swallowed. *Calm down, you idiot! He's just a man.* "I don't want to sound rude, or appear ungrateful—"

"It's okay. I'm used to it."

Pia inwardly winced at his reference to their conflict six months ago, but she caught a hint of humor in his eyes. "I'm sorry. Truly. And I'm sorry about that last time I saw you as well. There's just something about you that…" Pia broke off, searching for the right word.

Nate's lip twitched. "Yeah. There's something about you too."

Pia glanced up, and their eyes held a moment. It was nice to think Nate might be just as confused about her as she was about him.

"I appreciate you coming, Nate. For getting me out of there." She waved her hand in the direction of the station. "But I really want to go to Mark and the team."

To the familiar. To where she could breathe and get her thoughts under control. "They'll be as worried about me as I am about them," she added.

He eyed her, released a breath. "If that's what you want."

It was what she *needed.* "It is."

"Then that's where we'll go." He paused, then grinned. "You know, you're still as frustrating as you always were."

A smile kicked at the corners of her lips. "Likewise."

Across the street, a young girl was watching them closely. Pia saw her out of the corner of her eye, but when she turned to look, the girl was no longer there. She'd gotten only a glimpse of pale skin, a black vacant stare. But then she heard a familiar voice in her mind.

Why won't you help me? Why won't anyone help me?

Pia shivered.
It was the entity. And it seemed to have fixated on Pia. It was following her. Who—or what—was Sarah? And what did she want?

CHAPTER FIVE

Despite the warm, balmy evening, Pia was chilled to the bone when Nate's black Porsche Cayenne rolled to a stop outside the team's short-term Dunsborough rental. The tired old beach house was made from timber and had been painted a clichéd ocean blue with white accents on the window and door trim. On the front porch was a picnic table, and a barbeque that had seen better days was chained to the railing. The muffled voices and laughter of Mark and the *Debunking Reality* team carried out to the driveway through the open windows.

All she needed was a moment to herself, a brief second to clear her head. *To breathe.* Over the last twenty-four hours, she'd been continuously bombarded by thoughts and images from others as well as her own. Being around a lot of people for extended periods of time was emotionally draining, and being subject to Johnson's relentless questioning had been beyond taxing. She was exhausted, too tired to hold her shield in place, and it left her feeling exposed and vulnerable.

The afternoon breeze had kicked in, blowing cool and fresh off the ocean, flicking hair into her face. She shivered, and wrapped her arms around her stomach, then dragged in a quick but much-needed breath of salty air into her lungs.

Mark gave a low whistle of appreciation from the front door. "Nice car." Pia released a breath and turned from the ocean and walked around the car to Nate.

"Thanks. I like it," Nate said.

He waited until Pia reached his side, then they walked together toward the beach house. Mark Collins, Pia's friend since they'd met at university, was handsome in that head turning, movie star way. The type of outstanding looks that only a very select few had. Mark had an effortless, innate sense of style, as though he were born to be on camera.

This afternoon, he was dressed casually, wearing long board shorts and a fun, touristy, *I love Dunsborough* T-shirt, and Pia knew he'd carefully selected the outfit to keep the mood light. At the end of the day, Mark was passionate about his show—his life's work—and the morale of his team was essential. Despite the seriousness of what had happened last night, Mark was showing he wasn't letting it get him down.

"Must be doing all right then," Mark said as they approached, still ogling Nate's Porsche. "Didn't know they paid detectives so well. If this all goes to shit, I might have to consider a career change."

"My family is in the racing industry," Nate said, and Pia felt his tension as he said it. Why hadn't Nate followed in the family business?

"But you're a cop," Mark said.

"*Was* a cop."

"You're *still* a cop, Detective," Mark said, as Nate and Pia drew to a stop on the porch. "You just don't take your orders from the government anymore."

"Thanks for clarifying my job description," Nate said with a wry twist of his lip. "I did wonder what I was doing."

Mark laughed and shook Nate's hand. "Thanks for coming, mate. I appreciate it. Thanks especially for helping Pia. She was the one under the most pressure; I knew by the way they conducted the interview. They wanted to pin this on her."

They still do. Pia's stomach churned. Needing to think about something else, she looked over Mark's shoulder. Ryan and Joe were drinking cold beer at the kitchen table, and her mouth watered. She hoped they had something stronger. "You going to let us in, or leave us standing on the porch all night?" Pia said, angling her body to nudge him out of the way.

"Sorry." Mark immediately stepped aside. "I didn't know Nate was staying. I came out to thank him for his help before he left."

Was he leaving? She glanced up at Nate. *I'm not ready for you to leave yet.* Not when she'd just found him again.

Nate turned to her. "You want me to go?"

No! "Do you have somewhere else you need to be?" She tried to keep her tone neutral. Just because he'd dropped everything and had come when she'd asked, didn't mean that he didn't have something pressing to get back to. She'd be selfish to think otherwise.

"I always have somewhere else to be. But nothing is as important as you. As this, I mean. Right now." Nate cleared his throat and took a step back to include Mark when he spoke. "I know Johnson; he's good at his job. Your release doesn't mean you're off the hook; it just means he didn't have enough evidence to charge you. For now. I wanted to talk to Pia, to you all, and find out what really happened last night. Work out how I can help. Unless..." He paused, then looked at her. "Unless you want me to go?"

The thought of Nate leaving did extremely unpleasant things to her insides. And not because she was sure Johnson would darken her doorstep sometime in the near future unless new evidence surfaced to clear her. Seeing Nate again after all this time made her remember what it felt like to be around him. Of course, he'd leave again, eventually. Their lives would take them in different directions, but he was here, now.

And she wanted every second with him she could get.

"Stay," she said. Their eyes met, held. The energy between them sparked and sizzled.

"Well, what are you waiting for," Mark said, breaking the moment. "Both of you, get inside and have a beer."

------- ◆ -------

Nate sat at the wobbly, chipped kitchen table with its uneven legs, and watched Mark embrace Pia in a hug that went on. And on. *Okay, that's long enough.* He looked away. *Damn it, Ryder, they're like brother and sister. Get a grip.*

Nate had no claim on her. *Yet.* Even so, he studied them both, searching for signs of something deeper between them. Nate couldn't imagine working with Pia so closely for years and not wanting something more.

Was Mark Collins standing in his way?

"I was worried about you, Boo," Mark said to her.

Boo?

"I was worried about me too," she replied with an exaggeratedly solemn expression, and they laughed.

"Seriously though," she said, turning to address the others. "I've been worried about all of us. I'd prefer to keep the cops out of our next investigation if you don't mind." Pia kissed Mark on the cheek before moving past him and going to Ryan and Joe at the other end of the large kitchen table.

Ryan Donovan, *Debunking Reality's* lead cameraman, was a couple inches shorter than Nate and muscular, with light-brown hair cut short at the back and longer at the front. Beside him, Joe Clarke stared broodingly into a laptop computer. At five foot ten, with dark hair and tanned skin, Joe was the team's technical whiz and couldn't be further from the thin, pale, tech-geek cliché. Joe coordinated the setup of the cameras and the editing of the footage into a watchable forty-minute show for the network.

The team had built a huge following, a large percentage of it female, but their success was due to much more than their good looks. They all had degrees, and Joe was a near genius with programming. His services were highly sought after. Even Zach was impressed by the guy. Joe had funded much of the team's early work with sales of software he'd created.

Mark met Nate's eyes. "Thanks for looking after her, mate."

Nate acknowledged the sentiment with an incline of his head. He didn't want Mark's thanks, and the sense of ownership in his tone grated on Nate, even though it shouldn't. Nate hadn't helped her for Mark. But if he wanted to stay on Pia's good side, he needed to get along with Mark. Nate had a smidgen more sympathy for Ethan now. Mark had openly flirted with Sage. He'd even kissed her. If Nate saw him kissing Pia…

He unclenched his fists. *They're like brother and sister, right?*

"Want a beer?" Mark asked.

"Won't say no."

Pia took a seat next to Nate at the table.

He leaned in, his head tantalizingly close to hers. "Boo?"

"We called her Boo in university when she first told us she could see ghosts," Mark answered, his smile showcasing perfect white teeth.

Pia rolled her eyes, then grinned at the team. "And you idiots haven't changed at all."

"We have come a long way since then, haven't we?" Mark said fondly.

"Yes," Pia said. "Apparently now we kill people." Her comment hung heavily in the air. "Sorry," she murmured. "That didn't come across the way I intended."

"What the fuck was it that happened last night?" Ryan demanded. "One minute we were catching some great EVPs, and the next minute Tom was gone, and all hell had broken loose downstairs."

Mark cracked the cap of a bottle of beer with his keyring and shoved the empty too forcefully across the table, where it clanked against the growing pile of empties. The impact toppled a bottle, and it rolled off the table onto the floor where it connected with Pia's foot.

Nate rested a hand on her arm when she moved to pick it up. "I've got it." He retrieved the bottle. As he straightened, he found her blinking at him through long black lashes.

He was still touching her, her skin like silk beneath his fingertips. His chest tightened. With effort, he removed his hand from her warm skin and placed it around his cold beer.

He didn't know how she felt about him touching her or whether the connection let her see things about him. But he wasn't about to shy away from her abilities; he would embrace them. After all, he planned on touching her a whole lot more than that.

Ryan and Joe had shifted and were now seated on either side of Mark, peering over his shoulder at something on his computer.

"What do you have there?" Pia asked them.

"The only footage the cops *didn't* confiscate," Ryan said. "I'd slid the memory card into my pocket when it was full, before I inserted the new one the cops have."

"Fucking cops won't even know what they're looking for. Something in the footage might prove that Pia is innocent," Joe said. "That we all are."

Nate grabbed his phone and typed out a text message. He'd have copies of the confiscated footage here by the end of the day. The guys were right; something in the recordings might clear Pia from suspicion, something perhaps Johnson was unable or unwilling to see, taking into account his inability to consider the paranormal.

Nate didn't suffer from such a shortcoming.

If it had happened the way Pia and the team said it had, and he had no reason not to believe them, something supernatural had pushed Tom Kelly down the stairs and put a knife through his heart. Nate wasn't sure how it would hold up in a court of law, but if something on one of the tapes could prove Pia and the others were elsewhere when Tom Kelly was killed, that was all he was interested in.

"Johnson told me the footage went staticky about the time all the activity started," Pia said. "That there was nothing they could see."

"Yeah, they told us that too," Ryan said. "But I might be able to enhance the audio and run it through that new program Joe created to clear out some of the visual distortion. Who knows what we'll discover, if only we get the goddamned opportunity."

"What do you think happened?" Nate aimed the question at Mark. "Your real thoughts, not the answer you gave at the station, if they're different."

Mark leaned back in his chair, chugged his beer, then shrugged his shoulders. "My answer is the same everywhere. It's the truth. Tom's death was the result of a sudden burst of poltergeist activity. It was an unfortunate accident."

Nate watched him intently. His facial expressions, his body language. The dilation of his pupils… Nate believed him. Mark was speaking the truth. At least as he knew it.

"What I don't know is why he was going back downstairs," Mark said. "Johnson seemed fixated on that, asked me over and over."

Nate knew that from the police interviews. Some fact had stuck in Johnson's craw. Something he wanted the team to corroborate.

"I called out to him," Pia said. "I was in Cassandra's room when I sensed that Tom was in trouble. That something negative was focusing on him."

"So you shouted to him?" Nate asked.

Pia nodded. "It was instinctual. As soon as I received the impression, I automatically called out his name in warning."

"And he heard your call and started to come to you."

"You didn't hear me?" Pia asked Mark.

"No, but I was getting some great EVPs. Ryan and I were focusing on that. One minute we were recording some of the best evidence we'd ever filmed, the next moment Tom was gone, and it sounded like World War III had broken out downstairs. We must have made contact with something pretty serious to cause such a forceful burst of activity." He shook his head. "We pissed something off. Something evil." A shadow crossed his expression. Mark felt responsible for what had happened, for the situation Pia was in.

"This isn't your fault," she said, laying a hand on his arm. Nate forced his eyes away from their contact.

"Yes it is, Boo. What I haven't told you is that I was provoking it. When I knew I had it engaged, I got excited. I pushed it, wanted to see how much of a reaction I could get. How powerful it was. I've seen poltergeist activity before, but this was escalating to another level." He twirled the bottle of beer in front of him with both hands, not looking at any of them.

"What I suspect happened is that I stirred it up, and in the chaos, the knife flew through the air, and Tom was in the wrong place at the wrong time. I'm sorry." Mark's eyes glistened when he looked up. "After the attack on you last September, Pia, when I riled up that demonic entity—I should have known better. I should have been more careful." He wiped at his eyes. "I'm so sorry, everyone."

"It's not your fault," Pia repeated. "The entity in the house is unusually powerful. I think Tom's death is related to something from the past, something connected to the entity. Not something we did."

Ryan spoke up. "If we use Joe's program, we just might be able to clear enough of the static away to see the knife move toward Tom, and prove it wasn't in Pia's hand."

Pia's fingerprints hadn't been found on the weapon, but she could have worn gloves. And she'd been the only one on that floor when the incident occurred.

Getting Joe's program allowed in a court of law might be difficult, but Nate would leave that to the lawyers to argue. Of course, he hoped to clear the team's involvement before it got that far. The problem was that Johnson didn't have other leads to follow, and Nate couldn't point him in a different direction. Toward another suspect. The true killer was something paranormal, and as Johnson wasn't likely to concede that possibility, Pia was in trouble.

"Can they just steal our things like that?" Ryan asked Nate. "Those tapes and memory cards are our property."

"They didn't steal them. In a homicide investigation, they have the right to seize anything they deem to be evidence regarding the case."

Nate's phone flashed, signaling an incoming text message. "Copies of the tapes will be here in ninety minutes."

Mark raised a brow. "You can do that?"

"Not officially."

"Cool. Thanks, mate."

"Don't mention it," Nate said, then leaned forward for emphasis. "*Really*, don't mention it."

Mark smiled, tilting the top of his beer in Nate's direction, then took a swig.

"What I don't understand," Nate said, "is why Tom Kelly? If this entity was upset at you, why did Kelly get hurt and not one of the team?"

That was another thing that worked against the team and their poltergeist-activity theory, according to the notes Johnson had made on the file.

"Any thoughts, Boo?" Mark asked.

"I don't know specifically why Tom was targeted," Pia said after a pause. "Just that I'm certain he was. I don't think the knife through his heart was an accident. Actually, I'm fairly certain it wasn't. Whatever this entity is, it intended for that to happen."

"Fuck," Ryan said. "That's not good. What the hell are we dealing with here, then? It'd better not be another master demon. One was enough for me, thank you."

Mark leaned forward. "Boo, I think you know more than you've let on. Before we went upstairs, you were getting a vision. You were following your intuition about something, that's why you didn't come upstairs. It's time you told us what happened in Cassandra's room."

CHAPTER SIX

Nate and the *Debunking Reality* team watched silently as Pia closed her eyes, breathed deeply, and prepared to tell them about the events leading up to Tom Kelly's death last night. The soft golden glow from the waning sunset filtered in through the white shuttered windows, forming a halo around her red hair. Her face was creased into troubled lines, her breathing uneven.

Nate wished he had the right to hold her.

Pia opened her eyes. "I don't understand what it all means yet. Earlier in the evening, when I was by the window, I saw the knife with the eagle handle in a vision. The knife that eventually killed Tom. However, I didn't see it as a premonition, but as a vision from the past."

"I didn't notice that knife in the house earlier," Mark commented.

"Because it wasn't there," Pia said. "It materialized on the hallway table not far from where I was seconds before it flew in a direct line toward Tom."

"Jesus!" Ryan said.

"Before Tom was killed, I was getting visions. I saw a dark place. Perhaps underground. It was cold, bitterly cold. In the corner, there was a mattress, dirty and stained with blood. I felt unbearable pain, immense suffering, neglect, abuse. I sensed a girl, and I knew this had happened to her."

Pia glanced around the table, her eyes shining. "That was why I didn't follow you upstairs. I'd made a connection, and I had to find out what it meant. I felt led to Cassandra's room, and I ran with it."

Pia took a breath, tapped a long black nail on the table. "I saw a doll first, sitting on a chair. This doll… it frightened me. There was an energy attached to it. Something not good. When I lifted it off the chair to get a better look, I could have sworn that whatever was in the room disapproved. A music box began to play, and when I turned the box over, there were no batteries in the compartment. The cover was off, and I knew that someone, likely Cassandra, had experienced the same thing. It bothered me. Cassandra is just a little girl. I reached out to communicate with what I sensed in the room." Pia drained the remainder of her bottle of beer, and before Nate could react, Mark slid her another.

"The entity's name is Sarah," Pia continued. "She asked if I could see her, and at that time I couldn't, so I told her so. The rush of anger from Sarah was explosive. Things started flying off the walls and smashing on the ground. I hadn't expected a reaction like that from what I thought was a little girl. I wondered then if the entity was demonic." Pia glanced at Mark. "But then I sensed a flood of human emotion, a deep well of sadness, and I knew I was tapping into a spirit that had once walked the earth. She seemed disturbed that no one saw her. I asked her who didn't see her, and she told me 'they must pay.' Then she said 'he'—meaning Tom—'will pay.' And that's when I sensed Tom was in danger. I called out to warn him, but that turned out to be a huge a mistake. When it started hurting him, I tried to get to him, but the entity held me in place just outside Cassandra's door. I couldn't move, but I could see exactly what was happening to Tom. It was… horrific."

Pia broke off and swallowed. *To hell with it.* Before Mark thought to, Nate reached over and took her hand.

"And then I saw her," Pia said. "The girl, Sarah, standing in the doorway, the exact image as the doll."

Pia shivered, and everyone was totally silent while they absorbed her words. "She said it had been a long time coming. Like she'd been waiting to get revenge on him."

"So what we're dealing with is demonic?" Mark asked.

"Why do you think it's demonic when Pia just said she saw a manifestation of a girl called Sarah?" Nate asked.

"Demonic entities have been known to disguise themselves as children," Mark said. "True evil will use any tool it can to prey on humans. A demon has no scruples; it will use our most vulnerable as bait. It's our policy to always be wary if you see the ghost of a child and to make sure you know what really lies beneath before you allow yourself to get close."

"So the child Pia saw might be a demon in disguise?"

"Yes. That's why it appeared in the image of a doll. It's just taken on a form. It looks like we're dealing with a powerfully evil spirit. Only the darkest entities have the substantial power needed to reach across the veil and cause that kind of damage."

"I'm not convinced that's what we're dealing with, Mark," Pia said.

"But you have to agree it's demonic. That much we've confirmed, right? Otherwise Tom wouldn't have been hurt, much less killed. Spirits can be active, but they don't hurt people intentionally like that unless they're evil."

"Something isn't right, I agree. But the emotions I felt from it… They were real. Demons can't fake what I was feeling."

"What is it, and what does it want?" Ryan asked. "Any thoughts, Boo?"

"Not yet. Everything happened too fast. Sarah was connected to Cassandra's room somehow. The jewelry box, the doll. Cassy is only nine. I don't like the thought of that family returning to the house after what happened."

Nate leaned back. He couldn't offer much help in the way of supernatural theories. He'd leave that to the team. His main priority was proving that Pia didn't have anything to do with Tom's death. He needed to clear her. After that, it would be up to the police to decide what to do. As it was highly unlikely they'd list anything paranormal as the cause, Tom Kelly's death would no doubt join the long list of unsolved cases.

He was lost in thought when Pia said, "I need to go back into the house."

"Like hell," Nate said abruptly, and a little too loudly. Ryan and Joe eyed him curiously, and Mark narrowed his eyes.

"Excuse me?" Pia asked, twisting in her chair to face him.

"The house is sealed off; it's a crime scene." Nate kept his voice even, willing his pulse to return to normal. When Pia had suggested going into that house and putting herself in danger, his protective instincts had flared. Goddamn it, they'd just agreed there was a powerful entity—possibly a demon—in that house. One that had already killed someone. God knew they didn't need a repeat of what had happened to Sage and Ethan.

He took a deep breath. What the hell was wrong with him? Pia didn't take kindly to being told what she could and couldn't do, so he'd better keep his wayward emotions under control.

"*No one* is allowed in the house," he said, trying to sound reasonable. "Not even the owners, the Reynolds family. If you're seen trying to enter the house, the cops will assume you're trying to destroy evidence. It will work against you and have unfavorable consequences. Especially if this ends up in court."

"How long will the place be off-limits?" Mark asked.

"For as long as it takes them to finish documenting the scene and collecting evidence."

"Damn," Pia said. "Then I want to speak to Cassandra and her parents. They need to know what kind of danger they may be in if they go back in there before I can work out what's going on."

Mark was nodding. "I agree with Boo. We need more information. This could propel the show into the stratosphere if we get this right. People can downplay the footage we captured in Cryton and say we faked it somehow, but if we do it again? The evidence, the story behind it, will make for compelling viewing. And it's going to be lot harder for people to say it's fake."

Mark was looking at this through the perspective of the show. But Pia, Nate realized, cared not about the show but about the family who'd asked for their help.

Pia spoke. "I'm wondering what the connection is between the manifestation of Sarah and the doll and why that doll was in Cassandra's room. I know there's something significant in that; I just don't know what."

"A connection between Cassandra, the doll, and the entity?" Mark asked. "That's interesting."

"A young girl reached out to with me last night. I felt her pain, how much she suffered. It breaks my heart. I feel a responsibility to help."

Nate rolled his shoulders. He knew she was capable, but that didn't mean he had to like it.

"This… thing, it killed a man," Nate said, not wanting her to overlook that fact. "Demon or otherwise, you're risking your life trying to help." *A girl who's already dead.*

This was Pia's world, but how the fuck was he supposed to keep her safe from something he couldn't see? For the first time, Nate understood, *truly* understood, how Ethan must have felt wanting to protect Sage when she was the target of a demonic entity. Powerlessness was a crippling emotion.

And not one he intended to get used to.

Pia looked directly at Nate. "I won't be able to let this drop until I work it out. Just so you know. And now it looks like I'm going to have to dodge the cops while I do it."

Nate inwardly groaned. But what could he say? He'd be a hypocrite telling her to walk away. Not when, roles reversed, he wouldn't. He'd never let a case go until he was satisfied he'd tied up all the loose ends. But that was him. Dealing with death, murder, and evil was a way of life. *His* life. Pia was… well, with her gift and dealing with such unknown entities, she was vulnerable. Sure, she wasn't lacking in courage, but how did she fight something powerful enough to kill a burly old salty like Tom Kelly? Would it try to kill her next?

Nate clenched his jaw in an effort not to argue with her. Giving her the freedom to find out what was going on, while keeping her safe *and* out of jail, was going to be a delicate balancing act. He could try to get her to change her mind, but it would be a waste of breath. He'd gotten to know that stubborn streak very well six months ago.

If he was inclined to look deeper, he'd realize he'd fallen half in love with her and her powerful will back then. When Sage had come to Pia for help, Pia hadn't hesitated, unmindful of making herself a target for a demon-possessed serial killer.

She hadn't shied away from danger then, and he'd be a fool to think she'd shy away from it now. The best he could do was keep her safe while giving her the opportunity to do what she felt was needed.

"You're going to need to think of a plan B," Joe said, looking up from his laptop. "Getting the Reynolds to allow us back in the house isn't going to happen." Joe spun the laptop around, swiped his finger across the keyboard, and an interview with a major television network filled the screen.

Chad and Monique Reynolds were wrapped around each other, their daughters, Cassandra and Rebecca, clutching their legs.

"*Debunking Reality* destroyed our house," Monique said tearfully. "All our beautiful things, a lifetime of memories, broken. We bought this house hoping for a fresh start. *Debunking Reality* ruined that."

"Mrs. Reynolds," a reporter called out. "Who do you think killed Tom Kelly?"

"*Debunking Reality* obviously," Chad Reynolds answered, as his wife buried her head in his shoulder. "They had our house all locked up, and there was no intruder. It had to have been one of them. I don't know why the police released them. They're a menace to society. Dangerous."

"Mr. Reynolds," another reporter called out. "Why did they invite Tom Kelly into your house with them?"

"We don't know," Chad Reynolds said. "But the man ended up dead. The house is a disaster inside. The poor man must have fought for his life."

"Mr. Reynolds, Mr. Reynolds," another reporter said, shoving a microphone into his face. "Why did you call *Debunking Reality* in the first place?"

"We made a mistake. My wife heard a few strange noises, and considering the house has a reputation for being haunted, we called *Debunking Reality* in to *debunk* the noises. After all these years, we hoped to expose the truth about the legend. Put a stop to the superstition. We were hoping we could discover it was noisy water pipes or something like that to prove there's no such thing as ghosts. Especially ones haunting our new house."

"The rumors were starting to get to us," Monique picked up, and the microphone was transferred to her. "Everyone we meet asks us whether we've seen the ghost of Salty Simon Farrell. They joke, telling us to be careful not to get up for a drink of water at night, or Simon's ghost will get us. But the cruelest ones are the kids at school. They were scaring poor Cassandra with their stories. Cassy was starting to imagine seeing things in her room. She was having nightmares, but it was only because the kids at school were putting ideas in her head."

"Did *Debunking Reality* debunk the ghost?" One reporter asked.

"What they did," Chad said, his face red with anger, "is tear up our house. The damage they caused, the staging of a murder to replicate the ghost-story legend, is taking sensationalism to an extreme."

"So you think *Debunking Reality* killed Tom Kelly deliberately?"

"We're Christians," Monique said, her voice trembling. "I simply can't believe they did it intentionally. What kind of monster would do something like that? What we believe happened is that they were staging a reenactment that went horribly wrong." Monique broke off, blinking rapidly with a shaking hand placed across her heart.

"Only truly disgusting people go to such lengths for ratings. Fame has gone to their heads," Chad finished for his wife.

"And there you have it, folks," a pretty reporter finished, flashing a brief super-white smile before adopting a faux-serious expression and lowering her voice theatrically. "Did the taste of fame become too much for this paranormal investigation team? Did they take their attempt to remain number one in the ratings too far? You decide."

The story ended, going to an advert.

"Can they actually *say* that?" Mark asked, shocked.

Joe's face darkened. "They just did."

"Where can I find Cassandra?" Pia asked. "Where are the Reynolds staying? They need to know this is real. They could be putting Cassandra into serious danger if they don't understand that. You heard what they said about Cassandra seeing things in her room. I know there's a connection there. One that could cause grievous harm."

"You're not seriously—?" Ryan asked, looking up from the screen. "The media are going to be all over us now. This is a disaster! The negative publicity is going to kill us. Ruin the show."

"He has a point," Mark said, standing and beginning to pace. "I was hoping to keep the media out of this. I hadn't announced on any of our social media sites where we were filming."

"It was only a matter of time before the media got involved," Nate said. "The Reynolds are minor celebrities around here. Everyone knows they bought the haunted house."

Mark cursed, putting his head in his hands. "I haven't come this far to have it all blow up in my face now. We're the number one paranormal series. I was just beginning to cement my reputation in this business. The network is going to *freak*. What the hell do we tell them?"

"How are we supposed to prove our innocence and find out what's going on if we can't go back into the house and aren't able to communicate with our client?" Ryan asked, his face creased in worry.

Mark cursed under his breath and shoved two hands through his hair. "Maybe it's best to let things cool down a bit."

"I don't think so," Pia countered. "Yes, that may be best for the show, and I understand if you want to walk away. But *I* can't. That entity was in Cassandra's room. What if I'm wrong? What if it *is* a demon? And what if Cassandra is its next target?"

What if you *become the next target?* But Nate didn't voice his gravest concern.

Ryan shook his head. "You heard what the Reynolds just said. What they said about us. You expect them to allow us into their house again?"

"I didn't say anything about asking permission."

"You can't be serious. What if we're caught? We'll go to jail this time for sure."

Pia crossed her arms. "Well, I can't just walk away. How could I live with myself if something happened to that little girl, and I did nothing?"

Amazing. Pia was more focused on making sure Cassandra was safe than on the trouble she herself was in. She had no idea just how much influence Nate had had to exert to get her released.

But, as almost impossible as it was, Nate remained silent, listening to the crew as they bandied their options about and decided on their next course of action.

"Pia's right," Mark said. "We're used to forging ahead in the face of adversity. We fly in the face of skeptics and disbelievers all the time. Danger, controversy, and negative press have never stopped us before."

"But no one has ever been murdered during one of our investigations," Ryan argued. "That cop that interviewed me said they had enough evidence to arrest Pia, maybe even all of us. He told me if I admitted what happened, they would look favorably on me. The cops think we did it, the Reynolds think we did it, now the media and general public will believe we did it." Ryan's voice thickened. "Trial by media. It would kill my mum if I went to jail."

"No one's going to jail," Mark snapped, but a shadow crossed his eyes.

"What Ryan said is even more reason to not let this go," Pia said. "The cops *can't* solve this case. They don't even believe in this stuff. I need to talk to Cassandra. I need to know what she's seen. If the entity has spoken to her. What it has said. I want to find out where Cassandra found the doll, and why this demon—or entity—took the image of it. I need to understand the connection. To get rid of this entity, I need to start finding answers to these questions." She glanced at Joe, then Ryan. "I understand if you want to step back. Hell, it's the sensible thing to do. But I can't stop until I know for sure Cassandra and her family are safe to go back into the house."

She looked down at the table. "I feel responsible. What if I stirred things up? Yes, the house clearly contains an active spirit and has for thirty years, but it had never *hurt* anyone until I made a connection with it. I *know* I angered it. What if I caused this?" When she looked up, her eyes were shining with tears.

The team was silent.

"Well, you're not going to do this alone," Mark said, breaking the silence. "I'm with you one hundred percent."

"Thank you, Mark." Pia met his eyes with a small smile.

"Always, Boo."

Mark looked at Joe.

Joe released a heavy breath. "I'm in." He didn't appear too happy with the decision, but then again, he never looked happy, so it was hard to gauge.

"Ryan?" Mark asked. "No pressure, mate. I know your mum's sick. I'll understand if you want to sit this one out."

Ryan twisted his empty beer bottle around in his fingers. "I don't like it," he said eventually. "It's going to hurt Mum when she sees this on the news. But like it or not, we're already involved. We need to think carefully, be smart about how we handle this. One mistake could land us in jail." He glanced up at Pia. "But I'm not going to walk away. We're a team."

"I'm in," Nate said, even though no one had asked him.

Mark looked at him.

"No need to look so bloody surprised," Nate grumbled. "If you want to stay out of jail, you need me and my contacts, the information I can give you, and the resources I have access to."

Pia smiled, her eyes shining mistily as she met his gaze, and glanced around the table at her team.

"Okay then," she said, straightening. "Let's do this."

CHAPTER SEVEN

It was late in the evening, and Ryan and Joe had gone to bed an hour ago, having not slept at all since the night before last. Pia filled her glass of water in the kitchen after having showered and changed into a set of black sleep shorts and singlet for bed.

The team and Nate had spent the evening discussing strategy and their next steps. Nate had fired off a message to his tech wiz, Zach, and shortly after they knew which school Cassandra Reynolds went to and the park she played at after school.

Nate had explained that if there was a database, Zach had access to it. He was a ghost of the technology world. He hacked into systems unseen and left without a trace.

Nate had argued with Mark over who was accompanying Pia. Nate won, stating that it was a condition of his help that he accompany Pia everywhere. "They're my terms, take them or leave them," Nate had stated unequivocally. Mark had no choice but to agree, but everyone had to know Pia was safer with Nate and the security he could provide.

What Pia couldn't work out was why?

Nate surely had work he was supposed to be doing. Cases she'd pulled him off of when she'd made her phone call and he'd dropped everything to come. Nate was a busy man, his workload heavy. Their new company was in high demand.

Around six p.m., the first news crews had pulled into the driveway. When they'd knocked on the door, Nate had handled it. He'd put on his baseball hat and dark sunglasses and spoke to them, camera flashes going off like tiny explosions. He'd made sure they stayed off the property, but they were within their rights to hang around on the public street. Which is what they did. The timber-frame beach house would shake every now and then when a low-flying helicopter hovered overhead.

With the media camped outside their door, they'd stayed inside, spending the evening going through the arduous process of analyzing the footage from last night, including the copies of the confiscated footage that Nate had arranged. They had six units containing seven hours of footage each. It was a slow process that would continue over the next few days.

So far, they had captured lots of paranormal phenomenon—it would make a great show if they made it through this—but at this stage, they had nothing that would clear Pia or the guys. Johnson had been truthful when he'd said that all their electronic devices, video and audio, had gone staticky and shut down just before the incident.

Pia glanced over at the couch where Nate was arranging his body, his legs dangling over the armrest. He hadn't left. Why?

"Are you sure you're going to be comfortable there?" she asked, crossing the room to him.

He met her eyes, his half-smile doing strange things to her insides. "I've slept in worse places."

"You've slept in better too." Pia took a seat on the armrest of the couch. He put a pillow behind his back and eyed her. His hair was mussed like he'd been running his hands through it. Would it feel as soft as it looked? What did it smell like?

Pia cleared her throat. "Thank you, Nate," she said softly. She was now acutely aware they were alone. Nate's body temperature always seemed higher than other people's, and his heat rolled over her in waves that caused her pulse to skip and race.

"Of course." His tone was casual, but his eyes, more blue than gray in this light, were focused directly on her. It was a heady feeling being the subject of his attention. He studied her with such intensity she felt naked.

"I mean it," she said, struggling to find and hold onto her composure. "You didn't even have to physically come when I called. I had hoped you'd make a phone call for me. Help us out. I didn't mean for you to drop whatever case you were on to come here."

"Pia—"

"I just want to say thank you. I also want you to know that I don't want you to feel obligated to stick around. You've done so much already by getting us out of that tangle with the cops and getting us copies of the tapes."

"You're not out of that tangle with the cops yet."

"I know." She needed to stop rambling. Why did Nate always make her feel so awkward? "I… just don't want you to feel like you have to stay, that's all I'm trying to say. You can leave whenever you like." There, she'd said it.

So why did the words hurt so much?

Nate's expression hardened. "You don't get it, do you?"

"Get what?"

Nate sat up fully, bringing his head close to hers. His eyes darkened, some emotion she couldn't name swirling in their depths. "I'm not leaving you, Pia."

His intensity stole her breath. The way he said it implied he was sticking around for something other than the case. Impossible. Still, the rush it gave her was as thrilling as it was frightening. Nate Ryder was not your average man. He was powerful, successful, wealthy, and more handsome than anyone had a right to be.

I don't understand. Why risk tarnishing himself with this mess? With someone like me? *Unless…*

Pia straightened her spine. "You don't owe me anything, Nate," she said, feeling sick at the thought. "Neither do Ethan or Sage. We all did what we could to fight the master demon because it was the right thing to do. The necessary thing. Lord only knows what mess we would all be in if we hadn't."

"You think I'm here to repay a *debt*?" Nate's voice was lethally quiet. "Or worse, because Blade sent me to even a score on his behalf?"

Pia couldn't hold his gaze any longer. Too much anger and hurt were reflected in his eyes.

"Don't." She shifted uncomfortably. "Don't do that, Nate. I always end up saying the wrong thing to you."

"Likewise."

Why did things get so… *confused* when she was with him? They always ended up on opposite sides of the fence.

He put his hand on her knee, and his touch almost seared her bare skin. He leaned forward, so close his breath fanned over her cheek.

"I'm no one's puppet. Not even Blade's."

"I didn't mean to imply you were," Pia snapped. That wasn't what she meant, dammit!

Nate frowned. "I work *with* Blade, not for him. We're partners. The whole of Taipan are partners in our new company, TSI. I've taken personal time to be here."

"I… uh, I didn't know that."

"Clearly. Or you wouldn't have insulted me."

Pia shivered at the intensity of his gaze. "I didn't mean to insult you."

"And yet you did."

Her cheeks burned. "Damn you, Nate Ryder, I was trying to be nice for once. All I wanted to say is—"

His lips crashed against hers, and her mind blanked. Her heart raced, all of her overwhelmed by a tidal wave of sensation.

Nate tasted deliciously of mint. His full, firm lips moved sensuously against hers. Sifting his fingers through her hair, he cradled the back of her head, angling his head slightly to deepen the kiss.

When she breathed in his scent of spicy, virile male, her nipples tightened into hard points. Nate's tongue explored her mouth. With his hand on the back of her neck, and the weight of his body pressing over hers, he was taking control. Pia's first instinct was to push him back, but she quickly realized she wasn't discomfited by it. Allowing Nate to take control was a seductive thrill. Something she hadn't known she would like, although now found herself craving.

Pia was no innocent—far from it—but she'd never been kissed the way Nate was kissing her right now. His touch filled an emptiness inside she'd been unaware of, set a fire blazing in her soul. Another need she wanted Nate to fill burned urgently between her thighs. There wasn't an inch of her body that wasn't on fire.

Not a single cell that wasn't tingling and alive.

Nate ran his hand down the center of her back, then over her stomach before inching upward. When his hand cupped her right breast, he groaned low and deep in the back of his throat, her body absorbing the rumbling vibration, exciting every inch of her.

Abruptly he pulled back, eyes blazing, his breathing raw and ragged. He thrust a hand through his brown, sun-streaked hair, and her eyes were riveted to the bulge in his bicep as he moved. Nate Ryder was the epitome of strength, power, and masculinity encased in six feet of rippling muscle.

Holy fuck, she'd never seen a sexier man in her life. And she'd never been as turned on either. She gave serious consideration to shoving him back on the couch, straddling him, and finishing what he'd started. Giving her body the satisfaction she knew he was about to deny her.

The fact that Mark and the team were close by in their rooms and could walk in on them stayed her hand. For the same reasons, taking him to her room cavewoman style wasn't an option either. Her body rebelled from the frustration.

Pia peered into his stormy gray eyes, somewhat mollified to find the same torture there that she knew was reflected in her own. He licked his lips, the glimpse of his tongue momentarily mesmerizing her. When he spoke, his voice was rough, a low sexy rasp that sent her heart beating erratically.

"Make no mistake. I'm here because *I* choose to be. I'm staying, unless you tell me to leave. But Pia?"

He looked at her as though he never wanted to stop.

"Yes?" she managed.

"Don't tell me to leave."

Chapter Eight

A gentle sea breeze cooled Pia's bedroom, invited inside through the open window. The sound of waves rhythmically crashing onto shore was comforting, but Pia's body remained tense, her muscles taught and rigid. She fluffed and refluffed her pillow, pulled the blankets over her head, told herself sternly to go to sleep.

Yeah, right. When has that ever worked?

Her kiss with Nate replayed over and over in her mind, and each time their lips met, she was back on the couch, with her skin on fire and her heart racing. One minute she was arguing with him, the next she was about to tear his clothes off and have wild and passionate sex with him.

What the hell is up with that?

Okay, she was female, and Nate was beyond attractive. But he also knew exactly how to push her buttons, both good and bad. He was a mouth-watering aggravation, and her current state of sexual frustration only added weight to the aggravated side of the scale.

Last September, she'd been successful in keeping him at a distance, but this time it was proving impossible. Her attraction to him was powerful and becoming dangerously more so. It also didn't help that she had a vivid imagination. From that kiss alone, she knew he'd be a hot, adventurous lover, just as talented with that tongue in other, more intimate places. Her nipples were hard, her body still thrumming with the heat of desire. She resisted its demand for satisfaction. She wanted *him*.

More than she'd ever wanted a man in her life.

But she couldn't have him.

Aside from the not-small fact he was here helping her and the team stay out of jail, Pia didn't do relationships. Not that she didn't want to. She was a fit, healthy woman in her twenties—of course she wanted a relationship. The plain fact was that she couldn't have one.

The psychic abilities the universe had for some reason saddled her with made getting close to someone virtually impossible. Who wanted to hang around someone who could potentially hear their innermost secrets? People wore social masks in public because they wanted to control how they were seen by others. Nobody liked to be exposed. And being around a psychic meant running the risk of exactly that, especially if the thoughts carried heavy emotions. Those seemed to transmit most easily to her. And sometimes, just a single train of thought was shocking. Pia had been surprised and sometimes downright disgusted at what she'd accidentally heard. But people had a right to privacy. Not everyone *acted* on their thoughts.

So Pia built mental walls and made a concerted effort to keep herself a reasonable emotional distance from people so as not to unintentionally breach their privacy.

But that made relationships hard. If not impossible.

Except… there was one man who was potentially different. Nate Ryder, so far, was a closed book to her.

Would that change if they got involved? Perhaps he'd turn out to be no different at all, and she'd end up being hurt and disappointed like she always was.

The smartest thing—the safest thing—was to keep a firm distance between her and Nate Ryder.

No more fiery kisses. No more locked eyes.

Pia punched her pillow.

No more wondering what Nate was like in bed.

———◆———

Pia sighed deeply as she rolled over yet again. When was she going to be able to sleep?

She glanced at the clock on the bedside table. The digital glow clicked over to 3:01 a.m.

Dead Time.

The time of night that was the quietest. When the silence was the most complete. When the veil between the physical world and the ethereal one was thinnest. The time of night when darkness brought the shadows to life. Especially for someone with Pia's abilities.

Pia dropped her head back onto the pillow. Closed her eyes. *Sleep, damn it!*

She must have drifted off, because when her eyes sprang open again, she was wide awake, her heart racing, adrenaline flowing through her veins.

Why? The room was silent. And dark. She waited, sensing nothing out of the ordinary. And yet something was making the tiny hairs on the back of her neck rise.

She fluffed her pillow, closed her eyes.

Tap. Tap. Tap. Tap.

The sound of metal on metal.

Pia stilled. She sat up, peered through the darkness.

The sound had been loud. Close.

In her room.

Tap. Tap. Tap. Tap.

Pia searched the darkness until she found the source of the noise. The metal ring handles on the drawers of the tallboy were lifting and dropping back down by themselves. The warm ocean breeze blowing through the open window was not strong enough to move them, let alone pick them up and drop them.

The temperature in the room plummeted, and Pia shivered. An icy claw scraped down her spine, and goose bumps covered her flesh.

What was happening?

She hugged the blanket tight around her. Her abilities meant she was no stranger to the paranormal. That didn't mean she didn't fear it. For everything she thought she understood, there was a world of things that she didn't. For every question she could answer, a million more were raised.

The world of the afterlife was just as much a mystery to Pia as it was to everyone else. Everyone normal.

Scraape. Something moved on top of the tallboy, and Pia's pulse pounded loud in her ears. She had to clench her teeth to stop them chattering at the chill in the room.

In her experience, sudden temperature drops were caused by dark entities, not by a visit from Granny.

What was in the room with her now?

Pia reached over to the bedside table and grabbed the black tourmaline pendant she wore for protection against unwanted paranormal attention, wishing she had something stronger at hand. Everything else she'd brought had been confiscated by the police and packed in a box labelled "Evidence." The tourmaline would have to do.

She took a deep breath, struggling to fill her lungs. The air felt thicker somehow, as though the oxygen had been sucked out.

"Who are you?" Her voice sounded hollow and shaky in the small room.

And then she saw it. A shadowy mass starting to form at the end of her bed.

Pia's eyes locked on the shape, her heart skipping in her chest. What was it? What did it want? Nocturnal visits could mean a variety of things. Not all of them good. Either way, the entity shouldn't be there, and Pia was tired and not in the mood.

"Go away," Pia said to the inky shadow.

The black mass at the foot of her bed began to move back and forth, a brush of icy cold wind across her cheeks. A chill skittered over her skin and dread pooled in the pit of her belly.

Pia clutched the pendant of black tourmaline. Closing her eyes, she visualized herself being surrounded by a cocoon of white light and recited a passage of protection.

Something touched her right foot through the covers, and her eyes sprang open.

In the moonlight streaming in between the cracks in the shutters, Pia saw the dark mass materialize into the form of a young girl with long blonde hair. Dressed in a dirty white gown stained with crimson splatters of blood, she had vampire-pale skin and black circles where the eyes should have been.

It was the girl from Cassandra's room. The same face as the one on the doll on the chair.

Sarah.

"You followed me from the house?"

Pia focused, peering at the entity cautiously, remembering all too clearly the anger, the violence, it had caused.

This entity had killed a man.

Can you see me? The words pressed themselves into Pia's mind, even though the lips of the manifestation did not move. Sarah had asked the same question back at the house and had exploded in anger when Pia had said no.

"Yes, I damn well see you." She hoped she sounded forceful and in control. "And I shouldn't. You have no right to follow me here. Go back to the house." How had she managed to pick up an attachment? She always went to great lengths to cleanse herself before and after…

Oh shit. She hadn't cleansed and protected herself after last night's investigation. She'd been in the police station all day.

It was frightening, not to mention dangerous, when something followed you home. If you weren't paying close attention, an entity could oppress you, messing with your mind and confusing your thoughts.

Pia had investigated several houses where she'd discovered that the occupants had been experimenting with a Ouija board, having no idea just how dangerous the boards could be. It was quite possible to bring through something dark and malevolent. Once a person invited something like that into their home and into their lives, the entity could attach itself, causing the person to become severely distressed—or worse, go insane—as they fought ideas and thoughts not their own.

Pia knew better than to allow herself to be vulnerable.

As curious as she was to find out who Sarah was and learn her story, Pia needed to be careful how she chose to go about it. Especially as she didn't know exactly who—or what—the entity really was. Mark could still be right. It was possible that Sarah could be a demonic entity, manipulating Pia's good intentions.

Pia studied the manifestation at the foot of her bed, despite the chill doing so gave her.

You really can see me. The entity appeared surprised and excited. Pia guessed she was the first medium Sarah had come across.

Sarah glided a bit closer. She was now at the side of the bed, beside Pia's ankles.

"That's far enough," Pia said, pushing down a rush of fear. There was something particularly creepy about the apparition before her. Communicating with those who'd crossed over was not unfamiliar to her, but this figure seemed more solid, more calculating, *more forceful*, than those she normally encountered.

Even so, beneath it all, Pia sensed a deep and profound sense of pain and sadness. That glimpse of vulnerability called to Pia. She'd give Sarah the benefit of the doubt. For now.

"Who are you?"

Frightening images pressed themselves into Pia's mind. Darkness, blacker than black. Again, the filthy, bloodstained mattress, the taste of dirt in a dry mouth. Bone-chilling cold, and a body and muscles that never stopped aching. Tiny clawed feet crawling along tender young skin. *A mouse? A rat?* Pia's stomach clenched, and bile rose in her throat.

"What are you showing me, Sarah?" Pia tried to clear the disturbing images from her mind.

They never saw me. Nobody ever did.

"*Who* didn't?" Pia asked, her voice a loud whisper in the room. "Who didn't see you, Sarah?"

Nobody. The black holes where eyes should have been stared directly into Pia's soul.

"Did someone hurt you, Sarah?"

More images of horror and abuse assaulted Pia.

Yes. The bad people. I wanted to go home. I wanted to go home to Mummy and Daddy.

Intense pain, fear, isolation, and absolute devastation swept through Pia.

I never did.

Oh dear God, Sarah never went home. She was showing Pia the conditions she'd lived in before she'd died.

"Who are the bad people, Sarah?" Pia asked gently. "Was it Tom Kelly? Was he one of them?"

Yes.

Pia's stomach churned with anger. No wonder he'd triggered her survival instincts. Tom Kelly had done those unspeakable things to this girl? To Sarah?

He didn't see me.

It still didn't make sense. How did he not see Sarah, if he was one of the people abusing her?

"Sarah, was it you who hurt Tom? Did you do that deliberately?"

Yes.

An icy claw fingered its way down Pia's spine.

"Because he hurt you? Did you hurt Tom out of revenge?"

They all must die.

Pia's mouth was dry, and she couldn't swallow past the lump in her throat. She was still not entirely convinced that she was dealing with a human spirit. In her experience, dark entities and demons were the only spirits that wished to cause physical harm to humans. But at least Mark could take comfort from knowing Tom's death had nothing to do with anything he'd done during the investigation. Tom Kelly's death wasn't accidental. It was murder.

"You said 'they.'" Pia was trying to understand, choosing her words carefully to try to keep the entity calm and not have a repeat of the storm of rage she'd shown at the cottage.

"Who are the others, Sarah?"

The apparition didn't answer, just stared at her with those black holes in place of its eyes. A chill pierced Pia's bones.

The moment drew out, and Pia's unease grew. It was becoming nearly impossible for her to remain strong and not show fear.

"You look like Cassandra's doll."

Need her.

"Need who?" Pia shivered. "Cassandra? Or the doll?"

Both. Will you help me?

"Help you do what exactly?"

Get the others.

"Who are the others, Sarah?" She wanted to be sure exactly what Sarah was asking of her. She'd been shown images of horror that she believed Sarah had been forced to endure. Someone had abused and tortured this little girl.

Perhaps Sarah was tied to the earthly plane because justice had never been served. Her story had not been told. Was she reaching out to Pia for help, because Pia could see her? And what exactly was Sarah asking Pia to do?

"I can't help you kill someone, Sarah." That needed to be clear. "No matter what they did. I'm not a damn hit man."

Please? It's not right that they should live when I cannot. Sarah sounded so sad, so broken, Pia felt her grief as a terrible pain in her own heart.

You saw what they did. You saw it! I showed you. How can you know what happened and not help me?

Images flooded into her mind. A young girl, so frighteningly alone, so terribly afraid. So much pain, so much suffering. A constant flow of tears. A lifetime of cruelty endured. It was traumatic enough to watch the images; Pia couldn't imagine what it must have been like to live it.

"Look, if what happened to you is true, I don't disagree with you. They do deserve to die. But life doesn't work that way. When something bad happens, you have to tell the police about it, and then they'll put the people who hurt you in jail. If you'll tell me who did this to you, give me dates, details, I will do whatever I can to make sure those people are brought to justice." God knows they deserved to be punished, and severely, if what she'd been shown turned out to be true.

What if you warn them?

"Warn them?" Why the hell would she warn them?

And then it occurred to her.

"Trust," Pia said. "You don't trust me. You don't trust adults to help you, do you?" Pia rubbed at the tightness in her chest. No one had helped her, Sarah had said. No adult had helped her. They were the ones who'd abused her.

They'll get away with it, Sarah said, energy beginning to swirl around her. She was becoming agitated, and Pia's pulse started to race, her eyes darting to the door. Her escape. If only the entity would let her get that far.

They'll tell lies. Hide what they've done. There was no justice back then and there is none now. The only justice from here will be mine.

"I'm sorry." Pia's heart was in pieces, but what other choice was there? Pia could not be a part of someone's murder. Under any circumstance.

You know what it's like to be alone. Sarah's tone lowered and the icy chill emanating from her shadowy figure intensified.

You know what it's like to have nobody you can turn to. You know what it's like to be a child so alone. Adults let you down too.

Sarah's words hit Pia like a physical blow. How could she know that? Growing up with psychic abilities had left Pia isolated. An only child, she didn't have siblings to turn to, and Pia's parents had been emotionally absent for as far back as she could remember. They'd simply been unable to deal with the embarrassment of having a child that wasn't "normal." She'd been clothed and fed, but she certainly hadn't been loved. Not in the nurturing way parents should love their child. There'd been no cuddles, no stories before bed, no one to pick her up if she fell, *no affection*. At best, she'd been tolerated; at worst, her parents had looked at her with something akin to fear. And disgust.

It wasn't until Pia was nine, Cassandra's age, that she'd realized she could confide in her grandmother. That her grandmother had *understood*. But Pia had never gotten over the isolation of those early tender years, not really. There were scars, and they ran deep. Night after night for years, Pia had cried herself to sleep, telling God He'd made a horrible mistake when He created her, praying He would fix her so that she would stop bringing shame to her family. Prayed He would fix her so that her parents wouldn't wish her dead.

Yes, she'd heard them think that. It wasn't something a child ever forgot.

Or ever got over.

Yes, Sarah said, coming closer. *We are not that different. We both wanted parents we could never have. I never got to see mine again, but at least I knew they'd loved me.*

Ouch! That stung.

I need you to help me, Sarah said, placing her hand on Pia's arm.

Pia hissed in a sharp intake of breath at the icy burn of the entity's fingers brushing against her skin.

"You mustn't touch me." Pia scrambled back on the bed. There were lines she didn't allow entities to cross. She'd shown far too much vulnerability in front of Sarah for her own safety.

Sarah could still be a demon.

I'm not a demon! Sarah shouted into Pia's mind, the intensity sending needles of pain splintering through her brain. Pia squeezed her eyes shut, cradled her head with her hands.

"Calm down," Pia said, waiting for the severity of the pain to subside.

I'm not *evil*, Sarah said more softly this time. *I'm just a little girl who never got to go home.*

Sarah started to cry, her grief, raw and harrowing, washing over Pia. Pia felt tears well in her own eyes. She fought a strong impulse to take Sarah into her arms, to hold her, to give her the love she'd been denied. The love that had been denied to both of them.

But she needed to be careful. Forcefully, she bit back her natural instincts to nurture the child. She had to maintain the distance that she'd discovered early on was essential when dealing with non-human entities.

"Of course I want to help you," Pia said. "But I'm still not clear about what you're asking me to do. You want revenge, but what is it exactly you want me to do?"

They must die.

Again, those chilling words. Pia hugged her arms tightly around her body. "You can't do that," Pia said, shaking her head. "You can't just kill people."

They killed me.

Oh, hell. What did she say to that?

Will you help me?

"I'm sorry." How did she make Sarah understand? "You might have been too young to know about it, but Sarah, there's a justice system. A process…"

Sarah went still, and death's icy wind blew across Pia's face.

No one stopped them! No one helped me!

The atmosphere changed, becoming instantly charged. Pia gasped. Energy crackled violently in the room. A chair in the corner skidded across the floor, crashing into the opposite wall before falling to the ground. The door opened, then slammed shut. Pia's suitcase upended, spilling her things across the floor.

You will suffer too. Like I did.

Sucking in a breath, Pia gagged on a stench like rotten eggs. Her stomach roiled, and she instinctively clambered farther up the bed, moving too fast and falling off the other side. She hit the floor with a thud, then kicked at the blanket tangled around her.

Surely Nate or one of the guys would hear all the commotion and come to her rescue. Pia strained to listen, but there was no sound of footsteps approaching. Strangely, it appeared that the noise had somehow been contained in this one room.

Sarah floated up and across the bed to hover over her.

Pia tried to scream, but the sound caught in her throat.

I thought you were different. Sarah's voice was a clap of thunder. *I thought you'd care. I thought you'd understand. But I was wrong. You* don't *care. No one ever did. I hate you! I hate you all!* Sarah's words sliced across Pia's skin like razorblades.

You're just like the others. You don't *see me. I will get them, and I will get you too.*

And as suddenly as she'd appeared, Sarah vanished, leaving nothing but a bone-deep chill from the ominous threat.

Pia trembled, her heart pounding furiously. Her hands shook as she grabbed the blanket and climbed back into bed.

Tears rolled from her eyes, and she wiped them away with a trembling hand. As terrified as she'd been, she also been sick to her stomach over what Sarah had endured in her lifetime.

And now Pia was left feeling that she, too, had failed Sarah.

Was Sarah a demon, or a victim?

One thing was for sure: whatever this was, it was killing in revenge from beyond the grave.

Sarah had admitted killing Tom Kelly. And others.

And she'd said it wasn't over, that there were more to come.

How many more had to die?

And who? Pia started reflecting on the images Sarah had shown her. She wanted to help, and yet…

There was something unusually powerful about Sarah. Something malevolent.

What if Sarah had never existed at all? What if the entity really was a demon, and all this was a trick to mess with Pia's mind? A voice in her head, coaxing her to kill? It was well documented that demons caused people to act and do things they normally wouldn't. But Pia wasn't crazy. She was intimately familiar with her abilities and what were her thoughts and what weren't. The question Pia needed answered was whether this really was a dark entity, something evil and demented.

Was Pia playing right into its hands?

There was only one way to find out.

Pia needed to find out if Sarah had existed in real life.

And if anyone could help her answer that question, it was Nate.

CHAPTER NINE

Nate entered the kitchen of the beach house to find Mark peering through the shutters at the reporters in the front yard, a look of heavy concern on his usually carefree face. Like roaches they kept coming, swarming and chattering noisily in little clusters. The team silently ate a late lunch and cleaned the beach house. When they left here today, they weren't coming back. Mark's anxious mood echoed that of the team.

With the exception of Pia. Dressed in knee-high black boots, a leather skirt, and a figure-hugging black shirt, she looked ready to do battle. Her long red hair was slicked back into a tight knot, and her kohl-lined eyes were narrowed and focused.

Apparently, she'd woken determined to find answers to their mounting questions. She'd sat across from Nate with her knees touching his while she'd fired off requests about everything she wanted to know. The full history of the house, the deaths of Simon Farrell and Des Wilson. A background check on Tom Kelly, any other murders and suspicious deaths in the area over the last fifty years, and anything at all they could find on missing girls named Sarah.

Of course, Nate had already set Zach on those tasks—information had been coming in steadily throughout the night—but he didn't tell Pia that, instead enjoying watching her mind work.

Based on the information he'd received from Zach yesterday about Cassandra Reynolds, he knew she'd be at a particular park in about an hour, if she was following her regular after-school routine. Which meant Nate had barely enough time to escort the crew out of the house; lose the media; get Mark, Ryan, and Joe established in a safe location; and take Pia to the park in time for Cassandra's arrival.

Nate didn't know exactly what Pia hoped to gain from the park excursion—Pia had said she likely wouldn't speak to Cassandra and instead would only see what she could "pick up" from her—but it was what Pia wanted, so Nate would make it happen.

His phone signaled incoming messages. One more to come… *Bingo*. Everything was in place. It was time. "Ready to roll?" he asked Pia.

She slid her half-eaten piece of toast in the bin and slung her bag across her shoulder.

Tires screeched outside, followed by a loud crash.

"That's our signal. Let's go." He took Pia's hand, with Mark, Ryan, and Joe cued to follow.

Nate swung open the front door, and the crew made a short dash to his Porsche Cayenne. The reporters, as expected, were at the sight of the "accident," snapping pictures and barking out questions. Daniel Smith, former member of Nate's Special Operations team, now a partner in TSI, was deliberately "outraged," creating more of a scene than was necessary. The journalists were lapping it up; it was the first bit of excitement since they'd staked out the beach house yesterday afternoon.

Sheltering Pia with his body, Nate assisted her into the passenger side, before lunging into the driver's seat. Mark, Ryan, and Joe had barely shut the back doors when one of the journalists spotted them and began shrieking. The reporters came at them full charge, like a pack of hungry wolves.

Nate started the engine and threw it into reverse. The tires spun, then gripped as he whipped the vehicle around in a smooth one hundred and eighty degree arc, then with a spray of dirt and gravel, sent them hurtling forward. A quick glance in the mirror confirmed one… no, two of the leeches had made it into their vehicles to follow. He veered off the main road and began taking a series of side streets.

"Fuck, man," Joe called out from the back seat. "You a race car driver in a past life?"

Nate grinned, loving the speed. He always had. The family business ran in his blood after all. "Not officially. Trained with a few though." His father's business supplied a large portion of the parts for the Formula One racing industry. His dad was a major sponsor, the family business logo plastered across numerous cars. Nate had spent many weekends on the track, giving the cars a workout.

But that was then.

Nate picked up speed even more, raced down a few back streets, then pulled to a stop behind a black 4WD and a black semi parked on the side of the road.

Sean Wynter, another ex-Special Ops teammate of Nate's, now also a partner in TSI, and Rob Steel, a new employee Nate had met only once before, exited the vehicles, wearing black sunglasses, black shirts with a discreet TSI logo, and charcoal cargo pants.

In a blur of movement, an exchange of vehicles took place. Rob opened the rear doors to the truck and rolled out a black motorbike. Nate caught the keys Rob tossed him in one hand, and seconds later he had a helmet on Pia and settled her behind him on the bike. He barely glimpsed the Cayenne roll inside the semi before Sean closed the rear doors.

Mark, Joe, and Ryan were now in the back of Sean's 4WD and speeding off to the right, and Nate zipped past the semi as it took a hard left. The journalists wouldn't look twice at the truck, now taking a leisurely journey back to the highway, nor would they think to look at the motorbike or 4WD. They'd be looking for a Porsche Cayenne that had disappeared like a ghost.

———— ♦ ————

On the bike behind Nate, Pia slid her hands beneath his leather jacket and around his waist. She felt the coolness of his gun on her forearm and the rush of wind against her body as Nate skillfully navigated the winding streets. She tightened her arms around his rock hard abs, enjoying how they rippled and clenched beneath her fingertips as he moved with the bike.

Watching what Nate could effortlessly make happen reminded Pia of his background. He was ex-military, ex-Special Ops, now working for the most elite private investigation and security organization in the country.

To anyone else, Nate's little car shuffle might have seemed overkill; after all, they were being chased by journalists, not the mafia, but Pia knew Nate had just done what came naturally to him and his team. The exchange was practiced and fluent, as though Nate and his team would be as comfortable arranging an undercover operation as they would watching a matinée showing of the latest blockbuster.

She let her body meld with Nate's. The bike hugged the tight corners, and then they were on the open road. Nate rode the throttle, sending them hurtling through the air as one. It was exciting, freeing. Addictive. Every cell in her body was alive and tingling. She loved the speed, the rush of air on her face.

Being pressed against Nate's body.

All too soon, he pulled into the carpark of a playground in a wealthy neighborhood and cut the engine. He steadied the bike as she slid off. She removed her helmet and ran trembling fingers through her tangled hair, feeling a sudden sense of loss. Already she missed the speed and the thrill of being so close to Nate's hard body.

"You okay?" Nate assessed her through dark sunglasses.

Her mouth dried.

Was she? Pia was fairly certain now that she'd met Nate again, nothing in her life would ever be the same.

Shaking off thoughts of Nate and the future, she focused on what she needed to know.

Who is Sarah, and what is her connection to Cassandra?

Chapter Ten

Pia sat wordlessly on a park bench in Riverside Park, Applecross, next to Nate and squinted against the bright sunlight. Wind whipped her ponytail against her face and the strands caught on the side of her mouth. She brushed it back impatiently.

Nate's close proximity set her nerves on edge in a delicious, yet unsettling way. She still hadn't come down from the bike ride, her senses heightened, her nipples hard and tingling. She'd come alive in those wild, carefree moments.

She was left craving more.

More rush, more *Nate.*

In contrast to her inner turmoil, Nate appeared the epitome of deep, still waters. Leaning back with dark shades covering his eyes and his long legs stretched out in front of him, Nate affected the appearance of someone casually relaxed. A sexy single father perhaps, watching his child at the local playground.

However at ease Nate appeared, she doubted a single detail escaped him. He catalogued everything and everyone around him with a hunter's precision.

What he was thinking? What was he seeing that she wasn't?

I wonder what he sees when he looks at me?

She could reach out, get just a little glimpse…

She slammed that thought down before it could take flight. Not only was it a breach of her personal ethics to pry into private thoughts intentionally, for nothing but her own self-indulgence, she'd learned the hard way years ago that listeners never heard good of themselves. Nate's private thoughts were not her business.

And never would be.

That kiss last night had been like a bolt of lightning to a bar of chocolate, melting and obliterating something inside her. The power of that embrace had forever altered a deep part of her in a way she didn't understand. Left her craving something she'd long convinced herself she didn't want.

Or need.

Nate was too much and not nearly enough. Like a mere taste of an exquisite cake, knowing you could never have the whole thing. Or even a slice.

And the way he'd taken control of losing the journalists. The feeling of being at one with him as he rode the bike like the wind… Nate was an intoxicating thrill. If she were a normal girl, she'd jump into his bed if he so much as snapped his fingers.

But she wasn't a normal girl. It would serve her to remember that.

For Pia, that type of impulsiveness was dangerous. Sure, Nate had insisted he was staying to help her and the team out of this mess they were in, but every day he stayed increased the danger to Pia. Increased the strength of what she was already starting to feel for him.

That kiss had pulled the pin on a grenade, and the seconds before its explosion had already started ticking. If she wasn't careful, she'd begin to relax, open herself up. Allow herself to care too deeply.

It would then be only a matter of time before one of Nate's stray thoughts sneaked past her guard and she saw something she shouldn't. Something he wanted to keep private. Something not her business. He'd be hurt. Get angry. They'd fight. He'd leave. It had been that way with her ex, Adam.

It was no use telling herself that this time it'd be different.

It never was.

And this time, it would hurt not only her, but also Mark and the team. They all needed Nate and the help he was giving them. Pia couldn't afford to be selfish and take what she wanted.

A movement caught her eye and she tensed. Although he remained completely still, Pia sensed Nate's energy shifting, his senses becoming more alert.

Cassandra Reynolds, wearing pink shorts and a floral top, bounced into the playground with her mother and younger sister, Rebecca. Cassandra was a pretty girl, her waist-length ash-blonde hair pulled back in a chunky plait that ran down the center of her back. She was carrying a doll under one arm, its long platinum-blonde hair dangling toward the ground.

The same doll that Pia had seen on the chair in Cassy's bedroom. The doll that looked like Sarah.

"Isn't she a little old to be taking a doll around with her?" Nate murmured.

"That's not just any doll," Pia said, a heavy feeling settling inside her. "It's not even her doll. It's *the* doll. The one that was in the room when we did the investigation. That's what Sarah looks like. The apparition as it appeared to me."

Nate tensed beside her.

Mother and daughters walked to a bench on the other side of the small playground.

Monique Reynolds took a wide-brimmed hat out of her bag, slipped it on, and began typing something into her phone, her fingers flying across the screen.

"Mum?" Cassandra's high voice carried the distance easily in the light breeze. "Can I take Becky down the biggest slide?"

"Sure, honey," Monique Reynolds said absently, not glancing up. "Just don't let her fall off. I don't have time for broken bones today."

Cassandra placed the doll on the bench next to her mother, arranged it into a seated position, as though it were a real child instead of an inanimate object, then grabbed her younger sister's hand and took off to the slide, the brand-new, high altitude, tubular slide that made the park so popular with the kids. The doll stared out at the playground with strangely intelligent eyes.

"Creepy," Nate muttered.

Pia agreed. Something about that doll had unnerved her even before she knew that Sarah looked like it. The doll seemed to have an energy, a presence of its own. An eerily "alive" object that couldn't intake a lungful of oxygen, but seemed quite capable of taking a large bite out of your soul.

"How much can you... see?" Nate asked, his gaze not wavering from the playground.

"I can look at someone, and if I consciously reach out, I can often just 'know' things about them. Not everything, mostly what's active in their conscious mind. How they're feeling: happy, sad, angry. If I press a little more, I can sometimes know why."

"Sometimes, but not always?"

"No. It's actually pretty unreliable," she said, with a small laugh. "I get a lot of impressions I have to interpret. That leaves room for error. Sometimes, an impression I get is nothing more than a strong thought. It might be that someone is imagining doing something. Fantasizing. I get the impression, the thought, but I won't know if it's something that already happened, a memory, or something that will happen in the future. Or a fantasy that will never happen at all. It can drive you mad if you let it."

"Wow," he said softly. "How do you deal with something like that on a day-to-day basis?"

"Mostly, I do whatever I can to stay out of people's heads, the way I'd not look into someone's window."

"Can you see what Monique is so focused on?"

Pia glanced at Cassandra's mother, who was frowning in concentration on her phone.

"Probably. But I won't, because I don't think it's relevant." Pia could understand Nate's detective mind wondering, and once upon a time, she would have reached out. But not now. People's private thoughts were a line she had no business to cross. She'd seen women undressing other men while seated next to their husbands, and men inappropriately looking at small children, and countless other indiscretions that could leave a person cynical about the whole of humanity.

She tried to reach across only on occasions where she believed such a breach would be justified. Like with the detectives. She'd needed to know their angle for self-preservation. She was innocent after all, and those men were trying to arrest her for a crime she hadn't committed.

Pia focused on Cassandra, who was just starting to help her sister climb the ladder of the large tubular slide on the edge of the playground. Rebecca was a little scared; it was the first time she had ever been on it. It was new, and quite a step up from the medium-sized slide that had two curvy bends to slow the descent.

It was Rebecca's turn at the top of the slide, and Cassandra whispered a few words of encouragement. Rebecca took a breath, steeled her nerves, and shoved off. The wind pushed against her face, sending her hair flapping behind her. She screamed; she was sliding even faster than she'd imagined.

Cassandra took off after her sister, her feet soon skidding to a stop in the sand at the bottom. She jumped up, adrenaline racing through her veins.

"Mum! Did you see? Becky did it!" She looked over to her mother, who was still focused on her phone.

Oh. Cassandra looked down at the grass. Becky had just conquered one of her fears, but her mum hadn't seen. Did she even care?

Pia's heart reached out to Cassy. *You did good, sweetheart! You're such a great big sister!*

Cassandra's head whipped around, her wide eyes connecting with Pia's.

She heard me! Pia was stunned.

Cassandra ran over to Pia, Becky right at her side. "Did you see Becky go down the slide?"

"You were so brave." Pia smiled at Becky. Cassandra beamed. "You're lucky to have a big sister like Cassandra. I always wished I had a sister."

Cassandra hugged Pia impulsively, as though she sensed her inner longing, and Pia gave her a quick squeeze in return. She glanced over Cassandra's shoulder. Monique hadn't looked up from her phone. Pia placed her hands on Cassandra's shoulders and eased her back.

A high, off-key squeal raked across her nerves. Pia glanced to her right, seeking the source of the offending noise. An A-frame swing set, made up of three swings and a slide. On one of the swings sat a young girl in a flowing white dress, with long blonde hair and black holes where her eyes should have been.

"You can see her too, can't you?" Cassandra said excitedly. She'd lowered her voice so that Becky couldn't hear quite so clearly.

"You mean the girl on the swing?" Pia whispered back, suspecting, but wanting to be sure.

"Yes. Sarah," Cassandra said in a hushed voice. "I saw you looking at her. You can see her? You can *really* see her?"

"Yes."

The apparition was staring at them, malevolent energy building around it in a way that sent a chilling shockwave throughout Pia's body. Sarah's threat came back to her. *I will get you too.*

Oh God. This was not good, not good at all.

"Mum can't see her," Cassandra said. "She doesn't believe me." Her eyes took on a heavy shadowed look. "Nobody does."

Stay away from us. Sarah's warning rammed itself inside Pia's mind with the force of a hurricane.

Us. Sarah had attached herself to Cassandra. Would she use Cassandra now because Pia had refused to help her last night? Bile rose in Pia's throat. She didn't want Sarah to be a voice in Cassandra's head, urging her to do who knew what.

Cassandra was peering up at her curiously, and Pia took a steadying breath, forced herself to remain calm.

Cassandra glanced at Nate. "Is he your boyfriend?"

Nate raised a brow in response to the forward question only children seemed to get away with.

"No," Pia said. "He's just a friend."

"He wishes you were more," Cassandra said, and Nate coughed. Pia's eyes widened. Cassy was more gifted than she'd thought.

"I went down the big slide all by myself," Rebecca said, wanting to be included in the conversation.

"I know, honey, I saw."

"Mum didn't." The girl looked over her shoulder. Pia followed her gaze to where her mother was still glued to her iPhone.

"She loves you," Pia said, pleased she could say that and know it to be true. "She loves you both. Perhaps she's just busy."

"I know," Cassandra lowered her voice and spoke directly to Pia. "But she doesn't *see* me. Not the way you do."

Pia's chest squeezed, and for a moment she was thrown back into her childhood. Having abilities her mother feared and didn't understand was a terrible thing for a little girl to have to endure. There were a lot of similarities between Cassy and Pia's younger self.

"My name is Pia." She'd just realized she hadn't introduced herself. They'd connected at a different level.

Cassy smiled. "I know who you are. Mum and Dad think you ruined our house. That you killed that man." She lowered her eyes. "But it wasn't you."

"No, it wasn't me. Do you know who it was?"

Cassy looked down at her white tennis shoes. "You can tell me," Pia said softly.

"I'm not supposed to."

Cassy looked up, and Pia met her eyes. The deep sadness there broke Pia's heart. The things Cassandra must have seen, the things Sarah had shown her, must be a lot to process for a young girl. Like watching an adult horror film before she was mature enough to deal with the subject matter.

"Do you see Sarah in your room, in that special way, Cassy?" *She doesn't see me,* Cassandra had said about her mother. Sarah also felt she hadn't been seen. Was that why the spirit had attached herself to Cassandra? Because of her abilities as a medium as well as her life circumstances? A similarity that also connected Pia with both Sarah and Cassandra.

With Cassy's open heart and her yearning to be understood, a connection to Sarah couldn't bode well.

"She's my friend."

"Your *imaginary* friend," Becky said.

Cassandra angled her body away from Becky and lowered her voice further. "She's not my imaginary friend like Mum says. Sarah is real. Or, she was real. I mean, she was alive, and now she's not. But she's still real. Now, I mean."

Pia nodded. Cassandra was struggling to work all this out by herself. If only Pia could spend time with her, help her. Mentor her. Protect her from a world that just didn't understand.

Cassy's energy spread, pushing into Pia's; she was probing to see if Pia could be trusted. Pia projected confidence and reassurance.

She must have succeeded, because Cassandra relaxed. "Sarah is sad, and hurt. She wears a long white dress, but it's dirty. There's blood on it, and it won't come off. I have her doll," she added proudly. "It's called Angel."

Pia smiled at the way Cassandra spoke, just random thoughts coming out as they occurred to her.

"The doll you put over there on the chair next to your mother is Sarah's doll? Is that Angel?"

"Yes."

"Monique is heading this way," Nate said in an undertone, and Pia followed his gaze to see Monique Reynolds casually making her way over.

"I'm going back to Mum," Rebecca said, running off.

"How did you get it?" Pia asked, knowing their time together was limited.

"It was in the cellar."

"How did you know it was there?"

"Sarah showed me," Cassy said. "They put her in there."

"Who? Do you know who they are?"

Cassy shook her head. "The bad people put her in there. A bad man hurt her." A tear rolled down her cheek. "Sarah wants me to help her. No one ever helped her."

Pia's stomach twisted. The attachment was happening already. If the entity remained with Cassandra for much longer, it could lead to oppression, then possession. Pia had to pray it never went that far. Removing a spirit from a body in the grips of possession was extremely difficult, and often had dire, even fatal, consequences. This beautiful girl's life would be shredded if that were allowed to happen.

Pia had to act fast. Was it already too late?

Pia gripped Cassy by the shoulders. "Cassandra, listen to me. You *mustn't* help her. Don't tell Sarah you can help her."

A gust of wind whipped through the park, flicking sand into Pia's face. Sarah had stopped swinging and was leaning forward, anger radiating off her. "You've made her angry," Cassandra said. "It scares me when she's angry."

"Cassy!" Monique shouted, her voice high and desperate; she'd clearly just realized who her daughter was talking to. Perhaps Rebecca had told her. "Get away from her! Come here." She whipped out her phone and dialed a number.

"*Now* she notices me," Cassandra said.

Pia released a breath and rested her hand on Cassandra's arm. "Sweetheart, you need to be careful of Sarah."

Cassandra's eyes filled with tears. "You don't like her."

"I need to talk to you more about all this, okay? Another time. But just be careful of doing whatever she asks you. Especially if it sounds like something you wouldn't normally do."

The squeak of the swings started again, then Pia's throat constricted as though hands were squeezing it tight.

She coughed, struggling to breathe, and glared fiercely at the apparition. *Back off, Sarah.*

Cassandra looked at Sarah. *Please stop.*

Pia could suddenly breathe again.

Cassandra turned back to Pia. "She needs me. She has no one else."

Monique, breathing fast, grabbed Cassy's arm, her fingers digging into the flesh, and shook it. "Why don't you ever listen?" Monique demanded.

"Hi, Monique," Pia said, standing. "It's all right. It wasn't Cassy's fault, I called her over." It was actually sort of true.

Monique rounded on Pia, her hand raised to strike. "Stay away from my child!"

Nate rose and positioned himself in front of Monique in less time than it took to blink. "Don't you lay a finger on her." His voice was lethally quiet.

Monique lowered her hand, looked past Nate, and said to Pia, "I've called the police. Stay away from me and my family. You've done enough damage, you psycho!"

Nate made a low warning sound in the back of his throat, and Pia put a hand on his arm.

"Please, Monique." Pia kept her voice even. "I didn't have anything to do with Tom Kelly's death. You have no reason to be frightened of me. I won't hurt you or your daughter. Quite the opposite. I'm trying to help."

Pia heard sirens in the distance. *Sirens?* What had Monique told them?

"You asked us in to find out what's happening in your house." Pia blurted the words; she didn't have long. "I'm trying to do that, but I need your help. If you would give me a moment, perhaps have a quick coffee—"

"No! Stay away from us!" Monique shrieked, and suddenly everyone in the park was staring in their direction.

Monique yanked on Cassandra's arm, pulling her away as though running from a serial killer.

Pia's heart sank.

Cassandra glanced back over her shoulder to Pia.

Don't tell her about Sarah. Cassandra said without words. *Please. She will be even angrier with you if you do.*

Who will be angrier? Your mum or Sarah?

Cassandra didn't reply, but it didn't really matter either way. Pia slowly sank down onto the bench, felt the steadying weight of Nate's arm slipping around her shoulders.

"Are you all right?" he asked softly.

Pia glanced over at the swing set. It was empty.

"Dear God, Nate. That little girl is a medium. A powerful one."

"Just like you. So that's a good thing, right?"

"No." Pia shook her head, her throat tightening, suddenly on the verge of tears. "She's young and innocent and open to a world she doesn't understand with no one to guide her, or teach her how to protect herself."

Pia thought of Sarah on the swings, the spirit's anger and resentment. The way Sarah reached out and applied pressure to Pia's throat as though to strangle her, or stop her from saying something she didn't like. Sarah had power and abilities that were rare and frightening. Usually spirits were contained to a place, or an object...

The doll! The doll allows her to travel outside the house.

"Cassandra Reynolds is in far more danger than I'd originally feared."

Nate rubbed her arm absently. Like her, he was deep in thought.

"I've got to help her," Pia said. "Before it's too late."

"Do you have any idea how?"

"In an ideal world, I'd talk to her. Teach her how to protect herself, stop non-physical entities like Sarah attaching themselves to her. She has no idea the kind of trouble it can cause."

"Can't see Monique letting you anywhere near her."

"Then I have to try to send Sarah away myself. And the only way I know to do that is to get back into that house." If she couldn't get the doll, she'd have to use the other location Sarah was attached to. The house. She'd seen Sarah there last time. If she could call her there again, perhaps she could reason with her, send her away. Free her from whatever was binding her to this earth, so that she would leave Cassandra alone. Pia had no idea if it would work or even if it was possible, but it was the only thing she could think of to try.

"I already told you that's not an option. It's a crime scene."

"Will there be cops there 24/7?"

"Well, not exactly." Nate frowned. "Goddamn it, Pia, it's a sealed crime scene. An active murder investigation."

"So there's just a bit of tape across the doors, then?"

Pia was sure she heard his teeth grinding.

"Look, Nate, I know it's not ideal. But I need to get into that house. I have to try to help Cassandra. Did you see a cellar mentioned in any of the police reports?"

"No."

"Cassandra said she found the doll in a cellar. That Sarah showed her where to find it. I didn't see a cellar during the investigation. I want to see if I can find a cellar at the cottage, or if it's in another location."

Nate made a choking sound which she ignored.

The cellar had to be the place in the images she'd been seeing. The place where Sarah was kept. Perhaps if she found the cellar, she could work out who Sarah was. If she found out what had happened to her and had the perpetrators brought to justice, Sarah wouldn't be trapped here any longer. She'd be free to go.

The sirens were getting louder.

"We'd better hurry." Nate grabbed her hand and headed for the bike.

"Nate!" Pia hurried to keep up with him.

"What?"

"Where are we going?" They'd already reached his bike.

"Back to my house." Taking in her expression, he added, "Please?"

Despite everything, that tacked-on, desperate "please?" made her laugh. Being in charge was Nate's comfort zone. And it was hers too. She'd been on her own for as long as she could remember.

But if he could bend, she could too.

"Can you *please* take me to the lighthouse keeper's cottage?"

The police had pulled up in the carpark across from them. Two uniformed officers were heading down to the playground area to talk to Monique. She pointed over to them.

"I'll take you to Darwin if that's what you want. Just hurry up and get on."

Pia slid her leg over the bike and settled her body against Nate's back. His muscles rippled and contracted, his breath hitching. He felt their contact as powerfully as she did. Perhaps she *should* tell him to take her to Darwin. She could easily spend days wrapped around Nate like this.

"You're still the most exasperating person I know," he grumbled, starting the engine. The half-smile he slanted at her over his shoulder caused her heart to skip a beat.

"Likewise." She hid her grin in the back of his jacket.

Nate rode the throttle and spun the tires as they took off, the police looking in their direction as they sped away.

CHAPTER ELEVEN

The police were at the lighthouse keeper's cottage, so Nate took the opportunity to find them a late lunch. Or was it an early dinner? He'd long ago stopped giving titles to the meals he ate, eating only when the opportunity presented itself.

They found some great grilled fish and chips from a local place and brought their meal to the beach to eat. Pia was licking the salt and vinegar from her fingers as the sun slipped fully below the horizon.

They were at the most southwesterly mainland point of the Australian continent, on a white stretch of sand, looking back on the Cape Leeuwin Lighthouse.

Nate was waiting for Daniel's all-clear. The police had returned to the property a couple of hours ago, a visit that included Johnson. Apparently, there was some damage or something else had happened to the house. Nate was awaiting clarification and further information.

"The view of the lighthouse from here is spectacular," Pia commented. Nate agreed, but nothing compared to the view of Pia snuggled into the soft sand, the fingers of a light breeze tousling her hair. The same shade of red was in the sunset as in some strands of her hair.

"I have views from my house too," Nate said casually. "And a real table and chairs."

He was rewarded with a half-smile at his playful reference to her refusal to go to his house when he'd mentioned it. Twice now.

"It is an offense to eat fish and chips at a table," she said lightly, but a shadow crossed her eyes. "Aren't you Australian? Eating on the beach or a grassy lawn is a requirement." She brushed sand off her legs. "Do you really have views like this from your place?"

"There's only one way to find out."

Pia slanted a glance in his direction. "Why do you want me to go to your house so badly?"

Nate turned his head and looked out at the ocean in case she could read him too readily. It certainly wasn't common for him to invite women back to his place.

His Perth house was his home. His retreat. His private space. He traveled so frequently, it was the one place in this busy world that he thought of as his own, and he guarded its privacy fiercely.

It was also the one place he could assure her safety. There was no safer place in the world for her, than there. That must be the reason.

What a load of shit, Ryder.

He answered her question with one of his own. "Why do you resist going there so strongly?"

Pia rested back on her elbows and turned her face away, suddenly taking a great interest in the lighthouse. "You don't want this, Nate," she said softly.

"Don't want what?" He wanted her to be the one to clarify the "this" that was between them. "People visit their friends' houses all the time. It's what they do. Pop over for a coffee."

Pia turned in his direction. "Is that what you want? For me to be a friend who pops over for a coffee?"

No. That wasn't what he wanted at all. What he wanted was to grab her and not let her go. He wanted her permission to keep her safe. Not just for now, but always. To simply be with her. "Would that be so bad?"

Pia sat up, hugged her knees to her chest, and sifted sand through her fingers. "I'm not the visiting-for-a-coffee type."

Nate wanted to press her, but now wasn't the time. She didn't know it yet, but she was coming back to his house after she'd finished at the cottage. No use causing her to dig in her heels about it now.

"I'm so worried about Cassandra," Pia said, clearly steering the topic to more comfortable ground. "Not only about the whole Sarah situation, but in general. Having parents so adamant in their disbelief of the paranormal when Cassy knows for sure what she sees with her eyes and feels with her body." Her eyes welled with tears, and Nate's heart squeezed.

"Was it hard for you too? Your childhood?"

"It was." Pia's voice was hoarse with emotion. She cleared her throat and sniffed, and when she spoke again, her tone was flat, hard. "But I'm all grown up. I'm a different person now than I was back then. What doesn't kill you and all that." Pia shrugged, her stare defiant. Nate recognized that thread of steel and knew where it came from. Adversity either broke you or made you stronger. It was the latter with Pia. Rather than hiding her differences, she embraced them.

"Yours wasn't easy either," Pia murmured thoughtfully, then turned to him wide-eyed. "I'm sorry," she said quickly. "God, I'm so sorry. I didn't mean that to sound like I've been prying uninvited. It was only a general observation. Just tell me to mind my own damn business."

He placed his hand on her arm. "It's all right," he said with what he hoped was a reassuring smile. "Really." But she wouldn't look at him.

He couldn't imagine what it would be like to live with Pia's abilities. Sometimes it seemed as though she carried the weight of the world on her shoulders.

Nate forcibly removed his hand from her arm. The skin beneath his hand was so soft, her body enticingly warm. Much too aware of the woman beside him who was trying to keep her distance, he took a deep breath of salty air and stared out at the ocean. A cool evening breeze had picked up, causing whitecaps as the waves broke on their way to shore.

"See that seagull hovering just over there?" he asked. "That's the line where the Indian Ocean meets the Great Southern Ocean. You can almost imagine the two seas as roaring beasts," Nate said as though the line were real and not a geographical boundary. "Two apex predators colliding and fighting, competing for dominance, year after year, century after century, with neither of them winning or coming out on top. A continuous fight where there can be no victor."

A lock of hair escaped from her ponytail and danced in front of her eye in the gentle sea breeze, and he resisted reaching out and smoothing it back into place.

"You can't help but feel small when you look out at the enormity of the ocean like this," Nate said. "As insignificant as a grain of beach sand. Have you ever wondered what it would be like to live on the sea, to travel from land to land following nothing but a whim and the sunsets?"

Pia smiled. "I can't say I have. But that's a very romantic notion."

Nate shrugged. "Maybe I'm a romantic guy."

She turned to him. "Are you, Nate?"

"Why do you ask?" He kept his voice even so as not to betray his pleasure at her question. He'd love to get her to start looking at him like a woman looked at a man. Sure, they'd kissed passionately last night, but since then a chasm had opened up between them that he didn't know how to bridge.

"Romance is overrated." She picked up a handful of sand, letting it fall through her fingers like rain.

He'd never taken her for the hearts-and-flowers type, but still… "I thought women loved romance."

Pia shrugged. "It doesn't last. Romance is like the frosting on a cake." She picked up another handful of sand. "Frosting is sweet and tasty, but it's just window dressing. The real part is the cake."

Her voice was so small, so bereft, Nate's chest tightened. She'd been hurt. More than once. It didn't take a detective to realize that the men she'd been with hadn't been able to deal with the real Pia. Was that why she dressed the way she did? From her choice in hair color, to the leather outfits, the dark eyeliner, and the black fingernails. So that the icing made clear she was different, so there was no surprise when you got to the cake?

"Perhaps you just haven't found a man who likes your particular cake yet," Nate said, keeping his voice even. "Who wants vanilla when you can have something far more exciting?"

Pia's lips twisted. "I'm definitely not vanilla."

His body responded instantly to her words. *That's what I'm counting on. I'm far from vanilla myself.*

The phone in his top pocket buzzed, putting an end to a conversation he looked forward to pursuing another time. Soon.

The message was from Daniel.

Clear. Tell Pia the house is not quite how she left it.

Nate showed her the message.

She wrinkled her brow. "I wonder what that means?"

"No idea. Ready to do this?"

"Absolutely." Pia shook the sand off her leather skirt and slid back into her boots. She took his proffered hand and allowed him to help her to her feet. "You haven't been inside the cottage yet. It will be interesting to get your take on it."

Nate didn't need to go inside the house to give her his take on it. Instinct told him he wasn't going to like what he saw. He was fighting an extremely unsettling and overwhelming protective impulse to throw her over his shoulder and take her the hell away from here. It didn't matter where, just anywhere other than the haunted cottage she was determined to go back inside.

The cottage contained something powerful enough to kill a man. Something that was not yet finished with her. Pia thought it was *she* who couldn't walk away from this case.

Nate feared something far more sinister. The opposite.

What if it was the thing inside the house that wasn't letting *Pia* go?

CHAPTER TWELVE

Nate left his bike parked in a nearby cove hidden by bushes and held Pia's hand as they crossed the beach to the cottage. He was dressed in a black leather jacket, cargo pants, a black T-shirt, and a baseball cap. With dark shades covering his eyes, he appeared fiercely masculine and frustratingly sexy.

They walked across the soft, white sand a few minutes before they found the little beach-access track and climbed the sand dunes to the cottage.

The sky darkened, and sporadic, heavy drops of rain sprinkled Pia's face. On most days, she would have said she loved the rain. But not today. Instead of cleansing her and making her feel uplifted, the rain just made her feel all the more the suffocating sadness that saturated the air and pressed down on her shoulders, the weight increasing as they drew near the cottage.

It appeared the Reynolds were putting their heart and soul into the renovations. They had spent decent money making the cottage look less like a beach house and more like a modern luxury home. The three lighthouse keeper's cottages built directly next to the lighthouse were no longer residential. This cottage, set farther away, was the only one that still was.

Pia's heart went out to the Reynolds family. Buying a house that would be your family home was one of the biggest investments, emotionally and financially, people made in their lives. Creating a space where your family could be safe and happy was a priority for most parents, and Pia sensed this was especially true for Chad Reynolds. He was a proud family man who loved his wife and girls unconditionally.

This house was to be their new beginning. Pia slowed down a little to "read" the house as they walked.

Lots of work had been carried out on the cottage. The newly renovated glass doors on the beach side opened up onto the deck, a large alfresco area that contained a traditional Aussie wooden picnic table and a large barbeque to one side.

When they reached the wooden steps, Pia closed her eyes and took a deep breath.

She saw Chad Reynolds, tongs in his right hand, turning over sizzling sausages for his girls, Cassandra and Rebecca, and some prawn and pineapple kebabs for his wife. Monique's favorite.

An open bottle of beer sat on the preparation table to his left, with two empties resting side by side. Monique was at the table, sipping a glass of white wine, Cassandra and Rebecca coloring, one on either side. Every now and then a sea breeze gusted and a colored pencil rolled onto the timber floor, and a giggling Becky, with her platinum-blonde hair in shiny pigtails, crawled around to retrieve it.

Chad Reynolds was content. His family was happy here. This was going to be exactly what they needed. A fresh start. Monique had been unhappy in their marriage—unhappy with him—for a while now. Though Monique blamed him for the trouble in their marriage, it had more to do with her post-partum depression after the birth of Becky than the brief affair he'd had during the pregnancy. It was unfair of her not to realize the insignificance of a one-night stand on a weekend away with the boys. It hadn't meant anything. But it did to Monique. And he'd heard about it often over the last few years.

But the idea of Monique leaving him and taking his girls had shaken him to the core. He wouldn't risk doing anything that would bring him that close to losing her again. This house was their chance to do things over; everything old had been swept away and become new again.

And that was why Chad so vehemently refused to acknowledge the shadow he'd seen on more than one occasion. The one his wife had seen at the foot of their bed one night and screamed bloody murder over. He'd told her it was her imagination, but it hadn't been. He'd seen it too.

He worried about Cassandra and her imaginary friend. He wouldn't admit it, but it scared him to hear Cassy's music box turn on in the dead of night. The first time it had happened, he'd gone into her room and discovered her sound asleep. The music box had continued to turn itself on even after he'd removed the batteries. And he absolutely refused to spend more than a minute contemplating the fact that when he'd tried to turn her bedside lamp off, he'd seen that the plug was already not in the socket. Because if he did, he would have to acknowledge that Cassy had unplugged it for the same reason. Because these things were happening to her. And he couldn't talk about it because he didn't know what the hell to say. Daddies were supposed to know the answers to everything. So he'd worried in silence until the acid burned a hole in his stomach.

When Monique had suggested getting in *Debunking Reality*, Chad was secretly relieved. Outwardly he'd grumbled, then smiled indulgently, saying "Anything for the girls." He'd even joked about them wanting to be on TV, to be famous. But he just wanted the house to be theirs again. And he wanted whoever was sharing the house with them to leave. He didn't want this "ghost" to ruin his new beginning. Not when, for the first time in years, he felt like he had his family back again.

Pia shook off the image and took Nate's hand. He tightened his grip in a reassuring squeeze, and she silently appreciated the way he'd stood patiently at her side. He didn't ask questions, didn't pull on her, didn't tell her to hurry up. She'd never met anyone, other than Mark, who'd unconditionally accepted her eccentricities without question before. It surprised her beyond measure to discover it in Nate. She'd thought, as a take-charge detective, he'd be a big thorn in her side.

How wrong she'd been.

It was dusk, and even though the sun had set, they could easily see without torch light, but the clouds continued to darken in disapproval, as if Pia had failed to deliver on something important.

Although legend had it that the house was haunted by Simon Farrell, the cray fisherman who'd fallen on his own knife thirty years ago, it was Sarah who walked the halls at night.

Who are you, Sarah?

What is your connection to this house?

They walked around the back, Pia so lost in thought she hadn't immediately noticed that Nate had stopped dead still and was staring at the house wide-eyed.

"So this is why Johnson was back at the house this afternoon," Nate murmured. "And this is what Daniel meant in his message. What the fuck happened here?"

The house was covered in puffy white eggs. Pia moved closer to get a better look.

The eggs didn't have an outer shell, like a bird's egg; they were soft, like mushrooms. The eggs covered halfway up the exterior walls and spilled down into the front yard.

Pia moved forward, bending down to study them. *Creepy balls of fungi.* The warmth of Nate's hand hadn't left her back, a solid presence as once again, he appeared to let her take the lead.

"What the hell are these?" Nate asked, staring down at an egg that was… hatching.

"Some type of plant," Pia whispered. Closer to the house several of the eggs had broken open, revealing long, red, grotesque "fingers," that looked like the tentacles of an octopus.

"They appear to be something like Archeri." She swallowed her disgust at the odor they emitted, a stench like putrid flesh. "Devil's finger mushrooms."

Pia and Nate stared, riveted to the spot and unable to look away, as a crack appeared in an egg by Nate's left foot. As though on increased time-lapse photography, a revolting, blood red hand erupted, fingers together, rising toward the sky like a grotesque tower, before separating flower-like into sticky, mucus covered, talon-like tentacles.

"Like a hand with no skin," Nate said. Pia imagined bloodied, skinless fingers, and her stomach roiled. "Makes me think of a corpse reaching up from the grave," he added.

"Not helpful." Pia elbowed him lightly. Her imagination was vivid enough.

The plant that had opened atrophied in seconds, and it now lay wilted, a shriveled old hand coated with dried blood.

"If these really are Archeri, they absolutely should not be behaving like this. So many in a concentrated location, and they certainly don't open, then wither that fast. I've seen one or two in my whole life. They usually grow on a fallen tree, in thick forest, never on a house. I wouldn't have even believed this possible, if I wasn't seeing it now." Her voice faded. Jesus. More and more eggs were opening, all with the same fast cycle of "blooming" then dying.

"That's just not right," she said.

"No argument from me." Nate placed an arm around her shoulders as they surveyed the stinking mess before them. "This is a hundred shades of fucking wrong."

Now that the initial shock had worn off, Pia scanned the area with a cool, analytical mind. There were eggs dotted in clusters in the front garden, around the base of the trees, and growing on the timber frame of the house.

More eggs, the ones stuck to the front wall of the house this time, began to open, their red, finger-like tentacles rising up and outward, wriggling around like festering hands of rotting flesh. The noise accompanying the movement was a damp, viscous sound, like hundreds of maggots moving through raw flesh.

Sarah.

Was this her way of sending a clear message to stay out of the house?

"It's going to take more than some gross plants to stop me," Pia said out loud, and a sudden gust of icy wind blasted her. She swallowed, hard, and forced her feet to walk to the front door.

Step by cautious step, Pia and Nate picked their way to the entrance of the house. The stench was becoming unimaginable, like prawns rotting in the sun, and she kept her breaths short and shallow.

"Watch how our presence affects the eggs," Pia said. "Look how the ones we get near open faster."

The front door was practically encased in the eggs, as if to prevent entry. They lined the edges of the frame, even covered the lock.

With a look of distaste, Nate peeled a half-withered Archeri-thing off the lock and flicked it on the ground. It landed with a plop, the sound of a wet towel hitting the floor. Nate provided a swift keyless entry using a tool he pulled from his pocket. When he opened the door, there was the fleshy sound of a wound being ripped open, as the sticky Archeri eggs and half-formed plants tore apart.

In what appeared to be blood, so fresh it was still running down the wall facing the entry, were the words, *Go Away.*

Her last trace of doubt—if it had really been there—disappeared at that moment. The infestation of Archeri *was* a warning, and it was meant for Pia.

Nate stepped across the threshold and stilled. But he wasn't looking at the writing on the wall. He'd turned to look outside behind them. Pia followed his gaze and saw nothing. When she looked at the wall again, the words were gone. But the metallic smell of blood lingered.

Behind his dark glasses, Nate was still scanning the front yard with sharp, cop eyes.

"Hear that?"

Pia paused, hearing the click before she could use any extrasensory abilities. She looked again and saw a series of tiny flashes coming from beside a tree.

Nate pushed her inside the door, out of the photographer's sight line, but it was already too late. The pictures that had just been taken of her would be clear, indisputable; Pia at the open front door of the murder house she'd been warned to stay away from, staring directly at the camera.

When the police saw that in the paper, they'd think she'd returned to the scene of the crime to remove evidence that could implicate her. Would the Reynolds go public and imply that Pia and the team had somehow covered the house in Archeri themselves? She could almost see the headline: *"Ghost Hunter" Caught in the Act.* What reason could Pia ever give to justify being here?

I am so screwed.

She peered through the gap where Nate had left the door slightly ajar. He lowered the visor of his cap over his eyes and swiftly crossed to the photographer, the squishing of eggs loud beneath his boots. The photographer, a balding middle-aged man, his flanno shirt straining at the middle, stepped out from behind the tree he'd used for cover and began snapping pictures of Nate.

Towering above the photographer, Nate ripped the camera out of his hands and ground it beneath his boot.

The photographer's face turned beet red, and he began sputtering, spittle flying from his lips. Nate took a step back, reached into his top pocket, and handed him a business card.

"Email me a claim for the new camera."

Nate took out his iPhone and took a picture of the photographer, then his car parked in the nearby driveway.

"You will not call the cops," Nate said. "You so much as whisper about seeing us here, I'll find you." He leaned down for emphasis. "And you'll wish that I hadn't."

"Are you threatening me?" the journalist choked, stumbling back a couple of steps.

Nate straightened. "I don't need to make threats," he said casually, his voice low and even. "You'll learn that if you take me on."

The photographer didn't reply. Instead he scrambled back to his car, tires screeching as he drove away.

Nate crossed the lawn back to her, and Pia couldn't breathe. Was there anything sexier than a powerful man who took control so naturally? She wasn't the type to back away from a confrontation, but she would likely have just ended up in a shouting match with the photographer.

"He no longer has the pictures he took of you, but just like cockroaches, where there's one, there'll be more. We have to go. Now."

"Wait," Pia said, turning to peer inside the house.

"Pia, damn it. You can't go in right now. We've got to get out of here. There are limits to what I can do for you if Johnson catches you here."

Nate's voice faded into the background as Pia took a cautious step deeper into the house. She ran her fingers across the wall where the words *Go Away* had just been scrawled. The smooth surface felt damp, and when she checked her fingertips, they were covered in blood.

"What the hell?" Nate grabbed her hand. "What did you do?" Before he could wipe it off, the blood was gone.

His eyes met hers. "What the fuck just happened?"

Another icy breeze blasted them, and a heavy sense of dread washed over Pia's body, a premonition that something really bad was about to happen. The muscles in her legs quivered with the impulse to run outside, but she forced herself to go deeper into the house.

She walked slowly down the hallway, stopping at the entrance to Cassandra's room. Nate shadowed every move she made. His eyes were narrowed, his hand hovering over his weapon.

"Sarah?" Pia called out to the empty room. "Are you here?"

BANG!

The sound split the air, reverberating through the house. Before she could take a breath, Nate had thrown her to the ground, covering her with his body.

Lying beneath Nate, Pia realized the noise they'd heard had been the front door slamming shut. It hadn't just blown shut. It had slammed with the intensity of a gunshot.

The house had just swallowed them.

Nate rose, holding Pia's hand as he assisted her to her feet. His phone flashed.

"Two cars are heading this way at high speed," Nate said. "Daniel ran the plates, and they're journalists. It will be a only matter of time before cops are on their heels."

Nate grabbed her hand tight, and they moved to the front door. With each step they took, the air seemed heavier, saturated with emotion, as if sorrow had replaced the oxygen. Nate tried the door handle. It wouldn't turn.

"Stand back."

He kicked the door hard with his boot. The ease with which he did this showed he'd done it many times before. The door didn't budge.

"What the hell?" Nate frowned and kicked the door again, harder this time. Again, the door didn't give. They seemed to be in a vault made of solid steel instead of timber.

The air thinned, making Pia feel dizzy, as though she'd been catapulted to a high altitude without an oxygen tank. The edges of her vision blurred, and her knees began to buckle.

"Move away from the door," Nate said, drawing his weapon. Pia could feel someone staring at her, boring holes in the back of her head. But she couldn't think, couldn't breathe to clear her mind enough to reach out and confirm who it was. All she knew was that it hated her. Did Sarah detest her that much now? Or was something other than Sarah in the house?

Nate glanced at Pia, his brow furrowing. "Can you walk?" he asked, and she couldn't even answer. Couldn't move. He lifted her off the ground and set her just inside Cassandra's room. "You okay?" Pia nodded, even though it was far from true.

"I've got to get you out of here. Stay put."

Pia was shivering now. She could see her breath. The stench of rotting eggs washed over her, and bile rose in her throat.

Cassandra's music box began to play, its light, tinkling notes a sick contrast to the dark, swirling fury that tugged and pulled at her hair. The lamp in the corner of the room flickered once, twice, and then the bulb exploded, sending a spray of glass upward, fragments pinging off the ceiling.

Nate fired at the front door lock, making Pia jump. The noise was deafening in the confined space, and her ears rang. The room spun, her knees giving way. The floor was so hard beneath her chest, and then she was aware of a floating sensation. Nate had picked her up and she was being carried in his arms.

When they made it safely out the front door, Pia struggled. "Put me down," she finally managed through a constricted throat.

Nate set her down, carefully eyeing her, his face heavily creased in concern. "You don't look in any condition to walk."

Waves of sickness rolled through her, and she bent over at the waist, heaving. It felt as though she were being punched in the stomach or her internal organs were being attacked from the inside.

"Phone's dead," Nate growled. "Let's go."

Thwack! Something hit the back of her head. Surprised, she stood up straight, her hand moving to the spot. When she pulled it away, her hand was covered in sticky, foul-smelling fingers from the fungi. *Archeri.* Another one hit her dead center of the back, then another smacked into her thigh. Another splatted on her cheek, before slowly sliding down her neck. The world tilted on its axis as the unseen attack on her body continued.

Nate was tugging on her hand, and she knew he was saying words to urge her to hurry. But something was pressing down on her. She was sinking deeper into the earth.

"Pia!" Nate cursed, then once again she was weightless, Nate clearly deciding it was faster to carry her. As he ran with her in his arms, they were pelted with sticky eggs and sickly fingers that smelled of rotting flesh.

When they reached the beach, Nate set her on her feet. "Goddamn it, Pia." His voice was a low worried rasp. "Tell me how I can help you. Tell me what you need, and it will be done. You scared the life out of me back there." Nate whipped off his T-shirt and used it to wipe the sticky residue off her face and body.

"I'm okay," she said, her voice just as hoarse. She sucked in air. The oppressive weight that had been thrown over her had lifted. Pia glanced at the house. She would have died if Nate hadn't gotten her out when he had. The whole experience had been nothing short of terrifying.

What are you, Sarah?

Nate removed the bulk of stinking Archeri from her body, then crushed her to his bare chest. "I was so worried for you. So fucking angry at what was happening to you, and I couldn't do a damn thing to help. A lifetime of training, all of it useless." Pia pulled back, struggling against the waves of emotion radiating from Nate. She felt his fear for her, his frustration at not knowing what was happening, and his white hot anger at the entity for doing it to her.

Her weakened state from being oppressed by the entity made it hard to get her own emotions under control. She needed Nate to calm down so that she could begin to think straight herself.

"You did help by getting me out of there." She ran her hand soothingly down his arm. "I hate to think of what would have happened if you hadn't acted so quickly to free the door. I know it's hard to protect someone from something you can't see, but you did everything right, and it was enough. We are safe. *I* am safe," she added, and some of his tension drained away.

The sound of cars screeching to a stop in the driveway reached them.

Nate's phone flashed with several messages. "I have to tell Daniel we're okay," he said, his fingers flying across the screen. "He heard the gunshot."

Pia looked up the beach back at the house. On the outside, it appeared to be a typical two-story cottage. Quaint and inviting. Innocent.

On the inside, it was anything but.

Her pulse was slowly returning to normal. She had to hand it to Sarah. The entity was not to be underestimated.

But neither should Sarah underestimate Pia.

Sarah hadn't scared Pia away. If anything, Sarah had just made her even more determined. As if Pia could just leave an entity that powerful and dangerous and simply walk away?

More people could get hurt. Or worse.

The question remained: Who was Sarah? And what the hell had happened to turn a young girl into such a powerful and violent entity?

CHAPTER THIRTEEN

"Nate, I need to find out who Sarah is," Pia said, shivering. They had just pulled up at his two-story ocean-front house.

He'd gotten his way after all, and Pia hadn't fought him over it. He'd rather that she had. She was curled up in his jacket, heater going full blast, and still she shivered as if they were in the Arctic.

His chest tightened as he looked at her, and he almost had to physically pry his fingers off the steering wheel, his grip was so fierce. Fear over her safety had burned a hole right through his stomach. The drive had done little to calm his nerves or ease his temper. He ruthlessly reined it in as best he could, conscious of how fragile she looked right now.

Assisting her out of the car, Nate tucked her protectively into his side, supporting her as he guided her along the winding pathway to the entrance of his home. She was pale and shaking, and all she could talk about was who Sarah was.

"You really think that was Sarah back there and not a demon?" he asked.

"Yes."

"A young *girl* did that to you? I find that difficult to believe. I saw what happened to you, Pia, and whatever did that to you was not human. Whatever that was, it's pure evil."

Pia looked down at her shuffling feet. "She's angry with me now. Because I told her I wouldn't help her—"

Clenching his jaw, Nate cursed under his breath, entered his security code using the keypad by the door, then pressed his thumb to the screen. The lock disengaged with a click, and the front door opened.

"When I go back in—"

"Goddamn it, Pia!" Nate growled. "You're not going anywhere near that damn house. Do you *want* to get yourself killed?" His keys clanged loudly as he threw them in the bowl by the door. He thrust both his hands through his hair, struggling with a riot of emotions he had no idea how to calm.

"You don't understand. I don't have a choice. I have to." She hugged her arms around her middle and looked at him with sad eyes. "Sarah doesn't have anyone else."

"Stop talking about her like she's a real girl!" Nate shouted, and she flinched.

Fuck!

He sucked in a deep, shaky breath.

He was being an arsehole. But he'd never felt so out of his comfort zone in all his life. He was just so fucking worried for her safety. And there was not a single damn thing he could do to protect her.

Except keep her away from that bloody house.

And staying away seemed to be the one thing she was determined *not* to do.

"Pia, that thing nearly killed you back there. How do you think I felt?" His voice was thick with emotions he couldn't reel in. "Forced to watch while an invisible force choked the life out of you, knowing there was not a fucking thing I could do to stop it."

Pia was shaking, and here he was, shouting at her again, as though it had been her fault.

He wrapped his arms around her shoulders and pulled her against his chest. "I'm sorry. I don't mean to be an arse. I know I'm not handling this well, but I can't let you risk yourself again. Nothing is worth that. No case, no lost girl, even if she was real."

With a gentle grip on her chin, he angled her face upward and saw her eyes glistening with unshed tears. Something inside him shattered further.

She stared at him, her teeth chattering, seeming unable to answer.

His heart thundered in his chest; he needed to get himself under control. He took a deep breath and slowly blew it out, then put his arm around her again and steered her farther inside.

"Let's get you warmed up and give you something to eat. We'll talk about this later."

He guided her into the kitchen and watched as Pia's eyes went wide. She staggered over to the floor-to-ceiling windows that—were it daylight—had perfect views of the ocean. And his private beach. At the moment, a fresh storm was brewing on the horizon, flashes of lightning illuminating the scene.

Nate's grandfather had left him and his brother a sizeable inheritance when he'd died several years ago, handing the profitable family racing business to Nate's father. Nate's brother enjoyed a lavish party lifestyle and whittled away what had been left to him, whereas Nate, fully immersed in his career in Special Ops, had invested his inheritance in some very lucrative securities recommended by his partner Blade. So when Nate had seen this house come up for sale, he'd had the funds to buy and customize it, with plenty to spare.

"Climate control, on." The central air-conditioning unit immediately responded to his voice command, setting the house to a comfortable 24 degrees Celsius. He gave Pia some space, hoping the view of the ocean would help distract her from thinking about that thing she was calling Sarah.

Nate pulled a fresh towel from the linen closet and found the smallest T-shirt and tracksuit pants he owned and showed her into the master bathroom. *His bathroom.*

He didn't dwell on the fact that there were five guest bedrooms with en-suite bathrooms fully stocked and ready for use. One for all the other members of Taipan. Nate thought of Jake and rubbed at a pain in his chest. Only five original members were left.

He led Pia over to the massive shower. "Take your time," Nate said softly. "Clean all that gunk off you, warm yourself up."

He turned the water on and made sure she had everything she could possibly need before closing the door. He had to force himself to leave. The image of her soaked and shivering, eyes wide and haunted, triggered something deep and powerful inside him. He wanted to undress her, wash her hair, her body. And not in a sexual way. He wanted to take care of her.

But it wasn't his place to do so. Yet. He didn't want to scare her, or worse, make her push him away.

He showered in the closest guest bathroom, dressed comfortably in black sleep pants and a T-shirt, then moved to the kitchen, speaking the voice command that started the coffee machine. Or should he make her a cup of tea? Wine? Whiskey? What would she want? He wanted to know everything about her. To automatically know what she would prefer. In the end, he made all four.

Although getting her here had been a personal challenge he'd been determined to conquer, now that she was in his home, he felt out of his depth. This was an important step, and he didn't want to fuck it up by saying or doing something that would send her running.

He wanted to get to know her. *Learn her.* He'd never wanted that with a woman before. And he had no idea how to do it. Just like he had no idea how to protect her from what wanted to harm her.

Truth was, Pia Williams had sent his world into turmoil, and he was struggling to find his footing.

Nate lit a few candles, sat at the kitchen table, texted with Sam, Sean, and Daniel. Updated Blade.

And waited.

He was doing all he could to distract himself with the official side of this, documenting what happened at the cottage for his team, but really he was doing whatever he could to not picture where Pia was. Or that she was naked. Naked and wet. In his bathroom. Okay, now his thoughts *had* turned sexual. Who could blame him? He was a man, not a saint.

Nate drained his whiskey. When Pia finally appeared, he did a double take. His shirt swam on her, hanging halfway down her thighs. Her bare thighs.

"Sorry," she said. "The pants were too big; they kept falling down."

Nate swallowed. She was carrying her stinking clothes, rolled into a ball. "Let me wash those." He shoved them in his fully automatic washer/dryer.

"Care for a glass of red?" he asked when he returned. "Or perhaps a tea or coffee? Or whiskey?"

"I'll take the wine, thank you."

After pouring them both glasses, Nate joined her at the table and inspected her in the candlelight. She looked much better; the haunted look had left her eyes, and she'd stopped shivering.

"Are you okay?" he asked.

"Yes. Now that I don't reek of Archeri."

The candlelight flickered on her damp red hair, picking up vivid strands of burgundy. Her lips, usually painted the color of blood, were a soft pink, and her skin was pale, almost translucent. He had to restrain himself from running his fingers through the long silky tresses. Would they be heavy now, lush with moisture?

"I've got to find out who Sarah is," Pia said, reiterating the thing that seemed to be top of her mind. As far as he could tell, she was oblivious to his inner feelings toward her, which was curious, considering her natural ability to know otherwise.

Nate released a breath. As much as he believed Sarah was nothing but an evil, malevolent spirit, Pia's belief otherwise meant it was a lead he would follow until it was exhausted. "Zach's on it. If she existed, he'll find her."

Pia tapped a long black nail on his rustic timber table. "I'm just so frustrated. I can normally get a handle on what's going on, but this… the pieces I'm seeing just don't seem to fit together. It's like I'm watching two movies at the same time and not understanding the plot of either."

She rubbed the back of her neck, her brows pinching together in concentration. He remained silent, not trusting himself to say the right thing.

"I see images of the girl I believe to be Sarah," Pia continued after a moment. "She's in an underground room. A cellar perhaps. But what's strange is that there's no cellar in the cottage. So why am I being shown something that seems to tie together but doesn't relate to that place? What is Sarah's connection to the house or any of this?" Pia looked up, meeting his eyes. "Who was Sarah, and why did she reach out to me?"

Pia was so certain that Sarah was real, he had no choice but to run with the theory for now. "So you believe that Sarah intentionally killed Tom Kelly, and he had ties to that house. Perhaps the connection is the house? Perhaps it's something in the house that's killing people, and this Sarah is just a demonic ruse to get you in there?"

Pia wrinkled her brow, considering. "Of course, that's possible, and after what happened tonight I can see how you would think that. But I stand by my instinct that Sarah was real. She was alive once and horribly abused. I think she can't rest until her story is told, and the abusers held accountable. There is also a connection with the doll. Otherwise what happened with Cassandra at the playground doesn't make sense. Cassy has also seen Sarah, and she said Sarah led her to that doll in a cellar. If the cellar isn't in the house, it has to be close by. I can't imagine Monique letting her nine-year-old daughter wander off just anywhere."

Nate fired off a message to Zach, and moments' later the plans to the lighthouse keeper's cottage and the other nearby homes filled the screen. "There isn't a cellar marked as being at the cottage or at any of the properties nearby, according to the building plans. No permits were requested at any time."

"I didn't sense a cellar beneath the house either, and I didn't see a door. That was one of the reasons I wanted to go in tonight. Just to try to get something… be led to something… anything to help me understand how this all fits together. But I've damaged the connection by telling Sarah I won't help, and now she's blocking me. The Archeri at the house was a message for me to keep away. But I have to keep trying. I can't help Cassandra if I can't reconnect with Sarah." Pia's eyes were bright with emotion.

There was no use trying to change her mind. Pia was determined to help both girls, Sarah and Cassandra, and would see this through to the end. He didn't like it, but he had to admire her for it. It was time to show her what else Zach had dug up.

"This just came through. Zach first ran a missing persons search for anyone named Sarah for Western Australia, and then the whole of Australia. Sadly, quite a few names come up." Nate called the information up on his laptop, since the screen was bigger, and shifted it so that Pia could see. "He hasn't refined the search by any further criteria. Do any of these girls match your vision of Sarah?"

He watched her scroll through the pictures. As she moved from one to another, her eyes misted, and the hand not on the keyboard fisted at her chest. She struggled to swallow as though she had something stuck in her throat. Was she was picking up impressions from these girls?

He didn't ask, and she didn't offer.

Eventually, she pushed the laptop away, took the remainder of her wine in one swallow, and composed herself. "None of them is our Sarah." Pia shook her head, and Nate refilled her wine glass. When had she started thinking of the entity as "our Sarah?"

"You sound so sad when you speak of her," he said, keeping his tone even. "She terrifies me."

Pia bit her lip and twisted the pendant she wore around her neck. "I feel sorry for her."

"This Sarah entity was responsible for what happened to you tonight." Nate's voice cracked slightly. "I really think she meant to kill you. Like she did Tom Kelly." Nate's hands once again clenched into fists. What would have happened if Pia had gone in alone? If he hadn't been there to force their way out?

Pia's hand trembled slightly as she took a sip of wine. "The Archeri was a warning." The chink of the glass as it returned to the table was jarring in the otherwise silent room. "A warning I didn't heed. After thinking about it, I don't think her intention was—or is—to kill me. Not like she did Tom, anyway. If that were her intention, she could have killed me many times over tonight."

A low growl forced its way past his lips, and he clutched the edge of the table with white-knuckled intensity.

"She just wants me to back off," Pia said, nodding as though to convince herself as much as him. "And her display of power tonight was showing me that she'll go to any length to ensure I do."

Nate released the breath he'd been holding. "Which of course you will now, right?"

Pia looked up and frowned, shaking her head. "How could I possibly do that? What would happen to Cassandra? Plus," Pia tapped the glass with her nail thoughtfully. "I can't help but feel sorry for Sarah. She's a tortured soul crying out for help. Who will help her if I don't? At the moment, I am the *only* one who can help; therefore, it's my duty to do so."

He cursed under his breath, and he stretched his neck to relieve some of his tension. Failed. "Babe, she killed a man." He placed his hand on Pia's arm. How did he get through to her? How did he make her understand the danger? "This Sarah entity is a murderer. No different than any of the scores of murderers locked behind bars." Except this one was devoid of flesh and blood. "Each of them believes they killed for a reason too, but nothing makes that right. Or excusable."

Pia blinked and swallowed hard, and his heart twisted. "I understand all too well the compulsion to help the victim," he said, keeping his voice soft. "But honey, the victim in this case has turned murderer. A killer who threatened you directly, and from what you've said, fully intends on killing again." Nate's throat was tight. "And I won't stand by and let you be the next victim."

Pia shifted in her seat, but said nothing.

"Sunday night at the beach house, Mark questioned whether we were dealing with a demon," Nate said. "And considering we haven't been able to find a missing person matching her description, isn't it sensible to consider the very real possibility that we're dealing with something far more sinister than a girl?"

"Not in this instance. Spirits aren't supposed to remain on earth. And if they're trapped here, there's a reason. Sometimes, when people die suddenly, they have a hard time coming to grips with the reality that they're dead. And some have unfinished business that makes it impossible for them to move on until they've resolved it. There's a lot of anger in the entity, yes. An incredible amount. But it's not evil. It's about revenge. It stems from pain and intense sorrow. Anger caused from suffering. *Human* emotions."

She leaned forward. "Something happened to her, Nate. Something heinous and cruel. If I can work out who she is, I can work out what happened to her and how it ties in with the house."

Nate bit back a rush of frustration. Despite all the information he had access to, there was such a limited amount he could do to help.

"She was a good girl once." Pia rubbed her eyes. "I stand by that impression. Someone ruined her, someone stole her innocence and robbed her of her sweetness. She wasn't born evil. She was just a little girl, and someone snuffed out her life long before she died."

Nate released a breath. "I messaged Blade to update him on the situation. I'll see what additional resources he can provide. So far, we haven't been able to find anything at all on Tom Kelly or anyone involved that would hint at anything untoward with a girl."

Pia rubbed her temples, and he took her hand, waiting until he'd captured her gaze. "There's nothing more we can do tonight. Can we let it go until tomorrow? Until we get some information that might help fill some of these gaps? It's important for you to switch off, give your mind a rest."

Pia gave him a weak smile. Her eyes were heavy; she looked exhausted. "You're right. There's nothing more we can do tonight." She released his hand and took a large sip of her wine.

He ran a finger down her cheek, enjoying the way it made her shiver. He tucked a strand of hair behind her ear, resisted the impulse to lean in and kiss her.

"I like your nails," he said, watching her run a finger around the rim of the glass. Her hands were so soft, so delicate. Black polish, matching the black lace of the bra strap he occasionally glimpsed… He cleared his throat.

"They're not real," Pia said.

Nate blinked, momentarily confused.

"They're acrylic. I bite my nails. It's one of the many bad habits I have. I get acrylic nails so they're too hard for me to bite."

Nate stared at her a moment. Why did she find the need to point that out? Was she trying to turn him off?

Not possible.

"What are your other bad habits?" Nate deadpanned.

"I…" She frowned. "Why would you want to know?"

"So you can gross me out some more."

She smiled. "Well… I eat jam and cheese. Together, on a sandwich. Vegemite and cheese as well."

Nate scrunched up his face, although he'd tried those combinations too, and they were surprisingly good. "That *is* gross. What else?"

She'd raised her hand again, tracing little circles with her long, black, *acrylic* nails on the wine glass. Like he cared what they were. He just wanted to feel them scratching his back in the throes of passion.

"I eat chocolate in bed."

"That doesn't sound too bad." Especially if it was melted chocolate, and he was licking it off her delicious skin.

"But it is," she continued, warming to her theme. "When I read books late at night. Bits of chocolate flake off and leave nasty brown splotches on the sheets."

"I can see how that would be gross." He kept his expression serious. "What else?"

"Hmmm… sometimes I don't shower for a whole week."

"Really?" *That* surprised him. "A whole week?"

"No." Pia laughed. "What do you care what I do anyway?"

"Why do you care so much about trying to turn me off?"

A shadow crossed her face. "To save you a whole lot of trouble. And time." She looked at her nails. "And save us both a lot of pain."

He took a shallow breath, his chest too tight to take a full one. He wanted to take away her past pain, hurt whoever had caused her to feel that way.

How did he translate into words the intensity of the emotions warring inside him? He'd kissed her, but now he wanted so much more.

He was past merely wanting her. He physically *ached*. The fire burning inside him was bone deep.

But she didn't trust him to be different from the others. Not yet.

When the time was right, she'd surrender to him. On his terms. And the waiting would make the satisfaction all the sweeter.

He eyed her over the rim of his glass as he took a sip of wine. When he finally had her naked beneath him, emotionally and physically, her acquiescence would be absolute.

She drained her glass and yawned. It was very late, and he knew she'd slept little these last few days.

"Ready for bed?" he asked, and her eyes widened. He grinned, enjoying the pink flush spreading across her cheeks. Good. She wasn't unaffected by him after all.

Fending off her objections, he showed her into his bedroom, and forced himself to close the door behind him as he left. He took the guest room, enjoying the knowledge she was in his bed, her damp red hair spread across his pillow.

In the spare room, he stared at the ceiling. He'd be lucky if he got a minute of sleep. He couldn't help but think of the woman in the next room who had so captivated him. He hoped Zach would come through and discover who Sarah was. Pia had asked Nate for help, and he wanted to be the one to help her. He would move mountains to find what she needed.

Yes, damn it, I want to be her fucking hero.

And he still had to remove her as the primary suspect in the murder of Tom Kelly. He hadn't told Pia, but Monique Reynolds had filed a restraining order against her over the incident at the park. Johnson intended to serve the papers on Pia himself. Johnson had some more questions he planned on asking her at the same time. Questions he hoped would trip her into giving him what he needed for an arrest.

Nate's stomach clenched. He fought a powerful instinct to take her far away until the dust settled. Of course, Pia was determined to stay.

The trouble was, Nate's influence with the police only went so far. In the meantime, he'd do everything he could to answer the question that seemed key to solving the whole puzzle.

Who was Sarah?

Chapter Fourteen

Sarah
20 April 1981

Today is my eleventh birthday. Finally! I thought I'd be ten and three quarters forever.

Mummy is on a white sunlounge on the deck of our new yacht. Sorry. I mean Mum. *Big girls like me don't say Mummy anymore.*

Mum *is on the sunlounge wearing a two-piece bikini, her long blonde hair spilling over the edge. I eye her breasts enviously. Mine feel like they will never come. When I grow up, will my waist be as thin as hers? Will my hips catch men's eyes like hers?*

Daddy is sitting by her side. He's never far away.

He sees me standing there. "Here's my birthday girl." His smile warms me. The look he gives me is different than the one he gives Mum, but it's special all the same. And it's all mine.

He glances at the sky. Gray clouds have begun to form over the endless blue. "Princess, if you want to take that swim you've been talking about, you'd better make it quick. The seas are about to get a little choppy. There's a storm coming, and we'll need to start moving soon."

I glance at the water. The waves are forming frothy whitecaps in the distance.

"I'm going to go downstairs and write in my new diary instead," I tell him. I got it today. For my birthday. It's the most beautiful diary in the whole wide world. It has a purple and lace fabric cover and a fancy gold lock, and only I have the key.

In my room, I am drawn to my other special present. It's a keepsake, "an heirloom to be handed down to your own daughter one day," Daddy had said.

It's a doll, handcrafted in my likeness. The artist worked from a series of pictures, but right at the end, I had to sit still, like a real model for a portrait, while he made the finishing touches.

Mum has a designer doll that was created for her when she was the exact same age I am right now, and when we get home, I can put them side by side and see how similar we were.

But it's not a toy, Mum had warned. It's special. A family tradition where the growing collection will be handed down from generation to generation. Apparently, my great, great, great granddaughter will treasure it. I giggled at all the greats when Mum was telling me, and she frowned, warning me that she was serious, that I was a big girl now and old enough to appreciate something so valuable.

I smooth the blanket around my new doll on my bed, and spread out her hair on the pillow. My hair. Saved from an earlier haircut. Daddy said every detail had to be exact.

Daddy said there was not a human being alive who could recreate an angel, but I disagree. With her white gown and her long blonde hair, she looks like a princess.

I think she will be the sister I never had, and I will call her Angel, after Daddy's comment.

My best friend Debbie says we're rich, and I think she might be right. My friends don't have dolls made to look like them.

My new bathers are on the bed. They're blue with yellow trim. I'm too big for pink bathers now. I put them on, and eye myself in the mirror. I suck in my tummy and try to give myself curves like Mum has.

Now that I'm in my bathers, I might as well go swimming. I look at Angel on my bed. She wants to come too. I tell her she can't. She's not a toy, she's special, and I'll be in big trouble if she gets wet.

I hesitate at the door. Surely, if I look after her, it will be okay. If Angel is going to be my sister, a real sister would want to come too.

I carefully tuck Angel under my arm and head up to the deck.

Mum and Dad are on the other side of the yacht, but I can't swim there because I have Angel with me. I don't want to be in trouble on my birthday.

I place Angel on the steps of the landing so that she can watch, and I quietly slip into the water, careful not to splash her.

The water is warm, and I stare up at the clouds, making pictures out of them like I do with Daddy. There's a whale. There's a kitten chasing a ball of wool; you can see its little paw. The clouds are moving fast today, turning from white to dark gray. The approaching storm Dad was talking about.

The sound of an engine startles me. I look around to find the yacht off in the distance. I must have drifted in the current. My heart races in my chest, and I shout out to Mummy and Daddy. I swim as hard as I can, but the waves are pushing me back.

No!

I scream in panic and swallow a mouthful of salty water as I sink beneath the waves, splashing and coughing when I rise back to the surface.

"Mummy! Daddy! Wait for me!"

Frantically, I swim toward the yacht, not giving up even as my muscles begin to burn. I keep going, as though it's actually possible I could catch up with a moving yacht. My arms ache, but I don't stop. I have to keep going, or I'll die out here.

I see something white on the surface of the water.

A shark? Please *don't let it be a shark!*

My vision is blurry and my throat is tight. The yacht is getting farther and farther away.

After a while, I can no longer see it. I look around and see nothing but blue. Endless, frightening, waves of blue. With nothing to even tell me which direction I'm facing. I don't even know which way to swim.

My whole body is trembling. I don't know what to do.

Please God, I don't know what to do…

I glimpse the flash of white again, but this time I'm close enough to see what it is.

Angel!

She must have fallen off the step when the yacht left.

I swim to my doll. My Angel. I don't even care that she's wet. My tears rain all over Angel as I hug her as tightly as I can.

There has to be something I can do. It's so quiet, so terribly silent. Just the occasional rumble of distant thunder. I'm thirsty, and my throat is raw.

Twice, I think I hear a boat motor, but it's only my imagination.

There's just the two of us now, Angel and me, alone and lost.

The water is no longer warm, and I begin to shake. I hug Angel and tell her it will be all right. It has to be all right.

It will be all right, won't it?

Then, I definitely hear the sound of a motor in the distance.

They're coming back!

I knew they wouldn't leave me here. They love me. Mummy and Daddy have realized I'm not on the boat, and they're coming back to get me. I'm laughing, and sobbing, and shivering so hard my teeth are clacking together.

But the motor sounds different, and the boat that comes into view is not my daddy's yacht. But it's a boat just the same. I'm saved. They will take me to me to shore, and my parents will come and get me…

I don't want to remember what happens next. I want it to be my eleventh birthday forever.

I wish I'd never changed my mind about that swim. I wish I'd stayed in my room, where it was safe. I wish I'd stayed ignorant of all the bad things that can happen to little girls.

I never saw any of my pretty things again after that day.

Was never kissed by Mummy or hugged by Daddy ever again.

I wish I'd never learned that there were much worse things than dying alone out at sea.

Looking back, I wish the ocean had swallowed me up that day. But it hadn't.

And by the time the sun set on my eleventh birthday, my world was a totally different place.

Chapter Fifteen

Pia was pleasantly surprised and pleased to see Sam Wells, Daniel Smith, and Daniel's canine buddy Max in Nate's kitchen when she entered the next morning.

Her eyes sought out and found Nate's. He was just standing in the kitchen, making coffee, and her mouth was suddenly as dry as the Outback. She enjoyed this other side of Nate; his domestic self was softer than Nate the detective. They stood there awkwardly, and for a brief moment, she felt as though it would be natural to cross the room to his arms and kiss him good morning.

Instead, she turned to Max, Daniel's German Shepherd, who was wagging his tail excitedly. After receiving permission from his owner, Max bounded up to her. She lowered herself to her knees and buried her fingers in his sleek caramel and black coat.

"He's still wearing his police ID," Pia said, noticing the tag dangling from his leather collar that stated his name and rank.

"He earned it," Daniel said, coming over. The men of Taipan would lay down their lives for one another, and Max had proved himself their equal. He'd saved Sage's life months ago, at nearly the cost of his own.

"He was allowed to go with you?" Pia hoped Max was with Daniel and not on active duty still.

"He's mine," Daniel said, and his tone made clear that a separation would have been non-negotiable. The bond between them, the loyalty, went both ways.

Pia stood and offered her hand, but Daniel surprised her by bringing her in with a crushing hug. He pulled back. "Great to see you, Pia." A genuine smile lit up his face. Pia hadn't gotten the opportunity to know him well last September, but with his warm smile and clear affection for Max, she looked forward to getting the chance.

Daniel was tall like Nate, but had cropped brown hair and closely trimmed facial hair. He was handsome, but not as strikingly so as Nate or Ethan.

Sam greeted her next, also embracing her in a tight bear-hug. Slim and athletic, Sam was the youngest of the team. He wore his blond hair short at the back and fashionably long at the front.

"Have a seat." Nate invited Pia to join the team at the table. "I'll make breakfast."

"Do you need a hand?" She didn't want to be waited on.

"Sit down," Daniel said, answering for Nate. "It's Ryder's turn to cook. Have you seen this morning's news?"

"Not yet." Pia took a seat at the table.

Nate placed a hot coffee in front of her, and their fingers brushed briefly as he did, sending a jolt of electricity through her.

Daniel keyed something into his laptop and swung the screen around.

There was a picture of the lighthouse keeper's cottage, covered in Archeri.

"The Devil's House," the headline read.

Locals baffled by mysterious decaying plants covering old lighthouse keeper's cottage. Who put them there, and why?

According to local legend, the Cape Leeuwin Lighthouse keeper's cottage is said to be haunted by the ghost of Simon Farrell, who died in July 1986. The details of his death remain murky to this day. Two days after his mysterious death, his cray-fishing companion, Des Wilson, died in the same house, also under suspicious circumstances. Farrell's and Wilson's deaths were ruled accidents. Strange coincidence, or something far more sinister? You decide.

Farrell's wife, Meg, disappeared at the time of Wilson's death and has never been seen again.

Was this a love triangle that went tragically wrong?

The house has seen many different owners over the last thirty years. The latest owners, Chad and Monique Reynolds, bought the house in 2014, publicly scoffing at the idea of ghosts. However, it turns out the house was too much for even them, because on March 26 this year, they turned to the paranormal investigators of the popular TV series, Debunking Reality, *to investigate.*

Tom Kelly, a close friend of Simon and Meg Farrell, accompanied the paranormal investigators on their investigation, apparently to provide details of the house's history and the mystery surrounding the death of his close friends Farrell and Wilson. Sources say the paranormal investigation team are known for bringing "triggers" to their investigations, hoping to spark more activity for their show.

Seems this trigger may have turned out to be more than they bargained for. In the early hours of Sunday March 27, Kelly was found dead, yet another death occurring under suspicious circumstances. Did the paranormal investigation team stage a recreation of the deaths, only to have it go horribly wrong? Or are the team turning as evil as the entities they're famous for hunting?

Sources reveal the Debunking Reality *team was brought in for questioning, but formal charges have not yet been laid.*

The Debunking Reality *team have so far declined to comment, but someone close to the crew may have answers.*

"Pia Williams is a fraud," Adam Trey said from his wheelchair in an interview yesterday afternoon. Trey dated the team's alleged psychic medium, Pia Williams, for several months a little over a year ago.

During the time he was with Williams, Trey claims never to have seen her do anything that wasn't conjecture and guesswork. In fact, Trey insists, if Williams were really a psychic as she claims, wouldn't she have foreseen the car accident that Trey was in, a serious crash that caused the loss of his legs?

We agree that it is a very good question. Surely, a genuine psychic would have seen such a major and tragic event? And what about the death of Kelly? Why didn't Williams see that coming either?

And what, if anything, do the Debunking Reality *team have to do with the strange plants left rotting on the exterior walls and front yard? Theatrics? Will we find the answer in an upcoming show?*

Is anything about this team genuine? Or are the team smoke and mirrors, their evidence staged, as the last investigation seems to suggest?

The questions continue to mount about this paranormal-investigations team and what their true motives are. Perhaps the real evil are not the ghosts they hunt, but the team themselves, and we will be the ones who expose them.

Pia turned the laptop back to Daniel. Her mouth had dried again—and not for a good reason this time—and she took a sip of her coffee.

Adam Trey. The reason she'd sworn off men. A mistake that wouldn't stay in her past. She'd accidentally let down her guard around him and discovered something that had shocked her. When she'd confronted him, she'd learned there was a very ugly side to the man. To keep Pia from exposing his criminal activities, Adam now spent his days trashing her to anyone who'd listen.

"The house *is* haunted, but not by Simon Farrell, or even Des Wilson, as the article suggests," Nate said, turning over some spitting bacon. Pia met his gaze. No doubt he was curious as to who Adam was, why he'd said those things about her.

"I emailed you all a copy of Zach's report." Nate cracked some eggs into the pan. "Simon Farrell ran his family's cray-fishing operation out of the local area. Farrell married a local lass named Meg, and they lived there for thirteen years."

"Did they have kids?" Pia asked.

"No. And there was no one called Sarah in their extended family, or any record of Meg ever being pregnant or ever being seen with a child. The first thing I wondered was if they had a baby in secret, but there's no evidence of that being the case. Zach found some medical reports that indicate she had been trying to fall pregnant and the difficulty conceiving caused Meg a great deal of distress. Simon Farrell, her husband, died on the evening of 28 July 1986. They determined that Simon was carrying his cray-fishing knife down the stairs when he tripped and fell, the knife spearing him straight through the heart."

"And the knife had a wooden handle carved into the shape of an eagle," Pia said.

Nate nodded. "Apparently the same knife that killed Tom Kelly."

"How did the knife get back into the house?" Sam asked. "Hadn't the house been through several different owners over the years? How is it that the exact same knife just so happened to be in the house again now, and also happened to be the weapon involved in yet another death?"

"That's a good question," Nate said. "Any thoughts on that, Pia?"

Pia shook her head. "All I know is that the knife materialized on the hallway table moments before it flew in a direct line toward Tom."

"And by materialized, you mean not there one moment, and there the next?" Sam asked.

"Yes." Pia could add nothing further.

"Two days after the death of Simon Farrell, on July 30, Des Wilson died," Nate continued. "Wilson was part of Farrell's fishing crew. They'd worked together for thirteen years, were close mates."

"According to Zach, the papers said Wilson's death was the result of a robbery. That a burglar, believing Meg either alone or not there after her husband's death, broke in, stumbled upon Wilson, and in the fight, Wilson lost his life."

Nate turned off the stove. "That's what they thought initially. When the police arrived on scene, the place was a mess, items had been tossed all over the house, drawers emptied on the floor. They could hardly interview Meg; she was so terrified, she couldn't speak. The police file said her ramblings were those of a woman too distraught with grief to make sense. They ordered a psychiatric evaluation that she never attended. She disappeared that day, hasn't been seen since."

"But they didn't really search for her, not believing she was a suspect, right?" Daniel asked.

"That's right. They'd ruled her out as a suspect at the time."

"I have a copy of Zach's report on my laptop," Nate said to Pia. "Feel free to read it."

"That's okay. I don't believe Meg killed Wilson or her husband. How many were in Farrell's cray-fishing crew?"

"Three regulars, several casual."

"Simon Farrell, Des Wilson, and Tom Kelly," Pia said. "All dead. When Sarah visited me, she said there were more bad people. That she hadn't finished." Was one or more of the casual members of the crew also involved?

"You had a visit from Sarah's ghost?" Daniel looked up. Surprised, but not disbelieving, Pia noted. Last September had opened the team's eyes in a way nothing else could.

A chill trickled down her spine as she remembered that night. "I woke to find her at the end of my bed. She asked me to help her. I said no, and she got angry."

"She asked you to help her murder someone?"

"Not in so many words, but that was the impression I got, and that's why I said no."

"Who is this Sarah?" Sam asked.

"That's what we need to find out," Nate said. "Pia has reviewed the complete missing list of girls named Sarah throughout the whole of Australia ever since the early 1960s and doesn't recognize any of them."

Nate placed a large plate of bacon, eggs, tomatoes, and toast on the table, and Daniel and Sam immediately dug in.

"I've instigated a worldwide search." Nate took a seat next to Pia. "Zach's started work on it already. It'll take a while."

"The doll is in Sarah's image," Pia said. "I think. Or if not exactly the same, then similar to."

"Where's this doll?" Daniel asked.

"The Reynolds' daughter Cassandra has it. But Mrs. Reynolds doesn't want Pia coming into contact with Cassandra," Nate explained.

"I could try to sketch, but I can't draw to save my life," Pia said.

"Let's see what Zach can turn up. He's been known to come up with more from less."

"Are you working any other angles?" Daniel asked between mouthfuls.

"I've spoken to Mark this morning," Pia said. "We plan on going back into the house tonight."

Nate tensed by her side. He'd been adamant last night that she never go back in the house.

Sam looked up from his plate, surprised. "Ryder told us what happened last night, how you were attacked to the point of not being able to even stand and he had to carry you out of the house. Do you think it's a good idea to try to go back in? Overlooking the detail of course that it will be breaking and entering a sealed crime scene and risking pissing off a detective who already has it in for you."

"I agree," Pia said. "Best we overlook that."

Nate made a low noise beside her but otherwise remained silent. She took this as a sign to proceed.

"I angered the entity," Pia said. "When the spirit I'm calling Sarah asked me to help her, I told her I wouldn't." Pia could still feel the intensity of the anger that had poured off the apparition. Whatever Sarah was, whoever she had been in living form, she was now one volatile and powerful entity.

"What did she want you to help her do?" Sam asked. "Did she want you to help her kill the others that had hurt her?"

Pia looked down at her nails. *They all must die.* The entity—Sarah—had said. *They.* "Are there more?" Pia had asked. *Yes,* was her chilling reply.

"I can't be absolutely certain…"

"But that is how you interpreted it," Daniel pressed, reminding her she was at a table of former detectives.

"Yes."

"And you refused," Daniel said. "And now this thing is angry. Tried to hurt you last night when you went into the house. It wants to warn you away. So what I want to understand is why you think tonight will be different."

Pia felt like a bug under a microscope. She sucked in a breath, straightened her spine. "I want to apologize to her, tell her I'll help her."

Nate's fork clattered onto his plate. He picked it up and said slowly, "But you're *not* going to help her, right? Tell me you are not contemplating helping this—ghost or entity—kill someone."

Her face grew hot. He actually had to ask that question? "Do you really think I could kill someone?" Pia asked, facing him.

"No," Nate answered quickly, "of course not. But what exactly would you be agreeing to do?"

"I don't know. But I have to at least find out. For Cassandra's sake, if not Sarah's." Pia had told Nate she couldn't possibly hurt anyone. But was that really true? Sarah had shown her horrific visions of what had been done to her. What kind of monster could inflict that type of abuse on a little girl?

Could she assist in bringing a monster like that to justice, even the kind of justice Sarah was demanding?

Abso-bloody-lutely. Especially if there was a chance the perpetrator could get off scot-free.

But first, Pia needed to be certain her facts were correct. She didn't know for sure exactly what she was seeing. She needed more information, and for that, she needed Sarah. And to reach Sarah, she needed to make Sarah think she'd help so she would stop pushing her away.

"I want Sarah to come to me, not go to Cassandra. Sarah is powerful. Persuasive. I worry about her influence over Cassandra. If Cassy's not strong enough, and the entity gets too close, it can lead to oppression and even possession." Pia's chest tightened painfully, and she rubbed at her sternum. She couldn't let that happen. She'd seen possession before with Mark last September, and it was a horrifying experience. Dealing with spirits always carried a high level of risk. There were no rules. "Somehow, I need to talk to Monique. She needs to understand the danger her daughter could be in." Monique didn't even know her daughter was a medium. Pia scrubbed a hand over her face, then looked around the table. "I don't know if I'll succeed, but at least I have to try. Of course, I'm not going to take revenge"—*kill someone*—"on her behalf. But if I can discover who hurt her and bring them to justice, Sarah will be able to rest. To let go and move on."

"Sounds achievable," Daniel said, nodding thoughtfully. "Now tell me why Mark and your team need to be in the house? That increases the risk of being seen or something going wrong. I think the best option would be to bring you, and only you, into the house. Ryder will be with you on the inside, and we'll keep watch on the outside. We move in and out. Unseen," Daniel added with a twitch of his lip in what Pia knew was a lighthearted reference to the paranormal.

"Mark and the guys are just as involved in this as I am. Plus, this is the first time since September that Mark has something this big. This is a great opportunity, and I'm not going to deny him that."

"Right," Daniel said and looked at Sam and Nate, who both nodded. "So we secure the house, and you and the team go in and do what you need to. You get the answers you need, and we'll revisit and revise after that."

The tension drained from her in a rush.

"Thank you."

Pia finished her coffee and smiled at Nate. Thank goodness she didn't have to fight them on this. With or without their blessing, she was going, but she'd much rather have them with her. Their assistance raised the odds she'd leave the house alive.

One way or another, she had to get answers, and she had to gain Sarah's trust.

Or else Sarah would use the only weapon she had: Cassy.

And Pia would never forgive herself.

Chapter Sixteen

Later that morning, Nate and Pia said goodbye to Sam, Daniel, and Max. After they'd made their plan, Pia had visibly relaxed. Nate had actually enjoyed the last hour, watching how well Pia got along with Sam and Daniel. They'd already had immense respect for her after what had happened in Cryton, but that had only deepened now.

A warmth spread through him. It meant a lot that his mates and Pia got along so well. They genuinely liked her; he saw it in the admiring glances they gave her, in the secretive nods of approval they shot in his direction the way guys do.

Nate spoke a command, and the glass doors on the beach side of the house retreated into the walls. Pia smiled over her shoulder at him, then walked outside, her back straight, with a grace that was innate, not practiced. She was wearing a tight black skirt that ended just above her knees, ankle boots, and a fitted blue sleeveless shirt tucked in with a wide belt. She looked sexy as hell.

She stared out across the ocean. Last night's storm had cleared, leaving only a few wispy light-gray clouds and a fresh sea breeze. It had been a strange week, weather-wise. Stormy and unsettled.

"Wow," she said. "You really do have stunning views."

She was stunning. How could he not be captivated by her?

You're a rare woman, Pia.

"No, I'm not," she replied, gripping the railing, and turning her face to the sky in genuine pleasure. "I'm just different."

Nate's gaze didn't waver. "I didn't say that out loud."

Her reaction was the same as if he'd slapped her. Cheeks flaming, she stepped back, hugging her arms protectively around her.

"I'm sorry," she said, not meeting his eyes.

He wished he could burn away his comment. He wasn't at all concerned she'd heard something he hadn't spoken aloud.

But she was.

"I shouldn't be here," Pia said, angling her body away. "I should be staying with Mark." Her walls had gone up, and Nate felt the loss keenly.

"Don't run from me, or shut me down if something like that happens. It doesn't bother me. It shouldn't bother you."

"I can't be here," she said, her jaw set.

"Yes, you can." He poured all his confidence into the words.

Pia looked at him, her eyes glistening, and he glimpsed the vulnerability she hid behind her hard veneer.

"Why do you insist on doing this, Nate? Why don't you let me keep a distance?"

"Because I know who you are, what you can do, and it doesn't scare me."

She turned away, gripping the railing. "It should."

Nate shrugged. "I don't scare easily."

He moved to her side, shoulder to shoulder, and looked over the ocean with her.

"Does pushing me away have anything to do with Adam Trey? The guy in the interview?"

Pia squeezed her eyes shut, as though thoughts of the man pained her.

"Yes." She sighed. "Adam, my childhood. Hell, my whole damn life. Take your pick."

"Can we start with Adam Trey?" For the pain he'd caused her alone, Nate wanted to hunt Trey down and tear him apart. He ruthlessly reined in his emotions, affecting an outward calm.

"Adam and I were—" Pia stopped, swallowed, started again. "After sex one afternoon, I was lying next to Adam and I accidently saw something I hadn't intended to. My mind was open, relaxed. I wasn't thinking much of anything really. Just dozing. But Adam must have been thinking about it, quite strongly. I didn't do it deliberately. I honestly didn't."

"I believe you. Can you tell me what you saw?" *Tell me what that arsehole did to hurt you so badly.*

Pia rubbed her hands up and down her arms as though the afternoon sun wasn't shining on her skin. She bit her lip and stared hard out at sea. For a moment he thought she wouldn't tell him, but then she spoke, her voice flat and emotionless. "Adam was embezzling from his father's catering business. He had invented fake suppliers, and he was making regular payments to them, companies that fed directly into Adam's pocket. I couldn't believe that Adam could do that. To his very own father, no less. And—" Pia swallowed. "And what killed me the most was that I couldn't believe that someone with my abilities couldn't tell what type of person he was right from the start. How did I not know?"

She lifted her head and met Nate's gaze. "That was a pretty low point in my life. Not because breaking up with Adam was any great loss, but it deeply shook my confidence in my ability to judge character. Seems I'm only good at it when I'm not emotionally involved in the situation. I decided I'd focus on what I was good at and give relationships a wide berth."

"So you made a mistake. An error in judgment. So what? Name someone who hasn't? Seems to me you're just human."

Pia blinked at him in surprise, and he shrugged. "You don't have to be perfect. None of us is. Your gift makes you special, but it doesn't make you infallible."

Pia squeezed his hand, then let go. "Thank you, Nate."

"What happened with Trey? I assume you confronted him."

"Hell yes." She let his hand go and wrapped her arms around her middle. "When I confronted him, he denied it. But when I named specific company names, amounts, details, Adam went crazy." A shiver washed over Pia, and Nate gripped the balcony railing tight.

"He was looking at jail time, if it got out. He threatened me, he—" Pia shivered, and Nate didn't need the details to imagine how he'd reacted. "He crossed the line with his behavior," Pia continued, her voice firm and even. "Things went from bad to worse, and Adam left in pure rage. He T-boned a truck at an intersection at high speed, an accident that caused the loss of his legs. He immediately made it his mission to discredit my abilities, claiming I had even admitted to him I was a fraud and was only doing the show for the money. He played the sympathy card, making me out to be the villain in the story. When he got out of hospital, he told everyone that I had left him because he couldn't walk."

Jesus Christ! If he hadn't wanted to before, he was more determined than ever to find Trey and tear him a new one. No wonder Pia had trust issues. Was there one damn person who hadn't let her down? Mark, he supposed. Nate felt a rush of warmth for her best friend.

"Life hasn't been easy for you, I get that. You can't expect to come through what you've experienced unscathed. I don't know what to tell you, except that I'm not Adam Trey."

Pia glanced up at him, but her eyes were sad. "I know that, Nate."

"And I also know that shutting yourself down, not allowing yourself to feel, to *love,* is not the answer."

He pulled her to him, pressed his lips to the top of her head tenderly. They were silent for a long moment. He could almost hear her mind working, weighing the options, balancing the risks, overanalyzing everything that had to do with him. With them.

"I'm not going to freak out if you hear a stray thought."

She scrunched her brows together, clearly not convinced.

"I don't have anything to hide," he added. Well, that was not exactly true, not even close; his past was a sordid cocktail of death and destruction. But those were things he'd done on the job; things he'd done to protect others. Not things he'd done for his own benefit.

Pia pulled away, wrapping her arms around herself again. "*Everyone* has things they want to hide, Nate. The mask people show the world doesn't reflect who they are on the inside. I know that better than anyone."

Nate kept his tone even when he responded. "By now, you must at least know that I'm not a devious, narcissistic, lying fraudster like Adam Trey."

Pia's answering smile helped shift his attention from her arsehole ex back to her. He ran his fingers down her arm, then took her hand. She kept wanting to pull away, and he kept wanting to close the distance. He held her hand firmly in his grip, and she stared down at their connection.

Was she sensing who he was on the inside? Could she tell how he felt about her by just this touch if she willed it?

Nate found himself *wanting* her to know it all. The good, the bad, and the ugly. All of him. He wanted someone to know what he was capable of, *what he'd done*, and love him regardless. If anyone was capable of that level of empathy and understanding, it was Pia.

Sunlight glistened in her eyes and danced on her hair. Her long black *acrylic* nails contrasted against the white mug as she very gently released his hand and drained the last of her coffee.

He took the empty cup, his fingers brushing hers, and put it on the outside table.

"Come, let's walk."

"Where? Why?"

Nate ignored her questions and took her hand and began leading the way to the beach. She resisted.

"We can't do that." She looked mortified at the idea.

"We can, and we will." He kept his eyes steady, his voice even. In command. "Zach is working on the worldwide missing persons search for Sarah as we speak, and it's going to take some time. Mark and your team will be meeting us at the cottage tonight, as will Sam and Daniel. We can't risk going anywhere near the place during daylight; Johnson discovered the damage to the door locks."

And he's currently searching for you to personally serve Monique Reynold's restraining order.

"We've done everything we can for now. We have a few hours before we need to be anywhere." He softened his tone. "A short walk, Pia. You need it. I need it. Just a short walk along the beach. That's all."

"I'm sorry. I don't mean to be so uptight. I'm all wound up inside. It just feels somehow *wrong* to enjoy myself, walking on the beach, when all of this is going on."

Yes, she had a lot on her mind: a murder charge looming over her head, the weight of responsibility of a deceased girl reaching out to her for help, the desire to help Cassandra Reynolds cope with her psychic gifts—and avoid becoming possessed by a powerful spirit.

But Pia was also cautious around him, careful to always keep her guard up, and that was the one thing he could change. Who didn't relax during a nice stroll along the beach?

He opened the balcony gate, and they took the timber stairs down to his private beach. They walked through the soft white sand to the firmer damp sand near the water, leaving two sets of footprints behind.

Nate took a deep breath of fresh, salty air, and even though he was looking ahead, every cell in his body was attuned to her, aware of her slightest move.

The silence stretched comfortably, and rather than risk saying the wrong thing, as he often did with her, he remained silent.

"I don't do it deliberately," Pia said eventually.

He stopped, turned to face her, placed his finger beneath her chin, and raised her face to meet his eyes. "I know."

She held his gaze. "You might think you don't care about that now. But it causes problems. It always does."

She was thinking about Trey again, and he bit back a growl. How could he make her believe it would be different for them? That *he* was different.

"I'm not your past," he said, thrusting a hand through his hair. It pissed him off to be lumped into the same category as that criminal.

She raised her chin. "Then what are you? My future?"

He held eye contact. "Perhaps. Sure, why not? If that's what we decide we want."

She released a breath and looked away. "You don't know what you're saying."

"Don't I?" Nate caught the strands of hair blowing across her face and tucked them behind her ear. He couldn't fight the overwhelming need to touch her. "How about you simply agree not to overthink things and let nature take its course. Stop trying to protect me, and let me be in charge of that."

She closed her eyes. "Maybe I'm protecting myself?" Her voice was a whisper that barely reached his ears.

His heart twisted. If only it were possible to reach into her past and erase her memories of everyone who'd hurt her. Every single person who'd helped put that pain in her eyes.

Nate gently placed a hand on her shoulder and pulled her against his side, as they both looked out across the ocean.

"Relationships with people are hard, particularly romantic ones," Pia said. She leaned into him, and he held her a little tighter. "The closer I get, the more relaxed I become, and I let my guard down. Like what happened with Adam." She tensed every time she mentioned that creep. It only made him more determined to mend that wound.

"You're mostly a closed book to me," Pia said. "That's why, I think, I kept pushing you away when I first met you in Cryton. You were different. I couldn't read you like I could other people. It was refreshing, but frightening as well. I didn't want to make the same mistake I'd made with Adam. What if you were hiding something dark? What if you weren't who you portrayed yourself to be? It scared me, because I was also very attracted to you." She glanced up at him. "It was easier to push you away than work you out." She tilted her head up, and he met her gaze. "Just so you know, I still haven't worked you out."

She sighed and looked back at the water. "I thought you might be the exception, and then earlier on your balcony, I was enjoying the sun sparkling on the waves across the ocean, was so at one with the peace of nature, and your thought came wafting in."

"No harm done."

"Not then. Not that time. Not that thought. But it still happened. And what if it was something else? A different thought? Something you wanted to keep private?"

"I'll take that risk."

"Until it happens. Then trust me. You'll be pissed off. They always are."

They. "Don't put Trey and me in the same sentence again," he growled. "I am nothing like him, and I am not your other men." Fucking hell, he didn't stand a chance if she continued to do that.

Pia's eyes glistened. "And that's what makes it worse."

"How?" he demanded.

"Because I care too much already, damn it." Her eyes were so sad, his heart shattered. She lowered her voice. "The more you care, the more it hurts."

Nate took a moment, absorbing what she'd admitted to.

"I can't change what happened in your past," he said. "Although I'd give almost anything to make that happen. But I do ask that you give me a chance to prove to you that it can be different between us. I *am* different."

Pia began to tremble, and he lifted her chin so that she was looking into his eyes. "*We* are different," he whispered.

Her eyes glistened and he saw her swallow. She averted her gaze, looking back at the ocean, but he continued to hold her close. Although he wanted to know what she was thinking, he knew better than to push. She was a woman who relied on her natural ability to read people's thoughts. If she couldn't read him as easily as she could others, it would take time for him to prove she could trust him. He had no choice other than to give her that time, and show her instead.

Again, the silence stretched.

"Being around me is like going to the toilet with the door open," she blurted.

Nate laughed, and some of the tension was broken. The walls of protection she had constructed around her were beginning to crumble; he just needed to give a few more bricks a nudge.

They continued to walk.

"I suppressed my abilities for many years," Pia said. "Most of my childhood actually, as my parents didn't understand. Didn't want to understand. They looked at me with disappointment in their eyes, sometimes fear, sometimes loathing. They honestly believed something was wrong with me that they didn't know how to fix, and I tried so terribly hard to hide my abilities. Pretend they didn't exist. But I didn't know how. How could I? I didn't know what was wrong with me either. I didn't understand what was happening to me, much less know how to protect myself from the things I could see and hear that others couldn't. The good entities and the bad. It's why I worry so much about Cassandra. She's so young, so open and vulnerable. I remember all too well what it's like to be that age and have no one who understands."

Nate's chest ached. There was so much despair and sadness in her voice.

"Mark described my parents once as emotionally absent," she continued, "and that would be an accurate summation. I tried so hard to be normal, just so they would accept me. I thought that if I was normal, they would finally be able to love me." Pia's voice cracked slightly and she straightened her shoulders and cleared her throat. "But that was a long time ago. And trying to deny these abilities is like..." Pia searched for the words. "It's like trying to hold a large cork under water. You can do it for a while, but the resistance is always there, waiting to come to the surface."

"What changed?" Nate asked, trying hard not to show how pissed off he was with her parents. He'd known she'd had a difficult childhood. But this? What the fuck had they been thinking? Instead of looking at her like there was something wrong, couldn't they have looked at her as though she was special? *Because she is, damn it.* How could they not see that? He wanted to knock their heads together, make them see how much pain and damage their emotional withdrawal had caused their beautiful daughter.

On top of Trey, it was just that much more that Nate had to overcome in order to win Pia over. He made a silent vow that should he ever be so fortunate as to gain her trust, he'd willingly die before ever breaking it.

"What made you finally embrace your abilities? Accept what you're able to do?"

"Mark," Pia said simply, her face easing into a smile. "When we met in university."

"How so?" Nate asked, feeling a pinch of envy at how fondly she spoke of him. *I wonder if Mark appreciates just how lucky he is?*

"I guess my friendship with Mark was inevitable once we met. I could corroborate what he sensed, what he thought he saw. We were good for each other. I gave him the validation he needed to prove to himself what he was sensing was real, and his outgoing personality gave me the confidence I needed to stand tall against the world, to embrace my gift, no matter what anyone else thought. We were two misfits." Pia laughed. "And nothing has changed."

"How does your friendship with Mark work? How does he deal with the psychic part of you?"

Pia's brow wrinkled. "I respect him immensely, and he understands me. I try very hard not to breach his privacy, but if I do see something, he shrugs it off. He's a good person with a good heart. I've known him for long enough to know there's not anything I'm going to see that will shock me."

"You don't think I'm a good person?"

The question was loaded, and she knew it. "Are you afraid of what you'll see, Pia?" he asked gently.

Her face fell, and she looked down at her hands. "I never find out until it's too late."

Again, another reference to Trey. He ground his teeth and nodded. "Are you willing to roll the dice on me?"

She looked up at him, her eyes wide. "You don't know what you're asking."

"I'm sure I do." Nate met her gaze, but a shadow of pain crossed her face and she looked away.

"I want to, Nate. I just don't know how…" Her voice trailed off.

"I get it. Trust has to be earned, and I'm prepared to go the distance to prove to you I'm worthy. So how about, for now, I don't ask anything. How about you just agree to not shut me out. Can we start there?"

Pia gripped the pendant she wore around her neck, twisting it between her fingers.

"You will end up hating me." She spoke so softly, he barely heard her. But the words were like punches to his soul.

He didn't need to be psychic to understand how hard it was for her to make herself vulnerable to another. If her own parents couldn't love and accept her, how was it possible that anyone else could? He felt his own eyes sting, and he blinked rapidly.

"Pia," he said fiercely, gripping her shoulders tight. "I could never, ever, hate you. I have far too much respect for you, for the woman you've turned out to be, for that to ever happen."

"You can't know that." Her voice was small. She looked almost lost. He imagined her as a child, alone, not knowing which way to turn.

He fully understood now how it would be impossible for her to walk away from this case. From Cassandra, who was as lost as Pia was, and from Sarah, who was also alone, with no one to turn to. For those two girls, Pia was being the person she'd never had when she was a child.

He dragged a shaky breath of salty air deep into his lungs, overcome by how much respect he had for the woman in front of him.

"Yes, I can know that. Just like I also know I'm not worthy of you. But I want you to take a chance on me just the same." She said nothing. Perhaps she needed more time to think. "Come on, let's walk through the water." Nate lowered himself to his knees, placed her foot in his lap, and removed her shoe. He did the same with the other foot, cupping his hands over her silky smooth skin before setting her foot gently on the ground.

Her breath hitched, something he noted with satisfaction. Taking her hand, he led her down to the ocean. The water was cool and refreshing as they walked, waves splashing high on their legs.

"Can you help me understand how you do… what you do when you're with Mark and the team?" Nate wanted to know her, really understand her and how her abilities worked. He also wanted to show her—prove to her—that her abilities were a part of her he would embrace fully. He never wanted her to feel uncomfortable about them, or pretend they didn't exist.

Pia gave him a wry smile. "I'm not even sure *I* know what I do, much less how I do it. It just happens. But I do prepare before we begin investigating. While the team get the cameras ready, I try to clear my head, get into a type of receptive state."

Nate nodded as though he understood what that meant. "The best way I can explain it is that everything is made up of energy. It's all around us. It's in our houses, in the electrical appliances we use every day, in our cities, and in the transport we use, but it's also in the earth, the sky, and the air."

A large wave crashed beside them, sending salt spray up their bodies. Pia's laugh as she jumped out of the way tugged at a deep place inside him. She didn't laugh nearly enough. *I intend to change that.*

"Energy is everywhere in nature and in the environment around us," Pia continued. "You can see it easily in the power of the waves or an electrical storm, but it's there on a clear day as well."

Nate took her hand, but kept silent, not wanting to interrupt.

"But it's also in other things. A dog reacts to anger in someone before a single word is spoken or action taken. You can walk into a room and feel the tension in the air of a recent argument before knowing any details. You can often tell someone is upset, happy, or excited before they speak. Emotions radiate in waves. Communication is ninety percent nonverbal. People pick up these waves of energy subconsciously without even realizing it every single day.

"This same energy can be transferred from people to an object or a place, for example, becoming embedded in the walls of a house. That energy is like a vibration to me, like I can hear the notes of a song through the strumming of a guitar."

Pia paused. "I guess you could say I was born with a stronger antenna than normal. But we all have one; we just don't always know why or how to use it. My antenna just so happens to also be able to pick up on entities and the spirits of people who have crossed over, as they are energy too."

Nate squeezed her hand. "In the police force, we're trained to listen to our… we don't call it intuition, we call it gut instinct. It's more often than not the one thing that saves our lives. More reliable than any intel we have available. Perhaps you and I are not as different as you want to believe?"

"It's not that you and I are so different that's the problem. It's that you are so very different from the other men I've met. That's what makes you so dangerous for me."

He grinned at her. "Come on, you love a little danger. Think about what you do for a living."

She didn't return the grin; her eyes were solemn, her lips trembling slightly. She opened her mouth to speak, but looked away before anything came out. "But you're not dangerous to my body; you're dangerous to my *heart*." Her voice cracked on the last word.

That's when Nate finally understood: she feared that pain more than any wound to her flesh. What could he say to prove he'd be different?

Only time would tell.

And Nate was a very patient man when it came to getting what he wanted.

The lazy blue blanket of the Indian Ocean stretched outward to blend with the horizon. The sky was turning angry, the clouds swirling; were they on the ground, they'd have been pacing. Farther out to sea, the waves formed whitecaps high into the darkening sky.

"Looks like there'll be another storm," Pia said.

"We only have an hour or so. But we could both use the walk, the fresh air, to clear our heads."

"Tell me about yourself," she said. "Your family, your childhood, what made you enter the force. I only know what I've… seen." She smiled, a little embarrassed.

There were so many things she should know about him… but none of them were things he wanted to reveal. Not this minute, not while she still had so many doubts. But he'd have to man up soon and take the chance.

"Okay. But you tell me some more about yourself first. I only know what I've seen in reports."

She smiled at his quip. They both had access to information not available to the average person. They were not as different as she kept insisting.

But would she ever believe that was enough to overcome all the odds she thought were stacked against them?

CHAPTER SEVENTEEN

Pia walked with Nate through the sand, talking easily and swapping childhood stories: where they'd gone to school, where they'd holidayed.

Sporadic drops of rain turned into a sudden downpour. Nate grabbed her hand and dashed toward the sand dunes. Laughing, Pia ran with him, struggling to keep pace with his long strides as he bolted through the thick sand.

Nate ducked down, leading her into a limestone alcove that formed a large cave. They sat close, warm and dry, as the rain poured outside. The ocean had turned dark gray, and she could no longer make out the horizon between sea and sky. Salt spray misted off the crashing waves.

As they sat, shoulder to shoulder, Nate's scent filled the small space, causing her chest to tighten and her body to heat. Despite the distraction of her physical attraction to Nate, Pia felt a deep sense of peace and contentment. Opening up to Nate had released a weight she hadn't realized had been holding her down. He'd listened, and he hadn't judged. For the first time, other than Mark, she'd found someone she trusted enough to let inside.

Nate's thigh pressed against hers, and she shivered, not from cold, but he slipped his jacket off and placed it around her shoulders. She inhaled the sensual scent of worn leather and Nate's unique masculinity.

Now that his fitted T-shirt was visible, she was conscious of each and every well-defined muscle. He reminded her of the ocean, wild and untamed, mysterious and deep. Having Nate so close in such a confined space was intoxicating.

If she licked the fresh raindrops off his skin, would they taste salty? Her face heated, her nipples hardening at the thought.

She glanced at him out of the corner of her eye. He was staring at the ocean, the waves crashing on the shore.

"It's beautiful," she said. "Just as beautiful as when the sea is sparkling and the sky is endless blue."

"See, you are a romantic."

She felt the smile fade from her face. "No I'm not." Her stomach clenched. She knew what he wanted, he'd made that clear, but it was the one thing she couldn't give to him. *A normal relationship.* Pia was different. She was not like other women, and she needed to make that clear to Nate from the beginning. It was no good promising something she'd never be able to give.

He cursed softly. "I always manage to say the wrong thing with you."

"No you don't, Nate. You just think we can have something more than what we can."

He turned to her, his eyes intensely gray, matching the stormy skies above them.

"Too late," he said. "I already want more."

"I don't do relationships. I can promise you nothing more than this moment."

"It's not enough." His lips brushed against hers.

His heat washed over her. He was right there, a fraction too close, sending her nerves haywire. His shoulders were wide and square, his muscles rippled, clenching and contracting, when he moved. He effortlessly radiated power and strength. His sheer vigor called to a deep part of her, a hidden side that wanted to stop being so strong. If only for a little while.

"I don't believe you can say no to me—to this—any more than I can say no to you," he whispered.

Nate sealed his lips against hers, making Pia's mind spin. A soft sigh escaped her when he cupped one hand on the back of her neck and deepened the kiss.

The fingers of his other hand traced tantalizingly up and down her back, making her shiver. Her body heated. Already insanely attuned to him when he was across the room, this close, this intimate, Nate set off a series of explosions inside her.

"Did you think about me?" he murmured. "Even once since September?"

"Did you think about me?"

His eyes darkened.

"All the damn time." His voice was rough, his breath a caress across her lips. He touched his mouth to hers, feather-light. A question.

This time, she answered it.

She gripped the back of his neck, tight, opened her mouth, and deepened the kiss. Swallowed a low noise he made in the back of his throat. Nate quickly took charge of the kiss, fought her for control. The power struggle between them sent an electrical current shooting through her body.

She wanted him desperately. *Needed* him desperately. Like she'd been lost in the desert and Nate was a cool, refreshing oasis. She licked his tongue and drank deeply. It was thrilling. Intoxicating.

"Say yes," he said.

"Yes," she repeated breathlessly. She had no idea what she'd agreed to, but at that moment he could have asked her anything and she'd have granted it. He pulled back, eyed her questioningly. It was enough to clear her thoughts slightly. Then she remembered. "Tonight," she said. "I'll promise you tonight. That's all."

His gaze seared her skin as it raked over her.

He had a way about him, as though he saw too much when he looked at her. Far more than anyone should.

He looked beyond the surface, to the reasons behind what she'd said. He asked the questions and needed to know why. Nate had a powerful ability to focus, and right now the full force of that focus was on her.

He left her exposed, naked… excited.

"Tonight." His fingers grazed her knee and electricity raced up her leg. "Tomorrow." He traced circles on her inner thigh, stopping at the hem of her short black skirt, sending shivers across her skin. "And the weekend."

His eyes rested on their point of connection, where his hand moved on her skin. Desire radiated from him, washing over her, searing her. Nate's gaze was blatantly sexual.

"I can't think when you're—"

His lips caressed her ear, and his thick, silky hair tickled her neck. "When I'm what?"

"Th—that."

A soft gasp escaped her lips, an outward sign of her internal chaos. Blood thrummed through her veins, and energy crackled between them like a summer storm.

She pushed him away and tugged down her skirt, struggling to clear her head.

"What is it?" A thread of tenderness in his voice left her yearning painfully for something she could never have.

"I'm not like the other girls you've been with," Pia blurted.

"I know that already. You've told me. You're gross. You eat jam with cheese, chocolate in bed, and don't shower for a week."

Pia laughed, then turned serious. "This…" She waved her hand between them. "Us. Whatever this is can't happen. Not like you're thinking it will. I like you, Nate. A lot. I don't want to ruin that. You asked about Mark. We never did this. Never crossed this line. He and I are best friends. I could have that with you too."

"I don't want to be your damn *friend*, Pia. I want more. I want all of you." He caught her wrist, kissed the tender skin, his lips pressed against her racing pulse. "Did Mark make ever you feel like this?"

"No." Not even close. She'd never looked at Mark as anything more than a friend. A brother.

She blinked hard, her eyes stinging. Damn him for bringing back emotions she'd thought she'd buried forever.

"So you think the answer is to keep your walls up. Build those walls, and keep them strong. Keep everyone at a distance. Is that all you want from life?"

"It's the price I pay for being born this way."

"I don't accept that."

Her breathing sounded loud in her ears. She was aware of every breath he took, the way his mouth was slightly parted, the sight of his tongue, as it briefly touched his lips.

"Oh, fuck it." Pia lunged, throwing her arms around his neck, and pulled him close. His low groan was pure satisfaction.

"If this goes wrong, you have no one to blame but yourself, Nate Ryder," Pia said, straddling him. He let her take the lead, clearly spinning from the swift turn of events.

Sometimes a woman just had to stop thinking and give into her baser desires. And Pia's had been pent up for far too long. She wasn't waiting for tonight. She was taking him here. Right now.

She grabbed the bottom hem of his T-shirt and pulled it off and tossed it aside. Nate's chest was a masterpiece. Perfectly defined and sculpted. There were scars across the skin, evidence of a life fully lived, and they added to his appeal. Nate in real life was even better than in her wildest fantasies.

The waves of the ocean crashed behind her, and the sea breeze blew cool across her naked skin. But she wasn't cold. Not even slightly.

"What's this?" Pia asked, tracing her fingers over a tattoo of a snake on his upper arm. A name in calligraphy ran through the center.

"It's for Jake," Nate said, his voice tight, referring to Jake Brown, who'd died during the incident in Cryton. "The snake is a Taipan, representing our unit name."

Pia traced the winding snake, the ornate writing. It was an impressive piece of artwork, stunning enough to hang on a wall.

"Did your whole unit get them?"

"Yes."

Pia sensed a deep sadness in Nate that was far from healed. The events of last September were still fresh in her mind as well. She'd met Jake; he'd been a good man. He'd sacrificed himself to make sure Ethan was in the right place at the right time to help Sage. Had Jake not done so…

There was no way they would have won against the demon. Jake's actions had saved a lot of lives that night. Sadly at the price of his own.

It was something that no one involved would ever forget, especially the men of his unit. "I've got your back" was not just a phrase they bandied about.

And Nate was trying to make her a similar promise. A deeper one, if that was possible.

His phone buzzed, signaling an incoming text. He pulled his phone from his pocket. "Worst timing ever, but I've got to see what's going on." He swore as he read the message.

"Sam and Daniel are back at my house. They've been to see Mark and the team and have a few questions about the investigation. We'd better head back and begin preparations for tonight." He looked up at her, his expression filled with equal parts longing and regret. He ran a finger down her cheek, his lids heavy, then he fisted his hands in her hair and kissed her hard. When he pulled back, his eyes were glazed, his voice deep and husky. "But just to be clear. I fully intend to finish what we started."

She wanted that too. But beyond that?

As if he could read her mind, he shook his head. "Don't start doubting this."

Maybe he was right; maybe they weren't so different.

Maybe something more than simple friendship with Nate could work after all.

CHAPTER EIGHTEEN

Pia and Nate hid in the bushes outside the lighthouse keeper's cottage as a stiff ocean breeze buffeted their bodies, the *Debunking Reality* team hunkered down just behind them. Though it was dark, they couldn't take any chances on being seen.

Nate was waiting on a signal from Sam and Daniel that the house was clear. A moment later, he sprang into action, escorting Pia and the *Debunking Reality* team swiftly through the shadows to the cottage.

The Archeri, now dead, had left a putrid covering of dried and rotting plants that crunched beneath their feet as they rounded the corner to the rear of the house.

Using that nifty tool again, Nate provided a keyless entry in seconds, and Mark whistled low under his breath. "Nice skill. What is that? A bump key?"

Nate didn't reply, clearly eager to be inside the house and out of sight.

The smell of blood saturated the air. Did it linger from Tom Kelly? Or something else. Pia took a breath that tasted metallic and bitter on her tongue. No, the smell of blood was fresh. As though a large animal had been slaughtered right here and now in the living room. But the house was empty. Quiet.

Deathly still.

Pia took a few steps inside and instantly felt claustrophobic, unable to breathe. Nate shut the door behind them, and Pia fought an urgent impulse to run. *Get out now*, her subconscious was screaming.

She looked at the door, now closed, and swallowed down the rising panic. *Focus. Breathe.* But the memories of last night, the oppressive weight that had fallen over her, came flooding back. She had to try to talk to Sarah, had to get through to her before that near-paralysis struck again.

Nate was making sure all the blinds were down and the windows closed. The sense of confinement increased. She felt more and more unwelcome as the seconds ticked by. As though Sarah's energy was building.

"Have to open a window," Pia choked, hurrying to the kitchen at the rear of the house. She shoved open the sash and dragged in a breath of humid night air, looking out into the starless night. Tried and failed to slow her racing heart.

The quiet before the storm.

A chill raked down Pia's spine. Thick black clouds blanketed the moon, and the wind kicked up, buffeting the house in small gusty bursts.

"We need to keep the windows closed, so our torches aren't visible from outside," Nate said, reaching over to shut the window Pia had just opened.

She grabbed his arm. "No can do. I need air, or I'm going to be sick. This window is facing the ocean, so it's not as likely to be seen." *I'm worried I'll be overcome again. Ruin our chance to get answers.* It wouldn't be so easy to convince Nate to come back a third time.

Pia looked up into his eyes, a stormy gray that matched the night. They'd been flicking here and there, as though taking in the whole house at once, but they stilled when he met her gaze. Despite the shadow of concern that was there, Pia read determination. Clear intent. Nate was no stranger to dangerous situations, and she absorbed the calm confidence that radiated from his inner being.

"The house feels different than when we were here last night," he said.

"It does," Pia agreed, inwardly pleased he used the word "feel," as though he were trying to sense things from her perspective. "All I feel at the moment is lot of residual energy. It's heavy and intense, but not currently… *active*, if that makes sense." *But it could be. In an instant.* She'd seen firsthand Sarah's abrupt mood swings. From heavy sadness to blinding rage in a heartbeat.

She couldn't sense Sarah here at the moment, at least not in a manifest form. Pia hoped she'd be able to change that. She doubted she'd be able to get the clear information she needed from impressions left in the house, no matter how intense the emotional imprint left behind.

"We'd better make this fast." Nate's voice was somber. She understood his impatience. Sam and Daniel were keeping watch visually as well as monitoring the police scanners. Zach was also monitoring incoming reports made by the public.

But still…

Beneath the surface, Nate was supremely on edge, picking up the unsettled energy that had started to prickle in the air. Sarah was somewhere around. Keeping her distance. Watching.

Mark, Joe, and Ryan were aware of the change in energy too. They'd dropped the jovial banter they normally engaged in while setting up for an investigation, instead focusing on moving fast and efficiently.

Their time here was limited, the pressure keenly felt by all.

Nate, noticing Mark struggling with untangling some camera cable, moved across the room to help. When they'd finished, Mark indicated he'd check on Joe's progress in the front room.

"What do you want me to do?" Nate asked, turning toward Pia, his face set in severe lines. His hands clenched and unclenched at his sides, and he looked restless, as though out of his comfort zone. And he was. Far from being in control, Nate was waiting to act on the defensive. That had to grate on his nerves.

Pia moved away from the window and crossed the floor to him. He held up his hands in a gesture of surrender. "I'm to stay out of your way and let you do your thing, right?"

Pia wrapped her arms around him, and he stiffened a moment in surprise. Then he squeezed her tightly to him. His fingers brushed back a tendril of hair that had escaped its confines and tucked it behind her ear. She tilted her face upwards, and he touched her lips with his.

Pia felt some of his tension ease, and they pulled apart when they heard Mark's footsteps approaching.

In the distance, a flash of lightning lit up the sky, followed by a low roll of thunder.

"Done," Mark said, referring to the setup of the static night-vision cameras, a task made quicker since they'd repeated what they'd done only a few nights ago. Joe had set up a small monitoring station on a coffee table in the front room, and Ryan turned on his handheld night-vision camera and tested the battery level.

The team had conducted numerous investigations and knew their routine like clockwork.

But tonight was different. They were not establishing the presence of the paranormal. Pia had the single-minded goal of contacting Sarah, summoning her to the house.

And away from Cassandra.

Pia took a few deep breaths, quieted her mind. Became present, aware of her bodily sensations, of a warm breeze through the open kitchen window.

"We're ready when you are," Mark said, Ryan following him with the handheld camera. "Go do your thing, Boo. Ryan and I will do some standard EMF and temperature readings while you establish a connection."

Pia felt the weight of Nate's watchful gaze, but he kept his distance as she headed to Cassandra's room. To where the connection to Sarah had been the strongest.

Pia sat on Cassandra's bed and looked to the doorway, where she'd seen the manifestation of Sarah right before Tom Kelly had died. The first thing she noticed was the absence of the doll. Of course she'd seen it with Cassy on the playground yesterday, but Pia couldn't help noticing the room felt… different somehow without it.

She closed her eyes, took a series of deep breaths that brought her to a centered place within herself. A calm inner peace. Pushing her sense of self aside, she reached out and opened herself up.

Called out to Sarah. Invited her presence, here, in the room. Assured her she was no threat.

Pia tuned in, her psychic impressions very general at first as was often the case. Images deluged her mind as she opened up, became what she likened to a television or radio receiver. She saw the history of the house, different families, filtered through the images like flicking through a packet of photos.

But no Sarah.

Pia fell deeper into a dreamlike state. And then she sensed something. Floating images, vivid and shocking, began to push themselves into her mind as she attempted to tune in to the energy she recognized as Sarah.

A dark room.

Heavy chains were bolted to the wall, curling like serpents on the floor.

And blood, so much blood.

A man's wicked laughter, a child's pained cry.

A woman brought her food once a day. Threw it down the hole like she was a caged animal. *A woman?* Pia pushed down her surprise, fought to maintain her focus.

"Sarah," Pia called out to the room.

On a subconscious level, she was aware of Mark standing outside the room, observing, the red glow of Ryan's camera aimed in her direction. Nate behind them both, but no less focused on her.

Pia let their presence fade away, as she fell, fell, fell. Back in time. Calling out to Sarah.

A door slammed upstairs. Pia didn't so much as flinch.

The temperature in the room plummeted, and she hugged her arms around her stomach. Instinct. Protection.

She sensed a presence standing behind her. *Sarah.*

Fierce anger rolled off the manifestation in sickening waves. Pia turned to face her, and as her eyes met Sarah's black, lifeless ones, she felt a painful jarring to her very soul.

I don't want you here. The apparition spoke directly into Pia's mind. Loud. Forceful.

"Sarah." Pia spoke through a tight constriction in her throat. She raised her hands to her neck, feeling once again the intense pain of being strangled. "Stop that," Pia croaked. "Strangling me is not necessary. There's no advantage to hurting me. Stop it," Pia repeated forcefully.

Pia was aware of Nate tensing, standing in the doorway, holding back, but ready to take action.

You see me. And you don't *see me. Just like her.*

"I see you, Sarah," Pia said, understanding that Sarah was referencing the woman Pia had seen. The woman who had not helped her.

The constriction around Pia's throat grew tighter, and she gagged. Her fingers desperately clawed at the invisible binding, her nails scratching her own tender skin.

You won't help. Just like her.

"Stop!" Pia rasped.

Nate made a low warning noise from the back of his throat. She sensed the amount of self-control it took to hold back his natural instinct to intervene.

An angry gust of foul wind whipped through the room, and objects fell from shelves; the ground shook with the force of an earthquake. The cane chair the doll had been sitting on flew at the wall with such force it splintered to pieces.

The bedroom door slammed shut with the sound of a gunshot. The power, the sheer intensity of the torment, pain, and anguish Sarah had suffered was what she used to cross the veil, to affect this reality.

Pia was aware of Nate, Mark, and Ryan shouting and banging on the door from the other side.

Pia stood up from the bed, her head spinning from a lack of oxygen.

Sarah stood in front of her, waves of menacing energy rolling off her.

Pushing down a tremendous rush of pure terror, Pia faced her opponent.

"Stop," she choked, gagging.

You are just like her.

Pia was thrown back against the wall. The pressure on her neck didn't slacken as she was dragged toward the ceiling.

I see you, Pia said, the constriction around her throat making it physically impossible to speak. She had to get through to Sarah before she passed out.

I can help you, Sarah. I can help you. Stop hurting me. I can help you.

Pia shouted the words in her mind as clearly as she could, and eventually the pressure around her neck and body eased slightly. She sucked in as much air as the force against her lungs would allow.

How? Sarah asked. *How can you help me?*

The apparition floated a few inches off the floor, her blonde hair blowing back from the lifeless, spectral face.

"Show me what you want me to see," Pia rasped. "Tell me what happened to you. I see you, Sarah. I do. I can help."

BANG!

A deafening noise rent the room, and Sarah was gone.

Pia fell to the ground, her knees buckling beneath her.

She was in Nate's arms, the smell of gunpowder heavy in the room, and Pia knew Nate had shot the lock off the door the way he had last night. Mark and Ryan were shouting, but she couldn't hear them over the ringing in her ears.

The lights were blindingly on.

Damn it! She'd lost the connection again, before she'd gotten what she needed. What if she didn't get another chance?

"Pia?" Nate was shaking her, and she realized her eyes kept closing against the harsh light. "Pia!"

"I'm okay," she managed, her throat sandpaper, keeping her irritation in check. Of course Nate would rush to save her. It was just that… she wished he hadn't. Pia swallowed her disappointment.

"I'll get her a drink," Mark said, knowing that water grounded her after a vision. His voice sounded a million miles away even though he was in the same room.

"Pia, honey, what can I do?" Nate's voice was strained. "Tell me what you need."

I need you to trust me to do what I need to do.

His face was creased with concern, and she didn't have the heart to be angry with him. He traced a thumb beneath her left eye, then stroked down across her cheek.

"I'm fine. Can you turn the lights off?" she asked.

"We didn't turn them on. Every damn light in the place went on, and they won't turn off."

She struggled to swallow past the constriction in her throat, her heart still heavily saturated with a grief and helplessness she recognized as Sarah's.

Pia's gaze wandered around the room, through the door, and out into the corridor. "The crucifix on the wall is hanging upside down." Her voice sounded distant to her own ears. Inverted crosses were the hallmark of demonic influence.

Was that why Sarah was an unnaturally powerful spirit? Could she have risen from the dark side?

Nate glanced over his shoulder. "That's the least of our problems." He lifted her, held her tight against his chest. "We have to get you out of here. Daniel said a report was made, the cops are on their way."

"Damn. Put me down, I can walk," she said, not altogether sure that was true. But when her feet hit the floor, she realized that although the muscles burned, her legs as wobbly as though she'd climbed a thousand stairs, she could walk. *Damn it, she* would *walk.*

Mark, Ryan, and Joe tossed their equipment in their bags in record time and dashed in the direction of the front door.

Then, as abruptly as the lights turned on, they were plunged into darkness. A chair crashed loudly to the floor and Pia tripped over it, landing heavily.

Nate pulled her to a standing position.

Don't go! a voice shouted in her mind.

Sarah? Pia stopped, reached out into the darkness. Nate grabbed her shoulders, then pulled her against his body, supporting her weight as he half-carried her out of the house.

"Stop," Pia said.

"No!" Nate replied, ignoring her resistance. He was stronger than she was; she had no choice but to follow or be dragged.

The storm had hit and was at full intensity now, turning the ocean into a beast that roared its aggression with salty, icy breath. Through the howling wind, Pia heard someone crying. The sound ripped out her heart.

Outside, near the entrance to the beach, Pia finally got Nate to stop. Her teeth chattered as rain lashed at her face and gale-force winds whipped hair into her eyes.

She looked back at the house. The little girl called out to her from a time gone bye, asking her to stay. Begging her not to leave.

Don't leave me!

Pia wrestled herself from Nate's grip in case he thought to drag her along the beach. She was not leaving.

She had *gotten through to Sarah!*

The entity that had told her to leave was now begging her to stay. This was her chance. Her only chance to help Sarah and Cassandra.

"What is it?" Nate demanded.

Pia heard a car slide to a stop at the front of the house, its flashing blue and red lights reflected in the storm clouds.

"Pia, damn it. Let's GO!" Nate grabbed her hand and tugged. Mark, Ryan, and Joe were already out of sight, across the beach and into safety.

You said you would help me. Did you mean it?

Under the veranda, glowing translucently in the darkness, was a girl in a bloodied white dress, long blonde hair blowing in the storm winds. A flash of lightning that should have illuminated her, instead made her image disappear, then reappear in the darkness.

"Yes!" Pia shouted against the howling wind.

Pia started back to the house, but Nate grabbed and lifted her, throwing her over his shoulders. She struggled mightily, and he managed only a few steps before he gave up fighting her and set her back down.

Pia dug her feet in, her skin ripping on one of the scraggly bushes in the rough terrain that bordered the beach. Flashes of lightning light up the scene, the cracks of thunder so loud Pia felt the vibrations go right through her body.

Don't leave me! Sarah begged.

Sarah was desperately pleading for someone to save her. In death as she had in life. No one had helped Sarah then, and Pia vowed to help her now.

Stay. Sarah said. *If you stay, I'll show you.*

Ah hell. Nate was going to be furious.

CHAPTER NINETEEN

SARAH

20 APRIL 1984

SARAH'S 14TH BIRTHDAY

I *struggle to open eyelids crusted with grime. I raise my hand to rub them. The metal jangles, the cuff digs into my raw skin. I bite my lip until the sharpness of the pain subsides.*

Best I don't move too much.

Not until my wrists heal again.

It's my fault the shackles are back on. They're the ones from where they kept me before, the bedroom inside the house. I hated that room; now I wish I was back there. He promises me that if I'm good, he'll take me back.

If I'm good…

He wants me to do something I can't do.

Please, God, don't let me ever get that desperate.

With the bent tine of my fork, I make another scratch on the wall behind the mattress.

There are three hundred and sixty-five now. I've been underground for twelve long months.

That's how I know today is my birthday. I heard her complain it had been exactly three years to the day that they'd plucked me out of the water. And I still wasn't the daughter I was supposed to be.

How much longer will I have to endure this? A day? A week? A month? Please, God,

119

don't let it be another month.

Someone will find me soon. Daddy will come. He won't give up. Will he? Has Daddy given up?

But I'm still alive.

I heard them, when they discussed getting rid of me a year ago. Did they think I couldn't hear them, from my prison on top of the lounge room, where the sound travels upward easily? Or perhaps they just didn't care.

He said he'd get through to me. He was sure I'd break and do it soon.

She said it had been two years and he was a fool. She wanted to kill me. She said I'd get them all sent to jail. She wanted to give me something to put me to sleep so I never woke up.

They fought. Night after night. He said something about God's plan. She told him he was a fool.

In the end, he got his way.

And so did she.

The compromise saw me taken from the house and put in this hole.

I'm still alive. For now.

Some days, considering my life in the hole, I wish I wasn't. When it's stifling hot, or bitterly cold, or my stomach gripes painfully from hunger or thirst.

On the day of my thirteenth birthday, they shifted me here. The entrance at ground level wasn't large enough to get the mattress down. They had to make it wider. The hole was originally built to be a cool room, like in the olden days, one of them said.

I absorbed as much of the sun as I could that day while they argued and dug. I fought back the tears as I tried not to look into the darkness of that hole in the ground. Instead, I looked at the white clouds against the blue sky, found shapes in them like I used to with Daddy a lifetime ago.

I won't give them the satisfaction of seeing me cry. They wanted me to break. It's all I have left. They've taken my freedom, my life. They control everything else. I won't let them control my mind.

What he wanted? I'll never give. It's all I can do. It's everything I can do.

But still, I inwardly shivered as I stood at the top in the sun and peered into the dark hole. I fought an urgent need to be sick.

A grave, I thought. I am being put into the ground like it's a grave.

I didn't know when I would ever see the sun again.

Will I ever see the sun again?

I have to hold onto the hope that I will.

Hope is all I have down here in the hole.

I watched the mattress drop into the hole. One of them cheered. It landed with a thud. The hole looked deep. And dark. And cold.

And that was when I ran.

I ran, but there were shackles around my ankles. Someone grabbed me, sending me sprawling to the ground. I kicked and screamed and they looked at me wide-eyed, and I knew they were scared someone would hear. She slapped me hard in the face, using the full force of her arm. Pain streaked down my neck.

They didn't use the ladder to put me in the hole.

I don't know what happened that day, but I woke up with a white hot pain down my back and across my ribs. If I twist a certain way, or lie in the wrong position at night, it comes back. Something is not right in my body, but I don't know how to fix it. And I've developed a rattling cough that never seems to go away.

After thirty scratches on the wall, thirty days in the hole, he took my shackles off. Since he removes the ladder after each visit, he considered them unnecessary. Then last week, he saw I'd been carving steps into the limestone walls.

I thought he'd be angry, braced myself for the punishment.

But he looked sad as he shook his head. "I'll never give up on you," he said. "The hole will cure you. I know it will."

Cure me of what? Cure me of wanting to go home? To get back to my parents?

Never.

And now the shackles are back on.

And the pain of the metal on my tender skin is almost too much to bear.

I am fourteen years old today.

But there are no presents. No parties. No cuddles from Daddy, no warm smiles from Mummy.

I cuddle my doll and can't help but think of how different I felt waking up on my eleventh birthday. Before I was lost at sea. I never realized how significant a single decision could be. That one sunny afternoon on my birthday when I decided to go for a swim.

One day.

One decision.

That one single choice changed the course of my life.

I have a lot of time to think about days now.

A scratching sound, and I still, barely breathing. A movement, something dark scuttles into the opposite corner. I see two orange eyes peering at me through the darkness.

I hold my breath. I want to scream.

What's the point? Who would hear me?

The eyes come closer.

I shuffle as far away from it as I can get, until I my back is against the cold wall.

The eyes get closer still, until it is standing in the shaft of light shining through the edges of the overhead trapdoor.

It's an animal.

A rat!

Aren't they dangerous?

It doesn't look dangerous. It eyes me as curiously as I look back at it. It twitches its nose, and I watch how its whiskers move. It doesn't look scary, it looks kind of… cute.

It comes tentatively closer.

I grab some crumbs left over from my sandwich and place them arm's length in front of me. Perhaps if I feed it, it won't bite me.

After a moment's hesitation, it comes forward, sniffs the bread.

"It is not fresh." I apologize to the animal. "But it's all I've got."

The creature doesn't nibble the bread on the ground. Instead it grabs a large crumb in between its front paws and sits up, then brings the bread up to its mouth.

I expected it to eat like a dog out of a bowl. "You eat just like me," I tell it, fascinated. Holding the crumb, it pauses, turning its head to listen as I speak, then continues eating the remainder.

Paws back on the ground, it inches closer. The twitching of its nose moves the whiskers, helping it navigate in the low light.

I find another crumb, place it closer this time. This time there's no hesitation as it comes forward to eat.

It's small. Is it a baby rat, or is it a mouse? How can you tell?

My parents certainly didn't have creatures like this in the house.

I put my last crumb in my palm and hold it out. After a while, it comes close enough and eats right out of my hand.

It looks up at me when it's finished.

"You're going to be my friend," I tell it. "But you need a name. I'm going to call you—"

One of my favorite stories Mum read to me at night was Charlotte's Web. *The rat's name was Templeton.*

"Templeton," I tell him. "Your name is Templeton. Even though I think you are a mouse and not a rat. And you will help me remember story time at home." How soft my bed felt, how fresh and fragrant Mum smelled as she kissed me goodnight. Until I thought I was too big for story time. I wanted to read my own books, not be read to like a baby.

Now I wish Mum would read to me. I imagine I can still hear her voice in the darkness, laughing softly, telling me, "Don't be silly, Princess, there's no such thing as monsters."

She'd lied.

There are *such things as monsters.*

I used to think there was nothing worse than being in this hole.

I was wrong.

The monster that visits at night now is far worse.

CHAPTER TWENTY

Pia's nails dug into Nate's arm as the images Sarah had shown to her gradually receded.

Oh God, that poor girl!

Pia had to find the cellar.

The storm raged overhead, soaking Pia and Nate through to the skin. The bad weather turned out to be a blessing, however; the police re-secured the house efficiently and left, clearly planning to come back tomorrow to document and finish up. They'd left only one marked car in the driveway, the officer keeping watch from inside his vehicle.

A large gum tree was on Pia's right, its sprawling branches towering over a small garden shed. There was something about that tree, the way its leaves seemed to shake more furiously than the others. As though it were *trying* to get her attention.

Keeping the images Sarah had shown her in her mind, Pia braced herself against the wild weather and moved toward the shed. Nate kept pace at her side. She sensed his tension and was grateful he'd stopped trying to dissuade her from following this through. His unquestioning support shifted something deep inside her. Melted the last of her resistance toward him.

The tin shed was locked with a padlock. "You want to look in here?" Pia nodded and he flicked out a tool, and in less time than she could have used a key, Nate had the lock open.

The shed was dark and smelled of petrol and lawn clippings. Nate held the torch, allowing her to see that it was filled with garden-maintenance equipment: lawn mowers, chainsaws, rakes… Pia sensed nothing out of the ordinary, no entrance to a cellar. But she sensed it was close.

She circled the shed, raising her eyes to the tree overhead. A sleek black crow sat on a low branch, defying the rain and wind, eyeing her with eerie intensity.

Crows were often found near places of high paranormal activity and often served as a warning. She was close, so close.

Halfway round the shed was a full-sized wine barrel. Pia touched the rough wooden surface with her fingertips. She sensed a man had stood there regularly, his beer bottle leaving perfectly round stains on the top of the barrel. She couldn't see who it was, but the hairs on the back of her neck stood on end.

Why would someone position themselves here to drink beer when the view of the ocean was on the other side of the shed?

In this position, the person would be hidden from view of people on the beach.

Pia started back to Nate, but her foot caught on a tree root, and she fell hard on the ground.

"Pia!" Nate was immediately at her side, his eyes assessing her critically.

"I'm all right," she said, but her ankle was throbbing. She pulled herself into a sitting position, brushing wet leaves and sand from her jeans. "I don't have time for a damn injury," she mumbled, kicking away the leaves to take her annoyance out on the offending tree root.

But it wasn't a tree root.

"Nate, look at this," she said, the pain of her ankle forgotten as she rose up on her knees.

He knelt beside her, helped her brush away the debris to expose what looked like a wooden slab with a flat, round brass handle.

"It's a trapdoor," she said. "To the cellar." Her heart was pounding as she met Nate's eyes. "This is it!"

The heavy downpour eased, the storm ebbing to low rumbles in the distance and the occasional flash of lightning.

Nate flicked his eyes in the direction of the patrol car keeping watch. The officer inside was looking at his phone, not at them.

Carefully, so as not to draw attention their way, Nate lifted the trap door, and seasons of leaves, sodden with rain, fell into the deep, dark hole in the ground.

Her mouth had dried, and she was desperate for a drink. She became light-headed and dizzy, and Nate placed a steadying arm around her shoulders.

"Pia?"

Her heart began to race, and she took a deep breath of salty air. "No need for concern. They're not my emotions, but when I'm open like this, I feel them as if they were."

"Can it hurt you?"

Absolutely. The pain was often excruciating. "No." She didn't feel entitled to any sympathy. Unlike the victim she connected with, Pia could shake off the experience when she was finished. The physical sensation anyway. She wouldn't be human not to still be affected emotionally.

"I can't read minds." Nate held her a moment longer than necessary, his arm dropping from her shoulder slowly. Reluctantly. "Tell me what you need. What I'm to do. Promise me."

"I'm fine."

"I mean it, Pia." His voice was low, gravelly. "Every instinct I have screams for me to get you the hell out of here, out of harm's way, and come back here later with my team. If there is a Sarah, she's no longer alive. There's no rush to investigate this cellar during a storm in the middle of the night." He thrust a hand through his hair, his eyes blazing with intensity. "What the *fuck* am I thinking?"

"You're thinking I won't let you do that, and you'd be right."

"Fine. I won't waste my breath then." Nate flicked on his Maglite torch and shined the beam into the hole, both of them leaning forward for a better look. The smell was repulsive, like a porta-loo in the hot sun. Pia's stomach churned. The light illuminated an old, splintered, wooden painter's ladder, the type used for resting against walls of a house. The type just waiting to topple and kill someone.

"I go first," Nate said, positioning the ladder, and began the descent into the darkness.

A car door opened, and Pia could hear the short barks from a police scanner.

"Pia! Hurry."

Needing to get out of sight—now—Pia started down into the darkened space. Nate jumped the last steps and steadied the ladder before it—and she—came crashing down.

"Here, hold this." The torch was cool in her hands as Nate hurried back up the ladder, closed the hatch, and cut them off from the outside world.

When he reached her side again, he rested a warm hand on the small of her back, an unconditional show of support. He was trusting her, ignoring his instincts and his common sense, and that was no small thing.

He took the torch back from her and scanned the squalid space.

In the left-hand corner, an oil lantern sat on a set of drawers; in the right-hand corner sat a bucket and a roll of toilet paper, an empty tub alongside them. In the opposite corner was the soiled mattress Pia had seen in her vision. The heavy chains that had kept Sarah shackled were long enough to allow her to walk around the room, but not long enough to reach the top of the ladder.

It was silent, dark, and bitterly cold. Much colder even than it should have been, this prison beneath the ground.

Overhead, she heard the muffled sounds of voices, the short barks of a radio. Pia tuned out the distraction. Time was slowing down, fading away as she slipped into another place, another time.

Sarah—the imprint—was in the corner, her white nightgown dirty and covered in bloodstains, both fresh and old. Next to her was a filthy cloth, a gag, Pia realized with a sickening flip of her stomach.

For when he had his fun and she became too noisy.

Despite the isolation, he hadn't risked her screams being heard from inside the house.

Why? Didn't they know?

Perhaps the noise interfered with his perfect fantasy. Of having her willing and compliant. She sensed his increasing irritation as she continued to fight. Each and every time. No matter how worn down and weak she became. No matter what he did, how much pain and degradation he inflicted, he couldn't break her.

Not even at the very end.

Pia lowered herself to her knees on the soiled floor in the corner, amongst the decaying rags, the foul, and after all these years, now unidentifiable, refuse. Through her denim jeans, Pia felt the layers of muck and scum. Her heart shattered for a little girl locked up against her will and forced to live in such squalid conditions.

The stench was heavy and cloying, her every breath an effort not to retch. Pia refused to cower away from the unimaginable horror Sarah had been forced to endure. It didn't seem fair or right for Pia to do so, when Sarah hadn't been able to.

They didn't see me.

No one heard me.

No one came.

Pia sat on the stinking mattress with her back against the bloodstained wall. She pushed past her fear, the overwhelming instinct to flee this abominable, sickening place. To bolt back up that ladder into the fresh air.

Instead, Pia sat where Sarah had sat. Felt the helplessness, the despair, the miserable isolation. Alone, where memories of a happier time, a happier place, were so vivid they became Sarah's newest and worst torture. Even more than what he did to her body when he came.

When the monster came, she went there. Back to Mummy and Daddy. She clutched her doll in her arms and went back to a happier time. A place where she was loved.

The bad man could touch her body, every single inch of it, but he couldn't touch her mind. Occasionally the pain would shock her temporarily back into the hole, but it wasn't until after he'd left that she'd really felt what he'd done.

The pain of unset broken bones knitting together, of cuts that festered and bled. But worst of all was the terrible silence. The isolation and the endless loneliness.

To cope, to survive, she went back home. In her mind, she could live anywhere. She looked at her doll, her Angel, the mirror image of her, the girl she used to be, and imagined her beautiful and happy once again. She was in her kitchen, baking cookies with Mummy. Waiting those impatient seconds between when Daddy's car pulled into the driveway and when he opened the front door before she could throw herself into his arms. He caught her. Every single time.

Hot, bitter tears slipped behind Pia's lids and down her face. Sarah never saw any of those things again.

No one saw.

No one heard.

No one came.

Pia continued to sit and wait with Sarah.

Her mouth was dry, filled with dirt and grime from the last time he'd shoved the rag in her mouth. He'd forgotten to leave water, and the woman hadn't tossed any food down for two days.

"Pia!" Nate's voice bled through the veil, like a hand reaching into the space where she was, calling her back to a time she wasn't ready to go to yet. "Pia!" He sounded worried, his voice a little frantic.

"Not yet, Nate," Pia managed, focusing, holding her attention on the doll. Like Sarah did. "I'm not ready yet."

Pia would not leave Sarah. Not until she'd seen who the monster was that came down that ladder.

—————◆—————

Nate's gaze didn't waver from Pia on that filthy mattress in the corner. Back against the wall, she had her head on her knees and occasionally sobbed as she rocked back and forth.

It took every ounce of his willpower not to pick her up and haul her out of there. He had no idea if he should let her do what she was doing. Or for how long. He didn't even know if what she was doing was dangerous. There was so much he needed to know. So much he wanted to understand.

For now, he had to sit back, grit his teeth, and trust that Pia knew what she was doing. That she knew when to stop. Just like he knew his line of work, the dangers one faced out of necessity, he hoped Pia knew her limits. She had to be walking a fine line, staying with a victim in the past like that. Extreme mental duress broke people. Even the strongest.

Pia made another noise of distress and looked up, her eyes glazed and out of focus. She placed one hand on her stomach and the other fisted against her mouth.

His hands clenched at his sides, he watched. It killed him to see Pia like this. Suffering, taking on pain from a life that wasn't hers. Respect and admiration for her floored him. She was as strong and courageous as any of the men on his team.

And Pia had asked him what he saw in her!

Her reaction to whatever it was she was seeing changed. She took a series of short, shallow breaths, hyperventilating like she was having a panic attack.

He tensed, ready to intervene, but he wouldn't unless absolutely necessary. He had to pray he knew when that was and what he needed to do if it happened. How to bring her back to the here and now. Being in this filthy hole was terrifying enough, let alone doing an action replay with the victim.

If Sarah had died in here, where was her body? Nate had thoroughly searched the space. He'd lifted the corner of the mattress, lifted filthy blankets that had dried stiff with bodily fluid, likely blood judging by the dark crimson stains. There was no body, no bones. The floor was concrete, so she couldn't have been buried.

If Sarah had escaped, even briefly, she would have directed someone here.

The evidence suggested that whoever had done this to her had killed her before she made it out of here. Or before she was able to talk to anyone else.

If Nate was still a cop, he would have been compelled to call this in. Working for TSI afforded him a freedom he'd never had on the force, not even in elite Special Ops, while still allowing him to do the job he loved.

But this time, he'd keep all this away from the cops, and off the record, for now.

He needed to keep Pia off Johnson's radar.

He had to hope she could give him something, anything, he could use to find out who Sarah was and what had happened to her.

Only then would Pia have any hope of doing whatever she needed to do to put the restless spirit to sleep.

Pia moaned in distress, the sound desperate, broken, and he moved to her side.

Should he try to wake her from her altered state of awareness? How would he know when to?

The moan deepened and her head thrashed from side to side. He checked his watch. They'd been down here almost an hour. That had to be enough. More than enough.

"Pia, honey?"

Her eyelids fluttered, silent tears streaming down her face. Her chest heaved as she sucked in huge lungfuls of air. He wrapped his arms around her tightly as her body trembled. Her skin was cold, clammy, as though she were in shock.

She opened her eyes and looked up at Nate. "I couldn't see him." Her voice was a mere rasp. "I saw the monster climbing down the steps, but I couldn't see who it was." Frustration peppered her words.

Nate ran a hand over her hair, then down her back. He rubbed her neck, her shoulders. "Tell me what I can do." His attempts at comfort seemed inadequate.

Pia was oblivious to his ministrations in any case. Abruptly, she got onto her hands and knees and lifted up the corner of the mattress.

"What are you doing?"

She was running her fingertips across the lower wall. "Give me the torch," she said, holding her hand out for it without looking at him. She took it from him and ran the beam back and forth along the wall. She was staring at something he couldn't quite make out.

"Eleven hundred and ninety-three," she said, leaning back on her heels. Her distress was almost tangible and his heart twisted.

"Eleven hundred and ninety-three what?"

"See the scratches there?" She pointed to the wall. "They're markers. Of days." Pia took a breath. "Sarah was here for eleven hundred and ninety-three days. A little over three years and three months."

Nate reached for her. "She was just over sixteen when she died," Pia said, allowing him to embrace her. "That means she was thirteen when she was locked down here. And Sarah showed me that she'd been held somewhere else before even being brought here. The attic in the cottage." Tears streaked down her face, and she wiped them away with a shaky hand. "I couldn't see who the monster was," Pia sobbed. "I tried so hard, but I just couldn't see—"

Okay, that was enough. Pia was distressed seeing what had happened to Sarah, she wouldn't be human if she wasn't. But she was still wearing the emotions of someone else. She was too close, suffering as Sarah had suffered.

It was time to get Pia out. Nate pulled her to her feet, held her until she was steady.

He flicked the light across her eyes. Made sure her pupils were responding correctly.

"Pia, honey, look at me."

She blinked at him, her eyes glazed before they began to focus.

"You're going to let it go for now." He kept his voice low and calm. "We'll talk about it more when we're in the fresh air. For now, take a deep breath. Let Sarah go."

She struggled, really struggled, but when her breathing finally regulated, Nate fired off a text to Daniel. Seconds later, he heard Max barking in the distance. Daniel was creating a diversion.

"That's our cue." Nate urged her up the ladder. She stopped halfway up. "This is not goodbye, Sarah," Pia said, her voice wavering in the silence. "I will find out who did this to you." She climbed to the top.

"Oh, and Sarah?" she called out to the empty room.

"I see you."

"I hear you."

"I *will* help you."

Chapter Twenty-One

Back at Nate's house, Pia paced the lounge room restlessly. She'd showered and changed her clothes, but she didn't feel much different. Her body was heavy. Aching. She rubbed at a lingering pain at her wrists.

It was standard practice for Pia to "cleanse" herself after an investigation, to remove any attachments or energy not her own. She had deliberately chosen not to after that first visit from Sarah, fearful she'd lose the connection and not be able to get it back. Too much was riding on her need to communicate with Sarah to risk it. So she walked around the room, trying to separate her "self" from that of Sarah the best she could.

"She died in that hole, Nate."

Nate eyed her closely. "We don't know that. For sure, I mean. Do we?"

Nate was certainly wondering where the body was, where they'd buried her.

"It's a safe bet to assume that," Pia said. "She was in awful condition when I 'saw' her last image in there."

Sarah had never climbed that ladder to freedom. She'd never breathed fresh air again.

Pia blinked away her tears and pushed through what she likened to survivor's guilt. She had to. She'd learned long ago that if she didn't, if she carried around someone's pain and suffering for days, it became her own. Her very sanity depended on being able to separate herself from the victim.

Nate opened the sliding windows, let the cool breeze blow over them. The earlier storm had passed, leaving the air clean and fresh.

"Let's go for a walk," he said. He disappeared for a while, then came back with a packed backpack. He grabbed a bottle of wine, a couple of glasses, slung the strap over his shoulder, and reached for her hand.

As tired as she was, as late as it was, she wouldn't be able to sleep. She needed a distraction, if only temporarily. She needed to feel human.

She needed to feel alive.

Pia followed Nate gratefully, knowing the fresh evening air would go a long way toward helping her recover.

How did he always seem to know exactly what she needed?

They kicked their shoes off at the balcony, then walked down the stairs to the sand, damp but warm from the earlier rain.

Pia breathed the salty air deep into her lungs, listened to the roar of the waves as they crashed heavily onto the shore, the deep rumbling fading down the beach. They walked a short distance before Nate stopped, taking a large blanket out of his backpack. He spread it across the sand, and Pia sat down facing the unsettled ocean.

They sat side by side, shoulders touching. The almost full moon slipped out from behind a cloud, providing a surprising amount of light.

"I feel so sorry for her, Nate," Pia said, unable to simply forget, despair sitting like a stone in her stomach. "She was just a little girl. Three years and three months she lived down there." It was beyond comprehension how anyone could be so cruel.

She turned to look at him. "What I want to understand is why they did it. We aren't talking about a single deranged psychopath here. There was more than one person involved. A woman as well. What was the purpose? Why didn't one of them help her?"

How could these people do such things to a little girl and keep it secret all these years?

Unable to help it, Pia sobbed, tears sliding hot and angry down her cheeks. Nate wrapped an arm around her.

"This isn't your responsibility. You can't carry the whole weight of the situation on your shoulders."

"It's hard not to." Pia picked up a handful of damp sand and formed it into a ball. "I'm the one who can reach across to her. I didn't choose these abilities; they chose me. The cops have had this case for thirty years and haven't solved it. They haven't the means. How can I *not* think this is my responsibility?"

Nate was silent a moment.

Pia threw the ball of sand. It splattered on the beach before reaching the water. She picked up another handful and made another.

"I don't know how you deal with entities all the time," he said eventually. "It would freak me out."

"It's only natural to fear what you don't understand. From a very early age, I knew there were invisible forces hidden in the corners of our everyday lives. Things that exist that the general population is quite happy to pretend aren't there."

Nate pulled Pia into his arms, and she stared up at the sky, the endless dark night that held the twinkling stars suspended.

Pia sighed. "It's mind-blowing, isn't it? The universe so huge, endless. There's more we're discovering every day as our equipment to view it improves. I heard NASA found new planets last week. But they're not new. They're only new to us. They've been there all this time; we just didn't see them. That's how I feel about my abilities. I see what's there all along, only not everyone has the right equipment to see it."

Nate followed her gaze up to the night sky. "You're special."

Pia tensed. "I certainly don't look at myself that way." She was *different*. And people who were different weren't tolerated well by society.

Still, she did her best to embrace her differences in the face of adversity and often ridicule. "In your family, when you were brought up, did your family, your mum or dad, believe in ghosts?"

"No." Nate's lips twitched at the thought. "I come from an alpha-male-dominated industry that doesn't tolerate weakness."

"Weakness?" Pia asked, surprised. "That's an interesting choice of words."

"I didn't mean that to be offensive."

Pia smiled. "I know. Lots of people believe that only what you can see with your eyes and touch with your hands is 'real.' But how real is it to rely on only a couple of senses and ignore the others?"

"I didn't say I agreed." Nate's smile crinkled his eyes at the corners.

"I know." Pia released a breath. "It's a sore point with me, an argument I've long since tired of."

"It must have been hard being born able to see things not many others could."

"It was confusing. Luckily, I eventually discovered my grandmother had a similar gift."

"She didn't know you were psychic?"

"No," Pia shrugged. "My mother and her mother, my grandmother, didn't get along. Plus, I'd become quite skilled at hiding it. I was nine when my grandmother found out by accident when I slipped up, and the subsequent conversation we had changed my life. Mum isn't psychic and doesn't even accept it's real. She believes it to be a mental disorder and referred to my grandmother as 'that crazy old bag.' Apparently, psychic abilities can skip a generation."

"That's why you helped Sage. You related to her. Sage had only her grandmother, too."

"I like Sage," Pia said, smiling genuinely.

"I like *you*."

She rolled over and faced Nate. Being with him here beneath the stars, lying next to each other, made her crave something she didn't believe possible for her to have.

She wanted normal. She wanted romance.

She wanted to see where this could lead with Nate.

He was lying on his side, his head resting on his arm. He was still, gazing at her. His body was relaxed, but his eyes didn't miss a single breath she took.

Pia leaned in, their faces close. Nate's eyes searched her face, and she touched her mouth to his. His lips were soft and full, and sensuously warm. He smelled deliciously masculine, like the outdoors and the ocean.

The connection, as always, was electric. Something buzzed between them, crackled and sizzled as her body came alive. Would it always be this way?

Nate lifted her hair, cupped the back of her neck, and kissed her hard. He wrapped his other arm around her waist, pulling her flush against himself. She felt the hardness of his body, the evidence of his desire. The heat between them grew, a fire raging through kindling. Shifting in his arms, she altered their positions so that he was flat on his back and she was lying on top of him. She looked into his stormy eyes. His lids were heavy, his breathing labored.

She waited for a barrage of thoughts, of unwanted images, to flood over her. None came. There was just Nate, calm, still. Looking into her eyes. That had never happened to her before. Pia let herself go, willing the passion between them to consume her. She relaxed into the moment.

Into Nate.

The last of her resistance melted away as she deepened the kiss, swallowing his low moan when he responded in equal measure. The hardness of his erection pulsed beneath her stomach, and an answering heat pooled between her thighs. She sat up, straddling him. Nate's hair was sexily mussed, his shirt riding up his torso, allowing her to glimpse the ridged muscles of his abdomen. A shiver rolled through her body. He looked up at her, his smile crinkling his eyes at the corners, and her heart stuttered to a halt in her chest.

"You are a very sexy man, Nate Ryder."

He gripped her hips with large, strong hands, reversing their positions so that he was on top. With one hand he whipped his T-shirt up and off and placed it beneath her head.

It was then that Pia realized he'd been allowing her to set the pace, to take the lead. And he'd been fully prepared to stop on a second's notice should she decide not to go any further.

He was clearly aware that stopping was the last thing on her mind. In fact, it would possibly kill her.

She ran her fingers across his chest, tracing each well-defined muscle. His breathing was heavy and ragged, and the ocean rumbled in the background as the waves hit the shore. Nate leaned down, kissing her as she trailed her hands down his bare back, running her fingers inside the waistband of his jeans. She felt him tremble, sensed the tight rein he kept on his desire. Heat poured off him, warming her skin.

She tugged at the front button of his jeans, and he shifted so that he was on his knees in front of her. A lock of hair fell forward, dancing across one of his eyes in the cool breeze washing in from the ocean.

His expression was soft and tender, but Pia sensed the turbulence swirling just beneath the surface. Something possessive. A powerful desire he was keeping firmly in check, backed up by a fierce determination to make this work. If it had been anyone else, Pia would have been distracted with random thoughts, observations, insecurities. But this was Nate, and his touch was firm, controlled, and confident. Her mind remained silent, allowing her to feel nothing but the thrill his touch gave her. She savored his heated looks, the taste of his mouth, the saltiness of his skin when she leaned up to kiss his chest.

Driven by an urgent, primal, feminine need, Pia cupped his full hardness in her palm. He throbbed against her hand and let out a low groan. Pia lowered his zipper, tracing the thin trail of hair that disappeared into the V it made. She pushed his jeans down, her mouth drying at the sight of his erection straining at his black boxer briefs. He was hot and hard, his cock deliciously long and thick. She slipped her hand inside, tracing his length, and Nate groaned low and deep in the back of his throat.

Nate was so large, so strong, and so incredibly male. He was one hundred percent pure, raw sexuality. A man in peak condition in the prime of his life.

And he was looking at her like she was the only woman in the whole world.

He shrugged out of his jeans and knelt before her, confident in his nakedness. Pia tried not to stare. Failed. Her eyes wantonly traveled every inch of his perfectly formed body.

On his right shoulder was a thin white scar, and she traced her fingers across the line.

"Knife wound." Nate's voice was low and husky. On his side was another scar, jagged and red. More recent.

Nate answered her unspoken question. "Knife wound."

Pia smiled.

"And this?" she asked, tracing a long scar running from his left pectoral across his ribs.

"Knife wound."

Pia tsked playfully. "You seem to have a problem playing with knives, Detective."

"They aren't all from the same knife."

"Oh yes," she said, leaning up and licking across the scar on his side. "That makes it *much* better."

"The big one on my shoulder is a bullet wound," he said, and Pia could see the scar and a faint outline of stitches. It looked serious, like he'd needed surgery. She wanted to ask him what had happened. But that would wait for another time.

"You don't mind them?"

Her chest squeezed from the subtle thread of vulnerability in his voice. He wanted her to be pleased with what she saw. Didn't want her to dislike what he considered his imperfections.

In answer, she tenderly pressed her lips to the jagged scar at his shoulder. His body was perfect from the top of his head to his strong, large feet.

Nate rose and held out a hand, and she took it as he helped her up. Slowly, he unbuttoned her blouse, sliding the fabric off her arms, his heated gaze traveling over the black corset she favored.

"Turn around," he said, his voice low and gravelly.

Nate slid the zipper down and her favorite black leather skirt fell to the sand.

His hands were warm as he moved them across her skin. He fumbled with the corset's many hooks and huffed out a breath. With practiced fingers, she released the clasps that held the bodice closed.

Nate's eyes were dark pools of desire as he watched her breasts bounce free of their confinement. The cool air hit her skin, her nipples instantly pebbling.

He muttered something that sounded like a curse beneath his breath and cupped her breasts. "You are the most gorgeous woman I have ever seen."

Pia would have laughed if it weren't for the serious expression he wore. It was not a compliment. Pia sensed nothing contrived. He truly believed his words, and the effect they had on her was devastating. Her knees felt weak, and he pulled her flush against his body.

Holding one arm tightly around her, he knelt down with her, laying her gently on the blanket. Closing the distance between them, he kissed her deeply, languidly stroking her tongue. Pia's body was on fire, intense heat pooling between her thighs, her need for him a relentless, pulsing throb.

Nate broke the kiss, moved his mouth across her chin, down her neck, licked along her collarbone.

Pia still worried that she'd be unable to fully let go when the time came. She fervently hoped she wouldn't be holding part of herself back, waiting for an unwanted flood of thoughts to come rushing over her. She didn't want to know if, on closer inspection, he realized her thighs were thicker than he'd first thought. Or—

"Relax," Nate said, his lips brushing against her neck.

"I'm trying," Pia whispered, closing her eyes. Would there always be a part of her waiting for the other shoe to drop?

"Stop trying." Nate drew back and waited for her to open her eyes. "Stop overthinking this. Trust me enough to let go."

Pia frowned. "I do trust you. I'm—" She broke off before saying "trying."

"This is not your responsibility," Nate said, his voice all gravel. "If I do it right, you won't be able to think of anything else."

She clenched her thighs together. *Oh God.*

Nate lowered his head and drew one of her nipples into his warm mouth. She tangled her fingers in his hair as streaks of pleasure ripped through her body. He was right; her mind blanked to everything but Nate. To the feel of his warm tongue flicking her nipple and the gentle draw as he sucked the tip deep into his warm mouth. She cried out, twisting beneath him as her body burned. When he released her nipple, the cool air hit the hardened point and sent a bolt of electricity between her legs.

"You have the most beautiful breasts," he said almost reverently. He cupped one of them and squeezed softly.

Pia's mouth was dry, her skin scorched by each kiss he trailed across her ribs, then lower, down her stomach. She parted her legs and mindlessly clutched his hair. He licked at the cleft between her thighs, his talented tongue causing her to shiver and sending hot waves of pleasure pulsing through her.

"Oh, Nate!"

He flicked his tongue expertly across her folds, while one finger circled her opening before sliding inside. Pia squeezed her eyes closed, arching into him when he drew her clit between his teeth. Her orgasm when it came was as violent as it was unexpected, ripping through her with the force of a tidal wave. Nate groaned low and deep, the vibration adding to the intensity of her pleasure.

Nate fumbled in his jeans for his wallet and withdrew a condom. Slipping it on, he rested his cock at her entrance, then paused, raising a brow, asking if she was ready.

Oh, hell yes! Not trusting herself to speak, Pia wrapped her legs around his waist, urging him deep inside her. Her breath hitched and her body closed around each ridge of his erection. He withdrew fully before thrusting hard and deep inside her.

"God, Pia. You feel so fucking good."

Pia was still unable to reply, so she arched her back and encouraged him deeper. Nate placed one arm under her hips, lifted and supported her, then began to move rhythmically deep inside her.

Nate was a skilled lover, knowing exactly when she was close, slowing the pace, allowing the pleasure to back off before building it to an even higher pitch. He thrust inside her, faster, deeper, harder. The intensity, their hunger for each other, consumed her.

"Keep your eyes on mine," Nate ground out. "I want to watch you come."

She tried. Dear God, she tried. Pia was a writhing pool beneath him, unable to so much as breathe, let alone hold eye contact, before he finally allowed her release. Wave after wave of scorching hot pleasure, pure ecstasy, washed over her.

She watched his face contort with pleasure, couldn't breathe as he cried out her name. His body shuddered, and his weight pressed down on her.

Later, she lay in his arms and slowly relaxed into him. There were no stray thoughts from him, nothing but satisfaction and a deep sense of contentment.

That had never happened to her before. Nate was right. He *was* different. Maybe he'd stay that way. Maybe this would actually work.

Maybe she could be normal for once.

All Pia had to do now was bring the people who had hurt Sarah to justice, and everything in her life would be perfect.

Except…

Something hovered on the edge of her consciousness. Like a butterfly, it fluttered and teased. But not in a good way.

It wasn't a butterfly; it was a plain gray moth. And it was bringing a message of doom.

Something bad was on the horizon.

And it was headed her way.

Chapter Twenty-Two

Sarah
20 October 1985

He only comes at night.

It's dark.

I prefer it that way. It makes it easier to pretend it's not happening.

That it's not real.

But then he turns on the kerosene lamp.

He's carrying the knife.

I see the yellow glow as the light glints off the blade.

The eagle carved into its handle is a symbol of everything I don't have. An eagle is strong, free to fly above all others. It can go wherever it wants.

An eagle is free.

I'm not.

It hurts, the knife. The stinging heat of the blade piercing my flesh. I don't like the feel of blood, all warm and slippery on my skin. It turns sticky as it dries and leaves a bad taste in my mouth.

His hands are rough. Heavy. They scratch along my inner thighs, scrape across raw flesh that cries out in agony. I've begged, I've pleaded. I don't do that anymore.

No matter what he does, I don't cry out. He positions himself over me, his breath a warm, moist, stomach-turning cloud of something foul.

I have long since accepted I cannot fight him. It makes the inevitable so much more painful. More drawn out. The heavy bindings are no longer on my wrists, but it feels as though they still are. Ghost shackles. My bones ache, a persistent reminder of my lack of freedom.

He might have my body, but he cannot reach my mind.

There I can escape from the pain.

From his unwanted touch.

From him.

My fingers tangle in the satiny hair of my doll. Angel is pretty. Perfect. He has never touched her in that way.

I run my fingertips over her lips.

She is smiling.

Now I am smiling.

I am my angel doll, and we are a long way from here.

I fly across the seas, the ocean, to a faraway land.

Another time. Another place.

The comfort of the familiar.

I am in a pretty bedroom.

I am a present. I'm wrapped in glittery purple paper.

I am opened by a sweet girl who looks just like me.

Or I like her.

It really doesn't matter as long as we are somewhere else.

I am back in the hole. Brought sharply back by a tug on the rope of pain that binds me here.

His breath is foul, and I am sick.

He slaps my face but strangely I can't feel it.

My mind can leave here. One day my body will leave here too.

Sever the ties with him and this place forever.

I no longer believe in God. Did I ever? Perhaps He's just a story told to kids, like Santa or the Easter Bunny. I don't know what is real anymore. My mind has been my own far too long, fertilized with nothing but darkness.

What I do know is that I am alone down here. There is no one, no one, listening to my prayers. How cruel would it be if there was, and He didn't lift a finger to help?

If there is a God, why am I still here?

What did I do to deserve this?

There is no God.

Only darkness.

The darkness is my friend. I will make the monster pay for what he does to me. For the pain he inflicts. I will give it back tenfold.

Praying makes me feel helpless. But the darkness makes me strong. One day, vengeance will be mine.

Templeton shifts from where he is nestled in my hair at the nape of my neck. He senses when I'm upset, detests the monster as much as I do.

But I warn him to be quiet. I don't want him to be discovered again. We both remember what happened last time…

He is my little friend, and he was only trying to defend me. He almost died. Templeton is brave, but no match for this monster.

I am no match for this monster. Not now.

But someday I will be. The darkness tells me so.
My friend hides in the safety of my hair until it's over.
Until the peace of silence is once again upon us.
One day I won't be weak, I won't be a victim.
One day, the monster will be the victim.
In the cold darkness, Templeton and I plan.
I remain silent for now at the sight of the knife.
I hate the knife.
The eagle that can fly when I cannot.
One day I'm going to be the one holding the knife.
One day, it will be him who feels terror when he sees the eagle.

CHAPTER TWENTY-THREE

Pia's breath caught and slowly released at the sight of Nate in his kitchen, dressed only in faded denim jeans that hung low on his hips. Her pulse sped up as she crossed the room, removed his hand from the frying pan, and placed her palms on his bare chest. He had the most gorgeous body she'd ever seen on a man, even in magazines. She traced her fingers along the indentations of his six-pack, up his chest, and across his broad shoulders before wrapping her arms around his neck.

Angling his head, he leaned down and sealed his lips to hers. He snaked an arm around her, tugging her close. His cock pressed, hard and inviting, against her soft stomach. *Again?*

She was more than happy to rise to the challenge, to fulfill his every desire. Heat flared between them, and despite the number of times Nate had brought her to climax over these last twelve hours, her nipples tightened greedily and heat pooled between her thighs.

Would she ever get enough of him?

Nate broke the kiss with a soft groan and playfully pushed her away. "You taste so sweet." He licked his lips, slowly for effect. Did she also mention he was cruel? "But if you kiss me like that again, I won't be held responsible for the condition breakfast will be in."

Breakfast was certainly not what Pia was hungry for, but she had to admit the bacon and eggs *did* smell delicious.

"As you were," Pia said briskly. She slapped him on the arse—why not?—and turned to tackle the coffee machine. She poked at it several times, baffled by the lack of progress, finally working out that the machine wanted to grind up fresh beans *before* she could even begin to brew anything. *Argh!* "You do know it's much damned quicker to just toss boiling water onto instant coffee, right?"

"Now where's the fun in that? Besides, all the best things in life are worth a bit of extra effort."

He wasn't talking about the coffee machine, and the words warmed her heart. He gave her a contented half-smile as he flipped the eggs.

It almost felt surreal, making breakfast with Nate after a night of lovemaking. It felt almost… normal. Okay, "normal" might be going too far, but it did feel *right*. Certainly, it was far more than she'd ever believed was possible for someone like her.

Nate's laptop dinged, signaling an incoming email. He twisted the screen and read it. His shoulders tensed and his frown deepened the longer he read.

Pia resisted the immediate impulse to reach out, to discover what was troubling him in case she could help. Not that reading Nate was easy, or even possible, in the best of situations, but it upset her to see him so troubled.

"Are you okay?"

A muscle along Nate's jaw twitched, and his eyes narrowed as though what he was reading was really pissing him off.

"Nate?"

"What?" He glanced up, his eyes slightly unfocused, the bulk of his attention still on the email and the news it contained. "It's nothing."

Okay.

Pia swallowed a pinch of hurt. She had opened up and shared things—deep and personal things—about what it was like living with her abilities. How hard it was for to have relationships. She had never spoken to anyone about that before, not even Mark.

I made myself vulnerable for you, and yet you're still a closed book.

He turned back to the computer. "It's personal," he mumbled, the words a knife to her heart. After long moments of frowning at the screen, he finally looked up. "It's about my brother. But it's nothing for you to worry about. This is something I have to deal with." Nate fired off an email, his fingers tapping hard and loud as they flew across the keys.

A rock formed in her throat, making it painful to swallow, impossible to speak. But the words wouldn't stay locked up. "So I open up to you, something I never *ever* do, and you don't trust me enough to do it in return, is that it?" Her voice cracked slightly. *Damn it.* She looked away, sucked in a breath and tried to pretend there wasn't a burning pain in her chest.

Nate's fingers froze on the laptop and she felt the heat of his stare.

"Pia, look at me."

She met his piercing gaze head on. "You have to know that's not true," he said earnestly.

Her initial response was to want to back down, to tell him not to worry about it. That what he did wasn't her business. But she didn't want another empty relationship where she kept a cool distance.

Nate made her want things, made her dream of things she hadn't believed possible. That meant *both* of them had to open up. Both of them needed to take the risk of being vulnerable.

"Do I?" She struggled to keep her voice even. This kind of conversation was new territory, and it was scary as hell. But if she wanted things to be different with Nate, that meant speaking from her heart, and not her head.

"It doesn't take a psychic to realize that something you were reading in that email has you really concerned. I ask you about it, and you clam up. If it was work, I'd understand. Of course you can't discuss your confidential cases. But you tell me it's *personal*, and then follow up with, 'nothing for me to worry about.'"

Tears stung her eyes, and she angrily blinked them back. "Do you think it's been easy for me to get *personal*, Nate Ryder? Being *personal* isn't something that just happens for people like us. We both have to want it. To work at it." Pia swallowed, hard. "I was feeling so close to you just a few minutes ago, closer than I've ever felt to anyone in my whole life, but now I realize I don't really know you at all."

A fact that was all the more glaringly obvious because she couldn't read him like other people. The only way she'd get inside Nate's head was if he opened himself up and consciously allowed it.

Nate leaned back and thrust his hands through his still-damp hair. "I'm sorry. I… it's just that it's complicated."

Pia closed her eyes and groaned. *It's complicated.* When is life ever *not* complicated? She didn't want to make a big deal and *force* Nate to open up; she wanted him to *want* to.

And he clearly didn't want to.

"It doesn't matter," she said quickly, wishing she could eat the conversation back from the first word. Being open was overrated.

"Of course it matters," Nate said, staring intently at her. "And you're right. But you're wrong as well. You do know me, and believe it or not, this is me being more personal than I've ever been too." Nate leaned forward and grabbed her hands in his very warm, much larger ones.

"This is new for both of us. But you have to understand that I wasn't shutting you out just now. You have so much on your plate already with Sarah, I wasn't about to burden you with more. Trust me, the last thing you need to concern yourself with right now is my fucked-up family. You'll have the rest of your life for that, if I have my way. Plus, it's far too soon to risk scaring you off," Nate added lightly, his eyes crinkling at the corners.

Oh no, you don't! She wasn't letting him brush her off with a sexy smile this time. "If communicating with dead people and possessed dolls doesn't scare me, I'm pretty sure I can handle your family."

A shadow crossed his face, and Pia squeezed his hand. "I meant that as a joke."

"I know," Nate said, his smile fading as he realized he wasn't off the hook. "I don't even know how to do this. Where to start."

"Without too much detail, tell me something about your family. Let me start with what I know. Your family is in the car-racing industry, you clearly have a love of fast cars and spent lots of time at the track growing up, but you took the path of detective, then special operations, and not the family business. Why?"

Nate put some bread in the toaster. "Because my father and I don't see eye to eye." His jaw was clenched, his voice tight.

"About what?" Pia asked gently.

Nate thrust his hands through his hair. "About fucking anything at all."

Pia was stunned at the intensity of his response and what was clearly an open wound. Maybe this wasn't a good idea after all. She'd bring it up again another time, when they were finished dealing with Sarah.

"My father is an alcoholic," Nate said abruptly.

Damn, she hadn't expected that. "It's okay. You don't have to tell me now. I'm sorry for bringing it up like this."

His eyes were blazing. "You wanted personal. I'll give you a taste of my fucked-up life. My father races cars, but his love affair is with bourbon. He's an angry drunk, and one day when we're next discussing my scars, I'll show you which ones came from him."

"Jesus, Nate. I'm sorry, I—"

"And while we're there, I'll also show you which ones I received protecting my mother when I was old enough to stand up to the old bastard."

Jesus. She'd thought her childhood had been rough. And wasn't she selfish, demanding he share just because she had? Clearly, she sucked at this relationship thing. And it didn't help that she couldn't read Nate. He had the ability to shock her like no other. It left her feeling like she was treading on quicksand.

He blew out a breath and scrubbed a hand over his face. "I've never told anyone that before," he said, storm clouds swirling in his eyes. "It's not easy for me."

"Then don't."

"It's only fair you know what you're getting yourself into, while it's still early enough for you to back out."

"I'm not going anywhere," Pia said fiercely. "Whatever it is that you're about to say, it's not going to make one lick of difference. Your life made you who you are today, and I have to say, I've never met a better man."

"Fuck, I love you."

The impact of hearing the words coming from Nate's lips made her eyes sting and her throat close over. Her heart stopped dead in her chest, her breath leaving her lungs. She'd heard him think the words before, last night in the throes of passion, and again as he came in the shower this morning, but people often confused love with pleasure during sex. She couldn't take those thoughts seriously.

But now Nate had said it out loud.

Actually, he'd said, *Fuck, I love you.* And he kind of blurted it. He didn't say it in your typical wine-and-dine, look-deep-into-your-eyes kind of way. But then Nate wasn't your typical man.

Still…

Regardless of whether Nate intended them in a deep and meaningful way, the words had a powerful effect on her. The tug of longing now in her heart told her that.

This was the time to let him know what she felt for him too. She'd agreed to the relationship idea, and he was making the effort to open up to her, despite how hard it was for him. It was time for her to tell him that she'd fallen for him. Hard.

Nate had come to mean many things to her, but did she *love* him?

Did she dare?

And how did she tell him she was scared? Terrified? Handing your heart over to someone else had the potential to devastate you. That she knew, better than she knew anything else. Loving anyone, even her own family, had caused her nothing but pain. Nate too, by the sound of it. Was it even possible for them to make love work?

Pia looked away, blinking back hot stinging tears.

She heard him take a long, shaky breath before he spoke. "I know it's early. I don't expect you to say anything in return."

Pia looked up quickly. Her stomach twisted, but the words to tell him how she felt wouldn't form on her tongue.

"I was telling you about my family," he said, straightening.

"Nate, I—" She swallowed. "I'm sorry. I… just need time." She had no idea how to put into words what she felt.

His smile made her heart skip a beat. "Take all the time you need. I'm not going anywhere either."

He buttered the toast and began plating up the breakfast. "My mother won't ever leave him," he said, picking up the story from where he'd left off.

Pia's mind was still reeling from the heady rush of emotion Nate had evoked in her when he'd told her—out loud—that he loved her. And here he was, showing it again with his actions. He didn't pressure her, didn't pause with weighted expectation so she'd feel guilty for not saying it back. He just let the words wrap around her like a deliciously warm blanket and continued his story. Opening up and giving her the personal details she'd asked for, something that was painful for him to share. Her heart squeezed inside her chest.

"Mum leaving would mean admitting there's a problem, and family, reputation, and status in the community are important to her. Correction: they are *everything* to her. More, it turns out, than her own flesh and blood."

Nate's eyes hardened. "Her friends, the community, that's her life. It's all she's known. I asked her once why she stays. Why she puts up with Dad and his drinking, and she just looked at me wide-eyed and said, 'How can you ask that? Wherever would I go? What would I do? My life is here, my friends are here. I'm too old to start over.'"

He shook his head. "But don't get me wrong. Mum is no pushover. She'd rather put up with my father's temper than lose a lifestyle she loves." Nate shrugged. "It's all she knows, but believe me, she can give back as good as she gets. Violence has somehow become the norm between them. At the end of the day, it's her choice, not mine. But there was no way I was going into the family business and work with that arsehole until it was time for him to hand the business down to me." He broke off, and she saw the same shadow cross his face as when he was reading the email earlier.

"But your brother did," Pia said, piecing it together.

Nate released a breath. "Yes. Ben did. But he's not handling it, or my father, well. Mum is forever on my case to come back, take over, and make things right. Ben is my little brother, and I love him, but… sometimes there are too many cracks in a glass for it to ever hold water again. You know what I mean?"

Yes, Pia knew all too well.

"And I love what I'm doing. Making a difference. Making the world a safer place, even though that sounds like the worst cliché ever. I love cars, but it was never my thing. When I was in my teens, I dreamed I could fix the family. I'd grow up, get my dad into AA, clean up the shady deals, and get the business on the straight and narrow."

"But you have a right to your own life too," Pia said softly.

"Yes. Plus, I found out the hard way you can't force someone into AA. They have to want to do it, and if they don't, they certainly don't take too kindly to being told what to do by their son."

Nate squeezed his eyes shut, as though that particular memory brought him a lot of pain.

"I learned early on that getting into a war with my father has dire consequences. For everyone, especially Mum, who often copped the brunt of it. I encouraged Ben to leave home, do something else like I had. But Mum convinced him to stay. She can be very forceful when she wants to be, and she knows Dad needs someone to keep things running. He's dropping the ball left and right. He needs help, and if it wasn't me, it had to be Ben." Nate released a long, sad breath. "Ben isn't like Mum. He isn't strong enough to handle my father when he's been drinking."

Pia's heart broke for Nate, for Ben, for the whole situation. "You feel guilty that you got out, and your brother is taking over what was expected to be your role."

"Yes." Nate's eyes glistened, and for a brief, powerful moment, Pia glimpsed the broken man beneath the strong exterior. She understood why he'd been drawn to police work. Nate was a fixer. He'd felt powerless in his adolescence. When he was old enough, he'd embarked on a career where he called the shots. Where he was in charge.

In control.

Pia reached out and grabbed his hand. "Maybe your brother is stronger than you think?"

Nate shook his head, his jaw clenched, and Pia knew it had something to do with the email he'd received. News about Ben.

Nate's computer chimed, and his eyes lit up when he looked at the message.

"Enough of that for now. I've just received an update from Zach." He seemed relieved for the change of topic.

Pia took the plates to the table, and Nate grabbed the cutlery, bringing the laptop with him.

The smell of bacon made her mouth water, and unable to wait, Pia started her breakfast while Nate scanned the document.

An update from Zach meant, *Sarah.*

Pia desperately hoped for good news. Sarah was someone's daughter. Someone had loved her. Pia knew that for sure. Her parents had likely spent their whole lives wondering what had happened to their little girl.

"I think we found her," Nate said, glancing up from his screen and meeting her eyes. Pia's heart skipped.

"You have? Tell me."

"There was a little girl from England who matches the description and the timeline you gave me in the cellar exactly."

"England?" Pia sat up in her chair. The hairs on her arm raised, a sign she recognized as resonating with the truth.

They'd found her!

Pia choked up and she fought to remain calm as Nate relayed what he knew.

"You were right about her name being Sarah. There was a girl, Sarah Bradford, who disappeared off a yacht on holiday near Cape Leeuwin with her family on 20 April 1981."

"She fell off a boat?"

"Not just any boat, it was a private yacht. She fell overboard."

"But surely, they could have retrieved her?"

Something niggled at Pia regarding that detail. She sensed Sarah had not simply fallen off the yacht, but the details were hazy. She couldn't quite see exactly what had happened that day.

"The parents didn't notice she was missing for quite a while, believing she was down in her room writing in her diary. It was her eleventh birthday."

Pia let Nate's words sink in. They'd found her! They knew who Sarah was.

Nate didn't share her excitement. His face hardened. "Christ. She was eleven. Just a child." He turned to Pia. "I swear to you, I'll catch those responsible for this."

"And cut off their balls," Pia said.

A shadow crossed his eyes as though he'd like nothing more than to do just that. He cleared his throat before he continued reading Zach's report. "Sarah's parents were distraught. Sarah was an only child, no siblings. They launched a full-scale search using every resource available, but her body was never found. The parents continued funding a search party long after the police withdrew their resources. She was missing for long enough, she was eventually presumed dead. The family spent a small fortune trying to find out what happened."

"That would explain the doll. It was handmade in her likeness. The face is delicately carved porcelain. A family heirloom perhaps."

Pia caught Nate's shudder and raised her brow questioningly.

"Heirloom or not, dolls and clowns creep me out," he said coolly.

"A lot of people feel that way," Pia said but she suspected Nate's fear was deeper than he was letting on. "Just like energy can remain in a house, as we've experienced, energy can attach itself to an object."

"That's not making it better."

"Sometimes, it may be a doll's appearance that's creepy, but often people are subliminally picking up something 'off' about it. They know it freaks them out, but can't understand why. Don't want to understand why."

"Still not making it better."

Pia smiled at seeing her stalwart detective finally shaken by something. "Sarah's energy is attached to the doll in a very powerful way, which can happen when spirits carry the more intense emotions, such as anger or revenge."

Nate smiled. "*Definitely* not making it better."

"You want me to tell you pretty lies?"

He shook his head. "Enough about that creepy doll. So Simon Farrell and his crew must have been on their way back from a cray-fishing trip. They must have seen the girl in the water, and instead of reporting her, Farrell brought her home and kept her."

"What kind of people would do such a thing? Why wouldn't they just take her to the police?" It was such an inhumane thing to do, it almost defied belief.

Nate turned the computer, and a black and white, grainy picture of Simon Farrell and his cray-fishing crew filled the screen.

Pia took the hit of seeing Sarah's abuser on the screen in front of her. Her chest tightened, and a rush of anger and disgust flooded her body. Which one of these men physically abused Sarah? One of them? All of them? Who was the "monster" Sarah was most afraid of? Pia's stomach churned, her half-eaten breakfast threatening to come back up.

Nate angled the laptop away. "So if a spirit remains because of unfinished business, the deaths of Simon Farrell, Des Wilson, and her recent revenge on Tom Kelly should mean it's over."

But it wasn't. It was inconceivable that more people were involved, and that it had remained a secret to this day, but Sarah had been adamant. There were more people to bring to justice.

"Simon's wife, Meg Farrell," Pia said. "I wonder how much she knew about what her husband and crew were up to. I can't imagine a woman allowing abuse of that magnitude to happen right under her nose. But Sarah showed me that a woman was involved."

"Not much shocks me anymore, babe," Nate said absently, and her heart skipped over his casual use of the endearment. He scanned Zach's lengthy email. "Zach is already searching for her," Nate said, eyes still on his screen. "Meg Farrell disappeared off the grid the day after Des Wilson died."

"That sounds a little suspicious. We have to find Sarah's parents too. Tell them we found their little girl." Pia's heart clenched painfully. She wished she could be contacting them with better news.

"Do you think that's a good idea?" Nate asked, briefly taking his eyes off the screen. "Perhaps they've already made their peace? How can knowing what happened to their daughter, how much she suffered, make things better?"

Which was worse? If she were Sarah's mother, would she want to know that truth? Or spend her life wondering? In Pia's mind, the truth was always the best option, even as her stomach twisted painfully at how the truth would inflict even more pain on this innocent family.

"Closure," Pia said weakly. "I think I'd want closure. I think I'd want to know." *But would I?* Dear God, what a horrific thing to have to contemplate. After all these years, perhaps they would be better just imagining her being swallowed by the ocean?

"We'll hold off officially reporting any of this for as long as we can. We still don't have Sarah's body. And Johnson already thinks you're linked to Tom Kelly's death."

"I am, but not the way he thinks."

Nate released a long sigh. "Until we know who else is involved, who the other people are, and discover where Sarah's body is buried, we'll keep this off record. Johnson will have no choice but to clear you when presented with the full story and the evidence to back it up."

Pia received a text message at the same time as Nate's doorbell rang. She checked her message while Nate went to answer the door.

A beautiful, petite, well-dressed older lady came back with Nate, and Pia set the phone to one side.

"Pia, this is my mother, Naomi Ryder. Mum, this is Pia Williams."

Naomi was short, reed thin. It was hard to imagine her giving birth to the man who towered by her side.

"Hello, Mrs. Ryder." Pia offered her hand.

"Sit down, Mum," Nate said.

But Naomi wasn't having it, and she ignored Pia's outstretched hand. Naomi tugged on his shirt. "I need to talk to you in private."

"I already know what this is about. I've just received a full report on the situation in email. I can't help."

"Nathaniel Brandon Ryder! You do not mean that." She lowered her voice to a whisper, giving Pia a sidelong glance. "Let's not discuss this in front of your *company*."

Nate appeared to go from annoyed to angry in a single second. Pia smiled reassuringly, crossed the room, placed a hand on his arm. "You should go with your mum."

His face red, his eyes narrowed dangerously, Nate took his mum into another room, and Pia gave her full attention to her phone.

I need to see you. Urgently.

The message was from Monique Reynolds. Mark had received the message on *Debunking Reality*'s primary number and forwarded Monique's message through to Pia's mobile.

Pia's stomach clenched. She tried to reach out, get a read on the situation, but she couldn't achieve the clear, open state she needed. Often it was that way. It was so much easier getting a reading for someone else because she had no emotional investment in the outcome. When reading for herself, it was nearly impossible to sort out what was real from her own inner fears, wants, and confusion.

There was only one way to find out what Monique wanted.

Where and when?

Almost a minute passed before the reply came.

The park where I saw you last. 3pm

So she had chosen a public place. Pia had to trust it wasn't a setup, that she wouldn't arrive to find herself arrested by Johnson in front of a bevy of reporters. Mark always said all publicity is good publicity, but an arrest would be walking a fine line.

After about twenty minutes, Nate and his mother walked back in. Naomi, although still distressed, appeared marginally less so, and Nate's face was set in hard, unreadable lines.

Pia kept her walls up and firmly in place.

"Have a seat, Mum," Nate said. "I'll make you coffee. I want you to meet Pia properly before you go."

Stylish black coffee mugs clanged together as he set them on the countertop a little too hard.

"I'm sorry if I seemed rude," Naomi said formally, clearly at Nate's prompting before they came back into the room. "If I forgot my manners, it was only because there was something urgent, and private, I need my son to take care of for me. *A family matter,*" she said, in a mum-trumps-lady-friend tone of voice. "You understand, don't you, Peta."

"Pia," Nate corrected her from the kitchen.

"Right. *Pia,*" Naomi said with the expression of someone trying a foreign food the first time, only to decide they didn't like the taste.

Then Naomi grabbed her phone from her purse, and her fingers flew over the screen. Dismissed. It seemed Naomi had forgotten her manners again. Although, Pia reminded herself, perhaps this wasn't typical of Naomi. Perhaps she was just consumed with whatever was troubling her.

In the kitchen, Nate jabbed at the buttons on the coffee machine, palming the side hard when nothing came out.

"It needs new coffee beans," Pia said, moving to the kitchen, remembering her earlier—and unfinished—battle with the machine. She was more than a little relieved to put some distance between herself and Nate's feisty mother. After hearing Nate talk about Naomi's situation with her husband, Pia had imagined she'd be softer.

"Go, sit with your mum," Pia said quietly.

Nate placed a warm hand on her shoulder. "Sorry about all this, babe."

"Nothing to be sorry about."

Nate's computer signaled yet another incoming email, and with a sigh, he walked over to his laptop. His eyes narrowed, and he cursed softly. He fired back a reply. "This is much worse than you know," Nate growled at his mother.

"Everything okay?" Pia called across the room, unable to shake off an increasing feeling of impending doom. Whether it applied to the situation with Nate or her own with Monique, she didn't know. Couldn't she just go back to last night on the beach with Nate, when everything seemed stable and she believed life would be normal and okay?

If Naomi weren't here, she would have told Nate about Monique's text, about arranging to meet her. But Nate looked to be deeply involved with whatever was going on with his mother, something that she guessed had to do with Ben. Her news about Monique would have to wait until later.

Pia sniffed the various bags of coffee beans she found in the fridge, chose a rich imported brand, and scooped some into the machine. She pressed what seemed like the right buttons, and it began making a loud grinding noise.

She inhaled deeply; there was nothing quite like the smell of freshly ground coffee. As the machine started bubbling and gurgling, Pia closed her eyes and tuned out Nate and his mother speaking in hushed tones at the kitchen table.

Pia cleared her mind, reaching out into the day to get a read on the situation with Monique. Was Monique planning to double-cross her? Was it a setup?

The meeting, Pia sensed, would be about Cassandra. Monique was concerned about her daughter. Pia could certainly relate.

Still in a light trance-like state, Pia placed a cup beneath the spout of the machine and reached out to Cassandra. Her image was bright and clear, her aura vivid. Not surprising given Cassy's own psychic gift. Unfortunately, Cassy was untrained. When a psychic was open and in a state of receptivity, the psychic let all energies in, good and bad. Pia had learned the necessity of focusing the hard way.

Nate and Naomi were still whispering to each other. Clearly, the purpose of Naomi's visit was something not easily resolved.

Pia reached out to Cassandra, wanting to make a brief connection. To help. To reassure her. The cocktail of emotions coming from Nate and Naomi was overwhelming. Although the kitchen area was spacious and the table at the other end of the room, Pia heard—and felt—the conversation as though she were on top of them.

"I don't accept that you can't fix this," Naomi said in a harsh whisper. She was wringing her hands beneath the table, her anxiety a pulsing red haze around her body, her heart racing so hard it was almost aflutter. She'd worked herself nearly into hysteria.

"I told you there'd come a time when I couldn't," Nate snapped, his voice low, a tangle of emotion—equal parts frustration, anger, and fear—rolling off him. "It's Ben's mess." He spoke through clenched teeth. "No doubt something that has to do with Dad. Did you ask him about it?"

"It's the *family's* mess," Naomi said. "And of course I didn't ask your father about it. Whatever this mess is, it wouldn't have happened had you not shirked your responsibilities. And don't think this won't affect you this time. Everything we all have built, everything your father spent his life building for *us*, will come crashing down. How will it affect your new job if your brother ends up with a criminal record? Or does time in prison." Her voice cracked. "God, Nate. You can't stand by and let your brother go to jail. You won't do that. If you do..." Naomi broke off, then looked at her son directly.

"Don't even think about threatening me, Mother." The tenuous grasp Nate had on his control was wavering.

Feeling light-headed, Pia gripped the cool marble counter in an attempt to defend herself against the intensity of Naomi's torment, but the thoughts slammed into her. Naomi didn't know where else to turn. Even though Nate didn't like to get involved, he always came through. Why was he being so difficult now?

"This will ruin us, Nate." Naomi dabbed at her eyes. "I can forget the hope of your dad ever getting better. You know it's the stress that makes him drink."

Nate too was in turmoil. Despite his outward frustration with the situation, he hated to see his mother cry, something Pia suspected Naomi knew and used to her advantage.

Nate reached out and covered his mother's hand with his. "Don't cry, Mum. We'll work this out."

"Find your brother, Nate," she pleaded. "You know how to do these things. Find him and make him tell us about the deal. Then stop it before it happens. He's younger than you. Not as street-smart. He's a sweet boy. He didn't mean to get into this mess, and he wouldn't have if you hadn't left."

"Damn it, Mum," Nate growled. "Enough with the guilt trip. It didn't work back then, and it won't work now."

But that wasn't quite true. Naomi knew her words would wound; that's why she chose them.

"You know your father's business acquaintances can be less than"—Naomi lowered her voice—"honest, on occasion, but whatever trouble Ben is in, he got into it by accident. He doesn't know your world like you do."

"*My* world?" Nate's hands clenched into fists at his sides.

Pia shifted her focus from Naomi to Nate. She got a rare insight, as Nate's highly charged emotional state opened him up without barriers. He took a long, deep breath and rubbed his temples. Aside from his mother's ignorance over what it was he actually did for a living, she was asking the impossible from him. Zach's emails this morning indicated that the Feds were already aware of the transaction Ben had apparently been instrumental in brokering. Ben's name was flagged on Taipan's system, automatically sending an alert to Zach whenever it popped up in any government record or online database. At this point, the Feds didn't have concrete proof against Ben; they had the word of a snitch, that was all.

Naomi wanted Nate to circumvent the delivery, stop it from happening, and extract Ben from the situation, thereby eliminating definitive proof of Ben's involvement before anyone was arrested.

"How did you hear about this, Mum?"

"Tash," Naomi said. Natasha had left him a few messages, but Nate had assumed she was ringing because she wanted to get together with him as she'd indicated at the station. He'd deleted them without listening to them.

Nate had messaged Blade as soon as he'd been notified this morning by Zach, and he knew TSI would be working double time looking for Ben and/or details of this delivery. His mum was right about one thing: the family would never recover from a scandal of this magnitude if it were to be made public.

Nate's stomach burned. Where the fuck was this deal going down? And when? How much time did he have?

When the desperation of Nate's internal questions washed over Pia, her instinct was to respond to his call. To help if she could.

An image began to form… It was dark, after midnight. The smell of motor oil and burnt rubber were strong in the air. There was a man, someone who looked similar to Nate, but younger, shorter, stocky. His brother. Ben was with a large bald man who had several visible tattoos, even more hidden beneath black leather. Club tattoos. Bikies. Organized crime. These were serious guys. Not ones you messed with. The leader was smoking, and the smell of his tobacco mingled with the pungent odor of marijuana in the air.

Ben's eyes were glassy; he was high on something, not thinking clearly. His addiction ran much deeper than anyone knew, well beyond the odd joint. Numbing himself was the only way he knew how to deal with his father's alcoholic rages.

The bonnet was open on a sleek black luxury car, one owned by the Ryder business; hidden beneath the engine was a specially manufactured compartment filled with white packages.

Nate's brother was helping a dangerous crime syndicate import drugs hidden in his family's luxury cars. Pia expanded her vision to take in the entire warehouse. There were several cars, each specially modified to hide its valuable cargo. Porsches, Ferraris, Lamborghinis. They'd done this before. A smaller shipment, marijuana, just to test.

This shipment was the real deal. Twelve cars, twelve million dollars, a million dollars' worth of high-grade cocaine in each car. The value after it was cut and hit the street would be exponential.

Where is this? Pia expanded her vision, saw the warehouse from the outside, searching for something—anything—that would give her a clue as to its location.

"Malaga," Pia said, the suburb name just coming to her. She ran with it, hoping for its accuracy. "The warehouse is... I think... in Malaga. Yes, I'm confident it's Malaga, Dyson Road. The Feds don't know where the drugs are coming from, but they know where they're going. They won't make their presence known until the goods arrive at the property near Serpentine... The drugs are being transported in luxury cars..." *When is it going to happen...?* Soon. Very soon. Pia concentrated hard on the timeframe. "The delivery will be made Thursday night, tomorrow night. Midnight."

Her concentration waned and the image faded. That was all she could see for now. Perhaps she could try again later; there might be other details she could see. *Is this enough to help Nate?* Pia opened her eyes.

And wished she could suck back every single word.

Nate was looking at her a little stunned. Naomi, however, was looking at her with cold, narrowed eyes. She stood abruptly, her chair falling backward and crashing to the floor.

"Mum—" Nate said, standing as well.

Naomi rounded on her son. "How dare you tell that... that... whatever-she-is our business," Naomi spat. "How *dare* you!"

"I'm sorry," Pia said quickly. She looked at Nate in apology, but he was too busy glaring at his mother to notice.

Now that she was fully back and present in the room, Pia felt sick.

What have I done?

She didn't need to be psychic to know she'd made a huge mistake.

"Oh God." Naomi's raised voice went up an octave. Already on the edge, she was perilously close to full-blown hysteria. "It's over," she wailed. "We're all ruined, and your brother is going to jail!"

"Mum!" Nate's voice whipped through the air. "Calm down."

"I'm sorry, Mrs. Ryder," Pia said, walking toward them. She'd caused this trouble, and she was determined to fix it. "I won't say anything to anyone, I promise. I'm only trying to help."

"Shut up!" Naomi screamed.

"Mother, you need to calm down."

"Don't order me around," Naomi shouted at Nate.

"Your son didn't tell me anything," Pia said urgently. "I—"

"Shut *up!*" Naomi moved forward, shoving Pia out the way as she stomped to the door.

Nate immediately caught Pia around the waist, steadying her, as he shook his head over his mother's dramatic exit.

"God, Pia, I'm so sorry. She can be such a bitch."

Pia gently pulled herself out of Nate's hold. "Don't worry about me, I'm fine. Go to her." She tried—unsuccessfully—to settle her stomach. "She shouldn't drive in her condition. She's too upset." Adam had driven off in a similar state and would spend the rest of his life in a wheelchair because of one of Pia's visions. Because she'd known something it was not her business to know. That wasn't going to happen to Nate's mother.

"No," Nate said. "Not after the way she spoke to you. Her behavior is inexcusable." But Nate's eyes, creased heavily in concern, flicked to the empty doorway.

"Anger makes you say things you later regret. I'm not mad. She's your mother, Nate. Take care of her."

Nate released a long breath and kissed Pia briefly on the lips. "Stay here. I'll be back as soon as I've taken her home. I'll speak to Dad; he can take her from there."

An engine revved in the driveway, and Nate sprinted through the door. A heated exchange followed as Nate replaced his mother as driver, then they left.

The warmth of Nate's kiss faded, and Pia touched her fingers to the spot. Slightly dazed, she dialed a taxi with shaking fingers.

In the silence, she tried not to think about where this left her relationship with Nate. Nate's mother had come as quite a surprise, her immediate dislike of Pia seemingly unjustified, even before Pia's psychic blunder.

To hell with it. Her abilities had already caused enough trouble today, they might as well cause some more. Once again, Pia bypassed her moral code and reached outward one last time, wanting to know what Naomi's instant dislike of Pia stemmed from.

Tash! The female detective Nate had run into at the station. Though they'd obviously shared a romantic history, Nate had brushed Tash aside. At least that's how it seemed.

Could she be wrong?

No. Nate had made his intentions toward Pia very clear. He'd even told her he loved her.

And she believed him.

It was Naomi who wanted Nate and Tash to be together for some reason. And that was the reason for Naomi's unexpected hostility toward Pia. In addition, there was the very likely possibility that Pia hadn't fit Naomi's expectations of what Nate's girlfriend should look like. Tall, blonde, refined…

But Tash did.

Well, too damn bad. Pia was who she was. And Nate seemed to like her just fine.

But… Nate might believe now that he could handle having a psychic medium as a girlfriend, but did he know, truly, what it would be like? Nothing about Pia was easy.

Tash, however, was easy. She was stunning, a detective who knew and understood

Nate's unconventional hours and lifestyle. And Tash already had the approval of his mother.

Pia heard the taxi and walked to the door, trying not to worry about just how much influence Naomi really had over her son.

Despite the abusive relationship between Naomi and her husband, that woman was no pushover. What if she told Nate outright that she wouldn't accept Pia? What would Nate do then? His family had heaped on the guilt. How broad was Nate's back? Where was his breaking point?

She closed the door to Nate's house behind her, a thousand razor blades slicing through her insides.

Could their relationship stand a chance when the odds continued to stack against them?

And now that she'd fallen so hard for Nate, how would she survive if it didn't?

Chapter Twenty-Four

Speed was not enough to calm Nate this time. He was pissed. He couldn't remember ever being as angry with anyone as he was with his mother right now. His grip on the steering wheel made his knuckles white. He clenched and released his fingers as he navigated corners and backstreets by memory.

His mother sat rigid in the seat beside him, not concerned in the least by how fast her son was driving. Racing was in her blood too. She was still tearing him to shreds over his perceived betrayal of family secrets. Her words were a jumbled mess of word vomit, and she didn't seem to care whether she made any sense. Nate silently allowed her words to wash over him as she emptied herself out.

Finally, she stopped. She sobbed for a moment, then glared at Nate. "Well? Say something!"

"Your treatment of Pia back there was beyond disgraceful." Nate's tone was low, even. Lethally calm. He had never been so furious with his mother as he was right now.

"*That's* what you've got to say? Is that *woman* all you care about?" She shifted in her seat, angling her body toward him. Clearly, there was still fight left in her.

"I do care about her. A great deal."

"Is that why you told her about your brother?" Her tone was scathing. "You fancy yourself in love or something, do you? How long have you known her? Two minutes? It took two *whole* minutes for you to forget about Tash? Peta must be a good lay."

Nate slammed on the brakes, the car skidding to a stop on the side of the road. Sweat beaded on his forehead, and a vein throbbed painfully at his temple.

"Get out."

"What?" Naomi looked stunned.

"I swear, if you speak about Pia like that again, I will walk out of your life, and you will never see me again." He took a breath. "You, Dad, the family business can all go to hell. You can sort your own shit out. I'm done."

His mother burst into tears. "I didn't mean anything by what I said. I'm upset and not thinking straight. This trouble with Ben is wrecking my nerves." She sniffed. "I'm so frightened."

"I didn't hear an apology anywhere in there."

Naomi pulled a tissue out of her bag and blew her nose. "You know I'm sorry."

"No, Mother. I don't," Nate bit out. "I suppose that's as much of an apology as you have it in you to give though."

"I am sorry," Naomi repeated, dabbing at her eyes.

Nate took a deep breath, tamped down his frustration, and pulled back onto the road. As much as he detested his mother right now, all he wanted was to deliver her safely home and hurry back to Pia.

"You'll apologize to Pia. And it will be genuine, and it better be a hell of a lot more sincere than the one you just gave me."

"I will, and I'm sorry I was rude to your lady friend."

"Pia."

"I'm sorry I was rude to Pia. I'll apologize properly, if I see her again."

"Fucking hell, Mum! I love her. And if you haven't just ruined it for me, you can get used to her being the most important part of my life."

"Don't swear around your mother. It's not polite."

"It's not—?" Oh, for fuck's sake! *How the hell can this woman be my mother?*

"Okay, so you fancy yourself in love her, but even that doesn't give you the right to tell her family business."

"What do you think I told her, Mum?" Nate barely reined in his impatience.

"You told her… um… you told her—" She broke off, brow wrinkling.

"That's right, Mum. How could I tell her something I didn't know myself?"

"How did she know about our warehouse in Malaga?" Naomi said, wringing her hands. The property Pia had described was his father's warehouse. For Ben to so blatantly and stupidly involve the family in that way made him sick to the stomach. "And how did she know that drugs were being imported in *our delivery* of cars?"

"*Finally*," Nate said.

Naomi frowned and bit her lip. "Who is she, a Fed? I'm not trying to be rude here, so don't lose your temper again. My heart can't take it. But you have to agree she doesn't look like a cop in that getup. Is she undercover or something?"

Nate eyed the side of the road again. "She's not a Fed," he ground out. "Anything the Feds know, Zach knows. I've already had Zach's report." The Feds knew the handover would take place at midnight in Serpentine, but they didn't know the departure point—thank God—or that the coke was hidden in the shipment of imported cars.

The Feds had logically concluded the drugs were being transported directly from the Fremantle wharf, and had arranged for the place to be swarming with undercover detectives searching for evidence to put away as many of Wilson's men as they could.

But if Pia was right, and he didn't doubt her, it meant the shipment was coming in earlier, perhaps even tonight, and held at Malaga. Was that to ensure the Feds couldn't track the drugs from the wharf to their delivery point? Or perhaps someone wanted to check the quality and quantity of goods before the handover? Mistakes, even unintentional ones, could cost you your life.

"Then how did she know?"

"Pia is a gifted psychic."

His mum opened her mouth, closed it again. She made a dismissive noise, then folded her arms across her chest.

"Now it's my turn to ask you. How did she know about our warehouse? That drugs were being imported in a shipment of our cars? *When I didn't.*" Nate of course, could ask his father for details of the incoming shipment of cars into Fremantle, but he wouldn't. He could also get Zach to check. But it didn't help their cause, and could only risk drawing the Feds attention and flagging the shipment. All that mattered was the transfer between Malaga and Serpentine, because that's where he'd extract Ben.

"Well, then, we can't believe a word she said. Psychics are just charlatans in cloaks behind curtains with crystal balls."

"Are they, Mum? You sure about that? And be careful how you answer, because I told you what would happen if you insulted her one more time."

"I… well." She frowned and fidgeted in her seat.

Nate was not interested in trying to convince his mother of anything she chose not to believe. He had neither the time, nor the energy.

"I've never known a psychic before," she said eventually. "You're telling me she's the real deal?"

"She's the real deal," Nate said solemnly.

His mother twisted in her seat to look at him. "You really believe that, don't you?"

"I *know* it, Mum."

She released a breath. "I know there's very few who could have you fooled. If you say she's a psychic, then she's psychic. You wouldn't believe something without a slew of evidence and proof. You've seen proof, right?"

"I've seen proof." Firsthand, last September. Enough to remove any doubt from his mind.

She sat up in her seat. "This information she gave you, do you think it's accurate? Is it enough to help Ben? To keep our family out of this?"

"You had better hope so."

"Then do whatever needs to be done. Whatever it takes. If you need money—"

"I don't need your damn money," Nate snapped. "*Jesus!*" Did she walk around with her eyes closed? His mother was so far removed from understanding where he was in life she might as well be on another planet.

What Nate needed was for his goddamn brother to stay on the straight and narrow for more than five minutes. Ben loved motorsports, but he loved the celebrity life that came with them more. Living beyond his means, Ben had always supplemented his racing winnings with gambling and flirting with a quick buck on the wrong side of the law. But he'd never done anything nearly as stupid as getting mixed up with running drugs for a crime syndicate. What the hell was he thinking? How had he even met people like that?

They finally reached the house. Nate slipped the car into neutral and left the engine running. He needed to get back to Pia. If his luck held, she hadn't run a mile at the thought of Naomi as a future mother-in-law.

He turned to his mum. "I'm going to do this, with Pia's help, but this is the last time. You've punished me enough for not taking over the family business. That has to stop. I won't spend my life being saddled with your guilt trips. Next time Ben gets himself into shit, he gets himself out of it. Or goes to jail. Whichever comes first. Family reputation or not, I'm done."

"You don't mean that," she said, opening the door.

"Try me."

"He's your brother, Nate. Remember that. We're family."

"And why should *I* be the only one to remember that?" he demanded through clenched teeth. "Did Ben think of family when he put you through this today? Will he be thinking of family when I meet a drug cartel in the dead of night, stopping the shipment before it reaches a warehouse where a task force of federal police will be waiting? Tell me, Mum, what will Ben be thinking when I risk my life and those of my team during what is sure to be an armed confrontation?"

"You chose your career. That sort of stuff comes naturally to you. Ben doesn't know about guns and bad people. He races cars."

"Ben clearly knows about guns and bad people, mother. That's how he got himself into this mess."

"Watch the way you speak to your mother. Show me some respect."

"Respect is something you earn, not demand. And right now, I can't summon an ounce of it. You use me when it suits you. You think it's okay to call me to sort out your mess without ever considering the cost to me. Never once have you asked me what I want. You decided that I would take over the business, and then you punished me for making a different choice. And you might not realize it yet, but you're doing the same thing to Ben. You're screwing him up with your manipulation and guilt trips. Dad's business is his life choice; if he pisses it down the toilet because he won't go to AA, that's his problem. Ben and I get to make our own choices. They're our lives to lead, not yours."

"Don't be so harsh," she said, reaching for another tissue. "My doctor says I can't be stressed."

Nate squeezed his eyes shut and seethed. She never let up. Always had another avenue to lay on the guilt. He might be going to hell for it, but sometimes he loathed his mother. "Get out of the car, Mum." He needed to get back to Pia. For his own sanity.

All he wanted to do now was wrap his arms around Pia and never let go. To breathe her in, so he'd feel the sense of peace he only felt with her. A sense of belonging he hadn't even realized had been missing in his life until he'd met her.

Damn Ben for putting him in this position, for diverting his attention away from helping Pia with Sarah.

If it were only Ben involved, Nate would have told him to suck it up. You take the risk, you pay the price. But something niggled at him. It wasn't just how Ben had ended up in this mess, but why? His brother was clearly an idiot, but he wasn't a criminal. Something had driven him to this. But what? Surely it wasn't just for money?

He needed to speak to Ben. If he found him before tomorrow night, they could avoid the confrontation entirely.

Nate clenched the steering wheel. He'd do what he could to stop the shipment before it reached the warehouse. But he'd need to scramble every available resource he had access to.

"You're a good son, Nate," his mother said through the passenger-side window. "I know you'll fix this. You always do."

Nate didn't reply as his mother walked inside. He pulled out of the driveway and didn't look back.

———————◆———————

Rain beat heavily on his windscreen as Nate dialed Blade through the car's Bluetooth.

"Blade, how are things back at base?"

"Good, really good."

Nate heard the smile in Blade's voice and was happy for his partner. His best friend. Of anyone he knew, Blade deserved a break in life, and it seemed he'd found it in Sage. Nate ignored a small stab of envy.

"How can I help?" Blade asked.

"If Sam's not needed elsewhere, can I keep him here? I want to keep Smithy too if he's free," Nate said, referring to Daniel.

"Do you need anyone else?" And that right there, was the best thing about Blade. Blade knew Nate's help with Pia was off the books, meaning she wasn't a paid client, but he didn't hesitate allocating company resources to help.

Over the years, Nate had gone through a living hell with his unit Taipan; the training alone had damn near broken them all. He'd seen a lot of horrible things, learned just how depraved a human being could get. But every step of that walk through hell was worth it when you forged the bonds he had with Taipan, but especially those with Blade, his partner.

"No. I only need them for tomorrow night," Nate continued. "That 1969 Ferrari convertible Sam and I lifted Sunday, is it back with the client yet?"

"Looking at it right now."

"Are you able to check something for me?"

"Name it."

"Under the engine cavity, can you see a modification? If it's there, you'll barely notice. It'd be very well done."

There was a moment of silence before Nate heard banging and hammering. After a minute or two, he heard the sound of steel on steel, confirming his fears. He'd suspected who this crime syndicate was, but Blade was about to confirm it. Nate unclenched his hands, but the sinking dread remained. *Jesus Christ, Benny. Do you have any idea who these people are?*

Nate heard Blade's low whistle before he picked the phone back up. "Son of a bitch. That's some pretty fucking high-grade cocaine under there."

Nate wanted to punch something. No, someone. *Ben, how could you be so bloody stupid?*

"What's going on, Ryder?"

"My fucking brother."

"I read Zach's report. Any connection between this and what you need Smithy and Wells for?"

"I see you've already done the math."

"Talk to me."

Nate's hands tightened on the steering wheel. "You've seen Zach's report. The Feds know when and where the delivery of cocaine will take place, but they don't know where it originates or how it's being transported. I do, and Ben's going to be traveling with it."

"Who's your source?"

"Pia."

"She's sure?"

"As sure as she can be, and that's good enough for me. The delivery is scheduled to take place in Serpentine at midnight. I need to extract Ben and the cars before that shipment reaches its destination. But..." Nate inhaled, then exhaled deeply. "Considering that the Feds are involved, it might be best if TSI stayed out of this one."

"We'll deal," Blade said, but his tone was grim. "That car we repoed full of cocaine was meant to be part of the delivery, wasn't it?"

Leaving one hand on the steering wheel, Nate rubbed his neck. "That would be a safe bet."

"Like it or not, we're already involved. If this bust goes down tomorrow night, the Feds will trace the Ferrari to our door. We already have questions to answer. You said Pia told you where they're holding the shipment before delivery."

"Yes. A warehouse on Dyson Road in Malaga."

"Your father has his warehouse there, right?" Blade didn't need to ask that. He already knew; his clipped tone confirmed it.

Nate rubbed his temples. "I'd hedge my bets that's where Ben joins the transfer, but it's too risky for us to try to remove him from there."

"You want to minimize any connection with Ben or your father if things turn sour. What's the plan?" Blade asked.

"Intercept the transport carrier en route, and remove Ben and the cars before the cops can make the bust in Serpentine."

Ben might avoid having to deal with the cops, but he might believe the police preferable after Nate was finished with him. Ben could look forward to a serious come-to-Jesus moment with Nate when this was over.

"Risk assessment?" Blade asked.

"I believe Daniel, Sam, and I can handle the guys on the transport carrier and any backup. There'd be two at most in the truck, probably a car of up to four following."

"Six to three odds at the confrontation point. What were you planning to do, negotiate Ben's release?"

"That's the plan. We tip Wilson's men off about the Feds waiting to bust them at the warehouse; in exchange, they keep the cocaine and let Ben go with no retaliation."

"Wilson gets to keep the drugs and his men avoid arrest, but he misses out on making the sale," Blade said. "Wilson won't be happy, but he'll be glad not to get busted. The Feds though will be sore about missing out on the bust. They absolutely can't know we were involved."

The last thing TSI wanted was to appear a vigilante group working against the force. Until very recently, Taipan had been the elite of the police force, and it would be beneficial to maintain that respect.

"I know. Maybe—"

Blade cut him off. "There are too many unknowns, and I don't like the odds with only three of you. You'll need the whole team. We'll mobilize your way immediately. Plus," Blade said. "This is your family. If it affects you, it affects all of us."

Nate took a moment, made sure his voice was even. "Thanks mate. But I absolutely understand if you don't want TSI involved. This will have long-term ramifications. If this goes sideways, we'll be making serious enemies out of this." Wild Wilson *and* the Feds.

"I'll pretend I didn't hear that."

"But this—"

"Ryder!" Blade was pissed. "Watch your back. I'll start the wheels turning." He ended the call.

Nate's fists clenched. Damn his brother to hell for putting him and his team in this position. The op was risky, even if it all went according to plan. There was no guarantee this wasn't all going to hell, and Nate would be carrying the handbasket.

He stretched the power of the car, let the engine have its head.

When he arrived at home and opened the door, he tossed his keys in the bowl, but knew the house was empty before even calling out for Pia.

His day had gone from bad to worse.

Pia had left.

Where had she gone? Had she decided after meeting his mother that he was too much trouble?

Nate typed out a quick message to Zach.

What was the good of having access to information if you couldn't use it when it was important? He'd have Pia's location in a matter of minutes. He grabbed his keys.

He already knew without a doubt that Pia was worth the fight.

Now he just had to convince her he was too.

Chapter Twenty-Five

"Thank you for meeting us, Pia." Monique clutched her bag tightly with one arm while twisting the large cross around her neck. Dark shadows ringed her eyes, and she had the nervous energy of someone going through a trauma. Despite everything, Pia's heart went out to the woman. To the mother whose family meant more to her than taking her next breath.

At a secluded beach, Pia sat with Monique and Cassandra on a large rock, weathered smooth over millions of years by the pounding waves of the Indian Ocean. A little way up the coastline, the Cape Leeuwin Lighthouse stood proud and solid as it looked out over the vast blue ocean.

At the last minute, Pia had changed the meeting point from Riverside Park, which Monique had suggested, to Cape Leeuwin. She hadn't been able to read whether Monique was setting her up to find Johnson waiting for her with cuffs. Pia had sensed there was something Nate wasn't telling her. Something making him even more protective than usual. But after what had happened earlier in the day with Nate and his mother, Pia's emotions were in turmoil. She couldn't trust her intuition when her emotional state was so unsettled. Best to err on the side of caution.

So Pia fell back on the standard self-preservation techniques anyone would use. The place she had chosen had a perfect view of anyone coming. Pia had her escape route mapped out. If Johnson or the cops showed up, she could duck through the bushes behind her and be in her car before they got near. She was not going to allow herself to be arrested. Or brought in for "questioning." They could word it any way they wanted; she wasn't going anywhere with them. Once she was in the station, she'd be behind bars in an eyeblink and lose any hope she had of solving this situation.

"I'm sorry about the restraining order," Monique said.

Pia raised her brows, unable to hide her surprise. "You issued a restraining order against me?" Was this what Nate hadn't told her? Of course he would have known. The betrayal stung. "Why would you do that?" Pia spoke more harshly than she'd intended, her anger for Nate, not Monique. "I'm not a threat to your daughter. I talked to Cassandra at the playground. *Once!*"

Cassandra sat by Monique's side, Sarah's doll beneath her arm, and looked disapprovingly at her mum. For such a young girl, she seemed far older than her tender years.

"I'll call Detective Johnson and get it revoked, I promise," Monique said. "You have to understand, this whole situation has been terribly upsetting for me, my family. You have no idea what a shock it is to learn that a man was murdered in your house. We were not allowed to come back to our own home."

Monique glanced at her daughter, then rubbed her hands up and down as though she were cold, even though the afternoon breeze was warm.

"I was scared," Monique said. "I believed the cops when they said you and your team were responsible. And you have to admit, that's the only thing that was logical. Their explanation was the only one that made sense." Her eyes begged Pia for absolution. "You were the only ones there."

We were the only physical *beings there.*

Pia glanced out over the ocean. How sad was it that in this day and age, people would still prefer to believe decent people like her, Mark, Ryan, and Joe, people who had never hurt anyone in their lives, were capable of murder than to believe something paranormal had occurred. No wonder Mark was hell-bent on providing irrefutable proof that entities other than physical human beings existed.

"I want to apologize to you," Monique went on, "for everything. The television interview. The things we said. What we told the police. Everything," she repeated weakly. "But... I, we... Cassandra needs your help," Monique said, her voice breaking slightly. She glanced nervously at her daughter.

"What makes you believe me now? What changed?"

"The same things are happening at the new house that happened at the cottage. I... don't know where else to turn."

Pia looked past Monique's shoulder to where Cassy sat. She'd managed to wiggle a little distance away, as kids had the tendency to do, and was piling up damp sand in the beginnings of a sand castle. Dark, heavy circles ringed her eyes, and her shoulders were slumping forward. Cassandra, just like her mother, carried the look of someone living a nightmare.

How are you? Pia asked silently, and Cassandra turned sad eyes in her direction, the only acknowledgement of the wordless communication.

"I see you have the doll again," Pia said, out loud this time. "Does she have a name?"

That got a reaction. Cassy stopped piling up sand, and looked directly at her. "Angel. You know that."

"Why would Pia know that?" Monique asked a little too sharply. She was on that slippery slope toward her breaking point.

Cassandra said nothing, just continued working on the castle.

"Don't be rude," Monique said, softer this time. "Pia doesn't know everything."

Monique turned to Pia. "You *don't* know everything, do you?"

Pia gave her a wry smile and shook her head. "Not even close." Sometimes she felt worlds apart from other people. "I forgot that Cassandra told me the doll's name in the playground." To Cassy, she said, "You must like that doll a lot to take it everywhere you go."

"She's far too old to be carrying a doll around with her," Monique scoffed. "Even a fancy one like that."

She didn't answer her mother back, but Cassandra's glare at Monique sent a chill down Pia's spine, the hairs on the back of her neck rising. Monique briefly shivered, a subconscious reaction, even though she hadn't seen the look her daughter had given her.

This was not good. Just how much control did Sarah already have over Cassy? Cassandra seemed withdrawn, and there was a sad, haunted look in her eyes that hadn't been there when Pia had seen her just a few days ago.

"Cassandra is making quite a fuss about wanting to go back to the house." Monique fingered the cross around her neck. "Of course we told her no and the reasons why that isn't possible." Monique visibly swallowed and lowered her voice to a whisper, oblivious to the fact that her daughter would likely "hear" her anyway. "Her reactions are... not typical. It's not like Cassy to behave in... *that way*."

"Do you want to go back home, Cassandra?" Pia looked out at the ocean, doing her best to appear nonchalant, schooling her emotions so that Cassandra was less likely to notice the way Pia's heart was pounding in her chest. "Why would you want to go back to that house after what happened there?"

"Tell her," Monique ordered her daughter. "Tell Pia what you told us."

A cold wind washed over them, and Sarah became visible a few feet behind Cassandra, as though she'd been there all along and only now chose to be seen. The hem of her white dress glided an inch off the rocks, her long hair wisping across her pale face with its round haunted eyes.

"Look at someone when they're talking to you," Monique said, mistaking Cassy's distraction with the entity as poor manners. However, despite not seeing Sarah, Monique had altered her sitting position, bringing her knees to her chest and wrapping her arms around her legs, an instinctive response to the entity nearby. That was something Pia often saw. People picked up a "bad vibe" but didn't know why.

Like Pia though, Cassy was aware, glancing in Sarah's direction as she moved restlessly before them. Cassy had learned to keep her ability to see Sarah private. Clearly because no one believed her, and Pia's heart reached out to the little girl.

"Sarah wants us to go back to the house," Cassy said obediently, her little voice sad. Defeated. This was a conversation, an argument, the family had had more than once before.

"What do *you* want?" Pia asked.

"I—"Cassy flicked her gaze to Sarah. "I want what Sarah wants."

Monique began to wring her hands. "Tell her, please, that this Sarah doesn't exist. She won't listen to me or her father. This nonsense has gone on too long. It's got to stop. It's... it's scaring her sister," Monique said, eyes shining brightly. "It's scaring all of us."

Cassandra's eyes narrowed, and her lips pressed into a firm line. *Cassy,* Pia said silently, repeating her name a few times before the girl finally looked up. Pia met Cassy's gaze, struggled for the right words. *You have to trust me. I'm here to help. I will help you.*

Cassy's eyes instantly welled, a tear rolling down one cheek.

Pia would need to be careful how she explained the situation to Monique. "Can I speak to you alone for a bit?"

"Why don't you go play by the beach for a while, honey? I'll watch you from here."

Appearing relieved, Cassy, clutching her doll under her arms, ran to the shore and kicked off her shoes.

"I don't like that thing," Monique said. "But she throws such a tantrum when we make her leave it behind. Sometimes it's just easier to not have the fight, you know? Our family has been through so much already. Chad is more of the disciplinarian, forces her into line, but sometimes I think she's almost... *frightened* to leave it." Monique laughed nervously and glanced at Pia out of the corner of her eye. "I know that sounds crazy."

"Crazy and I are old friends," Pia said lightly.

Monique flushed a deep red. "It's so lifelike. Sometimes I feel as though its eyes are following me around the room." Monique laughed weakly. "I know how that sounds. It's just a doll, right? I feel like I'm losing my mind, but I have to hold it together. I have a family who needs me. Chad's not coping with any of this very well. He's angry—" Monique broke off. "We're all very stressed, that's the problem. We need to put this behind us."

Pia watched Cassy play in the water, her bare feet splashing in the shallow waves.

"What else is going on, Monique?"

Monique wiped sand off her white cut-off jeans, her hands shaking.

"It hasn't stopped."

"The same activity you were experiencing in the cottage?"

"Yes. We moved into the granny flat at my sister's house. It's brand-new; she had it built for our mother so she doesn't have to go into a nursing home when the time comes. We knew the cottage had a reputation for being haunted, but Chad doesn't believe in ghosts."

He does now, Pia thought but didn't say.

"We didn't care about supposed ghost stories, and the price was well below market value. We could afford it and have enough left over to do renovations. We were going to turn it into our dream home," Monique said sadly. "So when we started to hear noises, we laughed it off. Well, Chad did. He had an explanation for everything. Possums, wind, hot-water service... It was a joke to him. He'd put on a mocking voice and say 'woo ooo, watch out, it's the ghost.'"

Monique shook her head sadly. "And then it wasn't funny anymore. The footsteps in the attic at night—they weren't a possum or the wind. They were human. And so was the crying that seemed to be coming from the walls themselves. And then there was the music box that played without batteries. The lights that turn on by themselves and wouldn't shut off, even though they weren't plugged in. Chad couldn't explain those away.

"When I suggested we should call you, Chad finally agreed. I think he thought we could call you in and you'd make it go away. Like an exterminator."

Pia understood. So many people called *Debunking Reality*, believing the team could come in, wave a wand, sprinkle some magic dust, and make whatever it was in the house leave. If only it were that easy.

Some things didn't want to leave.

"What are you experiencing where you are now?"

"Electrical equipment seems to have a mind of its own. This morning, the vacuum cleaner started up by itself as I walked past. It took me a full ten minutes before I could work up the courage to get close enough to turn it off. Yesterday morning, I woke up to find every cupboard door in the kitchen open. I closed them all, went to help Becky get dressed, and when I came back in, they were all open again. But the worst part is the unexplained sadness. I know our situation is distressing, but this is different. There's a heavy feeling, a sinking grief, as though you've been told someone has died. The emotions that come over you don't match what's going on around you. It's frightening. It makes you feel as though you don't have control over yourself."

Because Monique was subconsciously reacting to what her eyes couldn't see. For the first time in her life, Pia actually felt grateful for her abilities. It would be the worst type of torture to live in the confusion that Monique was in. At least Pia knew what was happening.

Monique placed a hand over her heart. "It happens only when Cassy is in the house. When she's at school or at her grandmother's, the house feels"—she waved her hands, searching for the right word—"sunnier somehow." She choked. "I know that's a terrible thing to say about my daughter. I love Cassandra, you must know that. It's just that when she's around, things are… they're starting to scare me. The way she talks to that imaginary friend of hers. The way she's started looking at me, as though she would like to… hurt me, or something?" Monique's eyes welled, and she choked back a sob. "What kind of a horrible mother am I to say something like that about my baby?" Monique put her head in her hands, her body trembling. "She's a little girl. *My* little girl. It's just that sometimes it doesn't seem to be *her* looking at me."

Pia placed a hand on her back and gave her a comforting rub. "You aren't a bad mother. The simple fact you're questioning that makes you a good mother. I know you love your daughter, your family, but you are all experiencing something out of the normal, something *paranormal*, and you're struggling to make sense of it all. It's only natural to not know how to deal with this."

Welcome to my life.

"Can you help her?" Monique sat up, the hope in her eyes heartbreaking. "She likes you. She'll listen to you. Can you get my baby back?"

Pia twisted her tourmaline pendant while she watched Cassandra walk along the shoreline. As much as she wished differently, Pia couldn't promise anything. How could she? Especially as Monique needed to know and understand about Cassandra's psychic abilities. The little girl Monique thought she had was gone. And Pia was going to be the one to break Monique's heart. Cassandra was a beautiful, sensitive little soul, but she wasn't like the other children. If she didn't get support from her loved ones, her life was going to be unnecessarily hard. Pia knew that firsthand.

"Mrs. Reynolds," Pia began, looking through Sarah's energy form to the ocean behind. "Sarah is very real in Cassandra's mind—"

"Yes," Monique interrupted. "I should deal with that, I know. This imaginary friend thing is getting out of hand. I just thought if life went back to how it was before we moved here, it would go away."

"Monique," Pia said, making her voice firm. "I've seen Sarah myself. I saw her at your house on the night we did the investigation."

"What? What does that mean?"

Pia desperately wished she didn't have to tell Monique any of this. But she needed her help for what she was about to do.

"I believe Sarah was responsible for the things going on in the cottage, and she's followed you to your new place."

"Oh dear God," Monique said, making the sign of the cross over her heart. "Are you trying to say that Sarah is real? That she is a…? What?" she stammered. "A ghost? My daughter is seeing a *ghost*?"

Sarah turned her unseeing gaze in their direction, and Cassandra stilled, her little body beginning to rock in place.

"It's quite common for children to see what adults can't. Sarah is real. Or rather, she was real. Something bad happened to the girl in her human form, and now her spirit isn't able to rest."

A cloud crossed the sun, casting them in shadow. The temperature dropped several degrees, and Sarah moved to the edge of the ocean and stared out at the water. A heavy sadness came over Pia. Sarah had been lost at sea, and she'd never seen her parents again. She deserved closure. To finally allow her soul to rest.

There was so much more to be said, but Pia was being careful to give Monique only what she needed to absorb for now. Enough, she hoped, to garner her trust without scaring her away.

"Your daughter is a very special girl," Pia said.

"I know," Monique said quickly. "I didn't mean to make her sound bad. I'm just confused. I don't understand—"

"It's okay. I know you love your daughter. You have to understand though. Cassandra is *special*." Pia let the word sink in.

"What do you mean?" The color drained from Monique's face.

"Cassandra can't just see Sarah; she can see and hear other things. Your daughter has special abilities, in a similar way that I do."

"What does that mean?"

"When Cassandra talks to you, tells you things she sees and hears, you should listen to her. Don't dismiss what she's saying."

Monique was struggling, thoughts fluttering through her mind, batting at Pia like mindless birds—*this is not a good idea, whatever was I thinking, how could this be happening, don't listen to her, she's crazy*—flitting around and around.

Pia rested a calming hand on her arm. "It's going to be all right." She hoped that was true.

"Is Cassy causing this? Did she invite this into our lives?"

"No. Cassy has done nothing at all wrong. She is *not* responsible for any of this," Pia said firmly. "It's important you understand that. Sarah was already in the house. You knew the house was haunted before you bought it. Cassy didn't call Sarah; if anything, Sarah is more attracted to Cassandra because of her abilities. It's not her fault. It's simply the way she is." The last thing Cassy needed was to blame herself for her family's problems the way kids tended to do.

"Cassy is still the same little girl, but now you know something extra about her. Something that adds to her. Something that makes her even more special."

"Chad is never going to accept this."

"Then you're going to have to help him." Pia's temper flared. "You're going to have to stand up to him on Cassy's behalf. Your daughter is open, sensitive, and how you handle this will affect how she feels about herself as she goes through life. I know this all too well."

"Can you help me to help her? Us?"

"Yes. But right now, I need to deal with Sarah. Help her… move on. I believe the connection is the doll."

Speaking rapidly, Pia continued. "Sarah has ties to the cottage; I'm still working on that part. But I think she was able to follow you to the new house because of the doll. Usually entities remain tied to a location, but you said things only happen when Cassandra is around. Cassy always has the doll."

"You're right," Monique said slowly, nodding. "Dear God, you're right."

"I want to take the doll from Cassandra today. I'm hoping at the least, it will stop or at least lessen the disruptions in your house. But I'll need your help. Cassy won't want to let it go easily." *Sarah won't let her.*

"Cassy, honey?" Monique called her daughter over.

"How did you find the doll?" Pia asked gently when Cassandra sat back down beside her mother.

"Sarah showed me."

"Was it outside the house?"

"Yes."

"Did you have to walk near the shed and go under the ground?" Pia put her hand on Monique's arm to keep her from reacting. "Did you find the doll in the cellar?"

"Yes," Cassy said, with a glance at her mother.

"It's all right. You won't get into trouble." Pia reached out. "Can you pass me the doll?"

When Cassandra hesitated, Pia tried to gently tug the doll from her arms. "I'm going to look after her for you tonight."

Sarah was now standing right in front of them, her anger an icy blast. Monique rubbed at the gooseflesh on her arms, unable to see the menacing presence glowering at them. But she sensed it. She shivered and hugged her cardigan tighter around her.

"No!" Cassy said, hugging the doll tight. "My doll."

"But she's *not* your doll, sweetheart," Pia reminded her. "She belongs to Sarah. I'm going to help Sarah now."

Cassandra held Pia's eyes.

Sarah moved closer to Pia, and a heavy, swirling sensation of nausea settled in the pit of her stomach.

No, Pia told Sarah forcefully. *Don't do that to me. I can help you now, remember. I know who you are. You are Sarah Bradford, and I know you disappeared from your family's yacht. I know what they did to you, and I'm able to help you get justice. I'll help you find the others involved. I'll help you see this through to the end.*

Surprisingly, Sarah still resisted.

Give me the doll, Sarah. That is non-negotiable. You will *leave Cassy alone. She's a child. Cassy can't help you get revenge on the ones who hurt you. I can.*

Why did Sarah still want Cassandra to have the doll? After Pia agreed to help, Sarah should be willing to leave Cassy alone.

"She wants the life she never lived," Cassy said, aware of their silent conversation.

Oh dear God! Pia hadn't even considered that angle. She remembered what Monique had said about different eyes looking out through her daughter.

"She can't, sweetheart," Pia said.

She is not allowed to do that, Pia said to Cassandra telepathically, with a forceful glance in Sarah's direction. *Your life is yours, Cassy. Sarah cannot live through you. No matter how sorry for her she makes you feel, you mustn't allow that to happen. That's called possession, and that is bad. Really, really bad.*

"What can I do?" Cassandra asked, wide-eyed and concerned for the first time. Good. Cassy should fear Sarah. Despite the fact Sarah had once been alive, she was now a non-physical entity, and her relationship with Cassy was extremely dangerous.

"You don't have to do anything, sweetheart," Pia said. "I will. I'm going to help Sarah cross over to the light, where she will finally be at peace."

"Oh God," Monique said. "You two are talking like this thing's an actual person!"

A seagull on a nearby rock suddenly screeched and took off, diving at Monique.

Sarah, behave, Pia warned her.

The seagull pulled up, its feet almost skimming Monique's hair.

"Sarah *was* a person once," Pia softly said to Monique. "An innocent young girl."

She turned to Cassy and put on a schoolteacher's tone. "Cassandra, I need you to give me Sarah's doll."

Cassy gripped the doll protectively.

"Cassy, give Pia the doll," Monique ordered.

Cassy refused, and while mother and daughter went to battle, Pia reached out to Sarah.

I won't help you without the doll, Sarah. Let her give it to me.

No.

Then I can't help you.

Pia turned her head away, pretending to be interested in something in her handbag.

A sudden gust of wind whipped sand into her face.

Ignoring the sharp stings, Pia began to hum a tune. A childish act she hoped

Sarah would respond to.

"Here you go," Cassy said abruptly, passing her the doll.

"Good girl," her mum said, clearly relieved.

Thank you, Pia said to Sarah. *I won't let you down.*

Promise?

Yes. But you must promise to leave Cassandra alone now, Pia said sternly. *The moment you interfere with Cassy or her family's life again, this ends, and you're back to being on your own. Do I have your word?*

Yes.

"I won't let you down," Pia said out loud. "Any of you." Sarah, Cassandra, or Monique. Pia hoped like hell she could keep her promise.

She had to.

With the doll in her arms, Pia was filled with a sadness so intense, she wanted to take herself somewhere alone to cry. The doll must be carrying the weight of Sarah's suffering, the torture she'd endured. Pia couldn't imagine the effect that would have on a nine-year-old girl.

Standing, Pia brushed sand off her clothes, and Monique and Cassy did the same. Pia took the opportunity to embrace the girl in a quick hug. "You've done the right thing. I'll see you soon."

Reach out to me if you need me, Pia silently added. *I'll hear you.*

Monique made a choking sound. "You're going to make this go away?" Her voice was broken, distressed. She wanted reassurance, a glimmer of hope in all the darkness.

Pia rested a hand on her shoulder. "I will do my best," Pia promised, turning to look at Sarah. "But first, I need to help Sarah."

CHAPTER TWENTY-SIX

Nate was leaning against the passenger side of Pia's small rental car, wearing worn denim jeans and a white cotton shirt with the sleeves rolled up, leather bands tied around one wrist. His eyes were covered with dark shades, his hair mussed by the light sea breeze. One glimpse of him had her body tingling with the thrill of sexual awareness.

Her step faltered as her heart skipped a beat. Keeping her eyes on her feet, she made her way to the car, overly conscious of his unwavering gaze focused on her.

Putting the car between them, Pia peered at him over the top of the little blue Astra.

Nate pushed his glasses to the top of his head, pulling long strands of hair with it. The result was breathtaking—revealing his devastating eyes and his signature *I'm a cop, don't-fuck-with-me* expression at the same time.

"How did you know where I was…? Never mind," Pia mumbled. Of course it would be easy for Nate to find her, even though she'd taken the taxi from Nate's house to the hire car company, paid cash for the car and driven to a secluded carpark below the lighthouse. He had her mobile number; no doubt he could track her phone's GPS if he wanted to. Not that she had been hiding from him. It just amazed her how damn good Nate was at his job.

"You know you could have just called me, right?" Pia said.

"Now where's the fun in that?"

Pia hid a smile. Nate enjoyed a challenge.

So did she.

Pia tapped her nails on the roof of the car and eyed him. "How's your mum?" she asked genuinely. As much of a bitch as Naomi had been to her, Pia understood the woman. She was protecting her family.

Of course, Pia was far from happy over the way Naomi had spoken to her.

Perhaps if they'd met at a different time, under different circumstances, they might have even liked each other.

But you didn't get a second chance to make a first impression. The damage had been done.

Pia set Sarah's doll in the back seat, then got behind the wheel. Nate slipped into the passenger seat next to her and closed the door. The space inside the car seemed to shrink. Nate pushed his seat back, as far as it would go, making way for his long legs.

"My car would be much more comfortable," he grumbled.

"I don't remember forcing you to get in."

"I'll go wherever necessary to talk to you." His masculine scent washed over her and filled the small space.

Her body heated, instantly responding to him. Her mind might have warned her away, but her body screamed for his touch, for the tender way he spoke to her after they made love.

Nate glanced into the back seat and shifted uncomfortably. "You didn't tell me you were meeting Monique."

"You say that like I should have sought your permission. How strange of you to be under the impression that I need to inform you of my movements."

Nate glanced down, but not before she saw the hurt that crossed his face. He was clearly out of his comfort zone. She felt herself soften, wanted more than anything to just fall into his arms, revel in the peace and comfort she never felt anywhere else. She resisted. From a sense of her own self-protection. And his.

"Why didn't you tell me Monique had a restraining order out on me?"

He shifted in his seat before meeting her eyes. "I should have. I'm sorry."

Pia appreciated that he didn't try to defend his actions. "I get it." She kept her tone soft but firm. "You wanted to handle it. But you still should have told me. I had a right to know. You can't pull shit like that again, okay?"

Nate nodded. "You have my word."

Pia frowned. This was almost too easy.

Nate released a long breath. "I really want to apologize for my mother's rudeness earlier."

Ah! He was feeling guilty over the way his mother had treated her. "You already apologized. Before you went after her. And I told you then, it was unnecessary." She started the engine. "I'm about to take off, so unless you want to leave your Porsche here and ride with me to Mark's, it's probably a good time to get out."

Nate narrowed his gaze, and she fought not to squirm. Being the recipient of his unwavering focus was an uncomfortable thrill. Pia swallowed hard, the air becoming difficult to breathe. She slid down the window.

"My mother is rude to you, and you shut me down?" Nate asked, his voice breaking slightly. "Just like that?"

Pia slumped back in her seat. "I'm not shutting you down. I'm confused." She rubbed her eyes, tried to assemble her tumultuous thoughts and emotions. Nate shifted again, took another look at that doll in the back seat. Then he shrugged out of his jacket and put it up like a curtain between the front and back seat so he couldn't see it.

Despite herself, she laughed.

He looked at her with a wry grin. "I told you that thing creeps me out."

Pia could understand that. It creeped her out too.

"I can still feel it looking at me," Nate said, and he shivered as though something unpleasant had walked up his spine.

"I need it for tomorrow night."

"What's tomorrow night?" Nate asked, frowning. "Look," he said, when she didn't answer the question, "can we go back to my place to talk? Somewhere I'm not cramped into a sardine can?" he added when again, she didn't answer. But only because she couldn't.

The problem was, Pia wanted to. In fact, she'd never wanted anything more. But memories of that morning rose to the surface, mingled with the many conflicts and battles her gift had caused over the years.

Nate would end up hating her. They all had. Her relationship with Adam was not that long ago, the sting of his betrayal still fresh.

"Nate," she said at length. "I told you—more than once—that I will cause you nothing but trouble."

"Yeah? Well, I just so happen to think trouble is sexy."

Pia felt her lip twitch, then she turned serious. "What are we doing, Nate?" she asked wearily, a weight settling over her.

Nate glanced around. "I don't know about you, but I'm sitting in a car that's too small for me, trying to ignore something extremely unpleasant in the back seat."

Pia found herself smiling, despite the heaviness in her heart. "I'm scared," she whispered, her voice wavering.

Nate moved forward, their faces inches apart. His eyes locked on hers, his breath a heated caress on her face.

"I'm scared too. But I choose to see fear as a challenge to overcome. Don't use being scared as excuse not to even try."

She blinked back tears. That wasn't what she was doing, was it? "It's not an excuse. I'm going to hurt you, Nate, and I really don't want to." *I'm going to hurt me.*

She felt his weight upon her as he pushed her back into the seat, turned the ignition off, and took out the keys.

"Not giving us a chance," Nate said, his voice deep and rough, "will hurt me, both of us, more."

He leaned forward, crushing his lips to hers. Hard. His mouth moved across hers, fiercely determined, and her traitorous body responded instantly. *Of course it did.* Regardless of whether they could make a relationship work, Nate owned her body. A part of her very soul would always belong to him.

Pia leaned into him, her arms encircling his neck. The center console was between them, and she briefly wondered why she didn't feel the hand brake digging into her thigh as she leaned across to get as close as physically possible to him.

For a moment, her mind blanked to everything but the feel of his mouth, his tongue as it caressed hers. To the pressure of his hand as it tangled in her hair, supporting her head as he deepened the kiss even further.

And then…

Then she felt his energy swell and expand as he consciously opened himself up. The sentiment hit her powerfully. Floored her, crumbled the last of her defenses. Once again, Nate was proving to her with actions, not just telling her with words, that he embraced her abilities and wasn't walking away. And goddamn it, she was tired of pushing him away.

I love you. His thought landed like a butterfly in her mind but with the impact of a hand grenade. Blood roared past her ears, and he held her even tighter as a choking sound rose out of her.

He knew! Nate knew she'd heard him, and he wasn't shying away from it. He was embracing it. Even though the words weren't spoken aloud, she believed them. Perhaps even more so, as she absorbed the truth in the waves of emotion pouring from him.

He'd said he loved her before. "Fuck, I love you," he'd said. And she hadn't known at the time if she could trust those words, blurted in the heat of an argument.

This time, she knew they were sincere. The words might have come from his mind to hers, but they'd originated from his heart. And he'd deliberately chosen a way to communicate them that would prove beyond any doubt he meant them.

Pia's throat was too tight to speak. Nate had not only fueled a craving to have something she'd thought long ago denied to her, but sparked the hope that it just might be possible.

Pia might not have said the same words to him, but that didn't mean she didn't have strong feelings for him. But love? Love was something she didn't even know she was capable of. She had no benchmark, no reference to draw on, no example to compare it to. And she wouldn't say the words until she knew, with total certainty, what it meant—for her—to love someone in *that way.*

She'd show him how much he meant to her instead.

She kissed him back with everything she felt, swallowed the groan that came from deep inside him. The kiss was rough and wild, and she loved it.

The energy between them swirled to a storm that sparked, set fire to her skin, to the core of her very being. His touch became rough, barely controlled. She moaned, felt her whole body weaken in submission. She gave herself over to him.

And then abruptly, he pulled away.

———◆———

The moment Nate sensed Pia's submission, he pulled back. She'd never know just how difficult it had been for him to stop. The urge inside him to possess her had the power to drive him insane. He took a series of steadying breaths before he spoke.

"I'm not going to lose you, Pia." *You belong to me now.* He allowed himself to hold onto the emotion it was in his nature to suppress. Nate had told her he loved her using his mind. *And she'd heard it.* She'd tensed immediately, her eyes widening in surprise. That they could even communicate like that blew him away. He'd tried it because he wanted her to *feel* it, not just hear it. She needed to understand his determination.

He'd told her he loved her once before, and she'd been unsure how to respond. He didn't want to say it aloud again, in case she felt pressure from not feeling the same way about him. *Yet.* He'd spend his life making that a reality. But Pia needed to *know* how *he* felt about *her.* Pia belonged to him now. How could she not? She'd stolen his heart. It was important that she began to accept there was no way in hell he was letting her go.

How would he ever be satisfied with another woman now that he knew her? For the first time in his life, Nate had found a woman worth fighting for.

And he was getting in the damn ring.

"Do you know the price of being with someone like me?" she asked, and his heart ached at how small her voice sounded. She'd been hurt. But so had he. They'd heal together.

"Whatever the cost, I'll pay it."

She looked at him then, and he saw the pain in her eyes. He swore to his maker he'd spend a lifetime if that's what it took to erase it.

"What makes you different is what I love most about you," Nate said, deliberately using the word "love" in a different way. A less threatening context, just to reinforce his wordless declaration and not make her uncomfortable.

"Your uniqueness was what first drew my attention." Pia had never been just another woman to him. She stood out. And from the very beginning he'd been drawn to her. Getting to know her didn't disappoint. Her inner strength, her courage. She had the same reckless drive for justice inside her that he did. The ceaseless desire to right wrongs. To balance the scales.

Nate danced to his own tune. And so did Pia. And he didn't have to be psychic to know that she was waging an internal battle over whether she could trust him with her most vulnerable possession. Her heart.

When he had his way, when she finally did acquiesce to him fully, her decision would be watertight. She'd be as staunch a partner as his mates in Taipan.

That was a rare trait these days. As valuable as a diamond, especially to someone with Nate's career. It was imperative he had a partner he could trust and rely on to have his back. To be strong. Capable. To have his team's back when he was away on assignment and they turned up needing assistance.

Someone soft, who would moan and bitch and whine to him, would never do. He needed someone who would roll up her sleeves and get things done. And Pia was that rare woman. He didn't need to guess; he already knew firsthand from what had happened in Cryton. Pia, without consideration, had risked her life—on more than one occasion—because her friend Sage had needed her help.

Nate had fallen in love only once in his life.

And he'd fallen hard.

Pia was his rare blue diamond, and he was not letting her go without a fight.

And Nate always fought to win.

He flicked his eyes to his watch. He'd allow her ninety seconds to believe she actually had a choice in this.

When the time was up, he exited the car and went around to her side. He opened her door, and she took his hand as he assisted her out.

"Your mother hates me," Pia said.

"Do I look like the type of man who lets my mother run my life?" Nate's lips twisted. "Okay, don't answer that. I am going to help Ben, but not because she asked me to. I can't sit this one out."

Pia smiled. "All right then, Nate Ryder, despite the fact that the odds are stacked against us, let's make this work. Really, this time. No more doubts. No more pushing each other away. Let's make this work," she repeated, then softened her tone. "Let's make *us* work."

He put his hands beneath her thighs, lifted her onto the bonnet of the car, and crushed his lips to hers. Nothing tasted sweeter than that moment. The moment she committed to making them work.

The moment she committed to him.

This was deeper than when she'd let him in at the beach. He'd knocked down a large chunk of her wall today, and it made him feel ten feet tall.

She might not have told him she loved him—with words—but he knew she did. And knowing it was enough. For now.

"You're mine now, Pia." His voice was harsh, edgy, his need for her urgent and powerful.

For a delicious moment, he imagined what she would look like spread across the bonnet. Decided her satiny white legs would look even better open across his black Porsche.

A low rumble came from somewhere deep inside him. Something raw, primal and possessive. He barely fucking recognized himself around her. He knew one thing for sure: If he didn't get her home, he was making the bonnet image a reality. In broad daylight. In the middle of a public carpark.

He'd rather it be his Porsche, in the privacy of his home.

"I need you. Home. Now." His voice was a sexy rasp, and she arched up, pressing her body against his aching cock. "You tease, but you have no idea how tenuous the grip on my control is right now."

Her eyes held a wicked gleam, and he closed his eyes as a desire to take her hard and fast surged through him.

"It's a rental. I can't just leave it here."

Fuck the car. As she slid off the bonnet and placed her hands on her hips, he let out a resigned sigh. Not wanting to argue over it, he took out his phone and sent a brief message. Nate left the keys in the ignition, not bothering to hide them.

"Nate—"

"Handled," he cut her off, keeping her moving toward his much more comfortable car. He might not have followed in the family business, but the taste for luxury modes of transport and speed were in his blood.

"Wait!" Pia raced back to the little blue Astra, grabbed that... *that thing*. Nate swallowed. He suppressed a shiver as she settled it into the back seat of his Porsche Cayenne as though it were a child.

Nate steered his car in the direction of his house, Pia by his side, and a possessed doll in the back that he could swear was boring holes into his head as he drove.

No, his life with Pia would never be normal. He'd be living forever out of his comfort zone.

And he wouldn't have it any other way.

Chapter Twenty-Seven

Tash's car was in Nate's driveway when he pulled in with Pia. "And the hits just keep on coming," he groaned.

"Who's that? Oh," Pia said, her eyes widening with recognition when Natasha stepped out of the car. Tash was dressed to impress in a low-cut shirt, red skirt, and matching heels.

Nate tossed Pia the keys. "You'll need these for the front gate, but I've programmed your thumbprint into the scanner. Make yourself comfortable. I won't be long."

Pia hesitated. "Are you telling me to 'run along,' Nate Ryder?"

"I—" *Jesus!* He thrust his hands through his hair. "That's not what I'm doing. Well, I guess it is, but I didn't mean it that way. Shit. Will you just please go inside and let me handle this?"

Pia stood there, one hand on her hip, one arm on the car door, eyes flashing dangerously. Nate's jeans tightened. Damn, she was sexy when she got fired up.

He crossed to Pia's side of the car, wrapped one arm around her waist, and kissed her hard on the mouth. There was no way Tash could miss that, or the clear message it sent.

Appearing mollified, and slightly dazed, Pia slammed the car door for effect, glared at Tash, threw her shoulders back, and went inside. Nate almost sighed with relief. After what had happened with his mother this morning, he didn't want to take any chances that Tash would say something to upset Pia. His mother and his ex in one day. What were the chances? He would deal with the issue of Tash once and for all.

"What are you doing here?" He allowed irritation to bleed into his tone as he crossed to her.

"You weren't returning my calls."

"What *are* you doing here?" he repeated, making sure his displeasure was clear.

"Don't be like that." Tash leaned in closer when she spoke, as was her habit, a move designed to make her necklace brush over her ample chest, drawing the eye to her cleavage. The lace of her bra showed through her camisole, but it wasn't half as sexy as Pia's corsets. Tash was a very attractive woman, but she couldn't compete with Pia's raw, natural sexuality.

"I miss you," Tash said, reaching for his arm.

Nate stepped away, and her arm fell back to her side. "What happened between us is in the past. It was a long time ago."

"Being with you now makes it feel like yesterday. I should never have taken that job."

"You made the right decision."

"No, I didn't. I was just too young to appreciate the type of man you are, Nate. I didn't realize that no one else would compare."

He shrugged. "I've lived a lot of life since then, and I'm not who you remember me to be. I've moved on. So should you."

"Give me one night, and I guarantee you'll remember how good we were together. It'll be even better now. I—"

"I don't think you heard me. I've moved on."

"With her?" Tash's eyes narrowed. "You can't be serious." Her gaze flickered over Nate's shoulder, and he realized Pia hadn't gone inside at all; she was standing by the gate, watching them intently.

"Oh, I am," Nate said, his voice lethally quiet. "And if you remember anything at all about me, you'll hear what I say when I tell you to be very careful how you speak about Pia."

Tash crossed her arms beneath her breasts so they pushed up.

Did she think he was a mindless dog? "Go home."

"Your mum doesn't like her."

"You spoke to my mother?"

"Of course. Who do you think told me to come here after you? She said you were back working on a case, but would love to see me. She told me about the psychic you were helping keep out of jail."

"*Did* she?" He heard his teeth grinding.

"Look, Nate, we seem to have gotten off on the wrong foot. We always were very… passionate."

"That's all we had."

"You didn't allow anything more." Her eyes flashed. "But you're older now, ready to settle down. Your mother thinks we're a good match."

Nate heard Pia's footsteps approaching from behind.

Tash leaned in, whispered, "I am so much better for you than she is. When you're thinking clearly again, you'll realize that."

Pia's step faltered, and Nate knew she'd heard.

"I will say this once more," he growled. "Loud and clear. I'm. Not. Interested."

"I could make you interested if you—"

Nate put his arm around Pia, who had stopped at his side. "Pia, I must apologize. I made the mistake of not introducing you at the station, but this is an old friend—"

"Oh come on, Nate. We were a lot more than just friends." Tash leaned in and spoke to Pia. "I broke his heart when I took a job interstate a year ago. He has a right to be angry."

Pia's fingers dug into his ribs, and he saw Tash close her eyes. She looked a little distant. Dreamy. Too late, Nate realized what she was doing. Knowing Pia was psychic, thanks to his mother, Tash was conjuring up images of them together.

The color drained from Pia's face.

Nate grabbed Pia and sheltered her behind him. Tash had gone too far.

"You stay the hell away from here. You are not welcome. And when you see my mother, make sure she gets the same message."

He wrapped his arm around Pia and steered her into the house.

Tash's tires screeched, but at least she left his driveway.

"Jesus, Pia," Nate said at the front door. "I'm sorry." He tilted her face up so he could look in her eyes. "Tell me you're okay. Tell me I haven't just fucked up again."

Pia gave him a small smile, but his heart broke at the tears glistening in her eyes. "It's not your fault. Though I could have done without the image of seeing you and her together." She squeezed her eyes shut. Nate had no idea what Tash had chosen to visualize; they had been very adventurous. Damn her for using the worst way to hurt Pia: turning her abilities against her.

Pia opened her eyes and touched his cheek. "It's not your fault. Anyway, it's not like either of us believed this was going to be easy. Against all odds, right?"

Nate scooped her off her feet.

"What are the odds you'll be able to walk when I'm finished with you?"

He kicked the front door shut, held her against the wall with her arms above her head, and kissed her until they were both breathless.

Then proceeded to make good on his promise.

———◆———

Pia sat on the edge of Nate's bed, wishing she had a wider selection of clothes in her one bag. She hadn't been pleased to see Tash at Nate's house, but she was glad in a way that it had happened. She didn't know exactly how everything would work with Nate, but he had proved he was as committed to giving it a go as she was. At least she was no longer worried about what Tash meant to him, or that his mother held any significant influence in that department.

Nate had been one seriously pissed-off male, brimming with a forceful passion that she'd taken full advantage of. First against the wall in the hallway. Next on the kitchen table, then on the balcony overlooking the sunset, then finally, and slowly, on this very bed.

Pia smiled at the rumpled blankets and planned what she'd do next, and how soon she could get him back in bed.

Argh! She felt like a horny teenager. She forcefully shoved all lustful thoughts of Nate aside and concentrated on what she needed to do for Sarah.

As she cleared her mind to reach out to Sarah, strangely it was Johnson's image that pressed into her mind. She sensed Johnson's intention to wrap this case up as strongly as if he were in the room with her voicing that very opinion. She "saw" him in his office, compiling his report, ordering his evidence. All he needed was to get her back in the station. Question her some more. *She'll slip.*

His fingers itched to put the cuffs on her. People higher up in the force were beginning to look at this case. Ask questions. He couldn't allow that. He refused to allow that.

All he needed was to get her into the station. But the damn restraining order he'd tried to serve had been withdrawn. The pencil in his hand snapped. He threw the pieces across the room, and they hit the wall, leaving a mark.

Where the hell was she? Goddamn Nate Ryder! He had no business being back here. Johnson's number-one priority now was to find her. Her defense was ridiculous. *Ghosts! Ha!* She'd be a laughingstock. It would only make his case against her all the more easy…

Stop!

Pia stood, shook her hands, cleared the energy, the impressions. Worrying about Johnson and his intentions was not helping.

Focus.

They'd made a great deal of progress in a relatively short space of time. Pia had connected with Sarah. Nate and his team had discovered who Sarah was, and it was only a matter of time before they located her parents. Pia had been shown what Simon Farrell and his cray-fishing buddies had done to Sarah, and what Sarah had done to them from beyond the grave. Pia needed to learn only two things now.

Where Sarah's body was buried.

And who the others were.

Sarah had said there were others who hadn't been punished yet. Meg Farrell was undoubtedly one of them, but who was the "monster" who'd tortured Sarah the most? Pia hadn't been able to see his face.

Nate's team would surely find Meg Farrell soon, and when they did, they'd hopefully have the last pieces of the puzzle of Sarah's life. Perhaps the others were occasional members of the cray-fishing crew? However, that thought didn't hold the ring of truth for Pia. Plus, that greatly reduced the chances of it remaining a secret all these years. Surely someone only peripherally connected would have come out with the truth, or let the story slip.

Pia's phone flashed with Mark's name.

"Hey, handsome," Pia said.

"Hey, Boo." Mark's voice was flat, containing none of its usual vitality.

"What's wrong?"

"My dad's in hospital." Mark's relationship with his father was tenuous at best. Mark was supposed to have followed in his father's footsteps. When Pia had first met Mark, he had been completing his accounting degree. But after she'd confirmed Mark's suspicions regarding the supernatural, he'd changed course. His father had been furious. Especially when he found out what Mark planned to do. His father didn't believe in ghosts. Only fools and the insane believed that claptrap.

The two of them had had a falling out, said horrible things in the heat of the moment, and in the end, his father had written him out of his will, refusing to even acknowledge he had a son.

"What happened to your dad?" she asked.

"Heart attack. He had surgery, but there have been some complications." His voice was tight, and Pia could feel his pain through the phone. Despite everything, the fight, their differences, Mark loved his father.

Pia reached out and silenced her own thoughts as she opened her mind. Mark needed to understand the situation. "You should go to him," she said.

Mark was silent a moment, as he absorbed the deeper meaning behind her words. His dad wasn't going to make it. "Will you go with me?"

"I can't. I have Sarah's doll, and I'm going to go into the cottage one last time. Now that we know who she is, I'm hoping to help her leave."

"I should be there to help you."

Pia hoped they could sort out their differences before Mark's dad left this world. His father should be proud of him. Mark was a wonderful man with a good heart.

"There's nothing you can do anyway, Mark," Pia said softly. "Johnson is really after me now, and I'm scared he'll follow you to me. I'm safe at Nate's; Johnson doesn't know the address, and even if he did, Nate knows how to avoid a tail. I'm so close to fully knowing Sarah's story, yet still feel so far. You know what I mean?"

"I do. Ryan and Joe want to come back to Adelaide with me, but I can ask them to stay if you want."

"No. For the reasons we just discussed."

"At least I can rest easy, knowing you have Nate with you."

Nate won't be with me tomorrow night.

He would be tied up with intercepting the shipment of drugs his brother had gotten tangled in. Pia kept that to herself though; Mark would stay if he knew she'd be going into the house alone.

Indeed, it didn't seem the smartest thing in the world to do. But she felt she'd connected with Sarah. She just had to hope Sarah didn't suddenly turn on her again.

Pia swiftly changed the subject. "You already have great evidence, don't you?" He'd managed to catch a clear picture of when Sarah had manifested the last time.

"The best yet. It's going to cause a sensation when it goes to air. I'll film an interview with you to get the conclusion of the story after the fact, but there's already enough paranormal documentation to make the show powerful."

Mark fell silent, as though reluctant to break the connection. "I'd better go," he finally said. "Call me any time. Day or night. If you need me, I'll drop everything and be there."

Pia smiled. "I'll be fine. Nate is here."

Mark was silent a moment. "I like him, Boo. He's good for you. And to you."

A lump rose in Pia's throat, and she blinked back tears. She didn't need his approval of course, but it meant more than she could ever tell him. Mark was as close to family as she had left. "Thank you," she said, the words so inadequate, but they were all she could force out.

"Stay safe," Mark said, then disconnected the call.

Pia held the phone in her hand a moment before slipping it inside her bag. An image pressed into her mind. Mark would reconnect with his father before he crossed over. It wouldn't undo the damage from years of cold silence, but at least it would give Mark a small measure of peace.

She silently wished him the very best.

Pia stood and went to search for the other man in her life.

Chapter Twenty-Eight

"W e've located Sarah's parents." Blade's voice was on speaker as Nate stirred the sauce for a marinara he was making for Pia, while she went to have a shower and catch up with some phone calls.

"And everything is in place for tomorrow night." If Blade was at all concerned with how the takedown of Wild Wilson's gang would transpire, his smooth tone gave nothing away.

"Good." Nate cursed heavily as he dropped the spatula on the floor, scattering blood red sauce over his imported tiles.

"Are you and the guys going to stay here?" Nate had the rooms set up with everything they needed.

"Not this time, mate," Blade replied. "I'm meeting with a potential new client, and he's booked us in the top floor of his hotel overlooking the ocean for the week. Sam and Daniel are staying on until Sunday. You, and of course Pia, are welcome to stay there too."

"Thanks, but we're good here."

"Any updates on Pia's case?" Blade asked, knowing Nate as well as he did.

"Zach hasn't been able to locate Meg Farrell yet," Nate said, frustration gnawing a hole in his gut. If he was going to be out of action as far as Pia was concerned tomorrow night, he wanted as much closure on Pia's case as he could get before he left. Locating Meg Farrell would go a long way to providing that closure. Nate's instincts told him that she was key to solving this thirty-year-old cold case. Johnson was only one step behind him, and Pia was still number one on Johnson's radar. He needed to change that. And fast.

"You're worried."

Nate released a long slow breath and started wiping up the sauce that had spilled on the tiles.

Worried didn't quite cut it. Nate was torn apart inside over not being around to help Pia tomorrow night when she went back into the house. He remembered all too clearly what had happened last time. He didn't want to contemplate what would have happened had he not been there to blast the door open.

Pia needs me, is what he wanted to say. But Pia hadn't said she needed him. She hadn't put pressure on him at all. Pia would do what she felt she needed to do, either way.

It was Nate who couldn't leave *her*.

"This situation with Pia is far from resolved." What if Johnson turned up for an arrest, imagining some piece of evidence? What if Pia came under attack from the entity again? It didn't even have to be at the cottage; the doll was with them now.

What if she needs me, and I'm not there?

"I'll send someone to watch over Pia tomorrow night. If all goes according to plan, you'll be back with her by 0600 Friday."

If all goes according to plan. When did it *ever* go according to plan? Every moment he was away was a moment he risked losing Pia. TSI employed only the best men in the business, but the very best were the members of Taipan, and they'd be with Nate.

"What about we leave Daniel here?" Nate suggested.

There was a heartbeat's hesitation on the other end as his best mate tried to understand the reasons for his request. "You want to split the team?"

Sure, there were other guys in the industry who were experienced and capable, but Taipan worked as a finely honed unit. They knew each other's strengths and weaknesses and abilities. Years of working together on dangerous assignments meant they could change their plans on the fly, knowing that everyone was on the same page. They operated as one; throwing in other operators upset the balance.

"You're going up against the biggest organized crime cartel in the country. And you want to do it without the full team?"

"Of course I don't want to split the team." Nate cursed. "But I can't be here." He broke off. How did he say he didn't trust anyone but him or his team to look after the most valuable person in his life?

"She's the one," Blade said.

"Yes." Nate didn't need to elaborate, knowing Blade would understand like no other.

People always said they'd die for the ones they loved. Blade had actually done so for Sage and their unborn child. That he was still walking the planet was nothing less than a miracle.

At the time, Nate had looked on in awe at the apparent ease with which Blade had come to that decision. The number of times they'd fought for survival, defeated the black dog of death, and Blade had so easily made the decision to die for the woman he loved. Nate admitted to being surprised, and more than a little envious of Blade for having someone so valuable he'd die for her. Nate hadn't believed love like that existed outside romance novels.

Until he'd met Pia.

And now he understood how Blade had made that decision. Already, there wasn't anything Nate couldn't imagine doing for Pia.

"I don't need to remind you who we're dealing with here," Blade said. "The cartel will erase Ben the moment he's no longer of any use. Or becomes a risk. Be that tonight or next time, it will happen."

Nate fell silent. As pissed off with Ben as he was, he couldn't stand by and watch his brother be killed. He was an idiot and had got in over his head. But he wasn't an evil man. Blade was right. This wasn't just a matter of his brother learning the hard way from his mistakes. There'd be no second chances for Ben in this.

An image of Pia struggling for breath in the clutches of something unseen rose in his mind. Nate believed that thing, that entity, would have killed her Tuesday night if he hadn't forcibly removed her from the house. It had already killed three adult males. It had proven its power, its capability for murder. He refused to lose Pia to this thing.

"Who would you assign, Blade?" Nate asked wearily. "Who other than Taipan would understand what Pia is up against?"

How would Blade even vet someone for the job? First question: *Do you believe in ghosts…?*

Nate released a long breath, the smell of burning marinara bringing his attention back to the pan. He killed the flame and put the ruined sauce in the sink.

"I'll replace myself in the op tomorrow with a few additional bodies. We could use extra hands anyway. I'll look after Pia for you."

Nate rubbed his eyes. *Thank you, Jesus.* "You'd do that?"

"I'll ignore that, Ryder," Blade growled.

Of course he didn't mean the words, he was just so damned relieved he wouldn't have to worry about Pia with Blade watching over her. He trusted Blade with his life. Therefore he trusted him with Pia's.

"But what about Sage? Can you leave her at the moment?" *What if something happens?* The unspoken words hung in the air.

"Did you think I wasn't coming tomorrow either way? Fuck you, Ryder. That's strike two."

"Settle down, Blade. This whole thing with Pia has thrown me for a six. It is just… *different* when there's someone other than yourself to care about."

Blade was silent on the line for a moment. "Don't I know it."

"All I meant is that now I truly understand what it means for you to leave Sage to be here." Nate couldn't imagine leaving Pia pregnant and in such a vulnerable state to fly across the country and risk his life going up against a drug cartel. Or possibly a demonic entity.

"Let me put this in perspective for you. Sage would kill me with her bare hands if she ever found out I was here with her when you or Pia needed me. Trust me, I'm more scared of her than I am of you, Ryder."

Nate let out a short laugh. Sage was a force unto herself. Just like Pia. No wonder they'd become fast friends last September.

"Who would have thought we, of all people, would end up at the mercy of our women?" Blade said.

"I'd say it was inevitable ol' buddy. Could you imagine either of us settling for any less?"

Chapter Twenty-Nine

The takeaway dinner Nate ordered had just arrived when Pia came out still fully dressed. She raised her arms and twisted her long red hair into a knot at the base of her neck without a mirror.

"You're dressed," Nate said. He'd been hoping she'd be wearing his favorite T-shirt like she had last night. The one that was just a touch too short and rode up her thighs when she sat.

"I thought I could smell seafood marinara," Pia said, eyeing the takeaway containers suspiciously.

"Trust me, takeaway is the way to go tonight."

Pia smiled and his heart squeezed. Damn, he loved her smile. He didn't know the words, but hoped she knew just how much she affected him.

"Food is not what I'm hungry for," she said, and he swallowed. Hard.

She came to him, and captivated, he watched every movement, every sway of her body as she crossed the room. He took her in his arms and breathed her in. He loved the subtle, fragrant scent of her skin. He tugged at her hair, and it fell from its tie, soft and silky through his fingers. Nipping at her neck, he ran his tongue across the column, gently sucking. She hissed in a sharp intake of breath, and he savored the sweet, sexual sound. He inhaled deeply, her neck the place where her scent was the strongest. Intoxicating. He was painfully hard, his need for her a constant demand.

"Blade will look after you tomorrow night," Nate murmured into her neck.

"What?" Pia pulled away. Damn she looked sexy when she frowned. And when she smiled. And when she…

Nate tried to focus.

"The team are coming to help me. Blade is staying back here to look after you."

Nate moved to grab hold of her again, and she sidestepped out of his reach.

"What did you do that for?" Pia placed her hands on her hips, and he tried not to stare as the fabric of her shirt stretched tight across her breasts.

Do what for? Oh, that's right. "I trust Blade with my life, and I trust him with yours." That was the easiest and quickest explanation his blood-deprived brain could come up with. "Now come here."

"Nate! Ethan should be with Sage."

He sighed. "I've just had this conversation with him, except in reverse. He's coming; there's nothing you can do about it."

Nate saw Pia's distress, and this time succeeded in grabbing her shoulders. "Don't be mad, babe. I have to accept you going out and doing what you need to do tomorrow night; you can at least let me do what I need to do. I won't concentrate if I'm worried about you," Nate added, hoping that would seal the deal.

Pia narrowed her eyes, and his heart skipped. She was a smart woman; surely she could see this was a losing battle. She wasn't going to enter into an argument she couldn't win. At least he hoped not.

He ran his hands from her shoulders down to her wrists and held them securely behind her back with one hand. He used his other hand to tilt her chin up so that she was looking at him. Her eyes were shining brightly, and her lips were moist and parted.

He didn't ravish her mouth, instead he licked along her jaw. She threw her head back, as he kissed and nipped a trail down the long column of her neck to her collarbone.

She let out a groan of pleasure that increased the pressure he felt between his legs. His whole body was hot and hard, his desire for her turning him virtually mindless. Single-minded at best.

"Somehow you turn me on more and more each time. It shouldn't be possible."

"If you let go of my hands, I might show you some mercy when I get you in the bedroom."

"Is that right?" He tried to sound amused, but the image sent a raging fire straight to his groin. "Do you think I'd let you get the advantage over me?"

There was a mischievous gleam in her eyes, and he was helpless to deny her a single thing. He released his hold and one of her hands immediately gripped the hardness between his legs, and the other wrapped around his neck, drawing his mouth down level with hers.

A low groan rose from deep inside him as she squeezed his erection tightly.

"I'd say I have you exactly where I want you, Detective." Her breath was a sensual puff of wind against his lips and he groaned aloud again. She was going to be the death of him.

He tried to kiss her, but she twisted away, her teeth nipping at his neck instead. Withdrawing her hand, she gripped his arse and pulled his erection tightly against her soft stomach. She planted tiny kisses across his shoulders and biceps while he traced his hands down the curve of her back. His pulse raced, his heart pounding a staccato in his chest. She was so beautifully curvaceous, desperately sexy, with a force of will to match his own.

He wanted her with everything he was. Every ragged breath he tried to drag into his constricted lungs.

Pia's fingers traveled beneath his T-shirt, traced across his stomach and up his chest. He closed his eyes as a moan left his throat. Her touch was magnetic, stirring things he hadn't known existed. She was a temptress, pushing him, constantly drawing out things he was scared to feel, yet powerless to stop all the same.

Pia tugged his shirt up and off. "I'm going to fuck you now," she said in a low sexy voice.

He almost came then and there. *Jesus!* At this rate, he'd embarrass himself before he even made it into the bedroom. He caught her wrists on their way down to his jeans and pulled them above her head. He sealed his lips over hers, thrusting his tongue deep into her mouth, enjoying the whimper it elicited from her. The heat between them grew. Her lips were soft and sweet, but her tongue was doing wicked things to his. His cock strained hard against his jeans, the pressure becoming unbearable.

As though fully aware of his delicious torture, she rubbed her belly against him, and he released one hand long enough to slap her on the arse. Her eyes widened with the sting, then darkened in arousal.

He glanced at his bedroom door. He could have her naked and on the bed in twenty seconds flat.

Scooping her off her feet, he carried her into his room. By the time he'd traveled the short distance, he'd mentally taken her in more positions than outlined in the *Kama Sutra*.

But then something caught his eye and shut him down. Like being thrown into an icy lake, his body cooled instantly.

The doll sat on the chair in the corner of his room, its porcelain features eerily lifelike. It seemed to be looking at them. Watching with strangely intelligent, staring eyes.

Nate shivered.

"What's wrong?"

Nate pointed to the corner, trying hard to be a man about it.

"Sarah's doll?" Pia asked.

"I won't be able to relax with that thing in here," Nate said, rolling his shoulders. "It's looking at me. At least that's how it feels. That thing gives me the creeps."

"It can't look at you. It's a doll." But he could tell she didn't believe the words even as she spoke them. There *was* something horribly unnatural about that doll.

And she damn well knew it.

It wasn't simply a connection with Sarah. It was as though a part of Sarah had infused itself into the object. And it wasn't the nice part.

"What do you want me to do with it?"

Toss it to a pack of hungry wolves, drop it in the middle of the freeway, or stuff it in a concrete suitcase and leave it at the bottom of the Swan River.

The room turned ice cold, dropping several degrees in a single second as though someone had turned the air-conditioning to zero. As though the doll could read his thoughts.

Nate cleared his throat. "Do whatever you want, as long as it's not in the same room as me." *And preferably not the same house. State. Country. Planet…* "The damn thing feels as though it's alive. And mighty pissed off as well."

"Well, you would be too, if those things happened to you," Pia said, crossing the room. She picked the thing up, cradling it in her arms. A chill raked down his spine. How the hell she could touch that thing he had no idea.

Nate shook his head in wonder. There was the woman he intended to spend the rest of his life with, picking up a possessed doll like it was a goddamned real child, and carrying it out of the room.

Pia took the doll from the corner chair in Nate's room. He'd said it felt like it was looking at him. She hadn't the heart to tell him that it *was* looking at him. Or rather, an entity was looking out through the doll.

Sarah's likeness in her arms, Pia walked to the nearest spare bedroom, paused, then walked to the next one.

She stood at the open door. The room was perfectly made up, the décor having a distinct masculine feel. The bed covers were black with thin streaks of gold from an artist's hand. A large Tasmanian oak desk stood prominent against the far wall, complete with computer, phone, tablets, notebooks. Each guestroom was ready for any member of Taipan to use at a moment's notice.

She walked into the room and sat the doll on the middle of the bed. She had the prickling sensation she wasn't alone. The air was thick, like a packed ocean-side bar on a sultry summer's night. Except there was no festive feel. Sadness, heavy and cloying, filled the space. Like she was at a funeral.

Placing her hands on her hips, she looked around the room. "Now, you stay in here and behave."

Pia didn't get a reply, nor did she see a manifestation of Sarah, but she was there just the same. A chill skittered across her skin and trickled down her back.

"I mean it," she said for good measure as she closed the door.

Pia walked the hallway back to Nate, shaking unwanted energy from her hands along the way. She took a few deep cleansing breaths and stepped into his bedroom.

The moment she saw him, her heart skipped a beat, all thoughts of Sarah and her doll pushed far, far away. Nate was sitting up in bed, a sheet riding low on his hips. Was he naked under there? Either way, Nate was so desperately sexy, her nipples hardened in anticipation of remembered pleasure.

His heated gaze followed her every movement with a heavy-lidded intensity that stole her breath. At the edge of the bed, Pia paused and unzipped her skirt, the fabric falling easily to the floor. She unbuttoned her shirt and tossed it on a nearby chair.

She stood in front of him, a little out of arm's reach, in a skimpy black G-string and black corset. She supposed some people would consider her underwear racy, to be saved for special occasions. But Pia dressed for herself. She wore tight corsets because they felt more secure in her line of business. She didn't want to be readjusting a wayward bra while her hands were full of recording equipment during an investigation.

She favored black because it symbolized power and confidence, vitally important for someone who couldn't show fear in the face of negative entities.

But standing here in front of Nate now, her confidence wavered. Did he like what he saw? Or did he prefer soft, frilly, and feminine, instead of something more at home in an S&M club?

In the past, she had never cared about pleasing men, but Nate was different. No great surprise there. Nate *was* different. But the real difference was that for once Pia cared what a partner thought. Deeply.

Could she change if he didn't like it?

She hoped he didn't prefer soft and frilly.

Pia could never be "that" girl.

But she needn't have worried; the rapt way his eyes traveled the length of her body took her breath away.

Though she dressed for herself, watching Nate draw in a shaky breath made her glad of her choices for a different reason. He licked lips that appeared dry, and he visibly swallowed.

They weren't touching, but the electricity between them crackled. Nate was the only man she'd felt this type of chemistry with. The only man she could be comfortable enough with to be herself around.

"You're too far away." He reached out a hand, his voice low and gravelly. God, what was it about voices like that? All malt whiskey, honeycomb, and melted chocolate. She bet she could orgasm from it alone if he spoke long enough. But men like Nate didn't ramble. His words were concise and well chosen. The state of absolute control he maintained was so damn sexy.

So undeniably alpha male. The alpha female part inside her purred in appreciation.

She'd been in a sexual dry spell for too long. Nate had ignited the flame within her last night; now he'd have to deal with the consequences. For the first time in her life, she'd been able to relax during sex. Nate was the only man she'd been able to let her guard down around and truly enjoy the sensation, the freedom, that sexual release can give.

Pia felt alive. Liberated. Like she'd been trapped in a bottle all her life and was now free to enjoy all the pleasures intimacy could bring.

She ripped the sheet down, noting with pleasure that he was indeed naked. She straddled him.

Last night, he had taken control. Her body tingled as she remembered the feel of Nate's tongue between her thighs.

But tonight, it was her turn.

She wanted to see him undone. Wanted him shaking, on his knees begging.

She wanted to shatter his control.

The way he'd shattered hers.

She reached over to the bedside table where he'd placed his 9 millimeter Glock and cuffs, and chose the Smith & Wesson bracelets. His eyes widened, then darkened, when she grabbed his arms, the metal clicking as it locked around his wrists. His hands felt large and heavy as she took his cuffed hands and tied them on the timber bedhead with his leather belt. He dutifully gripped the wood as she tied the knots, his eyes darkening further.

He tested the bindings, but didn't resist. He just watched her with heavy lids, the way a caged lion watched through its bars.

Pia was not a fool. She knew full well she was in control only because he allowed it. So she ran with the advantage, determined to make the most of it. She took her time. Savored the feel of his skin under her fingertips, the way his muscles rippled as she traced patterns along the ridges of his abdomen. His masculinity was rougher, raw and primal in his heightened state of arousal.

Leaving her corset on, she unclipped the elastic at the shoulders, turning it strapless. She took a deep breath, knowing her full breasts would puff out above the tight material. Nate hissed in a breath. The scent of his warm skin was intoxicating. Pia cleared her mind and focused.

She placed a finger across his lips, an instruction that from now on, he was to be silent. He immediately opened his mouth, drew her finger in and sucked. A streak of white heat tore through her body like a bolt of lightning, and it was her turn to suck in a breath. She quickly removed her finger and waved it in front of his face. "No."

His eyes met and held hers. Holding his gaze, she placed her hands over his lips, and this time he let her. "No talking," she whispered.

She lowered her head, letting her hair trail across his skin as she kissed and licked his naked body. Her mouth ravaged every inch of his heated skin.

"You take my breath away," he said, his voice low and husky.

Pia ignored the thrill his words gave her and shot him a warning glance. "What did I say about talking?"

His lips gave a slight twitch, as she felt his desire for her intensify. It was with some satisfaction that she unintentionally read that Nate had never relinquished control in the bedroom before. He was not a man who liked to be outside his comfort zone. Especially in the bedroom, where by nature he took charge.

And yet he was trusting her. And enjoying the hell out of it.

She leaned forward, his darkened eyes lowering to her cleavage. His fingers flexed, causing the metal cuffs to jangle.

"You want to touch them?" Pia said, trailing her fingers across the soft skin pillowing out the top of the corset. She raised her arms above her head, felt the corset slide farther down.

Nate cleared his throat, then raised one brow as if to say, *I'm allowed to at least do that, aren't I?*

Pia smiled. Brought one hand behind her and slapped the side of his thigh. Hard. A warning. A reminder of who was in charge. Nate grinned wickedly, and she knew he was planning what to do with her when he was free. But for now, he was trapped.

And all hers.

Still straddling him, she gently lowered her body, allowing it to brush across his erection as her mouth ravaged him. The heat between them intensified into a scorching wildfire.

Pia kissed her way down his chest, his abdomen. Deliberately. Sensually. Teasingly.

She licked and tasted his skin, savoring every inch of his perfectly defined body.

By the time her lips reached his cock, his chest was heaving, his breathing ragged.

"Jesus, Pia. You're going to kill me."

The metal cuffs jangled as he flexed his arms and tugged on the restraints.

Pia's hand closed around his length, his skin a silky glove over an erection as hard as steel. Nate groaned as she moved her fist over him from base to tip. Moisture pooled at the tip, and she lowered her mouth and licked it off. His jaw was clenched hard, and Pia didn't need to be psychic to read how tenuous his hold on his control was.

She took the whole of his considerable length into her mouth and sucked hard. Nate cursed. "Yes. Fuck, babe, that's good."

Pia licked and sucked, taking her time, continuing her delicious torture, backing off every time she sensed he was about to come, repeating, and teasing.

"Goddam, Pia! You're killing me."

Pia took him even deeper, continuing her relentless assault.

"You have to stop, or not stop. You're a wicked, wicked woman."

Nate swore as his hips arched into her.

It was only when he was begging for release, his words an incoherent, deliciously sexy jumble of masculine need, that she relented.

She preened with feminine satisfaction as his body trembled. Then she closed her mouth over him and sucked in a long, deep, hard rhythm. He came in her mouth, pulsing streams of salty cum in the back of her throat. Slowly, she eased her lips from him, his eyes dark and heavy as he watched her lick her lips.

Nate lay on the bed, seemingly exhausted. She slid up his body, reaching for the handcuff keys. She would make love to him leisurely now, gradually stoking the fire again.

The moment she took the cuffs off, he pounced on her, tossing her over, reversing their positions. She gasped in surprise as she bounced on the mattress. She'd been fooled. But she didn't really mind.

"And now, beautiful vixen, it's my turn to ravish you." Nate held her down, his stormy gray eyes glinting wickedly. "Hand me the cuffs."

Pia's eyes widened. Nate's determined expression sent a thrilling ripple of anticipation through her body. "No," she said, but her body screamed, *Yes!*

"It wasn't a question." His voice was a raw, roughened rasp. With ease, he wrestled the cuffs from where she'd been trying to hide them beneath the pillow and slipped them over her wrists.

The metal locks clicked into place.

"Pia, Pia, Pia," he tut-tutted. "Did you think you could torture me like that and get away with it?" Nate lowered his head abruptly and bit her nipple, the sweet sting making her gasp again.

"Guess you better teach me a lesson then," Pia said with a wicked grin.

———◆———

Nate eyed the voluptuous, naked woman on his bed. "You are so fucking beautiful." He barely recognized his voice, it was so filled with gravel.

Her nipples were tight points, and when he bit them, she squirmed deliciously beneath him. He wanted her so fiercely, he struggled for the most basic semblance of control.

He'd never find the words to tell her, but letting her cuff him to the bed had been a powerful moment. One he hadn't been sure he'd be able to go through with. It took every ounce of his willpower to surrender to her.

Without words, she'd asked if he trusted her.

And by God, handing over the reins to her demonstrated more to him than it possibly could have to her. It had felt damn good to not have to be in control for once. Even for the briefest of moments. To have found a woman strong enough to make it real brought him to his knees.

He tongued the soft cleft between her thighs, and she trembled beneath him, her hips rotating sensually.

"You like that?" Nate teased, sucking her clit, reveling in how it made her writhe and make the sexiest sounds. She arched her hips upward, striving for release, but he held her waist firm and continued his torture.

He watched her, from his position between her legs, and thought she was nothing short of a goddess. Now that he had her, he'd fight to the death to keep her.

"Say there'll be no other," Nate said.

"What?" Pia lifted her head a moment, looking sexily mussed and confused. "You can't be serious."

"Oh, I've never been more serious. From now on, there'll only be me."

Pia was watching him intently with heavy, hooded eyes.

"I've dreamed of you looking at me that exact way," Nate said. "I have ever since I first laid eyes on you back in September. I've wanted you every day, every night, since then. I've imagined what it would be like to touch you, to kiss you. What you would feel like, what you would taste like. Not to mention the countless different ways I've pictured having you beneath me."

Pia chuckled softly, the sound warming his heart. "I dreamed of you too. And nothing I imagined in my wildest fantasies compared to how it actually feels to be with you."

"I love you," Nate said. "And now that I finally have you, I'm not letting you go. Ever."

"Oh, Nate—"

Nate silenced her with a kiss, knowing she'd be able to taste herself on his tongue. He didn't want her to feel pressure to say it back if she wasn't ready. For now, it was enough for him to make how he felt clear. She'd come around. She had to. He wouldn't stop until he possessed her body and soul.

Nate pulled back; her lips were swollen and puffy from his kisses. He cupped her face. "You drive me crazy, and I love every insane moment of being with you."

"I love being with you too, Nate." But her eyes, swirling with intense emotion, said so much more.

He pressed a kiss to her temple. She might still be in denial, but Nate knew better. The truth written in her eyes was as plain as words on a page.

He moved down and flicked his tongue across her nipple, then sucked deeply.

She threw her head back, sending silky strands of crimson across his white pillows.

He spread her thighs and positioned himself at her entrance. Slowly, he inched inside, felt her relax, opening to accommodate his length. Her sigh as he filled her was as sweet as honey. Once he was sure she was ready, he took her harder, withdrawing all the way, then burying his cock deep inside. It didn't take long until she was on the verge of orgasm. On the ragged edge, right where he wanted her.

"Please, Nate," she cried out, breathy, desperate sounds, her eyes blazing brightly. "Faster, harder," she panted. "Don't make me beg."

"Begging is exactly what you'll be doing," Nate said. "After what you just did to me, you're dreaming if you think I'll go easy on you, babe." Nate gripped her hips, causing her legs to spread farther. "Don't expect to be free of those cuffs before daylight."

CHAPTER THIRTY

Pia's eyes sprang open. She'd been asleep only a few hours. She could see the faint outline of daylight behind Nate's block-out blinds.

Something had woken her up.

Nate, true to his promise, had kept her in cuffs until sunrise. Her body deliciously sated, she'd fallen into a deep boneless sleep, her limbs entwined with Nate's. She still felt the warm, sated sensation of a golden afterglow.

Nate's breathing was regular and warm on her skin. She closed her eyes.

Tap. Tap. Scraape.

Something was moving on the dressing table across the room. Whatever it was that wanted her attention, she was not interested.

Not now. Pia radiated the message forcefully outwards, deliberately not peering into the darkened room.

Tap. Tap. Tap. Scraaaape!

She rubbed at a faint ache in her wrists and carefully untwined herself from Nate's arms, sat up, and took a sip of water from the glass on the bedside table, then stilled, holding the cool glass in her fingers a moment before gently setting it back down.

Something was watching her.

Pia closed her eyes and sighed heavily. *Leave me alone, dammit.*

She'd had such a great night with Nate; it would be nice to feel "normal" for a bit longer. At least for a few more hours. Until lunchtime.

She lay back down and closed her eyes, but the sensation of being watched increased, and a cool breeze blew across her cheeks.

Something was still trying to get her attention.

Go away!

The prickly sensation persisted, turning from insistent to angry. Pia cautiously sat up, reached out to sense what type of energy she was dealing with. *Who is it? What do you want?*

She rested on her elbows, peering around the room. No shadowy figure standing at the end of the bed. Nothing standing in the open doorway. No visible manifestation at all.

And yet, something was here just the same.

Maple Street.

What? Pia shook her head in confusion. *What the hell does Maple Street have to do with anything?*

Maple Street! The words hit her more forcefully this time.

I heard you, Pia said. *I don't need to hear it louder. What does it mean?*

Her.

She recognized the energy now. Sarah.

Pia was instantly awake.

Meg Farrell lives on Maple Street?

The air in the room changed abruptly, the electrical charge leaving the air. Pia peered through the darkness, surveying the room. Everything once again felt normal. There was only Nate and her in the room now. Pia was about to exhale when…

She blinked, then blinked again. Sarah's doll was no longer in the guest bedroom two doors down.

It was sitting in the chair in the corner.

Chapter Thirty-One

Nate paused, coffee mugs in both hands, and took a moment to savor the image of Pia on his balcony, the way the late morning sunlight caught and highlighted strands of her red hair. She wore it long and loose this morning, her face bare. He loved the way she dressed, her clothes, her makeup. She looked so fierce, so confident, and so damn sexy.

But he loved this Pia just as much, if not more. The tender side she hid behind the layers. Fresh-faced, dressed in nothing but his T-shirt. She was still living out of a suitcase, having only what she'd brought for the investigation with the team. Nate wanted to broach the subject of her staying here with him, but the timing wasn't right.

Would she be willing to move to Perth? Nate hoped she'd be open to the idea; there would be nowhere safer for her than here with him in this house. Being his girlfriend would mean she'd be seen as Nate's weakness to the people he'd helped put behind bars. To the type of people he and Taipan pissed off on a regular basis, there was no such thing as scruples; family often became a target designed to inflict the most pain. Or extort the biggest ransom.

Nate didn't know how this was all going to work out just yet, but one thing he knew for certain: Pia had become as essential to him as oxygen.

He crossed onto the balcony. She turned and smiled, and his chest squeezed. She looked so stunningly beautiful framed against the backdrop of the sundrenched coastline. The Sunset Coast of Western Australia was his favorite place in the whole world. He hoped to share it with Pia. He'd prefer not to have to relocate to Adelaide, but he would.

For her.

Already, there was nothing in his power he wouldn't give her.

"Morning, babe," Nate said, kissing her cheek and inhaling the scent of his shampoo on her still-damp hair. "Sleep well?" He ruthlessly pushed aside a rush of desire at the question. He'd like nothing more than to drag her back to bed, continue what exhaustion had forced them to abandon in the early hours of the morning.

Not today. Not now. There was no time. The whole team would arrive in the next few hours, and they needed to go over the details for tonight, choose the exact spot for the takedown. Talk strategy, weapons. How to handle Ben...

But as he passed Pia her coffee, he noticed a shadow in her eyes. "Everything okay?" He knew she'd risen before him, but now he wondered if she'd been up for hours. Was she worried about Mark? Or worried about Sarah? As soon as Daniel had told Sarah's parents, Patricia and Henry Bradford, they'd insisted on flying in. To see where Sarah had been kept.

Nate was less than happy to learn that was the case; he'd intended for the Bradfords to just be informed for now. He'd wanted to speak to them as part of the investigation. Perhaps they knew something, anything, that could give clues as to how the Farrells tied in. Was the whole thing random, or did the Bradfords know the Farrells somehow?

Nate had originally thought the kidnapping might have even been some sort of extortion attempt. Speaking to the parents of the victim was a standard avenue of questioning. But there was nothing to be done; the Bradfords were landing at ten p.m. this evening. He wouldn't be there when Pia met them. His grip tightened on the railing.

Damn Ben to hell and back. Nate wanted to be with Pia every step of the way. Having to leave her, only for a second, was the worst type of torture. "I'm sorry I won't be with you tonight."

"You have more important things to concern yourself with." But that wasn't true. Nothing was more important than Pia.

Then why am I going? Nate's frustration level increased.

"Is that what's worrying you?" Nate asked. Pia was staring into her coffee cup, her brows furrowed together.

"I think I know where Meg Farrell is," she said softly. Whatever he'd thought she was going to say, he hadn't expected that. He frowned; he hadn't heard from Zach.

"You do?" Nate took a sip of his strong coffee. "Where?"

"Maple Street." Pia waved a hand to indicate the outdoor table full of papers. Nate had been so focused on the image of Pia against the ocean, he hadn't even noticed the off-road map of Western Australia she had open. *Or Sarah's doll sitting right next to it.*

What the hell was that thing doing out here? Nate shivered and averted his gaze. Pia should be more concerned about that object. The doll looked, and worse, *felt* sinister. He didn't like the idea of it being in his house and couldn't wait until this case was over and that thing could be removed. Even better, destroyed.

"Okay, back up." Nate drew his attention back to Pia. "What makes you think Meg Farrell lives on a Maple Street? Has Zach been in contact with you directly?" It would have been highly unusual for that to be the case.

"Nothing that concrete. Sarah told me."

Sarah told her. Of course. Nate tried to unclench his twisting stomach. "She didn't happen to tell you a house number and suburb?"

That got a small smile. "If only it worked that way. I've searched online; there aren't that many Maple Streets it could be, and looking at the map, I sensed which one it could be."

"But you're not sure."

"I'm never sure. I'm never sure," Pia repeated intensely, eyes glistening.

"What?" Nate prompted, his already considerable inner turmoil ratcheting up another notch. "What aren't you telling me? Don't hold anything back. I need to know everything."

"Oh, Nate. What if I'm wrong about tonight?" The hand that brushed the hair out of her face was shaking. "What if I gave you the wrong location, and you and your team have wasted all your time and resources. What if Ben gets—"

He leaned in, silencing her with a kiss. "They don't know the shipment is coming from Malaga, but our own intel has confirmed it as highly likely." Especially as it was his father's warehouse, and Ben was involved.

"So you've double-checked my information," Pia said with a little relief.

"Nothing personal. It's what we do."

"No, I'm happier that way. I'm never a hundred percent sure—especially when someone I care about is involved—and I'd hate to be a laughingstock."

"You could never be that," Nate said, and meant every word. Taipan respected the hell out of her.

Pia shook her head sadly. "You're wrong once, and people instantly think you're a fraud. It's like they're waiting for you to slip up so they can say 'I told you so.'"

Nate's heart twisted. "Any information you provide me or the team will always be taken as a lead, nothing more, nothing less. Often our leads turn into dead ends. It's never an issue. We simply revisit and revise. And if a lead turns out to help, all the better."

"You're such a cool customer, Nate Ryder," Pia said, and he felt her smile all the way to his toes.

Her smile faded, and Nate immediately tensed.

"I'm going for a drive to Maple Street. Good luck for tonight."

Goodbye? No! He wasn't ready.

"I'm coming with you," Nate blurted. He couldn't imagine not going. He certainly wasn't prepared to say goodbye to her now. Just let her drive off while he went in the opposite direction.

"No, you're not." Pia placed her palms on his chest. "You have the team arriving soon."

"I've got time," Nate said, not entirely sure that was true, only knowing it had to be that way. "I'm not letting you go see Meg alone. Why don't we wait until tomorrow? We can both see her together."

Pia's brow furrowed. "I need to act now. What if she disappears? What if she's not there tomorrow? What if she can tell me what happened to Sarah, and I can give the Bradfords full closure. They're arriving tonight. I can't put this off."

"What difference does one night make?" The Bradfords have already waited thirty years.

"Sarah has been living the life she never had through Cassandra. I... I don't know what she's capable of. And I can't take the chance. I can't push aside this restless feeling inside me, Nate. This feeling that something is going to happen, and it's going to happen tonight."

Tonight. When I'm not there to help you.

To save you.

With every fiber of his being, Nate needed to know she'd be safe. He felt like a drowning man. He was going under and there was nothing he could do to change that fact. He had to trust in Blade to protect her. But if Nate couldn't be with her tonight, the least he could do was visit Meg with her today.

Pia touched his arm. "I'll be fine. Who knows, maybe this Maple Street thing will turn into a dead end. I'd feel better if you just concentrated on yourself. You worry far too much about me."

"Get used to it, babe," Nate said softly. "It's only going to get worse. Listen, I have time if we move out right now." Nate looked at his watch. It was at least a good two hours' drive away. If they left soon, they'd arrive at Maple street, early afternoon. "How long will you need to get ready?"

"How long does it take to slide into a pair of jeans?"

"Settled then." Nate moved, but Pia stopped by the table.

"Do you have a safe?" she asked.

"A safe? Yes. Commercial grade. We use it to store weapons and goods we've seized. Why?"

Pia peered at the doll. "I think we had better put Sarah's doll in there."

Nate opened his mouth and closed it again. Why ask a question you didn't want to know the answer to?

"Good idea," he said. "But I'm not carrying it there."

Chapter Thirty-Two

Sarah
20 April 1986
Sarah's 16th Birthday

I hear footsteps overhead, and I barely open my eyes. I don't care anymore.

What's the point of opening my eyes when there's nothing I want to see? I no longer dream of leaving here.

What's the point when it's never going to happen?

Time stopped a long time ago. Froze me in Hell. What did I do so wrong as to deserve this? Is God punishing me for the time I took two biscuits when I was allowed only one? For the time I took a sip of Mummy's wine when she wasn't looking just to see what it tasted like?

A nose, whiskers on the skin of my arm, tiny feet scratching. Templeton hears the footsteps too. He senses my pain, the suffering that continues long after the monster leaves. Templeton jumps onto my lap, runs up my chest, and nuzzles my neck. With an arm that's almost become too heavy to lift, I stroke his fur.

"I'm tired, Templeton," I murmur. "So terribly tired."

He knows. He senses the end is near. Templeton has been my friend for two years. He's tired too.

Mice don't live very long. I think I remember that from a lifetime ago? There are so many questions I will never know the answers to still in my head.

What happens to the questions when you die? Will they finally be answered? Or will eternity turn out to be as cruel as life? Perhaps there's nothing at all. You close your eyes, and *it all becomes an endless darkness. What does it matter anyway?*

I just want to stop hurting. I want my body to stop aching.

I won't be getting out of here alive. Memories of my life outside the hole have disappeared into a hazy blur. I can't remember what was real and what is my imagination. Sometimes I wonder whether there even was anything else. Did I really have a mother and father? Or did I dream them from the start?

When the memories first began fading, I spent hours concentrating on every single memory from my life at home, replaying every single second. Desperate to keep the images clear and bright.

But like butterflies through a hole in a net, they've flown away.

I'm too tired to catch them.

Are they real? Are they not?

I'm too tired to even care.

Tiny feet run down my arm, and then Templeton nuzzles my palm. It's as though he knows I'm not strong enough to keep my hand raised to pet him.

I love you, little Templeton.

My bestest friend in the whole wide world.

The trap door opens, and blinding light hurts my eyes, even through closed lids.

There was a time I used to peer up through the hole, needing to know if it was him or her. Or him… Wanting those few seconds to prepare, to brace myself for what would come.

Now I don't care either way.

It's all the same.

I roll over onto my side, not even bothering to open my eyes.

Templeton climbs over, snuggles himself up against my chest. I kiss his tiny little head. "You can have all my food today," I whisper.

I'm tired.

And I continue to grow more tired.

The bigger my tummy gets.

Chapter Thirty-Three

A woman with a round face and sparse gray hair opened the door, peering through the crack. Pia knew her to be sixty, but her thin, time-ravaged skin and the heavy crow's feet around her eyes made her look so much older.

"Are you Meg Farrell?" Nate asked formally.

"Maybe." She eyed them suspiciously. "Who are you and what do you want?"

"Mrs. Farrell, I'm Detective Senior Constable Nate Ryder, and this is Constable Williams." Nate flashed his old police identification badge.

When she hesitated, Nate softened his voice. "We were hoping you could assist us with a case. Can we come inside? We only have a few questions. It won't take too much of your time."

Mrs. Farrell hesitated the briefest moment before she opened the door. Pia couldn't fault her; Nate had that way about him. A potent mixture of authority and persuasive charm.

"I suppose I can answer a few questions," she said, and led them down a dark hallway to the kitchen at the rear of the house. They walked in a direct line from the doorway at the front to the doorway at the rear of the house.

Bad feng shui. Although, looking around the dark cluttered house, Pia concluded that unlucky *chi* flow was the least of Meg Farrell's problems.

There was a cat on the kitchen sink, licking the chopping board, and another two cats sitting on piles of… garbage and dirty plates. Pia saw seven mouse traps from where she was standing. How did the cats manage not to get their paws caught?

The house wasn't just messy; it was chaotic. But the worst of it was the smell. The reason Mrs. Farrell didn't open the windows was because she clearly couldn't get to them.

Pia declined a drink—a quick glance at the overflowing sink confirmed there'd be no clean glasses—and stood near the kitchen table.

Mrs. Farrell shifted a mouse trap and began taking stacks of books, newspapers, clothes, and cat chew toys off the kitchen chairs and stacking them on top of the piles on the floor. She didn't apologize for the mess. It was clear she didn't have visitors often. Or at all.

"How do you stop the cats from messing with the mouse traps?" Pia asked, a little concerned for their welfare.

Mrs. Farrell rearranged some items on the table, but her skin reddened, spreading up her neck and across her face. "Oh, I set a few off in front of them; the noise scares them. You do that a couple of times, they soon know to stay away."

Pia and Nate exchanged glances.

"You have a big mouse problem then?" Nate asked, obviously noticing as Pia had that oddly enough, there was no evidence of mice droppings.

"Mice everywhere. Have been for years. Can't get rid of them no matter what I do. They wake me up in the night; that's when they're out and about, you know. Can't sleep. Never can sleep. Damn mice. Damn cats ought to do a better job." She narrowed her eyes. "Why are you here?"

"There's been another death in your old house," Pia said. "The lighthouse keeper's cottage." The color visibly drained from Meg's face. She stood there, an empty soft drink bottle in one hand and a fork in the other, and even though Pia asked the question, it was Nate she answered.

"The house is cursed. I told the police at the time everything I know about my husband's murder," she said. "Des's too. I don't want to talk about it anymore."

Outwardly, she portrayed a practiced calm, but her unease emitted waves of prickly energy that set Pia's nerves on edge.

"It's very interesting you chose to use the word 'murder,' Mrs. Farrell," Nate said evenly. "It was my understanding your husband's death was ruled an accident."

"Murder. Accident." She waved a hand dismissively. "What does it matter? He's dead and ain't coming back. All's I got left is me cats and these bloody mice." With surprising ease, considering she had to clamber over the stuff on the floor, Meg flicked a tea towel at a corner, apparently shooing away… something.

But nothing was there. No mice. Just clutter.

The mice weren't real.

The scent in the room strengthened, going from bad to repugnant. Pia could take only half-breaths, for fear of being sick, and looked longingly toward the kitchen window and the fresh air outside.

"Here you go. Have a seat." Meg indicated three grimy fabric-covered chairs of indeterminate color.

Pia briefly met Nate's eyes, and they both sat down.

"Do you really think your husband was murdered?" Pia asked. "And Des Wilson too?"

Yes, they was damn well murdered! The thought hit Pia in a rush.

"We never found out what happened," Meg said, affecting a sorrowful look that didn't match the anger Pia sensed in her. Meg looked down, apparently noticed her fingers shaking, and locked her hands together in her lap. "I don't like to think about it," she said abruptly, her voice rising an octave. "What are you doing, coming here after all these years, opening that can of worms? What's done is done. Ain't no changing the past. If you just want to dig around in what's none of your business, you can leave."

A cat sprang onto Meg's lap, and she jumped, before giving a short, slightly hysterical laugh. "Sammy could do with a bell. Damn cats always scaring the hell out of me." Meg turned her head, narrowing her gaze on Pia. "What do you want from me after all these years?"

"There are similarities between the recent death in the house to your husband's and Des Wilson's."

"How so?"

Although numerous newspapers were scattered around the house, none of them appeared recent. Pia leaned back, surreptitiously glanced at a stack of books and papers on the end chair, and pulled the corner of the newspaper out. 30 July 1986. *Didn't like to think about it?* How then did a newspaper from thirty years ago—from the day Des Wilson died—end up at the *top* of all this clutter?

"We think you may know the recent victim," Nate said.

"Who?"

"Tom Kelly."

A pot fell from a pile beside the sink, landing noisily on the floor. Meg placed a hand over her heart, her breathing becoming erratic.

"Tom?" Her eyes widened. "Dead? What was he doing back in that house? He should never have gone back. What was he thinking?"

"He was helping with an investigation," Nate said.

"Was he looking for me?" Meg said, turning.

"Why would he be looking for you?" Nate asked.

"I can't help you. I don't know anything. I haven't seen Tom in years."

Nate, apparently noticing her nervous reaction, began asking a series of questions rapid-fire, clearly a cop tactic designed to elicit the truth by leaving the interviewee no time to think about their answers.

Meg's distress was mounting, causing images to form in her mind that Pia could tune in to. Painful memories, as Nate's relentless probing caused her to relive the past. Pia kept her mind open, catching the images, rearranging and piecing them together like pictures in a storybook.

As Nate's questions continued, Pia was swamped by a barrage of heavy emotion pouring off the woman. Fear. She was scared of Nate. Of what his presence now meant. For her. But the most overwhelming emotion of all was hatred. Hatred for a little girl she held responsible for everything. For the loss of her husband, her marriage, her happy life by the ocean, for her current situation being trapped in this house.

There was a distinct absence of any sense of guilt or responsibility, only a black void where empathy should have been.

"How'd he die?" Meg asked.

"Knife wound," Nate said.

Meg sat up straight. "What kind of knife?"

"A fishing knife," Nate said. "Why?"

"Did it have an eagle handle?"

"Yes."

Meg visibly paled.

It can't be, Meg said in her mind. *I got rid of that. Dear God, I got rid of that once and for all. It's back. It's all coming back.*

"You've seen that knife before, haven't you?" Pia asked.

Meg folded her arms and closed her eyes in a way that suggested she was done talking to them.

But Pia wasn't done talking to her. "We know about Sarah."

"Who?" Meg said, but her eyes were open again. Wide open.

"Sarah." Meg winced, and her left eye began to twitch. "We know what your husband did to *Sarah*," Pia said.

"How?" *There's no way they can know*, Meg was saying in her mind. *They can't know. Tom wouldn't have told someone. Would he?*

"Was it Tom?"

"It doesn't matter how we know," Nate said. "All that should concern you is that we do."

"Tell us what happened," Pia said. "You've been keeping this bottled up for all these years. Getting this off your chest will unburden you from this terrible secret."

Pia expected to feel Meg's defenses crumbling. She imagined that Meg would have wanted, after all these years, to unburden herself. Surely she felt weighed down by her lies, by covering up her husband's atrocities all these years. The lies she told should feel smothering, much like the clutter filling this house.

Instead, Pia felt a wave of coolness. She shifted in her seat uncomfortably, unable to get a satisfactory read on the woman in front of her.

"Did you want to tell the police back then, when your husband died? Were you too scared that someone wouldn't believe you? What would they have thought if you'd tried to point a finger at a ghost?"

Meg narrowed her eyes. "What ghost?" But her eyes darted to the mouse traps dotted around the room.

"We know about Sarah," Pia repeated.

Meg twirled her finger around the cat's tail. She pulled too tight, and it lashed out with its claws. Abruptly, Meg hurled the cat off her lap, and it smacked against an old heater, letting out a mewl of pain as it did.

"Damn useless no-good animal," Meg grumbled.

Her hands clenched in fists, Pia leaned forward, and Nate laid a restraining hand on her leg. She nearly bit her tongue right off to stop herself telling this wretched woman what she thought of her.

Only the fact that she sensed Meg was about to open up stayed her. Pia couldn't wait until this woman was behind bars and these cats could be rehomed.

"Simon, my husband, wanted a son," Meg said, grabbing another cat by the scruff of its neck and setting it on her lap. It didn't attempt to jump off, but neither did it relax and purr.

"Just like all the men back then, he wanted a boy of his own to take over the family cray-fishing business. His father had handed down the cray license to him. The only way to be successful is to inherit a license; they're bloody expensive to buy. Simon wanted to hand the business down. That's what you do. That's what's expected."

Meg reached for a crumpled pack of cigarettes, lit one, then holding the cigarette in her mouth, reached for the nearby ashtray. It was overflowing. Meg tipped it over, emptying it onto the mess on the floor, and set it back down within easy reach.

Pia looked away.

"We tried and tried for a baby, but I was barren," Meg continued. "By the end, Simon wouldn't have cared if it was a girl. He just wanted a child. He was a good man," she said, and Nate and Pia exchanged glances.

"He blamed me, you know, for bringing that girl home," Meg said coldly. "Simon saw her floating in the water that day and thought she was a gift from God. An answer to his prayers. Too much bourbon, that's what it was. Too long at sea. That's why sailors see mermaids. They stop being able to think clearly, and they imagine things. Simon was coming home from a trip, desperate for a child, and there she was, floating in the water in front of him. What was he to do?"

Help her? Take her to the authorities? Find out where she came from? Save her?

A ginger cat walked past, and Meg dumped the black and white cat onto the floor, then grabbed the ginger cat by the scruff of its neck, put it on her lap, and began to stroke its back. "Finding that bitch ruined our lives." Pia flinched at the callousness in her tone.

"That night," Meg said bitterly, "Simon was so proud of himself, over what he'd done. Thought I'd be happy he'd solved our problems. He'd given us a child, he said. I couldn't do it, so *he* did."

Pia could feel Nate's disgust, his anger, at what this woman and her husband had done, but his expression was unreadable.

"He was an idiot," Meg continued. "I don't know what the hell he was thinking. The girl was eleven, for God's sake, not a baby. She had a life, a family she wanted to return to. The little bitch went on, and on, and *on*, about them. Wouldn't shut up. Made Simon real angry."

Meg shuddered. "Simon could get pretty mad when he was pushed, and she didn't know when to shut her mouth. 'I wanna go home. I want Mummy. I want Daddy.' On and on and on. But Simon didn't give up on her; he was convinced if we kept her for long enough, she would accept us as her new family. Said God wouldn't have given her to him if it wasn't meant to be. Simon had been shown the Divine plan, you see."

Meg mumbled something unintelligible as she stroked the cat, her eyes slightly unfocused, lost in memories of the past.

"Of course, this was easier to do all those years ago," she continued after a pause. "Before there was this Internet thing and social whatch-ya call it, where everyone knows everyone's business. A missing child from England barely made the papers here back then."

"So your husband found a young girl in the ocean and brought her home. What happened then?" Pia said, fighting to keep the disgust from her tone and failing. Meg didn't seem to notice. Or if she did, didn't care.

Pia didn't want her to stop talking until they knew the whole story.

Mrs. Farrell narrowed her eyes. "The ungrateful bitch wouldn't shut up. She fought us tooth and nail. Spat and kicked, refused to eat. After all we were doing for her!" Meg's face reddened. "We gave her a home. She even had her own room, pillow, and everything. It was her fault we had to keep the door locked all the time. If she'd stopped trying to escape, she could have done without the shackles. We gave her everything a kid could want. But was she happy?"

Meg shook her head and continued sarcastically. "No. Nothing was ever good enough for Princess. The spoilt brat couldn't appreciate even the smallest things. She'd have drowned out there had we not saved her. And did she thank us?" Meg demanded. "Not once! It was all wah, wah, wah. 'I wanna go home. I want Mummy. When's Daddy coming to save me?' Simon kept defending her. 'Some Divine plan,' I used to tell him."

Oh, this woman was too much! "Did you consider Sarah's family?" Pia couldn't stop herself from demanding. "That they might be worried sick over her? That what you did was wrong? That you should have done whatever it took to reunite her with her parents?"

"What?" Meg asked, blinking at Pia as though she'd spoken another language.

Nate shot Pia a speaking glance, and she tasted blood as she actually bit her tongue this time. How the hell did Nate do this calm-detective routine day in, day out? Pia wanted to choke the life right out of Meg Farrell.

"Simon and I began to fight. *Really* fight," Meg said sadly. "A child was supposed to make us happy. But it didn't. I could see it was useless. I was angry at her, but I was angry at him too, you see, that he got us into this mess. He said *I* got us into this mess. As if I asked to be barren! We argued day and night over what to do. He spent more and more time at sea. I stopped feeding her, thought if she was too tired and weak, she would shut up about going home. That didn't work. Her moaning and crying was just as irritating as her screaming. I tried to ignore her. Pretend she didn't exist. Then Simon would come home, feed her, look after her, and undo all my good work."

Pia was stunned. How could she be so coldblooded? Could she not see this through Sarah's perspective at all?

"I began to hate her," Meg continued. "She was a burden for me while he was away, but he said it was all my fault. He told me that a *real woman* would have been able to give him a child." Meg brought her grimy hands to her face, scratched at a small sore on her cheek with fingernails bitten to the quick.

Pia's stomach churned. These vile people. This woman with ice water in her veins. No wonder Sarah was unable to rest. *I won't stop until I have you justice either*, Pia vowed.

"Having the child in the house was a reminder of God's punishment. A constant one."

"Tell us what happened to Sarah," Nate's tone was even, controlled, but his jaw was clenched, and his hands were fisted at his sides.

"The months dragged on," Meg continued, seemingly wanting to get the story out at her own pace. She'd waited thirty years to tell it. "She still didn't accept us as her family. We were trapped. What could we do?" she asked, raising her brows. "You must be able to understand the position she put us in? We couldn't release her; we would go to jail!" Meg said, as if that would have been a gross miscarriage of justice.

"Des Wilson was over for dinner, and he heard noises upstairs coming from her bedroom. At the time, the little bitch was still doing everything she could to escape. She must have heard the car, knew we had a visitor. She broke the leg off a chair, used it to attempt to lever off the boards Simon had nailed across the window.

"Des hadn't realized we still had her at the time. Simon had told Des we'd handed her in to the authorities. Des was angry with Simon when he found out. They argued. I was so worried Des would dob Simon in. It was terrible, the situation she put us in. I told Des to help us get rid of her, but neither of them wanted to kill her. Bloody fools. In the end, it was Des who came up with the perfect solution. He helped Simon dig a cellar. After all, he reasoned, what if someone else had been over when Sarah made all that noise? That girl would have gotten us all in trouble. So Simon and Des built a home for her. A cellar close to the house, but far enough away that no one could hear if we had visitors." She said it as though it had been a great solution.

"We gave her everything she needed. Poor Simon never gave up hope that one day, he'd go down and find she'd forgotten her old family and would ask to come back to the house and be with us."

"But that didn't happen," Nate said, his voice tight, his disgust for this woman disguised from her, but not from Pia.

"No." Mrs. Farrell's eyes hardened. "Time went on, and I noticed a change in my husband. He began to spend longer and longer periods of time down there in between trips out at sea. He said it was because she was coming around, but I suspected she was seducing him." Her lips curled in disgust. "I knew what she was doing, teasing him with her growing titties."

Pia bit her tongue again to stop herself from doing this woman serious damage. Nate made a low noise in the back of his throat, his body tensed. Like her, he was using every ounce of willpower he possessed not to react, to let Meg Farrell finish her depraved story.

"Poor Simon did everything he could to teach her decency, to curb her wild and wanton tendencies." Meg shook her head in frustration. "Simon stopped coming to me, at night I mean"—her face reddened—"but I understood it was only because he was trying so hard to reform the demon child. It began to take all his spare time and energy."

I bet it did.

"Then one day, Simon came in happy again. 'Rejoice,' he said. He finally understood God's plan for him. Why He sent us the girl. She wasn't supposed to be our child; she was sent to *provide* us with a child. Simon prepared a nursery. We were so excited. At first."

Pia couldn't believe that even after thirty years Meg didn't seem to feel any guilt or shame over what had happened to Sarah. That her husband had raped a young girl under unspeakable conditions.

"Was the baby born?" Nate asked.

"Yes," Meg said, her eyes hard. "We had it for three days."

That revelation hit Pia hard, and she sat up straight in her chair. She didn't see the spirit of a baby with Sarah as she often would in such cases. She couldn't see the death of a child at all.

"Boy or girl?" Nate pressed, as Meg started looking around the room distractedly. As though the story no longer interested her.

"Boy."

"What happened to him?" Pia asked.

Meg shrugged and the cat jumped off her lap.

"What happened to the baby, Mrs. Farrell?" Nate repeated Pia's question using his cop tone.

"It was sick," Meg answered. "We couldn't take it to the hospital and risk questions. We didn't want to get in trouble. Not after it took us so long to achieve what we had set out to do. They do say that the Lord works in mysterious ways."

"So the baby was sick, and you refused to get it medical attention. What did you do then?" Pia asked.

"It up and died the same night as Des," she said abruptly, with the amount of emotion someone would use talking about what to make for dinner. Something was seriously wrong with Meg Farrell. She lacked the most basic human attributes, such as empathy and a conscience.

But still, Pia sensed they were not being told the whole truth.

"Of course," Meg continued in an odd emotionless voice, "I couldn't have kept it myself anyway. Not without a husband. It was Simon who'd wanted the thing so bad in the first place. And then he was gone. So what use was a hungry kid to me at that time anyway?"

Abruptly, Meg rose from the chair, kicking the cat at her feet, knocking it over, and watching as it scrambled to find purchase on the stuff on the floor.

"Useless animals, cats," she mumbled.

Between the horrific story, relayed in such a cold-hearted manner and the stench in the room, Pia's stomach began to heave and her head to spin.

She'd had enough of the way Meg referred to the baby as "it" and "thing." The fact she seemed to feel no guilt or remorse at all for what she and her husband had done was incomprehensible. This woman was pure evil.

"What happened to Sarah?" Nate pressed. Pia closed her eyes briefly and braced herself. She wasn't sure she could handle hearing Meg's cold summation of Sarah's death.

"Died."

"How?" Nate asked.

"Dunno."

But you do.

"Mrs. Farrell," Pia said, swallowing the bile that had risen in her throat. "Can you tell us what you or your husband did with her body? The bodies," Pia managed through a constricted throat. Nate reached out, touched her hand.

Meg's face hardened. "Buried them."

"Where?" Pia asked.

"What's it to you?" She narrowed her eyes. "What's in it for me?"

"It will go in your favor if you cooperate," Nate said, using the cop tone she seemed to respond to. She didn't respond to emotion, but she did when given direction.

"I'm going to jail, aren't I?" she asked.

"Yes," Nate said, the muscles along his clenched jaw twitching. "I'm taking you in." Nate was not officially on the force anymore, but his former colleagues still respected him. Pia knew he would take Meg directly to the station, to Johnson, and the police would "officially" take the matter from there.

Surprisingly, Meg seemed neither upset nor concerned by the idea of going to jail. She huffed out a breath and shrugged. "I suppose it doesn't matter to me now anyway. What have I got left? No husband, no children. My parents died many years ago. I have nothing left here for me anyway. Except my cats. If I tell you, you have to promise to take care of my cats."

"We'll find good homes for them," Nate said, rolling his shoulders.

"In prison there'll be company," she mumbled to herself. "I might find myself a friend. That would be nice. Been a while since I had someone to talk to. Someone other than cats, I mean. And there won't be mice in jail. And I won't have to cook meals." Pia glanced at the sink, at the dishes stacked so high it was impossible to even find the tap, let alone turn it on.

"Where did you bury the bodies?" Nate repeated the question firmly.

"I'll show you," Meg said. "Take me to the house first. I want to say my goodbyes to Simon and Des. Tom too now. We were all so close once. And now they're… they're all dead. S'pose I won't be getting out of jail now until I'm dead too."

"You're not in a position to be making demands," Nate ground out.

"Then you'll never find them," Meg said, her expression blanking. "You can't make me talk. I've already told you enough to get me locked up for the rest of my life. I'll die without telling you where they are."

Nate looked at Pia in question. Could they take the chance that Meg wouldn't ever disclose the whereabouts of the bodies?

"I need to know," Pia said quietly to Nate. Hoping he could read between the lines. Understand that Sarah needed her story told, and her body found for her parents to have closure. For her to have peace.

"You can make a deal at the station," Nate said.

An image, powerful, disturbing, flashed in Pia's mind. But it wasn't a vision of Sarah, or Sarah's baby, as she might have expected.

The image was of Nate.

His strong, muscular body streaked with blood. His body falling, hitting the ground. And he wasn't getting back up.

Pia gasped, her heart racing. She turned wide eyes on Nate. What was she being shown?

Oh God no! Not Nate!

Nate misunderstood, attributing her reaction to the situation with Meg. "Do you want me to take her to the house?"

Pia sensed Nate's deepening concern. He didn't like seeing her upset. He was impatient now, to wrap this up, to see Meg Farrell behind bars. Stat.

Pia placed a hand on his arm, and he immediately met her eyes in question. She focused on Meg and tried to push the disturbing vision of Nate away for the moment.

"Perhaps it would be a good idea to allow Meg a chance to go back to the house," Pia said. "For closure." Understanding slowly came into Nate's eyes as he absorbed what he believed to be her wordless communication.

To let Sarah get her justice. Nate interpreted her comment. *The way she did with Simon, Des, and now Tom.*

He raised his brow briefly in surprise, then nodded his agreement.

That's not what Pia had intended. *Was it?*

Pia needed to find out where the bodies were buried so that Sarah's spirit would be free to move to the light, to find the happiness she was so long ago denied. That had been Pia's only intention when she'd suggested the idea. Hadn't it?

Meg exhaled a stream of smoke over the cat, who closed its eyes and sneezed. The cat had no whiskers. An image of Meg burning them off with her cigarette flashed in Pia's mind.

Maybe subconsciously Pia *had* intended for Sarah to handle Meg. Her way.

Did taking pleasure in that idea make Pia just as bad as Meg, Simon, Des, and Tom?

And if she did help Sarah get her justice, her way, would it weigh on Pia's conscience years from now?

Somehow a prison term seemed inadequate. Meg didn't seem upset to be going to jail. And if anyone deserved to suffer, it was Meg Farrell.

"We'll take you to the house," Nate said, turning his gaze from Pia to Meg. "You can say your goodbyes and show us where the bodies are buried, *then* I'll take you in."

Pia read Nate's intentions clearly. He'd arrange to have Johnson there at the house when Pia, Ethan, and Meg arrived. Johnson would see what happened to Meg inside the house, and therefore he would then be unable to deny the paranormal aspect of her death—and Tom Kelly's.

Justice would be served all around.

Pia's stomach churned. Could she really lead a woman—no matter how evil—to her death? It was one thing believing someone deserved it, but to actually do it?

Undeniably, there was a part of her that could.

But *should* she?

Meg stroked the ginger cat for a few breaths and considered. "Give me a moment. I want to put some clean clothes on. Organize some things here. Put food in the cats' bowls. Say goodbye to them."

Pia could no longer suppress the vision she'd had of Nate. It surged back, overlaying the current situation, confusing her and making her head spin. She started to lose her balance, and Nate steadied her.

The contact brought the new vision to the forefront of her mind. *Nate!* She caught flashes of something so disturbing, she instinctively shut them out for self-preservation. *No!*

What was she seeing?

What was going to happen to Nate?

The emotion accompanying the vision was so strong, so overwhelmingly powerful, Pia's eyes stung with the acute sense of loss. It didn't matter that Nate was hale and whole in front of her at this present moment.

In her mind, he was dead.

Nate brought his face close to hers, looked searchingly into her eyes. "What is it?" he whispered. "Pia, honey, what's wrong?"

She couldn't breathe in this cesspool. The walls were closing in around her. The clutter. The junk. *The stench.* Pia placed her hand over her mouth, fighting the need to be sick. She needed fresh air. *Now.*

Pia moved as quickly to the door as wading through the junk would allow. She wanted to focus on the vision of Nate, and yet didn't want to.

No. No. No! That could not happen. Was there something she could do?

Can I stop it from happening?

CHAPTER THIRTY-FOUR

In a scraggly geranium plant out in front of Meg Farrell's house, Pia was violently ill. Nate stood by her side, holding her hair back, running a soothing hand across her shoulders, down her spine. Eventually Pia straightened and dragged in a ragged breath.

It was then she understood just how much the thought of losing him destroyed her.

I'm in love with you.

Of course she'd already known it; she just hadn't been ready to put it into words. What shocked her was how deep her feelings for Nate ran.

The vision she'd had of Nate had shown her the devastation she would feel over losing him.

I can't lose him. I won't!

Life couldn't be that cruel, could it?

Pia gripped the collar of his shirt as panic clawed its way up her throat.

She looked up into his handsome face, his eyes creased with concern and worry. She forgot about Sarah, Meg, and finding the bodies. Nothing mattered but Nate. Nothing was as important.

"I love you," she blurted. Despite everything they'd been through, she'd never put into words just what he meant to her.

"I love you," she repeated. "I really love you, goddammit!"

Nate grinned. "I was wondering how long it would take for you to finally realize what I've known for quite a while now."

"I'm sorry," Pia choked past the brick in her throat. "I shouldn't have waited so long. I should have told you a million times already."

"It doesn't matter. You can tell me a million times from now." His voice trailed off as his steel-blue eyes creased further in concern.

"Are you okay? Babe, you've got to tell me what's wrong. You're freaking me out."

What's wrong is that I could lose you tonight! No, that couldn't be right. She didn't get premonitions about people close to her.

And yet... her body shook, wracked and heavy with an ice-cold dread she couldn't shake. She stumbled, held her stomach, and was sick again.

"Pia, honey? Jesus!" He held her hair out of the way again and patted her back.

"I'm okay," she said, straightening. She wiped her sweaty palms on her jeans and took a deep breath.

"I seem to have missed a step," Nate said. "I'm usually fairly quick to catch on, but I'm at a loss here. One minute we're inside discussing Meg's imminent arrest, and the next you're throwing up in the bushes telling me you love me. I know you said romance is overrated, but I have to tell you, I expect a little more than that." His lips twitched into a smile.

Pia managed a wobbly smile of her own.

"I would have preferred that the thought of falling in love with me didn't make you physically ill. But I'll take what I can get."

Pia choked out a laugh that turned into a sob.

Now Nate looked even more worried.

"I love you, Nate. There, I said it. And I'm not even vomiting."

Pia tried to smile, but it slipped, and tears flooded her vision. She blinked them away. The image of Nate falling to his knees, his face hitting the dirt... no, bitumen. It was along a deserted stretch of highway.

Nate covered with blood. His body, so tall, so strong and muscular, crumpling as he fell. He didn't make a sound, didn't cry out. The only noise that accompanied the vision was a dull smack as the bullet embedded itself into his flesh, a *whoosh* as his breath left his lungs.

And the thud as his body hit the ground.

A lump lodged in Pia's throat, and she grabbed him by the shirt; this time, he caught her hands.

"Tell me." Nate pulled her close, cradling her head against his chest. "Tell me what's wrong, and what I need to do to fix it. You've got to start talking to me, and you'd better make it fast."

Pia sucked in a shaky breath and brought herself under control. Standing up straight, she turned her face to the sky and forcefully demanded that the images go away. Prayed she was wrong.

Knew she wasn't.

"Nate," Pia said, gripping his arm. Her nails dug into his skin, drawing blood, but she couldn't make herself stop. He didn't so much as flinch.

"Talk to me," he repeated.

"I have to somehow describe to you what I'm seeing. You... you need to be careful tonight."

"This is about *me?*" The furrow between his brows eased, and the tenderness in his eyes shredded her. "You're worried about me?" He smiled. "You are so sweet."

Pia glared at him. "I'm not *sweet!*" She palmed his chest hard. "And don't you dare do that, Nate Ryder."

"Do what?"

"You know what."

"What exactly did you see?" Nate tugged her to the car and gave her a drink of water from his bottle. As usual, he was more worried about her than himself.

"You," she said, taking another mouthful and handing him back the water bottle. "You were hurt. Seriously hurt, Nate."

"When?" Nate asked, fumbling around in the console and pulling out a packet of mints. He held the pack out and raised an eyebrow in question. She snatched a mint, mumbling her thanks. Why couldn't he take this seriously?

"Nate!"

"Sorry. Where and when was I hurt?"

"I… I'm not sure." The image had been so distressing, she hadn't held onto it long enough for details.

"Babe, what you need to understand is I take a calculated risk on every single case I go on. I've long since given up worrying about things like being hurt. If I ever did."

"This is not the same. I saw you fall, Nate." To the ground. The blood. *A bullet.* She blinked back the hot sting of tears. "I… I see you being shot. Tonight."

"Relax, babe. I've been shot before. More than once. You've seen the scars. You've even kissed them. If that's not incentive to get another one or two, I don't know what is." Nate gave Pia a half-smile, and she wanted to punch him.

Oh, she knew he was just trying to make light of it, to make her feel better. But nothing would. Not until she held him in her arms tomorrow. Alive and well.

"In my line of work, the odds are high I'll be shot again," Nate was saying. "Unless the shot is fatal, I'll live."

"Your blasé attitude can fuck off." She crossed her arms and conjured her most fierce scowl. "And your jokes aren't funny."

Nate just smiled. Then he grabbed her shoulders, pulled her flush against his body, and kissed her hard on the mouth. She was grateful for the mint then. After a moment, her mind blanked and she melted into him. And then she remembered what he was trying to distract her from and pushed him back. His lids heavy, he traced his tongue along his lips as though tasting her.

"I love that you worry about me," he said, then glanced at the house, and then at the watch on his wrist. "She sure is taking a long time. I'd better hurry her up. We should have headed back an hour ago."

He swiftly crossed the front yard and entered the house, calling out Meg's name. Pia heard Nate's heavy boots as he walked through the house.

"She's not here," he called out.

Nate performed a quick search of the house, yard, and immediate area while Pia took a deep breath and opened up, trying to focus on Meg and her current location.

The moment Pia quieted her mind, the gut-wrenching image of Nate, covered in blood, falling to his knees, filled her vision again.

"No!" Pia angrily forced the horror of the image aside and clutched her black tourmaline pendant.

"Can you see where Meg is?" Nate asked, walking back to her. "I keep forgetting there are benefits to being in love with a psychic." His tone was light, but he was breathing heavily, and he uncharacteristically bounced up and down on his feet.

"No, I can't."

"Okay. Back to the old-fashioned way. We didn't hear a car, which means she's on foot, so she can't be far."

Nate glanced at his watch again. "Fuck, I'm not going to make it back in time now. I'm going to have to get picked up from here." He fired off a quick text.

His phone pinged. "Blade is on his way. He's going to get you from here instead of at my house. Stay here; I'm going to search out back one more time."

Pia would be shattered if they lost Meg now. Pia didn't know exactly how, but she did know Meg was an integral part in helping Sarah move on. Sarah wouldn't have come through and given her the street name if that weren't the case. No matter what, Pia was finding a way for Meg to get to Sarah. Pia just hoped it would be in time for tonight.

Alone again, she tried to reach out, to focus on Meg and *only* on Meg, sure she'd be able to see where she was hiding. She'd been able to do such a thing on multiple occasions successfully in the past; there was no reason it wouldn't work now.

But as she cleared her mind, once again, the ghostly-real image of Nate, injured and falling to the ground, appeared vividly in her mind. For a long time, Pia persisted, fought under the strain. *I can do this. Where is Meg?*

But still, it was Nate's face she saw. Nate, covered in blood. Nate falling to the ground. Eventually it became too much, and Pia cried out. She closed her eyes, and blood rushed past her ears like a freight train. Her knees began to buckle.

Nate appeared just in time to see her fall. He was barking instructions into the phone against his ear as he ran to her side. Pia heard his voice in the background, behind a roar of staticky white noise, like a disjointed voice-over from a movie. He was coordinating men, revising the plan. She'd be saying goodbye to him from here.

Time was running out.

Pia experienced a floating sensation as Nate lifted her up in his arms.

"Jesus H Christ! What is going on, Pia? What the hell is happening to you? You were sick and now you're passing out. Should I take you to the hospital?"

"What? No!"

She clutched the collar of his shirt, felt her nails gouge the skin on his chest. She turned her blurry, unfocused gaze on Nate.

"You're not going anywhere tonight! You can't!" She shook her head wildly. "You *can't* go. I'm not going to let you." She was starting to rant. On one level, she was aware she was borderline hysterical, but was powerless to stop herself.

Pia felt the warmth of his palms on either side of her face.

"Breathe," Nate said, inhaling deeply, his breath warm across her face as he exhaled. Calm, controlled Nate.

"Breathe with me," he said, his voice deep, gentle and reassuring. "Breathe in… breathe out."

Pia followed his instructions, taking deep breath after deep breath until her mind began to clear. The horror of the image receded into a persistent, painful twist in her gut.

"What the hell is happening?" Nate asked. "Tell me what I need to do."

"I don't know." A vision had never affected her physically like this before, no matter how disturbing. With her abilities, she'd seen many shocking things, many gruesome deaths. Spirits trapped on earth often died under tragic circumstances.

Was Pia's strong physical reaction because she'd never been in love before? Or was it something else?

In her line of work, dealing with ghosts and spirits, Pia's visions were of what *had* happened. Only very rarely did she see what was *going* to happen. Was that the difference?

Please God, don't let that be the difference!

Pia pushed a wave of sickness back down through a constricted throat. "I'm okay." *Physically, not emotionally.* "But you can't go tonight, Nate. I won't let you."

Nate frowned. "I have to."

"No, you don't. I know you, Nate. You don't do anything you don't choose to."

"How can I *not* go? It's not that I want to; I'd rather be with you making sure you're safe. Leaving you tonight will be the single hardest thing I've ever done."

"Then don't do it."

Nate set his jaw.

"Please?" A tear rolled down her cheek, and she swiped it away, not wanting him to think she was manipulating him like his mother did.

Nate looked at her a moment, then turned away.

"Fuck! Fuck! Fuuuuck!" He cursed furiously, hands clutched into fists at his sides. He kicked the ground, sending up plumes of red dirt as he walked away, then picked up a large stone at his feet, and threw it hard against a rusty tin shed in Meg Farrell's backyard.

The jarring clang caused Pia to jump and sent her heart racing. She had never seen Nate less than cool and in control; even the threat of being shot hadn't fazed him. Watching Nate unravel was heartbreaking.

I caused this.

Pia silently cursed herself. But she couldn't lose him, not now. Not ever. She just couldn't.

"I'm not ready to say goodbye to you," Pia whispered, knowing he couldn't hear. Her body shook as shards churned in her stomach.

Nate placed his arm on a nearby gum tree and rested his head on his forearm, his back to her.

After a long, highly charged moment, he pushed off the tree and began walking back, his eyes wild and bright with emotion. The Nate coming toward her shredded her. A part of her wanted to tell him to go, to do what he must, that everything would be okay. Anything to get back the easygoing man he'd been earlier.

And yet… she couldn't bring herself to do it.

The vision came again, this time less vivid, a little faded and murky, the edges dark and blurred. Pia had no doubt: she was witnessing Nate's death.

Nate was not going to survive the night.

Tears streamed hot and fast down her cheeks, and this time there was no stemming the torrent.

She had an urgent need to be in his arms, to comfort him as much as she needed his comfort in return. But he stood just out of reach, his body as rigid as stone.

"You think it's easy for me to leave you?" Nate asked, his voice thick with emotion.

Pia's heart was pounding, but she raised her chin, and when she spoke, her voice wavered only slightly. "I have these abilities for a reason, Nate. What good are they if I can't save the man I love?"

He closed his eyes a moment, and when he opened them, they glistened brightly in the afternoon sun. His hair moved in the breeze, and she longed to run her fingers through it. Was this the last chance she'd get?

"Everything is in place," Nate said. "Everyone in Taipan has dropped what they were doing, and they've all flown in on a moment's notice. For no reason other than I asked them too. I said I needed them, and they came."

"Then let them do the op."

Nate shook his head. "I don't work like that. I stand with my team. It's how we operate."

"But Nate—"

"No!" Nate thrust his hands through his hair. "Damn it, Pia. I have to go. It's not even a question." He stared at her, and she stared right back.

Nate's expression softened. "I'm doing this for my brother. You know that, you know what will happen to him if I don't stop this shipment tonight. It will destroy him. My family. The business. Everything."

"Bullshit," Pia said.

Nate raised a brow. "Excuse me?"

"If you're going to go, you can at least be honest about why."

Nate narrowed his eyes. "And why would that be?"

"You feel guilty that Ben was forced into the role you walked away from. You're going out there tonight from a misplaced sense of responsibility. Your family was wrong to guilt you into thinking you had to take over. You are allowed your own life, Nate." Pia softened her tone. "Your own dreams."

"Ben's not strong enough; I've always known that. Maybe I should have taken him with me when I left to work interstate. Maybe I should have spent more time here, been around when he needed someone to turn to. Lord knows my father hasn't set the best example. Neither have I. I've been a disappointing son to both my parents, and I've been an absent and neglectful brother."

"No you haven't," Pia said, but Nate waved his hand, as if scrubbing her words from the air.

"All that psychological, poor-me bullshit doesn't change a single fucking thing. He's *my* brother. I have to go. I'll take extra precautions. That's all I can do."

Pia's blood turned to ice. There would be no changing Nate's mind. And damned if she didn't understand where he was coming from. Nate stuck by his moral code, his principles. Wasn't that one of the things she loved most about him?

Nate's phone pinged with a text. He read it, then looked up and sighed. "Blade is a few minutes away."

It was almost time to leave, and they'd wasted their last moments together fighting.

"Babe," he said, then began closing the distance between them. As he walked toward her, blood began oozing out of his body, staining the front of his shirt a bright crimson.

Pia blinked hard, and the blood was gone. She pressed her palms against her thighs so Nate couldn't see how much they were shaking.

"Don't do this, Nate. Please don't leave me." Her voice wobbled and cracked. "I can't love you for only a moment."

He cupped her chin and raised her face so that she was looking at him. Slowly, tenderly, he lowered his mouth to hers. Pia closed her eyes, and tears squeezed out their corners.

"I love you," he whispered against her lips.

She let out a moan, so raw it was embarrassing, and smacked him in the chest. "Damn you, Nate Ryder. You made me love you too."

He kissed her softly, and she clutched his shirt, tears running down her face. He was the best thing that had ever happened to her. And if this was all she had of happiness, at least she'd tasted it.

She had to hope her vision was wrong, that Nate could keep himself safe.

Otherwise, her future was nothing but ashes.

She'd tried so hard to protect Nate from herself, never guessing that he'd be the one to cut her to pieces, not from anger, not from spite, but because he was a man too good for this world.

Too good for her as well.

She'd known they wouldn't last; if only she'd listened to her abilities. They were never wrong.

———◆———

Two 4WD vehicles pulled into Meg Farrell's driveway. Blade exited from one and began walking toward them. Sean stepped out of the other, but stayed with the vehicle, leaning back against the front door.

"I have to go now," Nate said, a leaden weight inside his chest. He traced the silky softness of Pia's cheek, and when she turned her tear-stained face toward him, he dipped his head and touched his mouth to hers again. He closed his eyes briefly to memorize how soft her lips were, how sweet she tasted. Pia's warning had shaken him, far more than he'd ever let her know. But he couldn't allow himself to give it any consideration. A man had to do what a man had to do.

"Pia, Ryder," Blade said in greeting. He looked at Nate and raised a brow. "You let a *granny* get away?"

"Been busy with other things," Nate replied, wrapping his arm around Pia's shoulders.

"Nate!" Pia said wide-eyed. "We weren't doing that. Meg lied to us. We were waiting for her out front while she packed her bag and got changed."

"Oh, right," Blade drawled. "Never would have seen that coming. And by the way, what the hell have you got a doll on your kitchen table for?"

Nate exchanged a glance with Pia.

"Don't touch it," Nate said. "For fuck's sake, whatever you do, don't let anyone touch it."

"I suppose I don't need to ask if anyone else knows how to get into your safe, do I?" Pia asked.

Yes, Taipan had access to his safe, but none of them would withdraw anything from it without permission. There was one reason, and one reason only, that the doll was on the table.

A reason he didn't want to contemplate right now.

"Damn it, babe," Nate said, his voice low and fierce. "You be careful tonight. With that thing. With everything."

The thought of her walking around with that evil, possessed doll made his skin crawl and his stomach burn. She was taking on a spirit that had admitted to murder, that had almost taken Pia's life, not once, but twice. Between her and Ben, his heart was ripped in two. As he'd told her, he didn't have a choice. But it didn't mean he fucking liked it.

Pia's hand shook as she bought it tenderly to the side of his face. He leaned into it and felt the tremor of her lower lip as he kissed her.

Blade growled. "Jesus. As if I'm not missing my wife enough already."

"Thank you, Nate," Pia said softly.

"For what?"

"For everything," Pia said, her eyes shining brightly. "For making me whole again."

"This *isn't* goodbye," he ground out. He was not having this conversation. He'd be back later tonight. Nothing would stand in his way.

He kissed her one last time.

No, not *one last time!*

He simply kissed her. Ignored the question Sean directed at him, heard Blade tell Sean to let him go. Forced his legs to move to his car, his hands to turn the key in the ignition. He didn't know how the hell he managed to drive away from her.

But somehow he did.

Damn his brother to hell and back. Rage simmered, a stick of dynamite, the fuse lit and burning.

If something happened to Pia…

His hands clenched tight around the steering wheel, he stepped on the accelerator. The Porsche answered, like a stallion waiting for the signal to gallop.

Nate trained his thoughts on the night ahead. They'd be going up against the biggest drug cartel in the country, intercepting a major international shipment of cocaine, and pissing off some seriously nasty and heavily armed thugs in the process.

But none of that scared him as much as not being able to be with Pia.

She was going up against something far more unpredictable, something far more difficult to defend against.

Could life be so unfair as to give him what he so desperately wanted, only to yank it away again?

Yes. Tragedies happened all the time; he'd seen it again and again on the job, and not a damn thing made him exempt. He swore sharply, pounded a fist on the steering wheel, and blinked back tears.

He wasn't going to lose Pia. He couldn't.

He hit the open road, and as the sun slowly began to set over the Indian Ocean, Nate ignored the razors twisting in his gut and focused on, *and only on*, what needed to be done tonight.

CHAPTER THIRTY-FIVE

The moon was high in the night sky as Pia stood outside the lighthouse keeper's cottage, Ethan by her side. She stared up at the Milky Way, which, on this eerily still night, was a clearly visible artist's swipe of a brush over a backdrop of sparkling crystal stars, and tried desperately to distract herself, anything to stop worrying about Nate.

Ethan had told her that Meg Farrell had been caught hiding behind a burnt-out car several kilometers from her house. The meow of a cat had given her away, Meg having tried to take one with her when she'd made a run for it. To protect her from the mice, she'd explained.

That was just over two hours ago, which meant Meg was due to arrive any moment to show them where Sarah's body was buried.

The ocean pounded on the shore, its furious, ceaseless movement a sharp contrast to the overall stillness of the night. Not a breeze stirred a single leaf on the nearby gum tree. Clutched in Pia's right hand was the doll. *Sarah's doll.*

The eerily lifelike doll that had managed to get out of a commercial-grade solid-steel safe. An inanimate object that had been imbued with the vengeful energy of a desperate, fearful girl. It was sometimes easy to forget that Sarah had once been a normal little girl, full of hopes and dreams.

How would it have felt to be all alone in the ocean, paddling for your life, bobbing up and down with the waves, afraid at any moment you'd be eaten by a shark? Your limbs would tire, become heavy. You'd be thirsty, desperate, perhaps even delusional. Then, a boat appears. Saved at last! The joy so sweet, the relief so total. And then the ultimate irony: the horribly cruel moment when you realized you'd exchanged one hell for something far worse.

Pia imagined young, sweet, Sarah locked in a strange bedroom, unable to go home, crying herself to sleep each night, hoping her mother or father would come and save her. But no one came. No one heard her cries.

And then they'd put her in a dark cellar, where she'd lain on a filthy mattress day after day, year after year, fighting for a chance, a hope of being saved. Praying for someone—anyone—to see her down in that hole.

A beautiful girl, robbed of her childhood, abused, molested, and inevitably pregnant. Her only friend a mouse she'd named Templeton after a children's story her mother used to read her.

Silent tears trickled down Pia's cheek, and for once she didn't try to stop them.

She *wanted* to cry for Sarah.

Someone should have back then, but no one had.

It wasn't long though, before the tears dried and anger took the place of sorrow.

I won't stop until I get you justice, Pia vowed. *Whatever it takes, whatever the cost. Tonight, this ends.*

"Ethan, have you ever done something legally wrong, even though it feels morally right?"

He flicked his dark gaze to her. "All the time."

Okaay. What did she expect? This was Ethan she was asking. "Does that make it okay?"

"Depends on whose perspective you're looking at it from. Why? What's on your mind?"

Ethan already knew the details of the case, that Sarah's spirit was responsible for the deaths of Simon Farrell, Des Wilson, and Tom Kelly.

Pia released a breath. "Meg Farrell is just as responsible for what happened to Sarah as the rest of them."

"Agreed."

"Don't you think she should be punished for what she did?"

"She's going to jail."

Pia shuffled her feet. "I know but… she just didn't seem disturbed about that when Nate told her. She even seemed relieved. Talked about not having to cook her own meals…"

"Want me to give you some time alone with her before I take her in?"

Pia had to laugh at that. "Not me. Sarah."

Ethan raised a brow. "How so?" Then he nodded as he connected the dots about what Pia was asking. "You want to get Meg in the house, so Sarah can get her revenge the same way she did on the others."

"Is that bad?"

Ethan gave her a rare grin. "Yes."

He turned and looked back at the house. The silence stretched.

"Well," Pia said. "What does 'yes' mean? That we do it, or not?"

"What did Ryder say?"

"I didn't get a chance to ask him," Pia said, feeling a twinge of regret. There were lots of things she didn't get a chance to ask. But what *would* Nate say? Would he think less of her if she did it?

"Knowingly leading someone to their death isn't the question you should be asking yourself," Ethan said. "That part is easy. It's how you think you'll live with it after the fact. Do you know how you'll feel about the decision in five years' time? Ten? Twenty? When you're old and gray and looking back on your life. Wondering if there's an afterlife, and if there'll be consequences for your actions. Will you wish you'd have made a different choice?"

"Wow, that's the most I've ever heard you say all at once," Pia said, with a grin that quickly faded. He'd obviously given this subject a lot of thought. "That answer came so easily to you because you've wondered the same things yourself." Ethan, and Nate too, would have seen a lot in their line of work, been forced to make decisions that didn't sit lightly on their consciences.

"It's already too late for me," Ethan said with a twitch of his lip.

Pia turned serious. "You're right. I should trust in the legal system."

"Okay." Ethan cleared his throat. "If it makes you feel any better, Ryder won't judge you. No matter what you do."

Pia gave him a grateful smile. "Thank you." Although she already knew that to be true, it helped a lot to hear it. Nate wouldn't judge her. And that was good to know because there was a very real part of her that wanted Sarah to have her revenge. She was entitled to it for sure.

But Pia would let events unfold as they would. After all, it wasn't up to her to sway the hand of fate.

"The guys will be here any minute with Meg. Ready to do this?" Ethan eyed the house. The Reynolds' home, as it stood, didn't look formidable, much less malevolent. Its quaint beachside cottage appearance utterly belied the horror of what had taken place on the property.

Ethan's phone pinged. "The Bradfords' plane has landed," he said, reading another message.

Pia checked her watch. Ten p.m. If Meg arrived soon, they had an hour, an hour and a half with Meg to locate the bodies of Sarah and her baby before her parents arrived. Ethan had tried to convince the Bradfords to stay in the hotel tonight and come out in the morning, but they stubbornly refused. They were insistent about coming straight after they'd checked into the hotel.

"Any word on Nate?" Pia asked, even as she'd promised herself she wouldn't. Worrying about Nate, reliving her vision and everything that meant, would distract her from what she needed to do to help Sarah. The stakes were too high for her to mess things up. Nate had decided not to heed her warning and go. There was nothing for her to do but pray she was wrong. That he'd come home to her.

"He's fine." Pia frowned at Ethan's characteristically terse answer.

"Have you heard from him? Heard how the operation is going?"

"Don't have to. He's fine."

"But—"

"Pia," Ethan said, turning his unreadable expression in her direction. "He is fine."

Pia folded her arms across her chest. *I don't know how Sage puts up with you.*

The two best mates, Nate and Ethan, were handsome beyond measure, and together, they made a striking impact. Pia silently thanked the stars she'd fallen for Nate, who had at least mastered the art of communication. Ethan took the strong silent type to a new level.

A black 4WD matching Ethan's pulled into the driveway triggering the motion-activated floodlight, and two men began assisting Meg Farrell from the back.

At the same moment, two unmarked police cars pulled up alongside the 4WD, one carrying Johnson and Mulgrave, the other carrying two uniformed police officers she didn't recognize.

Pia could have kicked herself. Meg was still wearing the same clothes; she clearly had never had any intention of changing them as she'd said she wanted to. When Pia had been distracted over her premonition of Nate's death.

I can't afford to let that happen again.

As Meg stepped out of the car and peered at the house, the energy around them changed.

Pia's heart began to race, adrenaline kicking powerfully in as though someone was standing in front of her with a knife. The very air she breathed was prickly and unsettled, like a carbonated liquid.

Only not at all pleasant.

Johnson and Mulgrave reacted instinctively, Johnson in particular appearing to be on high alert while Ethan's men turned Meg over to the police. As Mulgrave read Meg her rights and handcuffed her hands behind her back, a chilly breeze washed over them.

Even Ethan's cool, unemotional appearance altered slightly. He widened his stance, his eyes narrowed, his right hand hovering over the hip where he kept his gun. Pia inwardly rolled her eyes. After Cryton, he should realize more than anyone here that a gun was useless against the paranormal. But instincts were instincts.

"Hi Darren," Meg greeted Johnson. "How ya doing?"

Johnson nodded. "Been a while."

"Thirty years." Meg stared at the house and chewed on her lower lip. For someone supposedly so determined to come back, she didn't seem keen to get too close.

"Show us where you buried the bodies of Sarah Bradford and her son," Ethan ordered, his even tone masking his inner turmoil. Pia got flashes of emotion from him; he was remembering coming face to face with evil six months ago. About to have a child of his own, Ethan felt no mercy toward Meg Farrell.

"Darren helped me when my husband was killed," Meg offered for no apparent reason. Except... the pointed glance she gave him as she said it.

Was she expecting his help here again today?

Meg began to walk toward the house.

The temperature dropped several degrees in a single second. Clouds appeared seemingly from nowhere and covered the moon, turning the sky above a murky gray.

Pia sensed Sarah's presence seconds before she saw her manifestation. On the doorstep of the house, watching intently with black, soulless eyes, stood Sarah.

Waves of unsettled emotion washed over them, swirling the air, picking leaves off the ground. In the distance, a dog began to bark. The darkness that had fallen was not just a lack of light, but something Pia felt deep inside. She shivered, turning up the collar of her jacket, but it did little to warm her against the chill.

Meg led them down the side of the house to the deck that faced the ocean. The same ocean Simon and his crew had plucked Sarah from, setting into motion the course of events that would end her short life. Meg walked around a little, her gaze occasionally wandering to Johnson. As the seconds ticked away, Meg appeared lost in memories of the past.

"Mrs. Farrell?" Ethan's voice interrupted her silent reverie. "The bodies?"

"Oh," Meg said, turning and walking around to the other side of the house. She pointed to the deck. "They're there." She waved her hand dismissively, pointing to the area the way one would point to an object of little interest. No, an object of inconvenience, Pia corrected herself. Meg was just as annoyed by the perceived trouble Sarah had brought into her life in death as she had been when Sarah was alive.

Was it possible to feel any more disgust for the woman than Pia did now?

The spot Meg indicated was the same place Pia had had the vision of the Reynolds, Chad standing at the barbeque, tongs in hand cooking his family lunch. Monique sitting, her youngest daughter on her lap, watching Cassy color directly on top of where Sarah and her baby boy lay buried.

Bile rose in Pia's throat.

Pia fought a powerful urge to throw herself at this abomination of the human species.

"It's only a timber deck," one of Ethan's men said. "Won't take long at all to pull it up. I've got tools in the back that will do the trick."

"Do it," Ethan said grimly.

"Why don't we wait until morning," Johnson suggested.

"Why the fuck would we do that?" Ethan snapped. "The Bradfords will be here tonight asking questions. What the fuck do I tell them? Your baby is likely buried under the floorboards, but we're going to wait for tomorrow to know for sure? This case is getting resolved now, if it takes all night."

Johnson's eyes narrowed. Was it over the effortless way Ethan bulldozed over Johnson's authority? Or something else? Pia reached out, but was interrupted by the sound of a car pulling in the driveway.

"The Bradfords," Ethan said, frowning at the notification flashing on his phone.

"What are they doing here so soon?" Pia frowned. *Dammit.* She had wanted to have the bodies uncovered and Meg arrested and away from here before they arrived. She was hoping to have a moment with Sarah, a final goodbye with her parents, before doing the ritual to send her to the light.

The Bradfords' inopportune arrival complicated matters.

"Apparently they didn't want to check into the hotel first, demanding to be taken straight here instead."

Leaving men shifting furniture and the barbeque off the deck, Ethan and Pia walked swiftly around the other side of the house.

Sarah's parents, Patricia and Henry Bradford, stepped out of a rental car, Henry supporting his visibly distraught wife. Patricia was wearing white pants and a silk shirt, her husband tan pants and a polo shirt with a logo.

Patricia had a diamond bracelet on her wrist that would be a house deposit. No doubt she'd give it up in a heartbeat to have her daughter back.

The energy crackled and shifted around them, and again, Pia knew Sarah was close before she saw her.

Sarah stood right in front of her parents and opened her arms. Sadness and grief poured out of her. Patricia instinctively shivered, wrapping her arms around her body. She thought it was a sudden chill, had no idea it was her daughter's spirit she was sensing. Henry left his wife's side briefly and came back with a white cardigan.

They can't see me. Sarah spoke to Pia with such deep, profound sadness. *How can my parents not know I'm here?*

They can't see you, Pia spoke to Sarah wordlessly.

Tell them I'm here.

Not yet.

Tell them I'm here! A fierce blast of cold air blew the hair back from Pia's face.

Not yet. I need to explain, to prepare them. You have to wait, Sarah. I'm sorry.

It wasn't that easy for some people to understand the paranormal, and it was even harder to explain. Pia had no idea whether they would even be open to the idea.

Patricia's eyes kept darting to where Sarah stood, only feet away. That was the usual experience for most people; they could see something with their peripheral vision, but not when they looked directly on. Different senses were needed to see spirits in manifest form.

What would Patricia say if she knew it was her daughter's spirit she was sensing? Would she be open? Or would she shut her down with a burst of anger? Pia had experienced both extremes.

"So this is where Sarah was, all the time we were searching for her?" Patricia said brokenly. Deep sorrow lines etched her face. Clearly, even after all these years, she'd never come to terms with her daughter's disappearance.

Patricia gasped and placed her hand over her mouth, eyes wide as saucers.

Pia glanced over her shoulder to discover what had shocked Patricia so much, when she saw her eyes on the doll tucked in Pia's arms.

Sarah's doll.

"It *is* her," Patricia said, through choking tears. She began to sob, her fingers like bony claws digging into her husband's arm. "It is my baby. You really *did* find her."

Patricia's knees started to give way, and Ethan was at her side, her husband on the other. Patricia needed to sit down. The only outside seating was on the ocean side of the house, where Meg and the detectives were.

"Take her inside," Pia said.

"Is it safe?" Ethan gave Pia a pointed look.

Pia glanced at Sarah, then the house. "Yes." Sarah wouldn't hurt her parents. Pia couldn't say the same for anyone else. She started to follow them in, intending to turn on every single light she could. Pia didn't know if it would make the house any safer, but it sure as hell would make her feel better.

"Ryder said you weren't to go inside," Ethan said pausing halfway down the corridor, but still supporting Patricia.

"Yeah, well, Nate's not here." Pia swallowed a rush of irritation.

"I can tell you now, he won't be happy about this. He was very clear."

"I intend to be just as clear. Nate doesn't make choices for me. Not now. Not ever." Pia couldn't be sure, but she could have sworn Ethan chuckled.

Inside, the house was still a mess, objects strewn all over, drawers upended, a pool of congealed blood at the bottom of the stairs. Its pungent, metallic scent filled Pia's nostrils.

Patricia gasped when she saw the large crucifix in the hallway hanging upside down. "Dear God! Are the family who live here devil worshipers?"

"No," Pia said. "They are lovely people. Victims in this nightmare just like you."

"Then who would do that?" Patricia looked at the cross again.

"I don't know." Pia didn't have the heart to tell her it was her daughter who had done it. Patricia wouldn't want to know the full extent of her daughter's suffering, the horrors she'd endured that caused her loss of faith in God. Better she remember Sarah as the sweet eleven-year-old she'd been when she'd disappeared.

For a long time, Pia had been forced to consider whether Sarah could be a demon, or if at some point she'd become possessed or under the influence by something evil. Her actions had been hostile, murderous, and her power far beyond anything Pia had ever encountered in a ghost.

But Pia had come to understand that Sarah's unnatural power came from the extremes of human emotion. Sarah had died with a seething and hostile fury at the injustice of what had happened to her. Just like an abused child could grow up to do wicked and heinous things to others, something similar was true for Sarah. Her body was gone, but her energy, her spirit, was left restless and smoldering with rage.

Sarah had lost her religious faith during her time in the cellar, had become angry with a God who'd never helped her, and she'd begun to court the opposite, the dark side. Pia suspected that was how Sarah had been able to imbue her energy into the doll.

Sarah had inverted the cross because of her disillusionment with God. It was a sign of her loss of faith, not a sign of demonic possession. Pia could understand Sarah's driving need for justice. No one saw her. Not back then. Not for the following thirty years. Sarah wanted her story told. And she needed revenge.

And who could blame her?

"This is where they kept our daughter prisoner?" Henry said through clenched teeth, glaring around the room.

For a while. Before they moved her to the outside cellar.

"Upstairs," Pia said, opting to share only a half-truth. "There's a room upstairs." Henry glanced up the stairs, and his face hardened further. Fortunately, he made no move to head up there. Henry was sixty-six, his wife sixty-three. The last thing Pia wanted was for them to suffer from any health conditions while they were here. She could just see Johnson's reaction if that happened.

"I'll try to find you something to drink," Ethan said, clearly concerned by how pale Patricia was.

"I remember sailing around this place," she said. "I remember the lighthouse." She began to shake and was unable to hold the glass Ethan brought back to her.

Water splashed onto her pants before he took hold of the glass again.

"We came back to search," Patricia continued, her voice choked with emotion. "We did! We went down to her room when it was time for dinner, and she wasn't there. We searched the boat from top to bottom as we retraced our path through the ocean."

"How did she get here?" Henry asked.

"A cray-fishing boat picked her up."

Patricia paused a minute, eyes round. She placed her hand over her mouth. "I remember seeing a trawler now. Oh dear God! She was on it? She was on that stinking old fishing boat, and we sailed straight past?"

Patricia looked as though she was about to pass out, and her husband wrapped his arm tightly around her shoulders.

"Sweetheart, calm down. Your blood pressure, remember? Take a breath and calm do—"

"How dare you tell me to calm down! How can I live now, knowing our little girl was on that boat, and we sailed straight past her?"

"Mrs. Bradford, you couldn't possibly have known," Ethan said reasonably.

"Our little girl was on that boat, and we didn't save her!"

"Honey, we weren't to know," Henry said.

"Not knowing doesn't make it better," she snapped. The utter devastation on her face was complete. "It was our job, our responsibility as parents to keep her safe. And we failed. We failed our little girl, Henry. She needed us, and we let her down."

She began to cry, huge wracking sobs, into her husband's chest. Pia couldn't think of any words that would make one iota of difference. Nothing could ease the pain and guilt this poor woman had been carrying around. At the end of the day, she'd sailed off in her yacht and left her daughter behind in the water. Not just to drown, but to end up in the hands of abusers and suffer unimaginable horrors in a dark hole for years.

How did one even begin to reconcile that?

On one level, Pia wished Meg were here to witness the grief these lovely people had suffered all these years. Would it make a difference? Would Meg finally realize the gravity of what she and her husband had done? Would she feel any guilt? Any remorse?

Probably not.

"I'm sorry." The words were insufficient and useless, but Pia uttered them anyway. What else was there to say? She set Sarah's doll on the kitchen table and stepped forward, trying to think of something, anything, to say.

Patricia's eyes snapped to the doll.

"That's why we never found her doll," Patricia said, sitting up suddenly, then frowned. "Why would she take her doll swimming? That doesn't make sense."

"She put it on the steps so the doll could watch her swim," Pia said automatically.

"Excuse me?" Henry looked at her strangely. "How could you possibly know that, Ms.... Williams, isn't it?"

"Plausible scenario," Ethan interjected smoothly. "Since we found the doll."

"And how did you know she went swimming?" Henry said suddenly. "The police reports said that she'd fallen overboard. It wasn't until much later, after the police had given up searching that we discovered her bathers gone and realized she must have gone for the swim she'd been talking about earlier." Henry's eyes narrowed. "Well? How did you know that?"

"It's okay," Pia said, placing a hand on Ethan's arm when he stepped forward. "I'll tell them."

"Tell us what?"

Pia had to be careful not to burden them with too much at once. They had so much to process with finally finding out what had happened to their daughter after thirty years.

"I'm a psychic," Pia said, leaving out the "medium" part for now.

Patricia took her head off her husband's chest and met Pia's eyes. "You can talk to Sarah?"

Pia swallowed her surprise. Usually that statement was met with disbelief and even anger. Being psychic and being a medium were also two different things. Pia ignored the technicalities.

"Yes," she replied.

"Ah hell and tarnation," her husband growled. "Not another bloody crackpot. Don't tell me we flew all the way here for nothing."

And there it was.

Pia inwardly sighed, and Ethan tensed beside her.

"I won't have my wife subject to any more of this nonsense," Henry said. "For years, we went from psychic to psychic to work out what happened and were told something different by every charlatan we saw."

"That second-to-last one was quite good," Patricia said. "When Sarah came through to tell us she was at peace and happy."

Pia thought of Sarah's restless spirit and her quest for revenge that had involved the murder of three people. So far. Not quite Pia's definition of peace and happiness.

How easy was it for someone claiming to be psychic to say a loved one who had crossed over was happy? It was, after all, what everyone wanted to hear about those who'd departed.

Sarah appeared on the other side of the room, moved until she was standing just behind her parents. Slowly, tenderly, she reached out and placed a hand on her mum's shoulder.

Pia's throat closed over.

Tell her I love her.

Pia closed her eyes, released a shaky breath. "Sarah wants you to know she loves you."

Henry stood, his chair scraping back loudly. "Shame on you!" he shouted. "Get up, Pat, we should never have come here."

Patricia started to rise from her chair, her shaking legs making her unsteady.

"Please stay," Pia said, resting her hand on Patricia's knee.

Sarah, who'd moved back at her father's outburst, came forward again.

Tell her my favorite bedtime story was Charlotte's Web.

"You used to read Sarah *Charlotte's Web*," Pia said. "It was her favorite."

Patricia sucked in a rush of air.

"Lucky guess," Henry said and snorted. "We're leaving."

"Sit down, Henry," Patricia said forcefully. "Of all the children's stories in the world, she chose that one. What else does Sarah say?" Patricia asked cautiously.

Henry gave Pia a withering look, a look that said she had better not hurt his wife any more than she'd been hurt already.

Tell her, Sarah said, *tell her about the time I knocked Dad's chess set over when he was in the middle of one of those extended games he played with his neighbor that sometimes took a week. I thought he was going to kill me, but Mum and I put the pieces back all jumbled, and he never noticed.*

"She said to remember a time she knocked her dad's chess set over..." Pia paused as the color drained from Patricia's face, turning so pasty white Pia thought she was going to faint.

"Go on," Patricia whispered.

"You helped her put the pieces back on the board, but they weren't in the correct places."

Patricia's hand flew to her mouth, tears streamed out her eyes, falling in a river down her cheeks.

Don't cry, Mummy, Sarah said. *Tell her not to cry.*

"She doesn't want you to cry." Pia could barely speak through her own tears.

"I remember that happening," Henry said, his lower lip trembling. "I accused Brian of cheating over that."

Patricia and Sarah laughed matching laughs, though Pia was the only one who heard them both.

"Where is she?" Patricia asked, her teary eyes searching the room.

"She's standing behind you. Her hand is on your right shoulder."

Pat's hand immediately went to her shoulder, and she released a gut-wrenching sob that broke Pia's heart.

"You're covering her hand right now," Pia said.

No one spoke. Barely anyone breathed, as Patricia closed her eyes as though she really were holding her daughter one more time.

"I'm sorry, baby," Patricia cried. "I'm sorry Mummy didn't protect you like I was supposed to."

I don't blame her, Sarah said. *Tell her I don't blame her. Either of them.*

"Sarah doesn't blame you, Mrs. Bradford."

"She doesn't?"

"No," Pia said. "It's time to forgive yourselves. You've punished yourself enough over something you had no control of."

Just then, Johnson stepped up to the open front door and nodded to Ethan. Sarah instantly reacted—the lights flickered on and off, and a nearby door slammed shut with the force of a gunshot. Patricia gasped, and Henry wrapped his arms tight around his wife.

"What's happening?" Patricia asked, a hand to her chest.

"Faulty wiring in the house," Pia lied. "Problem caused by the renovations." Pia rose and made her way to the front porch.

Johnson took a few steps backward, seemingly not willing to enter the house.

Curious for someone who didn't believe in the paranormal. Pia also didn't remember seeing him the night of Tom Kelly's murder. His partner, Mulgrave, was on scene, but Pia hadn't met Johnson until she was in the station. Was that deliberate?

Something about Johnson pricked at her instincts. Was it just because he had been so intent on arresting her and pinning this all on her? Or was it something else?

Pia followed the men to where they'd stopped on the front lawn, presumably so they could talk without the Bradfords hearing.

"They found her," Johnson said to Ethan, his face creased into hard lines.

Pia felt a mixture of sadness and relief. It was a tragedy, but at least Pia hoped Sarah could get this last piece of closure. Would she be able to rest now that she'd connected with her parents, her body was found, Meg arrested, and her story finally told?

Would that be enough justice for her?

Just then, Meg let out a loud shriek, two police officers struggling to hold her as she rushed toward them.

"What did you do with him?" Meg demanded, lunging at Johnson. "Where did you put the boy's body?"

Chapter Thirty-Six

On a deserted stretch of highway, between the Malaga warehouse and Serpentine, Nate, Sam, Daniel, Sean, and Max waited, unseen in the shadows.

The sky was clear, the moon full and bright. The Milky Way a white hazy stream through the middle of a thick blanket of stars. It was a night made for lovers.

Nate's thoughts immediately turned to Pia, and he ruthlessly crushed them. He had to remain focused. A transport carrier, carrying twelve rare cars modified to conceal stashes of high-grade cocaine, would drive past in—Nate pressed a button and checked the glow of the digits on his watch—two minutes. He'd received confirmation from the men tailing it. Wild Wilson's crew—and Ben—were headed their way.

TSI needed to intercept the shipment and forcibly immobilize Wilson's men long enough to talk to them—hopefully without bloodshed.

The terms were non-negotiable. TSI would take Ben in exchange for telling the cartel about the Feds waiting for them at the warehouse. If Wilson's gang played nice, they would be free to keep the cocaine and disappear into the night. They'd miss out on a lucrative deal on the other end, but that would be preferable to going to jail.

A twig cracked in the night, the noise causing Nate to still. On high alert, he waited. He heard a snort, then the sound of chewing, followed by the breaking of more twigs. He let out a breath. It was just an animal moving through the bush behind him. Something large. Probably a kangaroo.

Nate thought about Pia, tried to sense if she was okay the way she could sense him. Nothing. He inwardly cursed. His muscles were rigid steel, his stomach a tight fist.

One minute.

An engine rumbled low in the distance. He tensed, his pistol cold comfort in his hands. He'd prefer not to have to kill anyone tonight. But what were the chances of this ending without bloodshed?

Part of him relished the idea of spilling a little drug-dealer blood, of getting his own back on this gang who had, through his brother, caused his family, and now Pia, so much pain.

Headlights through the trees. The truck's engine drowned out the sound of nightlife as it bore down on them.

Three… Two… One…

All hell broke loose as the truck's tires burst on the metal teeth lying across the highway. The semi swerved, shredded tires peeling off the rims, as the driver tried to control the weight of the vehicle and bring it to a stop. Pistol gripped in his hands, Nate ran toward the truck. Jumping on the step, he swung the door open, gun aimed at the driver, before he had come to a full stop.

"Pull over! Stop the fucking truck!" Nate barked the order, his gun trained on the man closest to him. Sam did the same to the passenger on the other side. Knowing the small space would be filled with weapons, Nate kept his focus on the men's hands. The truck jackknifed violently before finally skidding to a halt on the side of the road in a spray of gravel.

"Move! Get out of the truck."

The heavily tattooed driver put his hands on his dark head of hair, and Nate stepped backward down the steps, allowing the man to follow. Keeping his eyes trained on the man's every move, every flicker of his eyes, Nate heard the same instructions being handed out by Daniel and Sean to the men in the car behind them. There were four men in that car—one his brother—so he needed to work fast.

"Keep your hands behind your head, and get on your knees." Nate kept the gun trained on the driver who had overcome his initial shock, his expression pissed.

"Who the fuck are you?" the driver said, his eyes narrowed menacingly.

"On the fucking ground! Now!"

The driver complied—albeit slowly—and Nate could see his mind calculating. Anger made people reckless; Nate had to wrap this up fast to keep the upper hand. When the shipment didn't arrive in exactly fifteen minutes, Wilson would begin asking questions. And when he did, it wouldn't be with words.

The moment the driver's knees hit the ground, Nate was on top of him, pressing his face into the dirt, placing the cuffs over his wrists.

"Get down next to him!" Sam had cuffed the passenger, brought him around the car and now had his gun trained on both men. "I've got them," Sam said, his gaze darting toward the car. Gun drawn, Nate moved to the car to assist Sean and Daniel.

Sean had the car's driver on the ground and was handling the passenger in the front seat, and Daniel had one from the back seat out of the car and was cuffing him. That left one other. Ben. Nate looked inside the car and met his brother's widened, glassy eyes.

"What the fuck are you doing here?" his brother asked, stunned.

Nate grabbed Ben by the collar and dragged him off to one side so as not to be overheard by Wilson's men.

"Feds are waiting for you at the warehouse," Nate said fiercely, keeping his voice low. "What the fuck were you thinking?" His brother's eyes closed, opened, struggled to focus.

"Are you stoned?" Nate asked, not bothering to keep the disgust from his tone. Ben smirked. "A bit."

"What did you take?"

Ben's bloodshot eyes flashed. "What the fuck do you care? You're too busy with your own life to give a shit about me or what I have to do."

"And what is it that you do, exactly?" Nate asked. "Get high and get involved in shit that's way out of your league? Do you have any idea who these people are, dickhead? Do you think they intended to let you live after the delivery? These were your last few hours alive, and you're a fucking fool if you think you'd be safe from them behind bars."

"How else was I going to get the money?" Ben shouted.

"Keep your fucking voice down." Nate looked over Ben's shoulder. Wilson's men were cuffed on the ground at gunpoint, not paying attention to Nate's conversation with his brother. Sean was explaining to them how this was going to go down.

Ben lowered his voice, but his tone was rough and aggressive. "Dad was about to lose the whole business when Mum came to me begging that I sort it out for him. How else was I going to get three million dollars in five days?"

"Mum came to *you*?" Nate couldn't conceal his surprise. Then anger. "Did she know about this?"

"Not the details. But she said to do whatever was necessary to get the money."

"So you thought you'd involve Dad's warehouse and Dad's car shipment, jeopardize the family business."

Ben shrugged. "Why not? It was Dad who needed the money, and the best way to hide something is in full view. You were the one who told me that. Anyway, Dad had a small shipment of cars coming in, so the boys and me, we made it bigger." Ben's grin was a fraction too wide to be normal. "Wilson had a little something he wanted brought in and needed the extra cars. It was the perfect solution. That is, until you butted your ugly face in. Fuck off, or Wilson will think I set him up. Do you want to get me killed?"

Suddenly, a figure emerged from the back of the truck and took off running across the road toward the bush. What the fuck? How had they missed someone hiding in one of the stolen cars?

Shots were fired from somewhere, and the night turned to instant chaos. Bullets sprayed the area, hitting the road, pinging off the metal of the car near where Nate and Ben were standing.

The runner was shooting at Ben! Wilson's men did think he set them up.

Nate shoved Ben out the way behind the shelter of the vehicle, then bolted after the man. About to lose him in the dense bush, Nate squeezed off a shot. The man stumbled, before dropping to the ground.

Nate was scanning for the fallen man when something slammed into him. There was no pain, just the bullet's punch in his shoulder, accompanied by the sound of gunshots. He zeroed in on the muzzle flash, then closed the distance, throwing himself on top of the shooter, twisting his body face first into the dirt, and zip-tied his hands together behind his back.

Ignoring the searing pain in his left shoulder, Nate yanked the man to his feet, escorting him roughly back to the others.

"Are there any others?" Nate shouted. Daniel and Max had already been searching the truck, and Daniel came back shaking his head. They hadn't missed anyone else.

Goddamn, how had they made such a critical error? They weren't amateurs.

Pia's prediction had come true. Nate had been shot. Good news. It wasn't fatal.

All the men were on the ground now, and Sean was reiterating the terms. They'd either agree, or die on the side of the road. Nate's ears were ringing too much to follow the swearing and abuse being hurled at them by the men on the ground. Sam climbed onto the truck and hammering noises confirmed he'd begun removing the modifications to get to the packages of cocaine.

"You've been hit," Daniel said at Nate's side.

"I've had worse cat scratches," he lied. His shoulder was throbbing; most likely some bones had been shattered. He'd already had one shoulder reconstruction on the opposite side. "Go help Sam clean out the cars."

Daniel moved off, Max at his side to make sure no packages of drugs would go undetected. Nate secured his gun in its holster and headed back to Ben. A quick glance confirmed Sean had the situation with the cartel guys well in hand.

He'd taken two steps toward the car when he heard a gunshot. Nate assessed the scene through the moonlight, trying to make sense of the commotion.

What the fuck? Who the hell fired a shot? They were all on the goddamned ground!

Sam, from his position on the truck, had his gun raised at an assailant in the shadows but didn't take the shot.

Why was he hesitating?

Daniel also had the shooter in his sights, but like Sam, he didn't fire.

"Ryder!" Sean shouted. "Make the call."

The shooter turned, his face catching the moonlight.

Ben! Nate walked slowly toward his brother, his good arm raised in the air. "Put the fucking gun down, Ben," Nate demanded.

"No!" Ben backed away, the gun wavering dangerously in his shaking hand. His eyes were wide as saucers. *Fuck!*

Frustration surged like a scorching wildfire through Nate's veins. His brother could be a loose cannon at times, but Nate had never known him to be this reckless. Or this wasted. Something twisted heavily in his gut. *I should have been paying closer attention. I should never have left Ben alone with Dad and his shoddy business dealings.*

Ben blinked rapidly as though having trouble focusing, and wiped an unsteady hand across his forehead.

"Benny, give me the goddamned gun." Nate walked toward his little brother with his hand out. Ben matched his steps moving backward, looking over his shoulder like he might take off running.

"You won't get far," Nate said. "Calm down and give me the gun, or you're going to get yourself hurt." Nate took another step forward.

"Stand back!" Ben roared, eyes darting erratically around him as if he were surrounded by a pack of hungry wolves. What had he taken? He was off his face.

"Ben, we don't have time for this. We have to go. You're coming with me, and these guys are going to forget they ever met you." Nate continued to speak to his brother in a low cajoling tone, inching forward. They were now far enough away to be out of earshot of Wilson's gang. "Ben, you're going to put the gun down and get in the car. These guys are going to go one direction, and we'll go another. The Feds won't get the bust, and there will be no connection to you if we do this my way. Right now. If you're going to be a dickhead about it, you can go down with them. Trust me, Dad's not worth it. I'll get you the money another way. I'll help you."

Ben's glassy eyes blinked rapidly. He seemed to be struggling to make sense of what Nate was saying.

"I need the money. They'll kill Dad."

"You've got to be fucking kidding me," Nate said. "If you need money, you come see me. You don't get involved in shit like this! Jesus! Why didn't you tell me Dad was in trouble?" *Why didn't Mum?* Why did she come to Nate only after Ben was in this deep?

Because you told her last time to never ask for help again…

"I'm not running to Mr. Perfect," Ben sneered. "You left me on my own. Mum came to me, not you, this time to help Dad. You don't get to come back and criticize the way I choose to do it."

What the fuck? Nate didn't have time for this. He was keenly aware of the seconds ticking away.

"Put the gun down. You're coming with me. This is your first and only chance. I'm trying to help you, you idiot. Put. The. Gun. Down."

Ben kicked his feet, as though something were biting his legs. "Get away, get away!" he shouted.

"Ben, there's nothing there."

Ben waved his gun at something near the ground only he could see, squeezed the trigger, then jumped backward, tripping and falling hard. Nate took the opportunity and lunged forward.

Before Nate could reach him, Ben raised the gun and squeezed off another shot. The bullet hit Nate directly in the chest. His body jerked from the impact as the bullet embedded in his Kevlar vest. The next bullet hit him in the thigh.

It took Nate a second or two to move past the shock and register what had happened. He took a step, but his knee gave way. Another step and he dropped like a stone, blood running a red river down his leg. He'd already lost a substantial amount of blood from his shoulder wound.

Daniel and Sam jumped Ben, disarming him, pushing him face first into the bitumen. Brother or not, Ben had forgone any further leniency. He cried out as Daniel secured cuffs around his wrists, spitting out a few choice words.

Sam was at Nate's side, slicing his jeans open. "Son of a bitch!" Nate could feel the heat of the blood coursing from the wound, the scent turning into a bitter metallic taste in his mouth.

"Let's hope it hasn't pierced a major artery," Sam said.

Nate took a tentative breath, felt the sharp sting of pain. Assessed it coolly. The shot to his chest hurt, but it would be just a bad bruise. He could breathe, wasn't coughing up blood. No lung puncture from a broken rib. "I'm good," Nate decided.

Daniel dragged Ben to his feet and forced him headfirst into the back seat of TSI's 4WD, hidden in the shadows off the side of the road. He then retrieved the medical kit and tossed Sam the black case. Sam and Daniel went to work with the bandages, wrapping them tightly around Nate's thigh to form a tourniquet, and a tight bandage around his shoulder to stem the flow of blood.

"I'm good," Nate repeated.

"Don't talk," Sam said. "You're pissing me off."

I've been shot by my own brother.

Nate closed his eyes, the pain from his brother's actions more piercing than that from his wounds.

Nate's phone vibrated, and Sam slid it out of his pocket. Zach's name showed on the screen. "Answer it," Nate rasped.

Sam pushed the speaker button.

"There are more cars coming," Zach's voice came fast and strong down the line. "Two, maybe three. One of them called for backup when the truck's tires blew. A black sedan with four men arriving first, another not far behind that. You have minutes, a few at most. And Sam?"

"Yeah?"

"They're armed to the teeth. Machine guns, grenades, the works."

"Roger that." Sam disconnected the call and pocketed the phone.

Sam and Daniel lifted Nate. Pain exploded through his body, and he gritted his teeth as his mates half-dragged, half-carried him off the road and positioned him behind Sam's 4WD.

Nate struggled to rise to his feet, the world spinning for a moment. He'd instigated this; he couldn't sit there helpless.

"For fuck's sake, stay down," Sam barked.

"Help me up," Nate said, his fingers, slippery with blood, struggling to draw his gun.

Sam released the holster snap, withdrew his weapon, and secured it in Nate's hands. "You can't stand right now." Slapping him on his good shoulder, Sam said, "Don't be a fucking hero. Stay out of sight. You've got your gun just in case. Shit's about to get real."

"Call Blade. I want to talk to Pia."

"No time," Sam said, eyeing him with concern. "She'll be okay. Blade won't let anything happen to her. Worry about yourself." Nate didn't know why he wanted to speak to Pia, he just wanted to hear her voice. Not to say goodbye. Never that. He just wanted to know she was okay. To tell her he loved her. To hear her say it in return.

Sam went around to the back of the 4WD and pulled out a selection of weapons, handing them to the team. Daniel gripped an assault rifle in one hand and a handgun in the other, a grim look of determination on his face.

A black sedan rounded the corner and skidded to a stop. TSI sprang into action. Through the hail of gunfire, Nate's thoughts kept drifting to Pia. Fuck his dad for not being a stronger man, for not being a better father. For becoming an alcoholic and not having the balls to admit it. And fuck his mother and her lies. His family were seriously screwed up. No wonder he'd left the moment he could. His only regret was not taking Ben with him when he went.

Nate never should have allowed his team to risk their lives for this.

He never should have left Pia.

Lying helpless and bleeding on the side of a road in the middle of fucking nowhere, the priorities in Nate's life become crystal clear.

His vision darkened around the edges. He blinked it away. He had to remain clear. Alert.

Had his realization come too late?

What were his chances of making it out alive?

Nate jerked as a stray bullet grazed his shin.

What were the chances of *any of them* making it out of this alive?

CHAPTER THIRTY-SEVEN

Pia doubled over like she'd taken a fist to her stomach, and her chest burned like fire. Nate!

Dear God, no! Something had happened to Nate; she was sure of it. Her shoulder throbbed, her thigh stinging in agony, and she knew this was Nate's pain. A sob rose up and out of her, and she straightened, struggling to take a series of deep, calming breaths. She couldn't afford to break down now.

Ethan placed a steadying arm around her shoulders.

"I'm all right," she managed and brushed his hand away. Meg's tirade dragged her attention away from Nate and to the here and now. Ethan was as tense a predator about to strike, his sharp eyes watching everyone's slightest movement.

"Where did you put the boy's body?" Meg Farrell was screaming at Johnson, spittle hitting his face as she hurled abuse.

Johnson's face was a mask of fury. "What the hell is she still doing here?" he barked. "I told you to take her in after she told us where she buried the body. Get her out of here!"

The uniformed officers began leading Meg away, but she kicked and twisted out of their hands. She was frantic. "Nooooooo!"

Pia had a brief flash of an image. A young man in a uniform out behind the cottage, here in the present day, uncovering the bones of Sarah.

What am I seeing? What's the connection?

Pia bit back her frustration, tried to hold onto the image, to see more. It was like trying to catch a fish with her bare hands. She reached out, grabbed Ethan's arm. "Wait. Don't let them take Meg yet. Something's not right."

"Riley. Schmidt. Wait." Ethan's words were a command the men instinctively responded to. They immediately stopped, keeping Meg restrained between them.

"What the fuck do you think you're doing?" Johnson yelled. "I said take her in!"

The cops looked at one another, then back at Ethan. Though they took their orders from Johnson, there was something about Ethan Blade people instinctively didn't disobey.

Johnson walked up to Ethan and shoved him hard in the chest. "You are out of line, Blade. You have no authority around here anymore."

"What's your problem?" Ethan demanded. He turned to Meg. "What did you mean when you said, what did you do with the boy?"

"The baby should be buried with her."

Ethan turned and began making his way to the porch, indicating for everyone to follow. Meg calmed down, much to the relief of the two cops holding her.

Pia noticed that Johnson hung back, leaning against his car and eyeing them in a way that made her shiver.

The porch was lit up like daylight by large portable floodlights. The timber deck had been entirely removed, boards stacked into small labelled piles, and another officer was taking photos. Bags containing what Pia suspected were Sarah's bones had been meticulously labelled.

"There's a baby buried there too," Ethan stated grimly, and the detectives continued to carefully shovel and sift through the dirt.

Pia watched wordlessly, trying to get a read on the situation, but it was useless. Every time she reached out, it was Nate's image that rose in her mind, just like it had back at Meg's house.

Even still, it didn't feel to her as though a baby was going to be found where they were looking.

Another hour passed, and they still hadn't found a body. A nice lady detective had made the Bradfords another cup of tea as they waited patiently inside.

Pia wondered what Johnson was up to, as he'd stayed away this whole time. Was he worried about setting Meg off again? Meg had more than implied Johnson knew the whereabouts of the baby, even to the point of accusing him of having something to do with it. Johnson had claimed Meg was delusional—no arguments there—but she'd sounded convinced of her story just the same.

Johnson was hiding something. But what? And just as importantly, why?

Just then, Ethan started to move toward the back of the house. "Stay there," Ethan said to Riley and Schmidt, who were still holding Meg.

Curious, Pia followed. Ethan began speaking into the phone, his face set in a mask of steely intensity.

"It it's about Nate, put it on speaker," Pia said, reaching his side.

Ethan shook his head, no.

Pia snatched the phone from his hand and pressed the speaker button herself.

Ethan's eyes widened in surprise, then narrowed into a glare. She ignored him, and handed him back his phone.

"Smithy, you're on speaker," Ethan said through gritted teeth. "Pia's here."

"How is Nate?" Pia asked, unable to hold back the question.

An image rose in Pia's mind. Nate, wearing his leather jacket, and underneath white bandages stained with large patches of blood. So much blood. Nate's knees giving way. Nate falling.

Nate *had* been shot. Her vision had come true. The pain in her shoulder, in her thigh, returned.

Is he alive? Where is he?

"He took a hit to the shoulder and one to the thigh," Daniel said, confirming Pia's worst fear.

"How is he?" Pia demanded, gripping Ethan's arm for support. "How bad is it?" She could barely get the words out past the constriction in her throat. The image of Nate covered in blood, falling to the ground, replayed over and over in her mind.

Daniel didn't reply immediately, and Ethan's gaze met Pia's, his jaw clenched.

Something was wrong. Very wrong.

"Where is he?" Pia demanded.

"We don't know," Daniel said.

"What do you mean, *you don't know*?" Ethan's voice was cold steel.

"Sam and Sean have mobilized a team to search for him. He wasn't where we left him."

"You *left* him?" Ethan roared.

"Shit went from bad to worse when the cartel's backup arrived, triggered from the delivery not turning up at the appointed time. Nate had already been shot twice by then, once in the shoulder, the other in the thigh. We dragged him off the road, held our ground, took them down. Six seriously injured, but only one fatally. The last two men took off in a car. We gave chase, and lost them. When we came back for Ryder, he was nowhere to be seen. He just vanished. He couldn't have gone far; he could barely walk. All we can think is that Wilson's men managed to take him when they left with the drugs, or he was in the boot of the car that we gave chase to and lost."

Ethan cursed heavily, and thrust a hand through his hair.

"You're going to find him, right?" Pia's voice was almost unrecognizable as hers, and her heart pounded an uneven beat in her chest.

"We're tracking him down now, with the help of Zach, who is monitoring all communications in the area." Daniel paused, then softened his voice. "Pia. I don't want you to worry. We're good at what we do. The best. We'll find him, I promise you. We won't stop until we do." Daniel's voice again turned business-like. "Blade, our best guess at this stage is that they've already swapped out vehicles, stashed the cocaine, and are hiding in a nearby bush property. They're not on the roads, and we've got the chopper up for eyes in the sky."

"What about the modified cars?"

"Wilson's men have the drugs, so no risk for us there. There was one death, one of Wilson's guys, and they've taken their wounded. Our exposure is limited there; Wilson's men won't talk to the authorities, we know that for sure. They may retaliate for the death of the guy, but we'll deal with that when and if it happens.

"I've mobilized another small team to put new tires on the truck and transport the cars to Ryder's place, where they'll be cleaned of all traces of drugs and fingerprints. The truck carrying the cars will pull into Ryder's parents' warehouse by sunrise, as though nothing ever happened. The Feds will no doubt trace it there, but there'll be nothing left for them find."

"Except you don't have Nate." Pia's hand shook as she rubbed at her eyes.

"Fuuuuuuck!" Ethan cursed heavily. "Find him. And don't stop until you have. Clear?"

A sob tore from Pia's throat.

"Don't worry, Pia, he's tough," Daniel said. "After his brother shot him—"

"*Ben* shot him?" Ethan asked.

"Yes. He's now in the underground holding cell at Ryder's house coming down from whatever trip he was on. Pia, when he was shot, before the cartel's backup arrived, Nate wanted to call you. To tell you he loves you."

Ethan growled, and Daniel hurried on. "But I'll find him, and he can tell you that himself."

"You're damned right he will." Ethan disconnected the call.

Ethan met Pia's gaze. He opened his mouth to say something, but a loud crash came from the house, followed by a scream. In the melee, Pia saw Johnson barking out orders. Where has he been, and what has he been up to?

"Stay the fuck here," Ethan ordered Pia as he moved swiftly toward the door to the house.

You've got to be kidding me. Pia ignored Ethan's order and followed him. From the entrance, Pia heard crockery shattering and Patricia's frightened screams.

"We have to get the Bradfords out of the house now," Pia said. "I know Sarah won't deliberately hurt them, but they're no longer safe inside." Pia remembered Sarah's fury, the flying furniture and objects. The Bradfords could inadvertently get hit with debris. What had set Sarah off?

Pia walked inside. The energy was a swirling vortex of tempestuous emotion. Pia couldn't breathe. The air was heavy, saturated in sadness and simmering rage. The kitchen cupboard doors swung open and plates and cups flew out, smashing on the floor.

Someone screamed hysterically. Meg!

Meg had apparently escaped the hold of the officers and was standing at the entrance to the house. "Where's that Johnson?" she shouted. "Is he in there?"

"No!" Pia shouted back, fearful of what would happen if Meg came inside before she'd got the Bradfords out. Pia had seen Johnson out front a moment ago, so where was he now? The two officers who had been responsible for holding Meg were again at her side. Yanking her arms roughly behind her back, they cuffed her. Pia saw an angry red scratch down the side of one officer's face and the other was limping as they led her away.

A toaster hurtled off the counter and smashed into the fridge. There was no telling what Sarah was capable of. "Get everyone out. Hurry!" Pia shouted at Ethan over the noise of roaring wind and smashing crockery.

Ethan managed to get the Bradfords out of the house and to his vehicle. At least they would be safe, which was more than could be said for her at that moment.

Sarah's doll was still on the kitchen table, and Pia left it there as she ran out of the house. She had no intention of being trapped inside a second time.

On the front lawn, Meg was screaming and kicking at the officers. A madwoman, she'd finally snapped. Her head was rolling on her neck, her eyes unfocused.

"Get her out of here! Now!" Johnson demanded. "She's lost her mind."

"The boy!" Meg shouted at Johnson. "What did you do with the baby?"

Again, Pia had a vision of a young man in a police uniform. One of the officers who had been helping dig up the area underneath the deck. He was somehow connected to this. But how?

Ethan was still with the Bradfords, probably reassuring them that everything was okay.

"You told me you'd take care of it," Meg shouted at Johnson, fighting the officers as they attempted to drag her away.

"I don't know what you're talking about, woman."

"The boy!" Meg screamed.

"You're mad." Johnson's eyes were ice cold.

"The whore's baby! The devil's spawn! You said you'd take care of it."

Johnson's body became rigid. "Come with me," Johnson said, his voice an eerie calm amidst the violent storm surrounding them. His face shifted into an expressionless mask. "I'll take her into the station myself."

With Ethan not there to say otherwise and seemingly not willing to disobey a direct order from his superior a third time, Schmidt handed Meg's handcuffed hands to Johnson. Pia was startled at the abrupt turn of events. Unwilling to make a mistake around Johnson and risk being taken to the station along with Meg, Pia held back. She couldn't get a read on Johnson's intentions. But something was wrong. That she knew in her gut.

"Where is he going?" Ethan demanded, returning to Pia from the car where he'd secured the Bradfords.

Pia peered around the moving bodies of policemen and Ethan's team, through the dim light and the noisy commotion surrounding them.

The house! Johnson wasn't taking Meg Farrell to the station, he was taking her *inside* the house.

He knows!

The realization hit Pia all at once, and she struggled to catch her breath. *All this time, he knew.* Johnson had convinced her he didn't believe in the paranormal.

Pia shouted after him. "You knew!"

Johnson looked over his shoulder at her briefly and sent her a cold smile that didn't reach his eyes. The effect was chilling.

Johnson pushed Meg through the entrance to the house. She stumbled with the force, landing hard on her hands and knees. The front door slammed shut.

"What the fuck?" Ethan demanded.

Everything happened in an instant.

The roar of a hurricane rattled the windows, an earthquake shook the walls of the house. Two officers tried to enter the house, but were immediately hit by flying debris, halting their progress and driving them back outside.

The front yard was filled with voices and shouting as everyone involved in digging up Sarah's remains came to see what was going on. The front door slammed shut again, and Pia knew this time, there'd be no opening it.

Pia raced to the front window, helpless to do anything but watch as Meg's body was lifted off the floor inside the cottage. She floated to the ceiling like a ragdoll and then dropped abruptly to the floor. Her head hit first, bouncing once.

But Meg was still alive.

Meg raised her head and looked around. To those watching through the windows—to everyone but Pia—the house was empty aside from Meg, but whatever Meg was seeing had induced pure terror inside the woman. Her skin was deathly pale, her lips white, her skin as devoid of color as a corpse.

Pia tried to feel something for her, empathy of some sort, but felt nothing. In Sarah's eyes—Pia's too—Meg was getting what she deserved.

Meg continued to scream and stutter, unable to form the most basic of words as she thrashed her cuffed hands about in an attempt to remove invisible objects from her body.

"What the hell?" the cop beside Pia shouted, staring through the window in open disbelief.

Pia glanced at him, then did a double take. It was the cop she'd been shown in her vision.

"What's your name?" Pia asked.

"Mike Johnson," he replied absently, riveted to the scene in front of him.

Johnson! She could see the resemblance now. He was Detective Chief Inspector Darren Johnson's son. How was he connected to this mess?

Through the window, Meg's body began to break out in red welts, the blood running freely to pool beneath her. She was thrashing around on the floor, fighting invisible assailants. Those around her couldn't see what was ripping at her skin. But Pia could.

Mice.

Meg's body was covered with crawling mice, biting every inch of her skin.

Unable to continue watching, Pia stepped back from the commotion. Every cop and detective, Ethan included, were either staring in shock or banging on the doors and windows, trying to get into the house. Trying to stop what was happening. Ethan smashed at the window with his Maglite torch, but it bounced off the glass like it was rubber.

There was no saving her.

Sarah wouldn't stop until Meg was dead.

Pia walked away from the horror inside the house and rested her back against the gum tree. She covered her face with her hands as she tried to put the pieces together.

Johnson had believed in the paranormal all along. That knowledge hit her hard. All this time, Johnson knew that it was Sarah who had killed Tom Kelly, Des Wilson, and Simon Farrell. But he'd been hell-bent on pinning the recent crime on Pia. Why was that so important to him?

Pia closed her eyes.

What was Johnson's connection to all this? Meg had said he worked on the case thirty years ago. He'd have been a young constable. Had he made a mistake back then? Turned a blind eye to Meg's involvement? Was he worried he would be reprimanded for something he'd done deliberately or unintentionally overlooked?

Pia had been so concerned about Johnson's single-minded focus on arresting her, she'd not allowed herself to think about him. In fact, other than avoiding him, she'd deliberately blocked thoughts of him. It was time that changed.

What are you hiding, Detective Johnson?

Holding the Detective Chief Inspector as her focus, Pia turned inward. Only due to considerable experience and practice could she tune out such chaos and silence her mind. Her mind blank, she fell back… back… back…

It was 27 July 1986. Johnson was a young cop, twenty-two years old. He was good friends with Simon, Meg, Des, and Tom. He used to go out with Simon on cray-fishing charters before he got his job on the force.

He hadn't known his mate Simon had found Sarah floating in the water initially. Didn't know that the Farrells had kept her locked in a room on the second floor for two years, didn't know they'd shifted her to a cellar where she'd spend the next three and half years of her life.

He hadn't known at the beginning.

But somewhere during that time, he'd found out.

Johnson worked the case in July 1986 when Simon and then Des died. Meg had called him, confessed what had happened. Johnson never let on that he already knew.

Meg told Johnson the night that Simon died that Sarah had given birth to a baby boy three days before. Meg was convinced that Sarah had somehow killed Simon. Johnson couldn't understand that at the time.

Sarah was dead. How could a dead person kill someone?

The girl in the cellar had died in childbirth—or soon thereafter—due to the lack of medical attention. By some miracle, the baby had survived. Meg didn't want the baby, the demon child whose mother had killed her husband. She was convinced the men had been killed by a ghost. The child could not stay with her.

The woman had lost her mind.

Johnson told Meg not to worry, that he'd take care of it. But Meg would have to leave that very night. Vanish and live the remainder of her life off the grid. She was never to return.

Meg was only too relieved to have the mess taken off her hands. By that stage, after the murder of her husband and his best friend, with the threat of exposure over what they'd done to the girl, Meg was verging on a full-blown breakdown. Johnson couldn't risk that. He told her he'd take care of it, helped her disappear. Meg understood Johnson to mean he'd dispose of the baby, bury it with its mother under the back porch. He didn't disabuse her of that notion.

Johnson carefully wrote the report, arranged the evidence to clear Meg of suspicion, altered the details of the case to make Des's and Simon's deaths read like accidents. Seized the murder weapon—the fishing knife with the carved eagle handle—and disposed of it deep in the Indian Ocean.

No entry was ever made of a dead girl in any police records.

Or a baby.

They simply ceased to exist.

It was remarkably easy for him to do. Who would have believed any reference to the paranormal anyway?

Johnson hadn't murdered the baby, buried him under the porch with his mother. Instead, he'd taken the baby home where he still lived with his own mother. Years later, he brought the child into his marriage with his childhood sweetheart.

Why? Pia focused. *Why would Johnson keep the child?* Why not turn it over to the authorities? Hold Meg accountable? Why had he covered it up and kept the baby?

It didn't add up.

Pia opened her eyes. The vision she'd seen had taken only a few moments. The house was still in chaos. Ethan was still trying to get in the front door.

"She's dead!" someone shouted.

Then, across the lawn, Pia's eyes connected with Johnson's. He was watching her intently with narrowed hard eyes. He sneered, and Pia's blood ran cold.

He must have seen the recognition on her face because he rushed toward her. Pia bolted, but made it only a few steps before Johnson was on top of her, grabbing her and putting her into a hold with her arms wrenched behind her back.

"You knew!" Pia spat at him, disgust thick in her tone. "You knew what Simon and Meg Farrell had done. You were the first cop on the scene. Why did you let Meg go? Why did you keep the baby? Why didn't you see justice done?"

"Some secrets don't need to be told," he said. "They need to die."

Chapter Thirty-Eight

Ignoring the jarring pain in his shoulder and thigh, Nate crawled along the red dirt that lined the highway. Cicadas screeched loudly, and every now and then a kangaroo bounced across the road.

Nate's heart pounded in his chest, the thuds seeming weaker with every beat. Sweat beaded on his forehead, and he shivered uncontrollably. The only good thing was that it was still dark; he didn't have to contend with the heat.

He was alive, but he wouldn't be for much longer. He was lucky to have survived this long.

During the second fight, when the backup for Wilson's gang arrived, he had been roughly tossed into the boot of a car. For whatever reason, someone had decided he was worth more alive than dead. Whatever they had planned had not been good. Perhaps it had been their intention to torture him for information about who they were. Perhaps he would have been used in exchange for money, to make up for the huge loss they took tonight. Either way, it wouldn't have ended well.

The car had sped off, Nate's body being thrown painfully around inside. After several crazy minutes, the car's tires blew out in a spray of bullets and the car skidded to a stop. Nate heard Sam's and Sean's shouting; they had been the ones to stop the car. There was a period of rapid gunfire and of men falling to the ground. Nate shouted, pounded on the boot to get Sam's or Sean's attention. There was the sound of an engine—one Nate recognized as Sean's 4WD—and then there was silence.

Nate had groped in the darkness, determined not to die in the boot of a damned car. His hands found shotguns and other weapons and finally landed on a crowbar. Somehow, he managed to jimmy the lock and heave himself out. He was going to have serious words to Sam and Sean about their search-and-rescue technique. Fucking amateurs. Not that he hadn't made his own mistakes tonight. His only hope was that Sam and Sean would realize he was missing and come back to get him. Before it was too late.

The low rumble of an engine sounded in the distance. Nate dragged himself as far as he could into the dense scrub. The vehicle, a truck, likely a tow truck, slowed to a stop, and Nate held his breath, waiting to hear whether it was Sam and Sean looking for him. A short but loud burst of cursing confirmed it wasn't.

The beam of a torch moved over him a few times, and Nate held still. Wearing all black, he blended in well with the shadows. After several long minutes, the sound of a winch dragging a car onto a truck stopped, and the men left.

Nate crawled out of his hiding space and repositioned himself just off the side of the road, in the hopes he'd be seen by anyone not belonging to Wilson's gang.

He was alone on an open stretch of highway, in the middle of fucking nowhere, thirsty as hell, and getting weaker with every breath he took.

Nate struggled to keep his eyes open, his lids getting heavier and heavier until he couldn't hold them open any longer.

Pia's beautiful face floated to the forefront of his mind. She was so vivid. So alive. Her red hair spilled across her shoulders and down her back in silken waves. The tresses felt so silky when he tangled his fingers in the thick mass as they made love. Her long black nails dug into his back as she came, crying out his name.

Her green eyes smiled at him, crinkling at the corners mischievously; she was so full of intelligence, wit, and fire. She challenged his beliefs, grinning wickedly when she argued an alternative point of view. How she hated being told what she could and couldn't do, which only made him want to do it more. He loved the way she tossed her head back when she laughed. And then he remembered the way she'd clutched the collar of his shirt, begging him not to go tonight with wild, desperate eyes.

A warning he hadn't heeded, a request he had denied her.

She was his perfect partner, his ideal companion for life. In his mind, she reached out for him. He raised his arm but grasped nothing but air. She wasn't there.

And as the night receded, the sound of nightlife fading further and further away, he had to accept the fact he wouldn't ever see her again. Never hold her again.

Just as she'd feared, he wasn't making it back to her alive.

In the final moments, he clutched hold of his preciously brief memories of Pia, replaying every moment of their too-short time together. He wanted her face to be the last thing he saw when he left this world. Maybe, just maybe, he'd get to take it with him into whatever came next.

"I love you," he said into the darkness, and prayed she could hear him.

As Nate's vision started to wink out, he got his dying wish. Pia's smiling face and fiery hair were the last things he saw as the world faded to black.

Chapter Thirty-Nine

In the dark shadows of the shrubs at the side of the cottage, Johnson picked Pia up off the ground from where he'd jumped on top of her. Pia kicked frantically, tried to bite his hand, but his grip was too tight, too forceful. People were shouting, screaming, sirens blaring as emergency services rushed into the house to help Meg. It was too late. There'd be no saving her. Sarah had gotten her revenge.

Pia couldn't find it in her to regret that. Meg had gotten no less than she deserved.

Someone shouted that they smelled gas. People rushed out of the house. Although right there with them in the commotion, no one heard Pia scream. No one was paying any attention to her as Johnson dragged her kicking and fighting several meters, opened a heavy trap door, and pushed her down a hole.

Johnson didn't use the ladder leaning against the shed. Pia fell, hard, her body twisting awkwardly beneath her as she landed on the cold, filthy floor. She looked up to see the trap door fall back into place.

The darkness closed in around her.

Judging by the sounds coming from above, the heavy scrape of a large object, Johnson had positioned the wine barrel over the trap door, reducing the chance of anyone accidentally discovering it if they searched for her. It would also muffle the sound of Pia's screams.

Pia was locked in Sarah's cellar.

Who would find her in here?

Nate knew about the cellar.

Nate! Pia choked back a sob.

"I love you." Nate's voice pressed into her mind as clear as if he were right next to her. Except the words didn't feel like melted caramel the way they did the last time he said them. This time they sent a chill down her spine.

Nate was saying goodbye.

Her blood ran hot and cold and she shook her head from side to side. No, no, no. She refused to accept that.

Sean, Sam, and Daniel will find him in time. Won't they?

Pia remembered the strength of her vision. The message she received had been loud and clear.

Nate would not be coming back to her.

A gaping cavern opened up inside her, a hollow that would never be filled. She'd die with the emptiness, the loss of losing him still inside her.

Nate wasn't just her lover. She'd blinked, and he'd become her whole world. She'd only had him for such a brief time, a single page from a book. But she would never forget what he'd given her.

Nate had taught her the power of love. True love.

Was there a greater gift?

A shocking explosion rocked the ground, sending a spray of rocks and dirt raining down on her from the cellar's ceiling. For a heart-stopping moment, Pia thought the cellar was caving in, but the shaking stopped, and panicked shouts and screams came from the ground above.

What had happened?

Someone had smelled gas. Had the house exploded?

In the darkness, Pia was momentarily disoriented. It felt as though she was in a shelter and a bomb had landed on top of her.

But she wasn't in a war. Though it did sound as though the cottage had exploded into flames.

Feeling helpless and frustrated, Pia crawled across the grimy floor to Sarah's soiled mattress.

It was bitterly cold, despite the warmth of the day outside, the stench so unbearable she drew in only short, shallow breaths. She could hear muffled sounds, voices, shouts. She could scream all she wanted, but it would be useless. No one would hear. Like no one had heard Sarah for three long years.

The energy shifted.

Pia was not alone.

But she wasn't scared. The energy wasn't malevolent. It wasn't even angry anymore. Sarah was sad. Peaceful almost.

Pia cleared her thoughts, allowed her mind to blank. Reached out.

"Hi beautiful," Pia whispered to Sarah. "How does it feel after all these years being finally heard? You've had your revenge on Meg Farrell, and now the whole world will know what the Farrells did. They will know that Simon's mates, Des Wilson and Tom Kelly, did nothing to help you."

Johnson had known. And he too had done nothing to help her.

Sarah had been let down by more adults than should have been possible. What kind of human being didn't help a child?

"I just don't understand why Johnson kept your baby," Pia said.

Sadness saturated the air, pressing down on Pia.

I'll show you, Sarah said.

I'll show you what happened…

CHAPTER FORTY

In the darkness of the stinking hole where Sarah had spent over three years of her life, Pia opened up, allowing Sarah's energy to meld with hers.

It's 27 July 1986. Sarah is sixteen years old.

For a moment, Pia was so shocked at Sarah's condition, she struggled to hold the vision, her immediate instinct to turn away from such horror. Sarah's face is hollow and drawn with dark shadows beneath her eyes, making the entire eye sockets look like big black circles. Lifeless.

The way they do in her ghostly form.

Sarah's mouth is open. Slack. She sticks out her tongue, and it drags against lips dry and cracked. She wants a drink so badly, but the water in the bucket in the corner is too filthy. The woman, who Pia understands to be Meg, hasn't lowered a clean bucket in far too long.

Sarah's tummy is sore. She can't sit, can't lie down, without being in pain. She feels the baby moving inside her. It's a boy. Somehow she knows that. She talks to him constantly.

Tells him everything will be okay.

And it breaks her heart to lie to him.

She tries not to wonder what will happen when he is born. Will they let him live in the sunlight? Or make him live down here?

The thought of her baby living life like this rips out her heart. *I hope they let him see the sunshine.*

It's July, the middle of winter, and Sarah is cold. So terribly cold. She can't get warm. Pia shivers along with her, unable to fight the acutely painful, to-the-bone-chill.

The rain beats down steadily overhead. A drip, drip, drip in the corner started as sometimes happened when it rained hard enough.

With concrete-laden arms, Sarah reaches for her water bottle.

She shifts Templeton, placing him on the mattress. The mouse doesn't move. Pia's heart squeezes. Templeton is no longer alive. But Sarah talks to him and cuddles him anyway.

Sarah slides across the floor, the smallest movement sending pain searing through her abdomen. She manages to roll to a sitting position, hissing in pain. Her head is pounding, her vision going in and out, her eyes so heavy they struggle to remain open.

Must make it to the dripping rain.

Not for her.

For her son.

The glass bottle is like ice in her hands, and she hates that she needs to put something so freezing on the inside when she's already so terribly cold.

But she keeps moving. Her baby is relying on her. She doesn't know how long it takes. What does it matter anyway? Eventually, she manages to crawl with the bottle to the corner. The rain has stopped. The last drop landed on the ground seconds before she put the bottle there.

She starts to cry. She cries a lot these days. She places her hands on her stomach. The baby has stopped moving. *He doesn't like it when I cry.*

Must be brave for my son.

She stills at the sound of footsteps overhead.

Was it her? Or him?

Or the other one?

Oh God, please don't let it be the other one.

The metal slides across, and the smell of damp rain reaches inside and teases her nose. She breathes the fresh air hungrily.

Her heart sinks.

It *is* the other one.

Her arms wrap protectively around her belly.

"Please don't hurt me," she whimpers, scurrying back to her corner as fast as the pain will allow. To the safety of her mattress. "Please don't hurt me," she repeats over and over.

But what she's really saying is, *please don't hurt the baby.*

Lying on Sarah's filthy mattress, Pia struggled to hold the vision as it wavered in and out of focus.

Usually able to get only short sequences, Pia was determined not let go until she saw the monster climbing down the hole. Her head ached, a sharp piercing knife to her brain.

But she focused through the splitting pain, forcibly held the image.

Heavy boots.

Uniform pants.

The monster got to the bottom of the stairs and turned around. A knife glinted in his hand. A fishing knife with a handle engraved like an eagle.

And then she saw his face.

Bile rose to Pia's throat.

The monster was Johnson!

That's why Johnson had kept the child. It was his son! Mike Johnson, the cop she'd met earlier, was Sarah's son.

Johnson was the monster Sarah was scared of.

Simon Farrell *hadn't* been the one molesting Sarah. His intention all along really had been to convert Sarah into the daughter he so desperately wanted.

Unaware of Johnson's nocturnal visits, when Sarah fell pregnant, Simon Farrell had actually believed God himself had given him the baby he so craved.

The deluded man had actually believed it had been divine intervention.

While right under his nose the devil walked in the shoes of Detective Johnson.

Chapter Forty-One

Unable to hold the connection any longer, Pia opened her eyes. Her body ached and her head throbbed.

The energy in the space crackled, and Sarah's ghostly form was a physical manifestation in the corner, her eyes black and unreadable.

"I'm so sorry," Pia said. "It breaks my heart what happened to you, sweetheart." There was nothing she could do. Pia had learned the truth about Johnson too late to help Sarah.

Pia closed her eyes. She'd failed Sarah. She hadn't brought the monster to justice. Her eyes grew hot with tears that she didn't let fall until she abruptly felt the departure of Sarah's presence. "I failed you," she whispered to the darkness, her voice choked.

Oddly, Sarah had seemed to have lost the edge of her anger. Was it because she'd connected with her parents? Did she not need the same justice for Johnson? The monster? Considering the depth of her quest for revenge, it didn't seem likely she'd quit before she'd gotten him too. Especially him.

Simon Farrell wasn't the one who'd abused Sarah. He really had believed that Sarah had conceived by immaculate conception. A gift from the gods.

What he hadn't known, of course, was that his good friend Johnson and his eagle-handled knife were visiting Sarah late at night.

When Sarah had spoken of monsters to Simon, Simon had simply thought Sarah was scared of the dark. He'd probably hoped it would help entice her into compliance and back into the house.

Meg had asked Johnson to destroy Sarah's child, but how could Johnson murder his own son?

Johnson eventually married and had kids of his own, raising Sarah's and his son with his other children. How ironic that Sarah's son might soon be involved in the arrest of his own father—if the others put it together.

Pia heard scraping overhead, and then the trapdoor opened.

Blocking the night sky, a brilliant light appeared.

Pia's eyes adjusted to the glare. Standing at ground level, at the top of the hole, was Sarah. She was holding her doll in her arms.

Sarah had opened the trapdoor.

Pia looked into her eyes and felt a different type of energy. There was a total absence of anger. Her energy was now that of a young girl. The sweet, innocent girl she'd been at eleven before she'd been taken by sick and depraved people.

Sarah smiled. *You saw me.*

Pia managed a smile. "I saw you, sweetheart. I still see you."

Thank you.

"Don't thank me. I'm thirty years too late," Pia said, pain twisting like a knife in her insides.

You brought my parents to me. You let me see them one last time. That's all I ever wanted all that time in the hole. Just to see my parents one last time.

Tears rolled freely down Pia's face, her heart shattered into a million pieces.

"I'll see that Johnson gets what's coming to him," Pia said.

It's already been taken care of.

"It has? How?"

He died in the explosion.

So Sarah *was* behind the explosion. And that was why her anger had left. She had been heard, and justice had been served. There was nothing left here on earth for her to hold on to.

I can leave now. But I wanted to thank you first.

Pia smiled through her tears. "As I said, there's no need to thank me."

Yes, there is. You never gave up. Even when your own life was in danger. Johnson was going to kill you later, did you know that?

Pia swallowed. Hard. "No."

He was planning your "accident." He didn't want to risk you ever talking about what you saw in your visions. He knew you were truly psychic. And it scared him.

It would have been easy for you to walk away, but you fought for me. And you kept fighting, even as the risk to yourself increased.

"The moment you reached out to me, I couldn't stop until I found out what really happened to you."

I was mean to you. I almost choked you. I'm sorry.

"You were scared. Every adult you'd ever known had let you down. There was no way I was walking away."

Many would have. Many did.

Pia's heart broke again, making her glad she wasn't one of the adults who'd let Sarah down.

I leave you with a parting gift.

The image of Nate's bloodied body rose in her mind. Pia gasped, surprised at the sudden intrusion. She squeezed her eyes shut, not wanting to see. Willing the image away.

It was his time tonight. His time to go.

Pia cried out, a ragged noise like the sound of a wounded animal. "No!" Even though after seeing the vision she had suspected that herself, to have it confirmed was devastating.

Calm yourself.

"How can I be calm when the man I love is dead?"

Then Pia had a sudden, shocking thought.

Was Sarah going to bring Nate through? Would she see him like she was seeing Sarah now? Was that the gift Sarah had for her?

Oh dear God, no! I'm not ready. I'm not ready to spend the rest of this life with nothing but the memory of his touch.

And how long would it be before the memories faded? She'd heard it happened fast. She didn't have even one picture of them together. Nothing she could put in a frame and place next to her bed.

How cruel could life be to let her love for just the briefest of time only to have it ripped away before it could fully bloom?

"Don't show me!" Pia cried. "I can't handle it. Tell him…" She choked. "Tell him that I love him. And that I'm sorry. I'm just not strong enough to do it. I… I just can't see him like that."

Maybe one day she'd regret not taking this opportunity to see him one last time. But right at this moment, she couldn't survive it.

An image of Nate, lying motionless on the side of a dark, deserted highway appeared in her mind. Surrounding him was a blinding white light. Sarah was standing over him.

Sean and Sam were travelling down the same lonely stretch of road, searching for the car they'd stopped earlier. There was no way they'd see Nate, wearing all black, his body so still.

The light around Sarah became glaringly bright, making Sam blink and forcing him to pull over, just meters from Nate's body. Sam stepped out of the car, looking for the strange source of light, and saw Nate instead. Pia then saw Nate a while later, surrounded by light, being tended to by TSI's private doctor.

My gift to you, Sarah said.

"Nate is alive?" Pia asked, not daring to hope.

Yes. You get your love in this lifetime.

Pia was sobbing hard now, blinded by tears.

"Thank you, Sarah."

Look after my son, Sarah said.

Pia blinked, surprised. "You know who your son is?"

Of course. He grew up to be a good man. Nothing like his father. Don't let him be scarred by this. One day, when he's ready, I want you to see him for me. Tell him… tell him his mummy loved him.

"I promise I will," Pia choked out.

Tell him about me, about my parents, his grandparents. He'll want to meet them, and they him. I want him to live the full, happy life that was denied me. He's the only good thing to come out of this. That, and meeting you.

"You would have been such a good mother."

Sarah smiled sadly. *That just wasn't my destiny.*

Something landed in Pia's arms.

And then Sarah was gone.

Just like that. Vanished. There was no fanfare, no haunting strains of violin music, no great show of brilliant light the way it was depicted in the movies. Sarah was simply there one moment and gone the next.

The air shifted and changed. Like someone had turned off the flow of electricity.

Everything was quiet.

Normal.

Pia looked down into her arms. She was holding Sarah's doll. It no longer held the same energy. There was nothing to fear about it now. No anger, no hatred. No ties to the spirit world.

It was simply a doll.

A handcrafted doll made in the image of a happy eleven-year-old girl before her world went horribly wrong.

Pia blinked back tears. Wherever Sarah had gone, she hoped she'd finally found peace.

Pia would never forget Sarah, the little girl no one saw.

The doll was heavy in her arms. Sarah hadn't given the doll to Pia to keep. It belonged to her parents. Pia would make sure they got it.

Ethan appeared at the trapdoor Sarah had left open, shining a torch down into the hole.

Pia shielded her eyes from the glare. She was safe.

And thanks to Sarah, Nate was alive.

Through the hole Pia looked up toward the night sky. She hoped that wherever Sarah was now, she'd finally be at peace.

Perhaps Sarah would be allowed to spend eternity living out the childhood that had been stolen from her on earth.

Pia prayed that it worked that way.

Chapter Forty-Two

One Week Later

Pia stood barefoot on the balcony of the house she shared with Nate and watched the sun set over the Indian Ocean. The breeze was warm and balmy, and there wasn't a cloud in the sky.

A soft smile played across her lips, as she let her gaze drift along the stunning white coastline, to the cave where they'd waited out the storm, to the stretch of sand where she and Nate had first made love.

Footsteps across the timber floor alerted her to his presence before her nose picked up the scent of a freshly showered Nate. She knew he was exceptionally clean; she'd washed every single inch of his six-foot-plus body personally. Showers these days took twice as long as they should have, but she could hardly be blamed. What woman could resist a naked and wet Nate?

She secretly enjoyed playing the role of nurse, Nate of course preferring when she played naughty nurse.

Pia turned and smiled as Nate placed a glass of red wine in her hands.

"Fuck, you're beautiful."

"Fuck, I love you," Pia said, kissing him hard on the lips. She nearly didn't get the chance to tell him that ever again; now she made sure to tell him all the time.

"How's your shoulder feeling?" The bullet wound on his thigh, although it had bled profusely, had not severed a major artery and was healing well.

"What shoulder?" Nate wrinkled his brow in faux confusion.

Pia shoved his good shoulder playfully, and he grinned. The doctors had said it would heal well, but he was going in for more surgery in the morning.

"Hey, haven't you already injured that shoulder once before?"

"That was my other shoulder. I had a reconstruction around six months ago. Pay attention."

"Paying attention to your scars is a full-time job. And anyway, you've officially run out of shoulders, Detective. You're not allowed to be shot anymore."

"I don't make promises I can't keep."

Pia leaned into him, tracing her fingers up his rock hard abs to link behind his neck.

"How's your brother doing?" Pia asked softly. Nate was closely following Ben's progress in rehab.

"It's a long road, but I think he'll get there. He's a good kid." Pia smiled. Ben was hardly a kid, but she knew Nate would always see him that way.

"Do you think he'll stay clean when he gets out?"

Nate nodded. "I think so. I got an offer for Dad's business yesterday. It was less than what I'd hoped for, but I think I'll take it. I'll make up the difference myself." Nate took a sip of wine. "Ben mentioned going back to university when he gets out, so that's promising talk."

"Your mother?"

Nate's eyes hardened. Pia knew he wasn't over his mother's lies and betrayal. "She'll make the best of the fresh start I'm buying them in Queensland." Nate stared at the ocean, and Pia didn't press him further. There were no quick fixes with family. People didn't change overnight like in the movies.

But Pia hoped, in time, that Naomi would find peace in Queensland and recognize the damage she'd been doing to her two boys over the years.

And apologize to both of them.

"I'm sorry I didn't see that it was your brother who shot you," Pia said.

Nate ran his palms down the outside of her arms and looked her directly into her eyes. "You can't save me. You can't even protect me. What's more, I don't want you to."

Pia frowned. "Why?"

"I don't want to be scared to take risks. I realized that, that night. You warned me I would get shot, and there was a part of me that was constantly aware it was going to happen. Whenever anything happened, there was a niggling thought, is *this* when I get shot? It affected my focus." Nate's lips slowly transformed into a grin. "The positive side is that I have Sam and Sean at my beck and call for... well, forever. They'll never live down the fact that I was in the boot of the car, and they drove off and left me. Blade was furious when he found out. Kicked their asses six ways to Sunday."

Nate's grin faded. "In their defense, it was an easy mistake to make. They couldn't have known I was in the boot at the time, and when they came back to search for the car, it was gone. Their primary focus had been locating Wilson's hideout, judging it more likely that I'd been taken and was being held by them. And they weren't wrong in that assumption. That had been Wilson's intention, which was why I'd been thrown in the boot in the first place."

"You had us beside ourselves with worry."

Nate smiled, and tenderly ran his hands up and down her arm. "I live with the fact my job is dangerous, that any case could technically be my last. I made peace with that years ago. It doesn't enter my decision-making process. I calculate what needs to be done, and I do it. That night, I knew it was coming, and it affected what I did, and how I responded to things." Nate smiled to take the sting out of his words. "It put me in more danger."

Pia nodded. She could understand that.

"So this isn't an issue then?"

"Honey, it's not your job to see me safe. It never was."

She looked down. "Adam didn't see it that way."

"Then he's a selfish arse."

Pia felt the weight of responsibility lift off her. It was a burden that came with her abilities, even though she rarely saw what was close to her. It wasn't just her ex, Adam, it was others too. How many times had she been asked by mere acquaintances, "Why didn't you tell me this would happen?" or she'd get a narrow-eyed, suspicious expression along with, "Why didn't you see this coming?" Like she didn't care enough to be constantly making sure everyone was safe.

That Nate didn't want to use her or her abilities in that way was freeing. Nate loved her for her. Who she was beneath her abilities.

Her eyes stung, and she blinked back tears. *Don't cry, dammit!*

"You're a rare man, Nate Ryder," she said, echoing the words he'd once spoken wordlessly on this very balcony. Nate smiled, wrapping his arms around her. He held her like he'd never let go.

And she didn't want him to.

Eventually, she pulled back. He always left her breathless. His eyes were glistening, his lids heavy.

"I love you."

Pia smiled. "I love you too."

Nate stepped back, bracing himself in faux tension.

"What's that about?" Pia asked.

"Just making sure you weren't going to be sick saying it. I'm always scared it will happen, and I'd like to be prepared."

Pia lunged at him, and being careful of his bandaged shoulder, grabbed him by the collar and pulled him into a hard kiss. This time he was the one who was left breathless. She grabbed his hand and tugged, urging him to follow her back into the house.

"What are you doing?"

"I'm about to remove any false ideas you have about exactly what it is that you do to me, Nate Ryder."

"Where are we going?"

"You've been a naughty patient," Pia said, mentally deciding which nurse outfit to wear this time.

"I have," Nate said with a gleam in his eye.

She led him into the bedroom.

This time it would be she who wouldn't remove the cuffs before daylight.

THE END

AUTHOR'S NOTE

The setting I chose for *Girl Unseen* is the scenically beautiful Cape Leeuwin, at the far south of the Margaret River region of Western Australia. The southwest region of Western Australia is one of my favorite places in the world to be, and I just had to set a story there.

Although Cape Leeuwin Lighthouse is a real lighthouse built in 1896 and is even purported to be haunted, the legends bear no resemblance to this story whatsoever. Additionally, I used literary license to create a lighthouse keeper's cottage in a small cove looking back toward Cape Leeuwin Lighthouse. There is no actual lighthouse keeper's house in that location, nor has there ever been, to the best of my knowledge.

Other than the geographical location, the story, characters, and events are entirely fictional and the product of my overactive imagination. I hope you've enjoyed reading *Girl Unseen* as much as I enjoyed creating it.

To hear about my new releases, you can sign up for my mailing list at:

http://www.athenadaniels.com/home/subscribe/

Thank you for your support!

Athena

ABOUT THE AUTHOR

Athena Daniels is the #1 International bestselling author of the award-winning Beyond the Grave paranormal romance series and romantic thrillers *The Scream Behind Her Smile* and *Desperate*. In 2016, Athena was nominated for Author of the Year and Best New Author in *AusRom Today*'s Reader's Choice Awards. Her latest novel, *The Scream Behind Her Smile*, won the Silver Medal in the 2019 Readers Favorite® International Book Awards.

Girl Unseen won the Silver Medal in the 2017 Readers' Favorite® International Book Awards and was awarded a Silver Medal in the 2017 Literary Titan Book Awards, and finalist in the TopShelf Book Awards 2018. *Girl Unseen* is a semi-finalist in The Kindle Book Review Awards, "Official Selection" in the New Apple Annual book Awards and nominated for 2017 Book of the Year in *AusRom Today*'s Reader's Choice Awards.

When Darkness Follows won the Bronze Medal in the 2018 Readers' Favorite® International Book Awards, Silver Medal in the 2018 Literary Titan Book Awards, and was nominated for the TopShelf Book Awards 2019 and nominated in the Australian Romance Readers Association (ARRA) 2018 awards for Favourite Paranormal Romance.

The Seer's Daughter was the solo Medalist Winner in the Suspense/Thriller category of the 2016 New Apple Annual Book Awards for Excellence in Independent Publishing.

The Seer's Daughter was also a finalist in the 11th Annual National Indie Excellence Awards in Suspense and in the 2016 Readers' Favorite® International Book Awards. Additionally, *The Seer's Daughter* was nominated for 2016 Book of the Year and 2016 Cover of the Year in *AusRom Today*'s Reader's Choice Awards.

Girl Unseen and *The Seer's Daughter* are both 5-star Top Picks at The Romance Reviews.

Athena holds several qualifications in metaphysics and natural therapies. She is a neuro-linguistic programming (NLP) practitioner, life coach, and feng shui specialist.

Athena lives on the northern beaches of sunny Western Australia. Follow her on Twitter @AthenaDaniels11 and on Facebook at /AthenaDaniels11.

athenadaniels.com